SECOND CONTACT

CHRONICLE ON THE SEEDS OF ORION

Kenneth E. Ingle

BooksForABuck.com

2012

BooksForABuck.com
January 2012
ISBN: 978-1-60215-164-2

Books by Kenneth E. Ingle

Science Fiction
SARAGOSA PRIME
FIRST CONTACT: ESCAPE TO 55 CANCRI
SECOND CONTACT: CHRONICLES ON THE SEEDS OF ORION

Mystery/Thriller
CROSS THE STYX: AND DANCE WITH THE DEVIL
TO KILL A THIEF
WHO KILLED THE KILLER

To learn more about Kenneth E. Ingle and his books, visit keninglebooks.com. Look for his books at BooksForABuck.com, Amazon.com, Barnes and Noble.com, your favorite eBook distributor, or ask for them at your local bookseller.

Author's note

As matters sometimes go, I couldn't get SECOND CONTACT to work. I started THIRD CONTACT and by the time that book took form, I knew the who's, what's and where's of SECOND CONTACT.

Preface

SECOND CONTACT, The Seeds of Orion chronicles is the second book of a series that sets out the spread of mankind and Orion's descendants into the galaxy. It takes the reader on a journey of the human race to new worlds. From populating one planet to expanding into the universe and as it has for thousands of years, doing what it had to do to survive.

Dedication

To Dr. G. Jordan Maclay who thought enough of my book, FIRST CONTACT to mention it in his paper, 'Gedanken experiments with Casimir forces and vacuum energy', published in the APS Journals Physical Review A, 10 September 2010.

Part One Prologue

1942 of the current era (CE),unknown to the humans, a space explorer visited Earth and left believing the inhabitants lacked sufficient social and political development to participate in the galactic community.

Twenty-five years later a laboratory explosion exposed eight of Earth's most brilliant scientists to an indescribable maelstrom of chemicals. Over the ensuing years, it became apparent they were aging very slowly; their life span had increased over five-fold. Their lives had changed forever. The choices: stay on Earth, become lab rats, and run the risk that whatever affected them would get into the general population, or leave. Joined by one hundred twenty others souls who had received blood transfusions from the eight giving them the long-lived gene, they chose the latter and began an epic journey that would take them into space to make a new life for themselves.

One hundred seventy-five years after their ambitious struggle and voyage began, it ended on 55 Cancri 'D' (named "New Earth" by the humans) in the Cancer System only to find a symbiotic troika made up of Kalazecis, Pagmok, and Rococo and the First, claimed the planet, Usgac, and ordered them to leave. Dominated by the Kalazecis, Pagmok warriors waged war to keep the planet. Having no other place to go, the intrepid humans fought to keep their new home and won. While capable of space travel, the technology the Kalazecis possessed was not of their own making and obviously came from someone else. As one New Earth scientist aptly put it, "These guys are not Mensa material."

In the first conflict between two worlds, New Earth defeated the Kalazecis and their Pagmok warriors. New Earth possessed minerals required for space venturing ships denying the Kalazecis the means to maintain their fleet of ships. Unable to breech New Earth's defenses, the Kalazecis, agreed to treat. During the negotiations, under orders from Kalazecis Emperor Djuc, Pagmok warriors attacked and killed Maria Presk, David Rohm, their son Michael, and Erik Svern, the three people most responsible for Orion's successful venture. Seven Pagmok died and fifteen New Earthers including the four leaders. Five Kalazecis diplomats spent the remainder of their lives in a New Earth prison. A state of war had existed ever since New Earthers denied the Kalazecis access to minerals needed to build and maintain space faring ships. Six months later, following Djuc's assassination his son ascended the throne. Myslac, the Kalazecis home world, entered a period of virtual dormancy.

Out there, somewhere an intellectually superior race had developed the means to travel space and weaponry to support that level of adventure. They gave the Kalazecis their space venturing ship technology. No one on New Earth doubted that the day would come when these beings would make their presence known.

For over one hundred years, that situation played out without the unidentified Kalazecis benefactor showing. Now, that had changed. One hundred fifty million kilometers above New Earth, an alien flotilla waited. The appearance of these beings would result in changes that our New Earth spacers had anticipated and ended with a Diaspora of Old Earth emigrants—not all of them friendly.

Our intrepid spacefarers had learned the hard way that space remained a dangerous place.

PART ONE

1: The Gathering

In long urgent strides, still in dress blues having just come aboard, Admiral Brogan Presk-Milar made his way along the passageway as he issued a stream of orders.

"Anything new on the mystery fleet?" the Admiral asked. Ten ships of unknown origin were above New Earth, whether friendly or not remained a question. He stepped into the carrier NES Lexington's CIC and studied the plot. Since the ships arrival almost four hours earlier, all of New Earth's electronic eyes remained locked on the aliens—his on the plot screen. Concern etched his face.

"Just that they're out there, Admiral, and showing no signs of leaving." Somewhat taller than her short stocky commander, the green-eyed auburn haired Captain Jeanne Swain had developed the habit of standing with her weight shifted to one leg minimizing the height difference.

"Recall Second Fleet. All speed," he said. Days earlier, he had ordered Second Fleet on a mission to the *void*.

"It will take Admiral Svern six T-days to get here." she responded. Swain dressed in khaki's and the traditional overseas cap, had served as flag captain for the last five T-years. If two people had learned to read each other, they had. He had an unfair advantage according to Swain, a sixth sense that seemed to defy logic.

Presk-Milar acknowledged with a nod. If Vice-Admiral Svern and Second Fleet were already in the *void*, contact would be problematic. Presk-Milar, great-grandson of Maria Presk, exhibited many of his ancestor's traits. He lacked the sweeping intellect she possessed—but only by a little. He had forgone the scientific field in favor of a naval space career and was recognized as a master tactician. The Admiral kept true to his scientific heritage, routinely offering technical suggestions that made their way into ships or equipment. During the idle times, and there were many, he took up exploring and platted the space within twenty parsecs of New Earth.

"I see we've got an effective track on them," he said studying the data stream at the top of the plot board. "Ten ships—one big enough to be a battlewagon—mass about the same as our Midway class. A few look like heavy cruisers on down to pinnaces and support. Don't see any carriers.

Maybe they don't use close fighter support. If they're as good as, over the years, we've made them out to be, they could rely on standoff missiles and energy weapons. Never get close enough to take much damage. And it gives them time to target our response." Presk-Milar had a habit of speaking his thoughts aloud and the staff knew the comments were rhetorical. He had expressed his concerns the drones that circled just inside New Earth's shield were seeing and relaying reliable data to receivers dirt side and Home Fleet.

"Has President Olivanta authorized us to engage them," Captain Swain asked.

"No. Says she doesn't want to come off as war-like. You know her pacifist thinking. She may be right this time. These guys haven't shown any hostile signs but just sitting there makes you wonder what they're up to. If they're waiting on an attack fleet, that's one thing. If they're just sizing us up we don't want to start the shooting."

Presk-Milar couldn't recall the number of times he'd sat around with fellow officers discussing what might happen when this day came and how New Earth would handle it. All of that seemed inane now that reality waited above the planet. He surprised even himself with the calmness that engulfed him.

They left CIC and walked the few steps to the bridge. Both took their chairs as the Marine sentry called out, "Admiral, and Captain on the bridge."

From her command chair, Swain could observe every working plot board and the weapons station; the Admiral had somewhat less visibility but his interest took in the entire fleet not just the Lexington. One design change made the bridge a self-contained unit, which meant that major portions of the ship could die but the command structure would remain intact to direct the fight for the surviving fleet. That added considerable mass but the newly installed matter-antimatter engines could easily accommodate the load. Early on, New Earth scientists had discovered that contained gravitational fields fore and aft of the spaceship permitted hyperspace flight speeds well above what the captured Kalazecis ships could achieve. It was a modification of the Casimir effect that had powered Orion from Old Earth. Transports and merchant ships still used a combination of the older Casimir engines and matter-anti-matter giving them more speed and load capacity but still slower than the combat ships. Brogan had devoted considerable time to the Lexington's design and the bridge reflected that effort. Access dominated every concept he put forward. To prove or reject an idea, sailors built mock-ups and checked times to station. Anything that failed to improve, in either time or ease of movement, went in the scrap bin. The result, as he would say, seemed choreographed although any reference to a ballroom brought a stern look that put a quick end to it. Few crewmembers saw his repeated drills as anything but drudgery yet declined to disagree publically. Capping off the effort, engineers provided the best current science could provide in electronics. Lexington's bridge layout and electronics defined state of the art.

"It doesn't make sense though," said Swain. "A flotilla is one hundred fifty million klicks above New Earth, just sitting there. I have to wonder why?" She fully understood how the element of surprise could shape a battle even determine its outcome. A tactic she'd never give away without a damned good reason and she'd never been able to think of one.

"Why?" responded Presk-Milar.

"Yes, sir: why? If they were here to attack us, why stop. Why not come right on in. Why give us a chance to prepare for an assault?" Now standing at the plot board of the NES Lexington, the two officers studied the image that had changed little since the alien fleet made its presence known.

"Think about it, Captain. The two times the Kalazecis and New Earth fought, we kicked their butts. The Kalazecis used these guys technology. That is if they're who we think they are. They know we're here. Furthermore, with our cloaking shield in place around the planet, they have to wonder what else might be waiting for them. Besides, a fleet of ten ships isn't about to start anything. They aren't here to fight."

Since the murder of their leaders, and being mainly scientists and engineers, much of New Earth's attention had been devoted to research and development of defensive weaponry. With applied foresight, that same armament in the right hands could become an effective offensive force— something that irked President Olivanta as it ran counter to her pacifist attitude. Presk-Milar had to admit he harbored some of those same views but he knew what his job was and would do it—with or without her approval.

"In any case, let's hope the gadgets the experimental physics boys and engineers cooked up can handle a deep space attack if that's what these guys have in mind," Captain Swain responded. She added, "I understand the entire academy has volunteered for active duty."

Presk-Milar gave out a short grunt and nodded. Presk-Milar's father started the school and named it Midway Military Academy after the ship lost in the *void*. Acceptance only started a student on his or her professional naval space journey, gaining them the nickname *Midwayers*. With New Earth's limited population, an applicant faced arguably the greatest non-combat test they would ever endure. Selection meant a candidate had submitted to a series of rigorous physical and mental trials. Physically, they were the best and mentally, some of the brightest. Name recognition or pedigree did not guaranteed admittance.

Retaking his chair, the Admiral looked at nothing in particular, his mind searching every possibility the enemy might throw at them; it they were the enemy. "Jeanne, we may have over extended ourselves. Bolivar isn't ready, can't space for at least a month. I wouldn't trust it to the rigors." Exploring the *void*, Second Fleet, led by the George Washington remained too far away and of no help. "Only the Gandhi and Home Fleet are space worthy," the Admiral added.

"Do they see us?"

"Don't see that it makes much difference. They've been here before so they know the planet's location. Not seeing it may give them pause. If it were me, I'd think twice about attacking a planet that I couldn't see, particularly if I knew it was there." As far as Presk-Milar was concerned, it stood to reason that these beings had been to Usgac, most likely as observers, any number of times when the Kalazecis had control of the planet.

With the arrival of the alien vessels, Admiral Presk-Milar had ordered the Ready Action Command from Home Fleet, twenty ships, to defensive positions two million kilometers out from New Earth just inside the shield. The remainder of Home Fleet would stay in close orbit. He tolerated President Olivanta's tirade for having done so without her authorization. The Constitution as amended by the Articles of War specifically gave him that responsibility.

"Second Fleet should be arriving at the *void* about now, said Presk-Milar. Sixty light T-days distant, the *void's* electrical disturbances made detection almost impossible. Although, if the uninvited guests had detected them, while doubtful, it could be one reason the unknown callers hadn't made a further move toward New Earth. Presk-Milar dismissed the thought. Second Fleet posed no immediate threat to their.uninvited guests.

New Earth's total complement of ships now numbered over two hundred of all sizes and armament that included two carriers provided the tactical clout to meet their strategic objectives: namely, defense. The inhabitants learned early on that to be unprepared invited unwanted guests and set out a plan to build a formidable fleet. Knowing what they faced in the Kalazecis and Pagmok, few raised objections. Either NES Lexington or the George Washington II served as flagships as had their namesakes. Only the Simón Bolivar remained from the original ships captured from the Kalazecis. New Earth's small population, just over forty-two thousand souls, mandated the ship's design minimize the crew size required to operate the vessels. Normal compliment of a Kalazecis ship numbered over four hundred. New Earth's designers had reduced that to less than fifty and at the same time doubled the ship's firepower. Following the strategic philosophy laid out by David Rohm over two hundred T-years earlier, New Earth's military design went for agility, long ranging weaponry and a quick strike force, as opposed to mass and heavy weapons. Inertial mass dampeners had given the fighters and corvettes maneuverability that few spaceship weapons could track, adding a sizable measure of survivability.

New Earth stood no chance in a battle of attrition. Despite a substantial birthrate, its population didn't allow for the kind of losses that would result from a major assault. Planners had estimated New Earth capable of supporting four billion people. Even with the death rate one fifth old Earth's—that would change in another fifty or so years when people reached their normal life expectancy of four hundred years—it would be that long before anyone got concerned about an accelerated birthrate. Stabilization wouldn't happen for almost twelve hundred T-years.

"And if the shields don't do the job?" Jeanne, her face scrunched asked.

"Well, I don't know if that really changes anything. Hell, we have no idea what we're up against whether they're the Kalazecis benefactor's or not. At least until we make contact. Seems to me it makes little difference." Presk-Milar was a pragmatist if nothing else. He left little to chance. "Nail it down," was a common utterance of his. "Do what you know how to do and do it well, the best you can."

"Ever wonder why they waited so long before showing up? As you said, they knew we were here." Every generation of New Earthers had anticipated this day. Many had become complacent even denying it would ever occur. That had all changed in an instant.

"Sure, just like everyone of the citizenry," Presk-Milar said. The admiral had worked constantly prodding the military to remain diligent.

"And?"

He watched Captain Swain and for a few moments and wondered as to why she'd never married. He'd not, so why should he question her desires? Maybe her career had gotten in the way; his sure had. But she didn't have to worry. Only fifty-five T-years and being long lived, she still had at least one hundred years before her biologic clock started ticking. He didn't answer his number two simply because he didn't have a considered answer. "Captain," he took a deep breath, "Have the fleet stand down from general quarters. Keep them on twenty-four hour alert."

"Captain, President Olivanta is on the comm for the Admiral," said the OD.

Admiral Presk-Milar hadn't talked with President Olivanta to get her thoughts since his original alert and didn't look forward to another conversation. She had a penchant for detail and the Fleet Admiral thought it led to meddling. Adding to his concern—her pacifist attitude was something his great-grand mother discarded quickly as not a good thing, more than that, suicidal.

The bridge crew could hear only one side of the conversation. "I understand Madam President, and I have the same questions. If I planned to attack, it would have happened before my enemy could prepare. They had to know we would use the time to marshal our defenses." Presk-Milar toed the deck plate as he listened. "I understand your position, Madam President but that doesn't mean we should be complacent." The remainder of the conversation just seemed to reinforce established attitudes. Presk-Milar would prepare for the worst.

Reclaiming his chair, the Admiral said, "She's concerned that we are projecting a war-like stance and sending the wrong message."

"Dangerous thinking, sir. What if they're like the Pagmok?" Jeanne said.

"We won't let our guard down nor will I reject the possibility they may be peaceful. We'll keep our options open."

"Yes, sir."

Admiral Presk-Milar knew his number two well enough to understand she would be the devil's advocate as her job required but the captain knew when to closet the adversarial attitude. She would keep everyone on their toes.

Lexington measured twice as big as its namesake. He punched the comm button, "Get General Jabari on the horn for me."

Less than a minute later, he'd arranged a meeting with New Earth's Marine Commandant.

James (Jimmy-John) Jabari remained one of the few from Orion's original crew who still had an active role in New Earth's government. Added to that, the Marine was the only person serving who had experienced personal combat. His war record prior to fighting the Kalazecis and Pagmok was remarkable enough. Added to that, the fight he led capturing all four attacking Kalazecis ships had become New Earth lore. Responsible for dirtside defense and space boardings, the man had few detractors. Some members of parliament thought he should retire, that a born New Earther should take command—a sentiment never openly broached with the Marine.

A few hours later, the launch arrived, clearing the massive hangar doors and settling on the second air lock landing bay retaining rails, not without some jostling. Six khaki clad Marines in visor caps snapped to attention and saluted as the bos'n piped his whistle ship wide. As the tattoo echoed off the landing bay's bulkheads, General Jabari, dressed in Marine blue and gold, black shined shoes you could see your face in, stepped onto the deck, and saluted the flag then Captain Swain.

"Permission to come aboard," he said in a deep resonating voice. Coupled with his size and bearing, it made the man seem even more imposing, maybe intimidating, not that he needed the added image. General Jabari was a living legend on New Earth. Few, other than President Olivanta, dared challenge the man.

"Permission granted General and welcome aboard." Jeanne returned the salute and extended her hand. Jabari had been a favorite of her great-grand father's and remained popular.

Standing almost two hundred centimeters, the man towered over the assembled group. Three hundred T-years had not diminished his imposing presence.

"Admiral Presk-Milar is waiting in the ward room, General. We can take the elevator or walk. What's your preference?"

"Captain, the Admiral keeps the ship running around the galaxy depriving me of a visit. I haven't been aboard the Lexington in over five years. Since you've given me the choice, let's walk." Preceded by two Marine lance corporals and followed by one, all from the ships company, fifteen minutes later they stepped through the wardroom hatch. Jabari had made the trip aboard the launch alone since most of his normal entourage, given the choice preferred not to ride with him as the General did his own piloting. They claimed 'reckless' failed to describe his skills something the man never openly challenged or denied. In fact, he seemed to savor their comparison. Admiral Presk-Milar often said he'd make one hell of a fighter pilot. Those who had flown in mock combat against the General agreed, and that delighted Jabari.

Arriving at the Admiral's cabin, Captain Swain rapped on the hatch.

"Enter. Welcome aboard, Jimmy-John." Admiral "Bogie" Presk-Milar extended his hand. "Have a seat, both of you. Coffee?" Anything but austere, yet short of plush, the Admiral's rooms reflected his tastes. Shelves lining the bulkheads were loaded with artifacts he'd gathered on exploring expeditions. Four good-sized rooms that included a bedroom, kitchenette, bath, and what he called the common area made up the suite. Form fitting chairs, fronted a desk made of something resembling wood, gathered from different planets, and polished to a high sheen.

Each doctored the brew to their liking, took a chair, and joined him. Those who knew Milar expected the small talk but they also understood it had its limits—only meant to get people to give honest opinions. Any officer who misread the Admiral's intention ran the risk of feeling his wrath for brown-nosing.

2: Talking To Them

"**Jimmy**, what do you make of our situation?" asked Bogie. Admiral Presk-Milar, even though Supreme Military Commander of New Earth, preferred first or nicknames when in private with those under his command. As such, until the President imposed Martial Law, the Marine reported to Milar. Jabari also carried the title of Military Academy Commandant and taught two classes, hand-to-hand combat and survival.

"Bogie, I'm at a loss as to why we were not immediately attacked. The only thing I can come up with is they really don't want a fight," Jabari said. "—that is if they're who we think they are. Even with the planet cloaked, they know where we are and a high intensity missile explosion would light up our shield."

"Jeanne seems to agree with you," Bogie said and added, "As do I. Think we can take them?" It was not a rhetorical question, the Admiral wanted honest answers. During his fifty years as head of the military, he'd rigorously tested every aspect to ensure their preparedness. While the enemy's capacity to wage war remained unknown, he stayed confident of New Earth's ability to take the fight to them.

Jabari thought for a minute. "I knew David Rohm. A most gifted engineer; light years ahead of anyone else. I doubt we have anyone who could compare with him. The one exception is his grandson. Hell, one hundred years after the Pagmok killed him, we're still working off the elder Rohm's original concepts. And that includes what the scientists and engineers are working on now—although our theorists have come up with some sophisticated ideas on their own. If these guys were planning to stand off and try to take us with missiles or energy weapons, I'd say we could handle them. We'll take some losses though." David Rohm II, grandson of Michael Rohm, son of David Rohm, now headed New Earth's highly regarded research effort.

Nobody saw fit to argue with the General's assessment. Most New Earthers never knew the grandfather but if they had to make a judgment, would put the grandson up against anyone.

"President Olivanta prepared a comm in all four languages," Bogie said. "If these ships are the ones we've been waiting for all these years, they'll be able to understand us. If they're the Kalazecis pals, we should hear something. If not, well, who knows what might happen."

"What's it say?" Jimmy-John asked. "I hope it isn't her usual touchy feely crap." Jabari's dislike of the President's pacifist thinking required no special insight and often sparked not so private exchanges between the two. He never crossed the invisible line of insubordination and firing him required parliament's approval, improbable as that was.

"The usual diplomatic jargon," Presk-Milar said. "Mostly that we don't want a war with anyone. Not bad really. At least the way it's worded, suggests we can and will resist any aggression."

"Makes sense to me. Have you talked with her?" A deep rumbling chuckle followed Jabari's question.

"She's something else," Bogie said. "After a conversation with her, you've no doubt about where she stands on a subject."

"Or you for that matter," added the General.

"Like her style of not, if her pacifist ways don't get in the way, she'll do alright. And we needed the religious nuts reigned in and she did do that." Admiral Presk-Milar had supported Olivanta for the presidency and the two shared some of the same views. Like his great-grand mother, he believed war was the last resort although in later years she had led her group through three wars, never hesitating to meet a threat head-on and never wavering. He likened her to a pacifist who carried a blaster pistol in her belt.

All three knew how Marie Presk had faced down the Kalazecis having a lot less with which to fight. Few put President Olivanta in that category, but no one considered her a pushover either. Quiet settled over the three.

Jeanne Swain stayed out of the banter between the two. She had grown up in a male dominated household and found it easy to sit and listen. Actually, that upbringing went a long way preparing her for a military career. By the time she received her officer's commission, few dared take her on in a hand-to-hand fight. Privately she would admit useful tidbits of information, pearls of military wisdom she called them, came from one or the other— particularly Jabari. No other person in the service, Marine or Navy, could match the man's experience. In her opinion, he had those rare qualities attributed to good if not great leaders. When he entered a room, just his bearing, how he carried and conducted himself could silence everyone. She mused for a moment realizing she'd never seen the man in civvies. Yet nothing seemed pompous or militant about the Marine.

"Bogie, you've said nothing about the president pushing to mothball some of the fleet. I damn sure think it's a mistake—crazy."

"Don't think it will happen," pensively Brogan replied. "Parliament won't go along with it. At least the way I count she doesn't have the votes. And if

I'm wrong, by my calculations, it would take at least fifteen years to pull it off."

"And she'll be out of office," countered Jimmy-John. That brought a nod and knowing grin.

With a reduced fleet, New Earth would have little chance to defend itself. The current ship count barely covered defensive objectives. Combat losses, if they occurred early in a fight would greatly diminish their ability to stop an assault. The weaponry they faced would determine how they handled their response. If the orbiting ships became hostile, launched an attack, New Earth's homing missiles, and energy cannons would be the first line of defense. Beyond any doubt, they planned to win never giving a thought to anything less.

Following Maria Presk's decision to provide New Earth with adequate protection from the Kalazecis or any other beings that might show, building of a fleet had gone virtually unabated. With her murder by the Pagmok, that intensity gained momentum although it wasn't without opposition. A number of citizens truly believed that the military had received sufficient resources and other matters needed attention. Admiral Presk-Milar even harbored some of those sentiments. Not building new ships was one thing, but reducing the fleet ship numbers was another matter altogether and would never happen as far as he was concerned.

"Hell, Bogie, send the damned message. We might as well find out what we're dealing with," Jabari said and added, "we need to know if these guys are the devil incarnate or something less than that."

Bogie leaned on the conference table plot board and pressed an icon. "Done, General."

"Jesus Christ, Bogie. You could have at least waited until I got back with my troops," Jimmy-John said as he jumped to his feet and headed for the hatch.

"Call the hangar deck and tell them to prepare my launch for immediate return dirtside," the Marine said to an orderly as he stomped into the passageway. The general's order brought a chuckle from Bogie.

Common knowledge had it Admiral "Bogie" Milar's ornery side would show and it had. But the antics were always with purpose. In this case, to break the tension building across the entire planet, and when General Jabari's told the story it would do just that. What the General didn't know: the signal was merely the stand-by to send alert.

"The drone's transmitter isn't FTL so the message will take eight T-minutes to get there after shield penetration, Admiral," the comm operator said.

Admiral Milar pressed the icon, "Once I give the command to launch let me know before it breaks the shield."

"Aye, sir. We'll launch on your order and advice."

Penetration of the shield created a momentary electronic disturbance. Launching from the far side eliminated detection by the unknown fleet. Once the drone established line of sight, transmission would begin. Whoever waited out there would be able to receive and should understand the message.

* * * *

Commandant of the Marines and Home Force General John (Jimmy-John) Jabari served at the president's pleasure and with the advice and consent of Parliament, but even she lacked the clout among the people to replace him; to them, he was their link to who they were. As the launch neared the landing platform, he hit the comm icon, "General," said the operator, "we just got word that President Olivanta declared martial law."

With that declaration, due to a quirk in how the framers wrote the constitution, General John (Jimmy-John) Jabari's position put him second in command with only the President outranking him. It wasn't uncommon for Olivanta not to give the man information on matters that directly affected him or his command. She disliked anything military and used every opportunity to make it known. Jabari immediately commed Admiral Presk-Milar and said, "The lady's hit the ML panic button; I'm boss now, Bogie."

With no rancor, acknowledgment came back immediately. "Aye, sir. The fleet awaits your orders." Presk-Milar knew the rules and as it concerned him and his command, ego had no place. He would follow orders and he had no problem with them coming from Jimmy-John. Aides on the ground put out the word on the change of command.

Jabari set the launch on the tarmac, entered his aircar, he drove himself, to the consternation of his staff as the most who rode with him accused the General of recklessness—and headed for planet's military headquarters, commonly but less than affectionately known as *The Box*. The oblong building covered six hectares on a peninsula. Established on the most defensible piece of real estate by the original settlers, ironically its isolated geography, now made it a most imposing target.

Jabari steered the aircar into his parking slot, double-timed to the elevator where his less than happy aide-de-camp and two enlisted men waited.

Military custom required Jabari's aide to accompany the General when leaving headquarters but all too often the officer found his boss had neglected to inform him.

Ten minutes later, Jabari walked briskly into his office in long heavy strides, his steps announcing his coming to all. Born in an old Earth bayou, the man seemed fearless, a by-product made necessary living in a swamp. Anything less than that and only a stone marker, or a wooden one if you were poor, noted your passage. To his chagrin, someone came up with vids of him in combat against the Pagmok and surreptitiously circulated those showing exploits that bordered on daring. That thinking, even more evident when civilians were at risk, earned him high marks with the people.

"General, the President has moved command to the bunker and requested you join her," said his aide, Colonel Mark Jackson.

"Tell the lady not now." He knew that wasn't going to happen. She would remember Jackson as the one who had delivered the *no* and remind him every time they met. She did demonstrate a visceral mean streak for those who opposed her and mostly that meant the military. Jabari sat at his smallish desk, seemingly made smaller with his huge size, and punched the icon.

"Madam President, I will join you shortly. I have a great deal that needs my attention here." The conversation lasted a few seconds and he cut the connection. Jabari knew his presence vital to embolden the population. His concern didn't include his Marines. They would follow orders no matter what.

"Colonel, anything new?" Jabari asked walking into the situation room newly set up two floors below his working office.

"No sir. The drone is prepped and ready."

Jabari commed the President and Admiral Milar to keep them both fully informed and issued the order to launch. The Admiral advised him the fleet would go to general quarters on his order.

"Drone launched, shield penetration in ten minutes," control said. They would wait.

Militarily, he had done what he could to protect the population. Telling the people to stay indoors seemed useless and in his judgment counterproductive. He did agree with the president that making contact with whoever waited out there had priority. "The response? Well," Jabari mused out loud, "that should tell us what kind of day we're going to have."

"Probe's transmitting, General," said the comm operator.

"General quarters," he ordered. "Advise the President, my orders," he somberly said.

He understood President Olivanta would take issue with the GQ status but so be it. The planet's military posture was his responsibility and he would exercise that obligation as he saw fit.

Quiet settled over the entire room. Almost to a person, their breaths measured, none wanted to be the one who made a noise.

All but Jabari bolted as the comm crackled, his reputation about having nerves of steel remained intact, "General, I think it would be a good idea to broadcast this to the entire planet," said President Olivanta. "Let them know what we know."

Jabari acknowledged and ordered the information released to the media. Along with their leaders, New Earth citizens would wait.

3: The Visitors

One month earlier Admirals Presk-Milar and Svern walked the Lexington's passageways.

"Magnus, it's time for New Earth to master the *void*." Presk-Milar knew the fleet had reached a point that only field trials could tell what technological weaknesses existed if any. "Take Second Fleet and see if you can find that planetoid Midway spotted before she disappeared."

Vice-Admiral Svern had pushed for just this kind of challenge for the Navy to evaluate their new electronics under the most severe conditions possible and that meant taking the big ships into the maelstrom. Losing any ship caused consternation but one the size of NES Midway added to that angst: the most severe loss New Earth had ever sustained.

Under the command of Vice-Admiral Magnus Svern, George Washington's penetration of the void would come about with extreme caution. Corvettes, pinnaces, and razors would make up the search teams. Slowly, they worked their way into the *void*, placing comm buoys to mark their return trail and maintain communication with the carrier. Captain Royce Ingram commanded the George Washington II. This was the first time they had taken this many ships into the space abnormality in almost fifty years. Loss of the Midway and over five hundred people put a stop to that practice except for an occasional foray into the outer reaches by small research vessels. Data sent back before the Midway's disappearance had identified a planetoid with unique and very interesting mineral properties. Not to mention it could serve as a military and scientific outpost. Advancements in electronics added a major degree of sophistication to the search capability but the downside, only the newest vessels had the capacity required to operate the massive power generators required. Finding the planetoid wasn't a sure thing, even with the new technology. Warnings sent back by the razors charted a clear path for the larger ships.

Every electronic sensor display had an operator intently scanning even though the ships computers processed the incoming data. Only the human eye could begin to deal with anomalies not known and therefore not programmed into their database.

Svern, now in his cabin, punched an icon on his chair arm. "Slow the fleet to fifty meters per second, Captain."

Lexington only a few kilometers inside the void, used thrusters to avoid collisions with rocks from one to one thousand meters.

"Captain, sensors picked up a small asteroid heavy in Terbium. It's on our list to bring back," said the electronics officer.

Svern stepped onto the bridge as the Marine quietly announced his presence. He stopped and eyed the plot board. "Captain, have the nearest ship launch a shuttle and bring it in."

Just as he finished the comm officer said, "We have the planetoid, Captain." One corvette had picked up radiation patterns that matched the computer and the size fit. "At our current speed, it will take another T-day to reach it."

Because of its maverick behavior, the planetoid could be dangerous. Svern wanted to make contact slowly.

"Launch drones two hours from rendezvous," Svern quietly ordered. Approximately one-fifth the size of New Earth, the asteroid's radiation appeared at an acceptable level, permitting uninhibited sample gathering. Sufficient gravity existed to allow something approaching reasonable movement. Admiral Svern order a landing party dispatched with a full array of scientific equipment.

Called it the *void* didn't come close to describing the area. That misnomer came as the result of a botched translation and it had stuck. One light T-year across and ten times that in length, disturbances made navigation tricky at best and often deadly. Maverick asteroids and quirky electrical disturbances filled the area. Small New Earth ships had disappeared before the loss of Midway without a trace. Clusters of asteroids, many with properties that caused navigation problems, populated most of the troublesome region.

"Captain, there's a tight beam comm from New Earth," said the comm operator.

"And?" The Admiral divided his attention between Captain Ingram and data received from the shuttles.

The comm operator, now standing next to the plot board said his voice filled with anxiety, "It looks like there's an unidentified fleet standing off New Earth. We've been ordered home."

"Interrogate the drone again. Put it on speaker." Svern's voice was crisp but without alarm. No bridge crewmember moved not wanting to be the one who might make a disturbing noise anticipating the replay.

"'Admiral Svern, there is a flotilla of ten ships standing off New Earth. Their coordinates are included in this message. You are to return immediately and take an offensive position,' Presk-Milar, Admiral Commanding." All eyes on the bridge swung in unison toward the Svern.

Without a moment's hesitation, the Admiral commanded in a voice that bordered on ferocious, "Captain, recall the shuttles and order the fleet to reassemble. We're going home."

Whatever caused the threat to New Earth, he feared the worst: an attack before he could bring his fleet to bear.

"It'll take some time, Admiral to retrieve all of our bread crumbs."

Standard procedure required navigation buoys set any time they entered a vexing area and the *void* certainly qualified. Instrumentation and navigation equipment readings often lacked reliability and experienced *void* spacers checked and rechecked readings and made good use of dead reckoning. Old-fashioned paper charts covered plot table streaked with red marks that traced every ships course. Spacers learned early on to leave a trail as they entered the *void* maintaining constant communication with their entry point and New Earth—breadcrumb as the chagrined Admiral's looks had suggested with the comm operator's announcement.

"Leave them," Svern ordered.

He'd spaced into the *void* a number of times and took nothing for granted. Running in close formation required precision navigation from the astrogator and helm—they would double check every maneuver ordered by the computer. Now wasn't the time to get careless. If the visitors were hostile, New Earth would need every ship in the fleet. Getting in position behind the unknowns would be as much a test of spacing skills as was navigating the *void*.

Increasing speed to fifty kilometers per second with razors leading the way, the corvettes, pinnaces, and fighters exited into clear space one day later completing Second Fleet join up.

"Set a course that will put the alien fleet between us and New Earth," he ordered and added, "Maximum speed, full stealth."

Maximum speed meant some of the support vessels would drop behind. Svern ordered two destroyers to remain with the slower resupply transports. Unless these beings had technology that bested New Earth's, the visitors were in for a surprise, if he could get there in time.

Six T-days later Admiral Svern positioned his twenty ships fifty million kilometers beyond the unknown armada and commed New Earth, giving his location and that he had the fleet positioned to take offensive action.

For reasons unknown, the aliens had made no effort to communicate with New Earth having ignored the message sent days earlier. Within the hour of Second Fleet's arrival, New Earth command headquarters again commed the alien ships in Pagmok, Kalazecis, and English advising them

New Earth required a face-to-face meeting. This time they did receive an answer to their astonishment—in English, a little cumbersome, but understandable.

"Greetings to New Earth. We are the Hommew."

"I'll be damned," the astounded General Jabari said. Something between surprise and anxiety permeated *The Box* CIC as the answer came through the speakers. "Looks like this bunch has a leg up on us. We better not take them lightly," In the back of his mind—President Olivanta's penchant for not coming off like some trigger-happy bunch. He would keep his finger on that trigger.

Transmitting in English, President Olivanta made it known New Earth would not look kindly on a withdrawal without face-to-face contact. To Jabari's amazement that sounded a little war-like. She added that any meeting between the two worlds required a peaceful resolution. To abandon the field and not establish some formal interrogatory must not happen. She reminded them of Second Fleets presence; something he suspected was totally unnecessary.

A comm from the aliens indicated that another ship, bearing an ambassador, would arrive in four days. No one knew what their reference to a day amounted to. One of New Earth's T-days an actual New Earth day; a Hommew day; how do they compare?

Prior to the emissary's arrival, President Olivanta had appointed Donavan Hillman, Secretary of State to head the delegation and meet with the aliens. A further exchange of comms led to agreement that the Mahatma Gandhi would serve as a meeting place. The Hommew would arrive on two unarmed vessels.

Both sides exchanged conventions intended to minimize surprises and prepare both groups. Pictures showed that the visitors were amazingly human like.

Excitement ran high. Everyone dirt side who wanted could watch events unfold as the Gandhi transmitted live vids of the fourth race New Earth had encountered. A number of comms preceded the launching of the visitors ships, agreeing on their vector, speed and final approach.

Secretary Hillman stood in the docking bay as the first alien ship, a pinnace, approached the Gandhi. Behind him, an unarmed honor guard prepared to receive the delegation. Cameras lined the catwalk ready to capture the moment.

The arriving ship cleared the hanger doors and two airlocks into the docking bay. It took the docking crew some time adjusting the locking rails as Gandhi's crewmen unrolled a bright red carpet. With that done, a lone figure stepped from the launch onto the hanger deck, sidestepping the mat. Taking his time, he (they assumed the alien was male) surveyed the entire area.

Apparently satisfied with what he saw, touched his belt signaling the pinnace.

Over one hundred New Earth civilians and crewmen, watched from the balcony surrounding the bay.

"Cautious bastards," Admiral Presk-Milar said from his command center as a second figure stepped through the hatch onto the bright red carpet. The alien's hands sported three fingers and an opposable thumb. Perhaps some lineage existed between them and the Kalazecis that went back a few million years. Light complected, his features were even more earthlike than the vids had suggested. He sported a sash not unlike those worn at diplomatic gatherings on Old Earth.

Secretary Hillman introduced himself and said, "Welcome aboard the NES Mahatma Gandhi and to New Earth. Whom do I have the privilege of addressing?"

The ambassador gave a slight bow and spoke in his native tongue which none of the New Earth delegation understood. With a smile, he repeated himself, this time in English. Hearing the raw words, Hillman, an anthropologist by profession, recognized similarity with old Egypt's language.

"I am Ambassador Lalost Fowoth representative of his Majesty King Resen and the people of Hommew."

Hillman, dressed in a pinstriped tuxedo, stepped forward and extended his hand.

Ambassador Fowoth obviously understood the gesture and reciprocated. Looking around the large bay the ambassador said, "Not much has changed."

His comment reaffirmed the assumption these were the Kalazecis benefactors and that the Hommew had designed and built the ship over two hundred T-years earlier. Hillman smiled and said, "Sir, your design has proven very good and we saw no need for change.

Ambassador Fowoth spoke into a shoulder comm. Six more Hommews, dressed as the ambassador, in tailored dark blue form fitting one-piece suits that sported light blue chest flaps, stepped into the bay.

Fowoth accepted a package from an aide, said, "On behalf of his Royal Highness Resen, King of Hommew, and the people of Hommew, please accept this gift."

Hillman took what appeared to be a book, thanked the ambassador, and handed it to and aide and accepted one in return. He handed it to the Hommew. "A gift from President Olivanta and the people of New Earth."

"Please, open it," Fowoth insisted still standing pointed to his gift. "It is in English."

Hillman shrugged and removed the royal seal, opened the book and read the first page.

"My god." Startled, he looked at the Ambassador. Hillman glanced down at the book again and read it aloud: "Account of the Expedition to the planet Earth. Circa 1942 CE."

"We are explorers," Fowoth said with a smile. It had taken some convincing to sell the public on the idea that making friends with the Hommew had merit but the fact they'd visited Earth years earlier—and done no harm—would remedy those concerns.

"May I invite you to join me in our conference room?" said Hillman. "I think you'll find it more accommodating."

Following a Marine honor guard, the group moved toward the elevators. General Jabari joined the New Earth contingent. His size awed the visitors. Everything about him dwarfed the aliens. Ambassador Fowoth offered a number of translation devices as not all Hommew spoke English.

Gandhi's engineers, using photos provided, had fashioned chairs approximating the Hommew form. Over the next few hours, the two worlds freely exchanged information. "Why did you not make an effort to contact us upon your arrival?" asked Secretary Hillman.

"Ha," exclaimed Ambassador Fowoth. "Frankly, it startled us when we arrived in-system and saw, or rather didn't see Usgac. To say we were concerned might understate it a bit. It took us a while to come up with the proper detection equipment to know you had somehow cloaked the planet. Our fleet admiral hadn't anticipated facing someone who could pull off such a feat and decided a diplomatic approach was in order. So, he waited for my arrival." He listened as Jabari ordered Second Fleet to stand down and nodded his thanks.

Fowoth's explanation fit reasonably well and satisfied New Earth's thinking. A few hours into the first session, Hommew's Ambassador startled every New Earth participant when he said, "Your Martin Grabel is a very intelligent man, but I must say a bit difficult."

"Martin Grabel? You know of him?" said General Jabari.

"We've dealt with him extensively," said Fowoth.

Not wanting to sidetrack the talks but more than curious about Martin, Jabari asked, "What have your dealings amount to?"

"Martin Grabel now leads the Kalazecis and Pagmok," said Fowoth. "As ruler after ruler died, some of old age although there was one assassination, dangerous events overtook Myslac. Both the Kalazecis and Pagmok turned to Martin Grabel for leadership. With him being long lived, his experience appealed to them. None could match him intellectually. He now is king."

"Good lord," said Jabari his voice had an incredulous tone. "Martin has a wife and three sons here on New Earth," he added. "I wonder how they'll react to this news."

"We have a vid for his New Earth family. He has taken a wife and has three more sons. His eldest is next in line for the throne."

"King Grabel." Jabari shook his head in disbelief uncertain if this was good news.

"He's a benevolent dictator. And it seems quite well liked by his subjects." Fowoth's voice remained casual and carried no sign of distress. "Perhaps the Kalazecis are not as fond of Grabel but with Pagmok backing, there's little they can do about it," he added with what seemed a bit of satisfaction.

Martin Grabel, volatile genius mathematician, had abandoned his family and New Earth, choosing to join the Pagmok and Kalazecis after New Earth defeated them in the first war between the two worlds.

"You understand a state of war still exists between Myslac and New Earth?" Jabari put his hands on his hips, his bearing bordered on belligerent.

4: Pacification

"About that," said Ambassador Fowoth. "Myslac is prepared to sign a treaty with New Earth to include a non-aggression pact. They want no war with New Earth."

Jabari reminded him when the Kalazecis had last offered to end the conflict, they attacked the unarmed New Earth delegation. He personally killed four of the Pagmok, but not before they had assassinated Maria Presk, David Rohm, and Erik Svern. He wasn't in any mood for another treaty but then it wasn't his decision. "Don't see us as a threat, is that it?" Jabari said his voice sinister.

"You are not the threat they face," said Fowoth, his face maintained the pretense of politeness. That got everyone's attention.

"There's another?" said Jabari his eyes riveted on the ambassador wondering what other threat existed.

"Yes. Old Earth mastered the technology of the ship you left, the Nelson Mandela, perfecting FTL travel. It seems your former home world has lost none of its belligerence. Something we've known for some time." Fowoth referenced the report from their earlier visit to Earth. "A number of skirmishes between your former world and Myslac ended in stalemates.

"Earthlings taken prisoner by the Kalazecis made it known you are on their list as well. Martin Grabel married one of captured Earth women." Fowoth said he had a substantial regard for Martin and his treatment of both the Kalazecis and Pagmok people. The Hommew accepted him with some major reservations. In fact, they had purposely minimized contact with the Kalazecis due to Martin's behavior and to the man's distress.

"But Old Earth's decision to attack them explains why you're here. You represent not only your interests but the Kalazecis." Jabari then added, "Looks like we're going to need the new gadgets our labs came up with after all."

Fowoth face had a questioning look.

"Over the years, our scientists and engineers cooked up a few surprises just in case you decided to evict us,—or tried," Ambassador Hillman said. "We're very pleased that they were not needed."

Fowoth apparently picked up on the threat as an eyebrow raised, then he nodded and added a smile.

Cynicism seemed to settle over the New Earth delegation. Maria Presk had expressed concerns that Old Earth's warlike predilection might surface once they worked out the spacing problems. From Fowoth, they learned the troika she'd required the United Nations to establish had failed, as did the world body—something that surprised no one.

Jabari asked for and received the information the Hommew had on Old Earth's fleet including, number of ships and armament. From what information they did get, Jabari and Admiral Presk-Milar agreed New Earth know-how remained significantly ahead of Old Earth's.

"Any idea of their time table?" asked Presk-Milar.

"Nothing for sure," Fowoth responded. "We can only tell you their fleet numbers over five hundred spaceships and twice attacked Myslac. At the time, their raids only used two hundred ships. It would seem they were testing their fleet and knowledge of how to use it."

"And you came calling. You must think we can make the difference?" President Olivanta entered the conference room.

The Ambassador nodded as everyone stood. She strode to the table, extended her hand to Fowoth, and motioned everyone to return to their seats.

"It would appear we have a major problem gentleman," she said turning to the Hommew Fowoth. "I assume you've given this considerable thought and have a plan to present."

Seemingly accustomed to how most members comported themselves, the Hommew took no offense at Olivanta's bluntness. New Earth would develop its own plan but hearing what Fowoth had to say might tell them if the Hommew's stated intention for showing up at New Earth bore out.

Fowoth seemed to sense the change, a wariness among the military people with the woman's arrival. "Madam President." Fowoth remained standing, "It is indeed a pleasure to meet you. My King offers his hand in friendship." He accepted his credentials from an aide and handed them to Olivanta. "As I said to Secretary Hillman, we are explorers not warriors." He explained that when they gave the Kalazecis space capability, a bitter war with the Pagmok had been going for some time and the Kalazecis were not faring well. "I should point out that only the Kalazecis were space capable and they just barely: the two worlds were close enough for rudimentary spacing. But as you know, the Pagmok are the warriors, not the Kalazecis. On the ground, the Pagmok were clearly winning. Since the Kalazecis had developed space capability, we knew someday they would discover our home world. We made the determination that intervening at that time might mitigate any attack on Hommew. Djuc's grandfather ruled at that time and was much loved by his people. As he lay dying, his son Cljuc prepared to take the throne. We were greatly disappointed when Djuc killed his father and seized power. The man, now dead for a number of years, was psychotic."

President Olivanta suggested the meeting move to the planet. Fowoth readily agreed, anxious to see the progress the inhabitants had made. "I've never been on Usgac nor met the Rococo and the *First*. Could that be arranged?"

Olivanta assured the ambassador he could spend all the time he wanted with the gentle beings as he called them.

Fowoth made it known he had another reason for meeting with the *First*. Hommew's fleet was aging and they needed raw materials only the First and New Earth possessed to keep their ships space worthy.

With assurances that both the Kalazecis and Hommew would get what they needed once New Earth had a signed treaty, the delegations moved to Government House.

General Jabari took up the conversation where it earlier left off. "What were they fighting about? What in the world could the Pagmok have done that provoked the war?"

"The Rococo and the *First*," said the Ambassador. "Some years before we discovered the three races, the Pagmok were breeding the *First* as food. After the Kalazecis defeated the Pagmok, really subjugated them, they put the warriors to work on their home world and continued to breed the *First* as a food source. The Kalazecis discovered minerals necessary for space faring on Usgac. Usgac being so far from Myslac, they decided to mine the minerals using the Pagmok. They objected amazingly at being so far away from their home. The Kalazecis didn't like the idea of a military presence on such a faraway planet. The Kalazecis found the Pagmok had a liking for a meat source on Myslac and the warriors came up with the idea of using the *First* to work the mines. Most certainly, cannibalism doesn't rank high on our druthers or the Kalazecis for that matter. However, once freed up, the Pagmok continue their warrior ways and again became a threat to Kalazecis. That resulted in those two going to war. We intervened and put a stop to it. Fortunately, The Pagmok possesses an amazing innate reasoning ability and we were able to come up with a solution that satisfied both."

That silenced the room. Ambassador Fowoth waited to take his seat after a few moments of observing some wall pictures and continued after General Jabari offered his chair to the president, "Our technology, while advanced, doesn't match yours. What you have accomplished in the short time you've been on Usgac, excuse me, New Earth is remarkable to say the least. Astounding might better describe your successes.

"About the Rococo and the *First?* How are they doing? Since the Kalazecis and Pagmok haven't visited New Earth in over one hundred of your T-years, we've lost touch with the gentle *First.*"

"Quite well, in fact," said Secretary Hillman. "They live near the mines and work them for us as they did the Kalazecis. We purchase the ore, and we have trade between the two nations."

"Nations? Finally. We had hoped the *First* would become self-sufficient and have their own government. My compliments for making this happen." Fowoth lightly applauded.

"Their slow birth rate makes them especially vulnerable," said President Olivanta. But so far, any illnesses they've had, we've been able to deal with."

"You can spend all the time with them you want before you leave if you'd like," Hillman said.

The Hommew ambassador nodded and responded, "I would indeed."

"Ambassador Fowoth, I must know," said President Olivanta, "Are there others?" referring to other sentient beings. New Earth did not know Hommew's location and as chance dictated, their explorations had simply not led them in that direction.

Fowoth picked up the essence of her question. "Many, Madam President. So far, only New Earth, Old Earth, Myslac and Hommew have spacing capability that we know of. Most are more like the prosimians, as you called them when you first arrived on Usgac, and there are others like the Rococo and the *First.* Some are more sentient than the *First* but haven't developed to our level of sophistication and therefore lack the technology needed for space travel. We have adopted a policy of non-intervention. That guiding principle applied during our visit to Old Earth. You will make your own policy, but we suggest a similar approach. We have found no other races that match our capabilities or the Kalazecis and Pagmok although we suspect quite surely, they are out there."

For ten days, the discussions continued. Neither Hommew nor New Earth seemed anxious to part ways. For the first time since leaving Old Earth, the humans had both neighbors and someone they could respect.

* * * *

"Gentlemen and lady." President Olivanta, dressed in a blue business suit, her graying hair neatly coiffed, addressed her cabinet with less than enthusiasm, "What do I do with this problem?"

A week had passed since the Hommew spaced for their home world. Before leaving, Secretary Hillman learned who would become Hommew's permanent representative to New Earth. Not anticipating the recent events,

Olivanta needed time to find someone to serve as ambassador to the Hommew world. It had become a bit of a concern. With what few efforts she had made, it seemed no one wanted to leave New Earth or more precisely, learning what little they had about the Hommew culture, no wanted to live in with the aliens. She accused her reluctant candidates of being arrogant since learning New Earth's technology topped the rest of the known galaxy. "Condescending," said the President as one after another refused the appointment.

Part of the problem, excluding the alien culture, stemmed from the discussion as to whether they should share technology with these new friends. New Earth had perfected FTL communications, along with other technologies the Hommew lacked. Whoever took the ambassadorship would have to face the question once in residence. No one cared to guess how the Hommew might react if refused the scientific advancements. Another concern: the Kalazecis and Martin Grabel. Other than a signed piece of paper, New Earth had no assurances he would be a reliable partner. No one doubted Martin wanted New Earth at his side if a war began, but afterward remained a large question. Meaningless chatter took the subject no farther, so the president raised another topic.

"With Admiral Presk-Milar here, I think it's time to discuss in detail reducing the fleet size." Olivanta turned toward Presk-Milar and added, "We all know your views Admiral, so I would like to hear other's thoughts."

Presk-Milar leaned back in his chair and looked steadily at her. "Madam President, I won't be intimidated. I will have my say!" Both stared hard at each other.

Standing, hands across her stomach, deciding not to retaliate at Admiral Presk-Milar's retort, she said, "I think the alliance we've forged with the Hommew and Kalazecis will permit us to safely reduce the fleet size. Considering the Hommew have approximately one hundred ships to add, we should be able to cut that number from our fleet and still maintain an effective force. I have savings estimates ranging up to over one hundred billion dollars per year that we can direct to other more important needs."

Appointed to the newly created Secretary of State office and a political ally, Donavan Hillman, cleared his throat. "Madam President, I think we should approach this with caution. After all, we have to consider that Old Earth, that is assuming the information from the Hommew is correct, may attack us. There is also the matter of our allies. What are they going to say if we proceed? Were I in their position, I wouldn't be happy learning New Earth had cut its fleet size as war loomed imminent." He kept his eyes on

Olivanta. For the first time anyone could recall, he'd openly opposed her by siding with Admiral Presk-Milar and others of a like mind.

In an exasperated voice Olivanta angrily said, "I've listened to most of you talk about Admiral Presk-Milar's order of battle. For the life of me, all I see is a lot of game playing. You have your plan, it's complete, you're prepared so there's no sense spending more time on it. Simply replace that portion of our fleet with these gift ships. Both the Hommew and Kalazecis need us and they know it. We hold the edge and I intend to make the most of it. You people are protecting your own interests and not those of the people. It must stop. I will hear no more of it. Anyone who can't follow my lead should submit their resignation."

Not ready to concede the point or the floor, Hillman said, "The difficulty isn't in our ability to gather an effective attack force but in defense. To prevail against a major attack, we estimate a minimum ratio of four to one, us being the four. With our current numbers, we stand at less than one to four."

Silence held for a few seconds. "Just numbers. Now let's get on with it. Admiral Presk-Milar, I want your plan on my desk in one week. Is that understood?"

"Yes," he curtly responded. He knew full well that parliament would have its say and he knew that outcome as well.

The slight of omitting her title didn't escape Olivanta as she glared at the Navy officer. One thing she had learned early on, Admiral Presk-Milar enjoyed wide public support and as such, cut loose would be a political rival. The fact he shared some of her pacifist feelings only added to the problem. She couldn't ignore his popularity, even within her party. Just evoking Maria Presk's name could put a crowd on its feet. So far, he'd shown no interest in politics. However, one thing she could do is appoint additional cabinet members—ones who more closely shared her views and would follow her lead.

Home Secretary Marsha Henderson stood, which was customary when addressing a standing president. "Madam, I have completed the details for the Rococo youth retreat."

She sat never having shown an iota of emotion—her face stoic and eyes straight ahead. Her reputation as Olivanta's lackey virtually isolated her from the rest of the cabinet but when she wanted something, somehow Olivanta delivered.

"A what for the Rococo?" questioned Secretary Hillman. "They have about as much need for a recreation place as I do."

"Madam President, when the newsies hear if this, they'll tear us apart," said Morrison Crest, Education Secretary. "This can't go beyond this room." Crest's word carried little weight, in or out of the cabinet, but the nodding heads clearly agreed with him. All but Admiral Presk-Milar—the grin on his face bordered on insubordination.

Adjourning her cabinet all stood as President Olivanta stormed from the room.

Two days later, her secretary ushered the parliamentary head into the office. Omitting the usual formality, her voice an octave higher than normal she said, "Mr. Speaker, I want these names approved without delay. Do you understand? Immediately." President Olivanta pounded on her desk.

Even though they were from the same party, the Speaker had a reputation for independence. He scanned the list. "For your cabinet? It isn't that simple, Madam. They must appear before the respective committees for vetting. Parliament will not brook bypassing the accepted process. It's always been this way. Trying to circumvent…" he stopped, "no, Madam President, I must say no."

"Bullshit," she yelled. "The constitution says nothing about interim appointments. I'll do it without you."

Speaker Myers left Government House knowing a political storm would come—more certainly a crisis of government.

Olivanta jabbed at the button, "Comm Jabari. Tell him to get here immediately."

Less than an hour later, the General walked into her office not pleased with the curt summons.

"You wanted to see me, Madam President." General Jabari remained standing as she offered no chair.

She recited the interim appointments to her cabinet.

"Well, Madam President, I'm in this job because you declared martial law and I have no say-so. I claim no political skills but I understand enough to warn you there will be a storm like you've never seen. You better get geared for a fight because that what you're going to get." After listening to her pronouncement, he still wondered why she was telling him. He had no role or place in this. It was a political fight, no place for his Marines.

"Just make damned sure the military stays out of it."

"I beg your pardon. Are you remotely suggesting I would permit anything like that? If so, you can add my name to those in opposition to what you're doing. Not as head of the military but as a citizen who thinks what you're doing is unwarranted."

"Good. I take that means you're resigning. You're only in that job because of a fluke in the constitution."

"Hell no, it doesn't. I'm keeping my job. If you want to fire me and make this a public fight, go ahead." Jabari left Government House never waiting for her answer, angrier than he could ever remember.

One month later, ignoring the storm building in Parliament, New Earth's lanky, bald headed Secretary of State Donavan Hillman said, "Madam President, it is my pleasure to present Ambassador Munn Authum representing his Highness King Resen and the people of Hommew."

Authum nodded, stepped forward and handed Olivanta his credentials.

"Ambassador Authum, welcome to New Earth. I hope our two worlds can develop a close and meaningful relationship." She studied the man for a moment and said, "Ambassador, the Hommew seem to have a firm grasp of New Earth's customs. I refer to the sash Ambassador Fowoth wore at our first meeting, and these credentials—very Earth like. How is that?"

Pushing away the translator, he said in very substantial English, "Madam President, may I remind you the Hommew studied your world, Old Earth that is, over three hundred years ago. Knowing our own habits, we hoped protocols hadn't changed all that much. It would seem we were correct. Being explorers, we have found that formal customs are the slow to change. Familiarity seems to have meaning and helps remove suspicion."

She started to say familiarity can be a two edged sword but instead smiled and said, "Well, I see you also speak our language as well as Ambassador Fowoth. My congratulations. Do all your people speak English?"

"No, Madam President. However, your presence on Usgac, excuse me New Earth, did suggest a day would come when having a working knowledge of your language would be useful." He smiled back at her.

She turned to the Secretary of State, "Secretary Hillman, how are we progressing with learning the Hommew language?"

Hillman cleared his throat. "Madam President, it is to my regret that I must tell you we have made little if any progress."

"I suspect little effort," she said.

A contrite look covered Hillman's face as he said, "Unfortunately, that's true."

Ambassador Authum made no attempt to stifle the smug grin and covered his face with a hand, arguably projecting an air of superiority. English had been the dominant language on Old Earth for years and that certainly carried over to New Earth and the expectation that anyone wishing to communicate with the Earthlings would learn their language. Ambassador Authum agreed and Olivanta felt a slight blush creep over her face.

"Please have a seat, Ambassador.

"In order to facilitate communications, I have decided to make our FTL communications technology available to your people. When our ambassador arrives on the Hommew world, he will have FTL equipment with him and all that is need for your engineers to develop your own."

"Our thanks, Madam. I will immediately send this information to Hommew. May I have the name of your ambassador? I will send that as well."

"My brother-in-law, Grandy Sashem will take the position. He is quite able and I think you'll find him easy to work with."

Secretary Hillman's eyebrows arched in surprise and his eyes fixed on Olivanta. Since he'd given her no name, her response stymied him. Sashem, in his opinion, lacked credibility as an emissary. Judged by most as a nit with the personality of a piece of wood—actually, President Olivanta had authored the description of the man. She had shoved him off on the Hommew. Since Olivanta won the presidency, Sashem had intruded into virtually every aspect of the government and she did nothing to curb the man. Comeuppance came when he ordered Admiral Presk-Milar to make a space ship available for his personal use. The Admiral laughed at him. That sent Sashem storming into General Jabari's office, told him of the slight by Presk-Milar and ordered Jabari to have the Marine contingent aboard Lexington arrest the Admiral. It didn't take long for reliable sources to spread the word that Jabari called a guard and had the guy removed with the admonition to shoot him if he tried to breached security again. Most likely, Hillman suspected, with Old Earth about to wage war, Olivanta named Sachem to the ambassadorship as the man totally backed her pacifist views and spouted it at every opportunity. His primary job would be to counteract any arguments the Hommew presented against mothballing a portion of New Earth's fleet. Part of his job would require selling the Hommew on the idea of talking with the Chinese instead of accepting war as the only means to reaching some accord.

Leaving Government House with the Ambassador, Hillman's eyes rolled. As they walked down the steps, he backed up his concern advising Ambassador Authum of Grandy Sashem's lack of respect for authority and he should not tolerate any impudence by the man.

5: Command Change

"**Who's** the twerp?" Grandy Sashem, New Earth's Ambassador to Hommew, looked out over the reception crowd and referred to a smallish man who had taken a seat on the dais.

Preparations to welcome New Earth's representative were extensive, with dignitaries from all walks of Hommew life. Response to the King's announcement to welcome their newfound neighbor resulted in over a thousand Hommew attending and the function moving outside to a tent. Had Sashem taken the time to check out the gala, he would have seen a number of joy rides similar to those on New Earth. The Hommew were not above borrowing good ideas, some a product of their Old Earth survey of over three hundred years earlier. Other exotic devices, perhaps from other civilizations or of Hommew design thrilled youngsters and adults alike.

Ambassador Fowoth, not given to histrionics, glared at the much taller Sashem dressed in a pinstripe tuxedo, common ambassadorial fare. "That, sir, is our King Resen."

"Not very majestic is he?" the mocking and unrepentant Sashem said. "Not one person bowed or even acknowledged his entrance. It would seem the crowd doesn't think much of him."

Recalling Secretary of State Hillman's admonition regarding the man's impudence, Fowoth turned to the ambassador, his voice filled with distain, said, "Sir, I resent your attitude. If your purpose is to antagonize the Hommew, you have made an excellent start. I hope you do not think your addressing our monarch in this manner will go unreported." Clearly perturbed, Fowoth stepped away from Sashem distancing himself, his eyebrows scrunched in contempt.

"Just stating fact," retaliated Sashem. "He wouldn't amount to much on New Earth. Not much of a commanding presence to the man. Being king must be hereditary. Nothing else would fit."

Fowoth made his way through the crowd toward the podium, leaving Sashem standing alone. He bowed to the King and took a seat.

A few minutes later, he stood at the speaker's dais and welcomed the exchange of ambassadors without mentioning Sashem's presence or inviting him to present his credentials to the king, something quite evident to the assembly. Ambassador Grandy Sashem had made an ungracious impression.

Two days later, New Earth recalled Grandy Sashem. A month following in a private ceremony, Ambassador Damon Watts presented his credentials to King Resen replacing Sashem as Ambassador to Hommew.

* * * *

"You imbecile," Olivanta scolded Sashem. "Why did you insult their King? I thought just the idea you could work with the elite of another country would mean something to you." She shook her head, "You even got all the trappings—including that damned spaceship you wanted for your personal use."

Sashem started to speak and she silenced him with a look that said more than 'don't speak a word—you'll regret every one of them." She dismissed her brother-in-law. She needed something she wasn't going to get—time to marshal her supporters to head off any action by parliament and Grady just made that more difficult, maybe impossible.

Olivanta keyed the comm switch on her desk, "Marsha, I need to see you immediately."

Less than an hour later Marsha Henderson, Home Secretary, stood in front of Olivanta's massive ornate desk. Hand carved from a single piece of wood, from one of New Earth's oldest tress very much like mahogany, she had staunchly defended her actions despite cries from within her own party not to cut the aged tree estimated at over a thousand years old.

"I need for you to buy me some time," she said. "Grandy's stupidity in calling the Hommew king a twerp may force a vote of confidence. I can persuade a number of parliamentarians to support me, I mean in addition to our party members, but it will take time." She laid out what she wanted Marsha to do. Home Secretary Henderson's successes made her popular on both sides of the aisle and now Olivanta needed her to use that influence.

A week later, standing before the great desk, as it had become known, Marsha Henderson said, "I'm sorry Madam President, I tried every trick in my book. Parliament is truly angry. Bypassing them with interim cabinet appointments caused an uproar on both sides of the aisle. There is talk of impeachment if the vote of confidence fails. And their dislike for Mr. Sashem killed any attempts I made to gain additional support." She left, knowing the next few days would determine the fate of this presidency.

The former emissary proved only one of President Olivanta's worries, yet his actions on Hommew did force the confidence vote in Parliament—just the opportunity her political enemies wanted. Naming the interim cabinet had members from both sides shouting for her blood.

Deciding it was best to frame the discussion, Olivanta decided to ignore the real reason parliament had summoned her. Standing in the *well* defending her pacifist policies, President Olivanta said, "We must not be afraid to show those who might do us harm our willingness to sit down and talk." Her voice rising about the shouts she continued, "Instead of preparing for war, a reduction in the fleet would send a better message, one of peace."

That statement fell on angry ears and alone could end her presidency. Even her silence about the interim appointments did not help as shouts of derision roundly drowned out her diminishing supporters. The list of grievances grew as her detractors clamored in the forum to air their complaints. More and more of the aggrieved rose to speak until the parliamentarian ordered an end to the tirades. Only a few of her most ardent supporters cried *no* when the order came for a vote.

President Olivanta failed to get the needed majority to continue her administration. In accordance with the law, the Parliamentarian immediately scheduled elections for president one month from that date. Olivanta could run for re-election as her critics knew and she wasn't without support although diminished by her attacks on Jabari.

* * * *

Following Parliament's vote, Olivanta resigned her presidency. Standing in *The Box* reception room among a dozen well-wishers, General Jabari took the oath of office as interim president serving until the people elected a new leader. In his first act, he issued an executive order that directed every governmental agency to continue as it had. There would be no changes in the government or policies except two. Joined by Fleet Admiral Presk-Milar, President Jabari ordered an end to the mothballing of any part of the fleet. In his second edict, he thanked the interim cabinet members for their service and fired them. For what he considered good reason, he would govern from his office in *The Box*, forgoing a move to Government House. After all, he would be President for only one month. Besides, there, he could control who had access and that included those who urged him to run for the office he now held. Or so he thought.

It took the better part of two days before the well-wishers stopped dropping by.

Interim President John Jabari walked from behind his desk and greeted David Rohm. "Hello my friend." He grasped the outstretched hand. "What do I owe this visit to? It's been some time since you graced this place."

His words brought a raised eyebrow from Rohm. Purposely, he'd avoided the early well-wishers.

Having personally known his grandfather, Jabari and David had a special relationship. The two had spent hours talking about David's namesake.

At David's request, Jabari started a journal detailing every item he could recall about the man. The idea caught on and Orion's four surviving scientists expanded the concept to include all eight of the original group. Of those who had received blood transfusions, one hundred nineteen, seven survived and took on the task of completing the now named *Chronicles of Orion*.

David Rohm took a seat, leaned forward hands on his knees. "Mr. President, have you ever tried your hand at acting? You know *damned good and well* why I'm here. I would like to see you as the next President of New Earth."

"Hell David, I am President," Jabari's voice boomed. "Don't you read the newsies? I don't need to run." He laughed but then grew serious seeing his guest didn't share in the humor. Rohm's demeanor left little doubt.

The President let out a pent-up breath. Standing, he said, "David, all my life I've avoided politics. It drove me out of the swamp. I enlisted in the Marines committed to steer clear of everything political. I've sworn allegiance to every president I've served. I am a Marine, nothing more. I'm in this job because someone miswrote the constitution and parliament never took it to the people for fixing. Nothing I've done has prepared me for this office. I would be a disaster."

"I disagree." David stood to his full height, still at least five centimeters shorter than his friend. "We're about to go to war, Jimmy-John." Rohm no longer talked to the President but to a comrade. "Old Earth will not be a pushover. From what we know, the Chinese are determined to subjugate us. It will take everything we possess to survive what's coming. You've been in battle. No other person on New Earth has ever fired a weapon in anger against an avowed enemy. We play war games with electronic rivals but that it is no substitute for combat. We need a leader who understands that and you do—someone who can order friends and our young people to their deaths." He stopped, took a step toward the president. "There are a number, like myself, who would support you in the office—serve in your cabinet if asked."

Jabari's eyebrows shot up. "You'd serve in the cabinet? David, you should be president, not me. Hell, you're twice as smart as I am."

"Maybe, but it isn't a matter of smart, Jimmy-John, it's about leadership. And you have what it takes to provide that. You have been tested in ways no other of us have. No, my friend, we need a proven leader and you're that person."

Jabari slumped back in his chair and sat silent for a moment, brooding. His massive hands brushed his face and hair. "My god man, I'd be lost. I wouldn't have a clue what to do." Desperation enveloped him.

"Leadership, Jimmy-John, leadership. That's what we want, what we need. Will you at least think about it?" David walked to the door stopped and repeated his urging, "We really need you, my friend."

One month and a week later following a robust campaign by the pacifists that failed at the polls by a vote of four to one, John (Jimmy-John) Jabari, a Cajun born in the swamps of Old Earth, took the oath of office as the twenty fifth President of New Earth to more pomp than he wanted.

He quickly learned even the president had only so much power—despite his protests, the ceremony went on as planned. Events had moved so quickly, he had little time to decide on a cabinet and quietly thanked David Rohm for keeping his word to serve. It unnerved some people when Jabari named three military men to cabinet posts. It didn't take the pacifists long to jump on him for being a militarist. His private response: "Assholes, what in the hell did they expect from a man who'd spent nearly three hundred years as a Marine." Naming Admiral Bogdan Presk-Milar as Commandant to head New Earth's defense post did quell most of the rhetoric. His being a direct descendant of Maria Presk, still meant a great deal and as a member of Olivanta's political party, the pacifists couldn't attack Jabari without denigrating Presk-Milar. That quieted them—for the time being. Jabari put them from his mind. He had much larger concerns.

A stream of orders went out from Government House as President Jabari prepared his world to meet their enemy. Emissaries made frequent trips to Hommew and Myslac as plans moved forward. Freighters loaded with the rare minerals spaced for Hommew as well as Myslac: material the Kalazecis badly needed to repair ships neglected for over one hundred T-years. In addition, FTL communications technology was shared with all the allies, including former enemies. Initially, some New Earthers voiced concern about how Martin Grabel would react to not being named to head the Tri-War Council but the diminutive volatile king quickly put those worries to rest when he sent congratulations on Jabari's presidency and the naming of Admiral Presk-Milar. The problem of sharing New Earth's advanced technology did cause a slight disruption but knowing voices reminded everyone it would take years to retrofit enough ships to make a difference in both the Hommew and Kalazecis fleet. Other than FTL communications, they would fight with what they had.

A month later, Bogdan Presk-Milar lamented the lack of intelligence. "It's not just *timely* intel," said the Defense Secretary, "we've received *no* meaningful word on the Chinese plan." Standing before the other members of the Tri-War Council he said, "Gentlemen, somehow we must remedy this problem. Suggestions?"

Secretary Presk-Milar had called the Tri-War Council meeting more out of frustration than strategic or tactical need. Added to that of the defense plans put forward, only New Earth's included dealing with Old Earth after the conclusion of hostilities—something for which the other worlds showed no interest.

The Hommew member had nothing to offer. Clearing his throat, the representative from Myslac, Kzasis leaned toward the human sitting next to him and to whom the Kalazecis had not been introduced, something not uncommon as presumed superiority plagued the relationship. Using a translator, he whispered for a few moments, received a nod, then said, "There is a way." Clearly, the Kalazecis wanted his human counterpart's agreement before committing his world.

"How?" said Presk-Milar. What had bordered on desperation quickly changed to hope. Penetrating the Chinese oligarchy had failed. He knew they must find some other way.

Being the only member who couldn't speak English, the Kalazecis deferred to the human as none of his race could get their tongues around what they called meaningless gibberish. Leaning back in his chair, hands folded across an ample stomach with a look Presk-Milar took for indifference he said, "I am Roster Philbin. I must declare myself. I formerly served on the PRC Golden Eagle. Badly damaged in the first war between the two worlds, we couldn't avoid capture. I opposed the war and given the chance, swore allegiance to the Kalazecis king, as I did to King Grabel when he took the throne, and have serve Myslac for twenty T-years. I have no regrets about turning on the Chinese."

Eyebrows raised, Secretary Bogdan offered a smile and nod.

"Our King has not been idle in this matter," Philbin continued. "Using the knowledge gained from those of us who have sworn allegiance to Myslac and the King, as well as captured prisoners, we sent drones using electronics only King Grabel understands to Old Earth. They are undetectable thanks again to his majesty's ingenious design. We made contact with a group committed to stopping the war."

"Great," Presk-Milar almost shouted. "We need this information, all of it, who these people are and how to contact them."

"It's yours. My aides will provide all the details," Kzasis grabbed the translator and spoke with unbridled pride.

Philbin's glance at the Kalazecis display seemed anything but pleased, probably over his pomposity.

He continued, "During production of the Chinese spaceships electronics, sympathetic engineers installed devices that will disrupt their electronics. Twenty of their largest vessels carry these chips. There are operatives aboard the Chinese fleet who share our concerns about attacking New Earth and will activate them once the battle begins. Hopefully when it will cause the most damage." He ended without fanfare.

Both the Hommew and New Earth delegates applauded the revelation.

Admiral Presk-Milar held up his hand. "Permit an interruption. Finally some good news. Do you know why the Chinese have chosen us to attack? Why are they by passing Myslac?"

Philbin looked at his Kalazecis who had the translator. With human like gestures, Kzasis shrugged.

Philbin paused, took a deep breath and said, "First, the Kalazecis have defeated them once and the Chinese leadership want your long life secret,"— reticence laced his voice.

Secretary Presk-Milar shot from his chair. "Goddamnit, why wasn't I told this? Shit, this changes everything. Answer me dammit." In one of the few instanced he'd ever lost his temper, Milar, angry with himself realized he'd overlooked the very reason for the attack on New Earth.

Kzasis, still seated raised the translator and said, "King Grabel thought you might fight harder if you feared annihilation as your fate." He laid down the device apparently not wanting to hear the response—Presk-Milar's glare carried enough of his message but didn't stop there.

Reaching across the table, he retrieved the translator and said, "You tell that little bastard I'll personally kick his ass for withholding this information," and stormed from the room.

6: The Order of Battle

"I know Mr. President, but I just couldn't contain my anger," said Admiral Presk-Milar. "This changes our order of battle completely. It's a problem you didn't need and I apologize to you but not Grabel. I don't like being manipulated and when the lives of our people are put to risk—it's downright deceit."

"That smart little son of a bitch had it wrong," said Jabari. "I doubt that we would fight any harder. At least we can be thankful that we know. I agree, it does change our thinking and we have time to make tactical adjustments."

"What about the spies on the Chinese ships? What do we know about them?" he asked.

"Sorry Mr. President. I left immediately after getting Grabel's thinking and headed over here. If you'll excuse me, I'll comm my second and see if he learned anymore."

"Jabari nodded and Presk-Milar touched his comm. For the next few minutes, he and the President listened to the recitation.

"Well, I don't see where that helps us other than knowing about the saboteurs. How much they will help remains to be seen," Jabari said.

"If we had some idea when they plan to disrupt the fleet, it would be helpful," Presk-Milar said. He paused for a minute recalling how David Rohm's grandfather had neutralized the Kalazecis ships electronics a few hundred years earlier. "Let me talk to David Rohm. He has a good understanding of the Kalazecis electronics. I doubt the Chinese changed much of the basic ship systems and we may be able to take advantage of that."

"Works for me, Bogdan. Keep me posted." They shook hands.

At the door, the Secretary paused, "Looks like David Rohm had it right about you, Mr. President."

Quizzically, Jabari looked up and leaned back in his chair, a slight grin crossing his face. "How's that, Bogdan?"

"Some people expressed strong doubts that you could do the job. David never flinched in his opinion that you were the right man. Even I had doubts. Shows how wrong a man can be."

"I'm not sure I should thank him. It isn't over and you may be right."

"I doubt that. But it would appear presumptuous of you to thank him so I will." Bogdan walked out the door not waiting for a response.

A month later, Admiral Presk-Milar, who had settled in as Secretary of Defense, and newly named Fleet Admiral Magnus Svern took seats offered by the President.

"Gentlemen, what do I owe this visit to? Magnus congratulations on your promotion."

"Thank you Mr. President," with a wry smile he responded. "I'm enjoying the new accommodations."

Secretary Presk-Milar gave a less than pleased glance at the Admiral. After all, Svern now occupied Presk-Milar's old haunt. These three men had served together for a number of T-years and traded lighthearted jabs, even welcomed them. To a man, they knew what the future held and it would leave little chance for humor.

"Gentlemen, what's on your minds?" asked Jabari. During the few months he'd held the presidency, Admiral Presk-Milar had made a number of trips to his office but the décor had changed since his last visit. The Cajun had seen fit to redecorate and the place had a distinct Creole flavor. Jabari had invited the remaining inhabitants of Orion along with the newsies to show off the changes. And not surprisingly, the public couldn't get enough about the unveiling. Most had never seen anything like it. Being original Cajun motif added to the mystique and their appreciation. Dealing with the upcoming war did little to detract from the liking the population had for anything Old Earth.

"Mr. President, the order of battle is complete." The secretary quickly added, "Subject to any suggestions you care to make of course."

Surprising even himself, Jabari had taken the reins of government, demonstrating a knack for handling the myriad of complex affairs laid before him. His most vocal detractors had admitted he seemed cut out for the job. His calm demeanor under pressure from any detractor worked its magic.

Fleet Admiral Svern laid out in detail how the fleet planned to handle the attack. "And if they breech our outer defenses?" asked Jabari.

"Of course, our orbital factories will be evacuated before hostilities begin. We have one hundred energy cannons in close orbit and another one hundred dirtside," Svern said. "The downside, if we have to use them, that means we will have lost the fleet and face the Chinese without that support. Mr. President, if we can't stop them," he paused a moment, "if they can get to the planet," he paused again, "we'll have a problem." A thorough study of the raids on Myslac showed the Chinese had developed rudimentary missile launch pads. Attached externally to the ships for transit, once they reached the attack location, they would deploy the platforms and launch their missiles. "There's every reason to believe they will have improved on that asset. It means each ship can simultaneously launch fifty missiles and repeat it every hour; we can't begin to stop ten thousand missiles coming at us at one time. They'll put troops on the ground once they've eliminated any resistance on the surface."

President Jabari sat silent for some time. "We have to prepare for that possibility gentlemen." Jabari looked out a side window.

The two admirals started to stand and were waved back into their chairs. "Admiral Svern, you found a class M planet on the far side of the *void*. Is it capable of sustaining life?"

Cautiously, Svern answered, "From what little we know about it, yes, sir. We did not make a detailed survey." He didn't add to the comment, apparently caught off guard by the President's question.

"I will not permit what started three hundred years ago to end," Jabari quietly said. "Secretary Presk-Milar, prepare a corvette and two transports that can take one hundred people and everything they need to this planet. They will be a hedge in case the worst happens. I will address our people in a nationwide vidcast and ask for volunteers. Any gaps we'll fill with a draft if necessary." Meaning he wanted a balance of men, women and skills. The group would have to carve out their destiny.

Stunned to silence, the two men gaped but met the president's steady gaze. In their most dire moments when considering the consequences of losing the war, they had not anticipated anything so startling.

After an interminable silence, Secretary Presk-Milar said, "Sir, you should be on that ship. I prefer to stay but we'll need a functioning government and you can direct that off-planet."

"No Bogdan, my place is here."

As Presk-Milar started to speak, Jimmy-John held up his hand stopping the secretary, "No discussion, my friends."

"Now, if Grabel is right, the Chinese will attempt a landing. They want prisoners," said Jabari. "How do you plan to meet that threat?"

"Mr. President, if they get on New Earth, we have no defense. They can land more troops than we have in our total population. A landing must not happen at any cost," the Fleet Admiral said. "We do believe the plan we have will stop that. Our combined fleet, two hundred Kalazecis, Washington class (three hundred Kalazecis Mandela's were mothballed due to lack of the minerals only found on New Earth), one hundred from Hommew, all less mass, and less fire power, our one hundred heavy cruisers, about the same number but mixed light cruisers and missile platforms along with our two carriers, the Lexington and Concord and their five hundred fighters. The best information we have on the Chinese fleet says their armada consists of two hundred Mandela class, cruiser size, forty troop transports and the rest support ships. With our fighters and energy cannons, we think, no believe, while we'll take substantial losses, the odds are in our favor."

From a thorough understanding of military history, President Jabari's knew a defender needed at least a four to one differential to have a reasonable chance of success. New Earth couldn't approach that. "Okay, go ahead with your detail planning but don't put it to bed yet."

"Care to tell me what you've got in mind, Mr. President?" Admiral Svern asked.

"Let me have a few days. Might be nothing." That signaled the end of the meeting. They shook hands and parted.

As the two approached the door, Secretary Presk-Milar asked, "Got a name for their new home, Mr. President?"

Jabari thought for a moment, smiled, and said, "I grew up in Alligator Bayou, Mississippi, no more than ten shacks, we called it Hope. It was supposed to be Jerusalem, but our mayor... don't laugh," he jokingly admonished his riveted listeners, "we had one, only he couldn't read or write. When he filed the papers making us legal, the clerk couldn't understand him, heard someone say hope, and wrote it down. The mayor couldn't speak English well either." Again, he cast a warning eye at his grinning audience. "My dream was to make Hope as important as the state capital, Jackson. Well, that sure isn't going to happen so, how about New Hope?"

With nods of approval, he closed the door and pressed a button, "Tell the Myslac ambassador I want to see him." Only this time, the momentary nostalgia had disappeared.

7: The Enemy

"**Is** the fleet ready?" asked General Yang Kuo Nu. As the People's Republic of China Commissar of the Army Navy, Yang had taken direct command of the space fleet. Normally in a high state of agitation, the intensity among the Army Navy command rose as the launch date to attack New Earth approached. Most everyone had experienced Yang's impatience and had suffered from it. His belligerence toward Peng Rui Bao had grown over the last few months. For over one hundred years, China had prepared for this moment. Yang's determined leadership led them through the plan laid out by his predecessors over a century earlier. One hundred years meant little to a society that had endured for over six thousand. Subjugation of Earth had taken fifty years—some countries succumbed under economic duress, others political and a number of nations required military intervention. But with China's massive manpower resources, building spaceships had proceeded unabated. Five hundred ships now orbited Earth and with rigorous training, proficiency met even the most truculent observers' standards. Yang showed little tolerance for his detractors as most quickly learned to keep their doubts to themselves. Even members of the politburo muted their discontent.

"It is approaching readiness, General. Admiral Yu's last report is most positive. He estimates another six months and they can launch all the ships." Despite his best effort, the smallish Peng sounded less than enthusiastic. He understood the general's real motivation—Yang wanted the long life gene New Earth possessed and their technology. And he wasn't alone. Many Earth people felt the same: that the New Earthers had cheated them of the opportunity, no the *right* to a much longer life. Support for Yang remained strong among many people, dividing nations as preparations for war moved forward. His power base capitalized on this silencing of the most vociferous critics. Leaders he'd helped appoint among the subjugated nations trumpeted the benefits of long life and viciously put down those who had the nerve to speak against him or the war or both.

"You are in doubt about this mission. Do you think we will not be successful? Do you not want to live another three or four hundred years?" Yang never permitted the use of the word failure. Sitting erect behind a large rosewood desk in an otherwise ordinary office, he eyed his aide. Resentment from nation states and influential people had grown, and the inept Nations of the World Organization (NWO) had privately approached Yang seeking to stop the upcoming war. Yang rebuked them with an admonition that if they persisted, he would have them shot. Even the NWO lacked independence from the General. They were expected to keep the subjugated nations pacified.

Knowing he could not speak his private thoughts, Peng said, "Your leadership has never failed us, General."

"That is no answer. If you are to be of use to me, I must know what you know." Yang's voice cut like a scythe as his tolerance lessened with each delay. Demanded loyalty remained a fragile matter with the General as the aide had seen people dismissed for little or no reason.

"General, information comes to me from many sources. There are nations against this idea. They are not to be discounted." Peng understood his master and the limits of any negative response. He had served the man for twenty years—something of a record for aides. Upon the younger man's graduation from the China University of Political Science and Law, Yang personally selected Peng and to refuse such an honor amounted to an insult. Peng had graciously accepted. His family and relatives all benefited from his prestigious position and he had become wealthy. But enjoying the prosperity eluded him. General Yang had never taken a vacation—the workaholic spent most nights at his office. "There are those who spread unkind words and plot to stop your plan," Peng said.

"Are these people known to us?" Yang stood, rocked back and forth on his toes, his jet black eyes unblinking, voice low, strained, the overhead light glistened off this clean-shaven head. He steadfastly refused to wear western dress and instead selected the Mao jacket and trousers. A portrait of the PRC founder hung behind the desk, the only item to adorn the walls.

"General, mostly they use surrogate sources to spread their poison," Peng said hesitantly.

"What have you done to stop them?" Anger dripped like acid from his words. As the time for launching the space fleet approached, Yang's temperament had worsened.

How he answered this question could determine how Yang would retaliate which he surely would do. Those who had experienced—there were many—and survived General Yang Kuo Nu's temper were few. In Yang's world, there were only two kinds of people—those who supported him and enemies.

"It is difficult, General. Microchips inserted in electronic devices of all kinds, particularly vid and HD's are used to interrupt and deliver slanderous remarks toward the war against New Earth." He purposely left out the most dangerous personal remarks against the General.

"Why wasn't I told this? You have deceived me keeping this threat from me." Yang walked from behind his desk and menacingly towered over the smaller man. "Leave me. I have no use for you."

Yang's words hit Peng like a sledgehammer. In the years he'd served the man, never had he suffered such venom. Fear gripped him—he knew the danger his family faced with his dismissal.

Peng left the command headquarters without stopping to gather years of accumulated personal items from his office. If any chance existed to save himself and family, he would have to move quickly. Outside the building, using the cell phone, he called his wife at their small home telling her he was on his way and ending with a cryptic message: "I have time to harvest the lotus," a reference to his hobby but also something only she would understand. Peng's efforts in cross-pollinating lotus flowers, genus Nymphaeaceae, had gained him considerable recognition. Now he would use that as cover for getting his family to safety. He and his wife had discussed this possibility numerous times and planned their escape.

At home, she gathered their children, the valuables they had decided to take, and left to pick up her husband.

An hour later, driving the family van—he'd left his government car in Yang's headquarters carpool and didn't sign it in, they drove to Beijing Capital International Airport.

Parking in the crowded public lot, they boarded a bus for the Beijing Railway Station.

Before boarding, he stopped long enough at a public telephone booth to make a call, one that would alert people dedicated to stopping the upcoming invasion, that he was fleeing his country.

At the train station, he purchased tickets for the port city Dalian where he bribed officials for space on a sampan bound for Hong Kong—a trip fraught with peril.

Ten day later, they found refuge in Macao. After doling out cash for forged passports and visas, he and his family book steerage passage on a freighter/passenger ship sailing for the Philippines.

A week later, they were on a suborbital flight for America.

Ushering his family from the plane—afraid for them—in a strange country whose language he didn't speak, Peng Rui Bao nevertheless followed the man dressed in blue coveralls through the now seldom used D.C. Ronald Reagan National Airport. The suborbital ship on which they arrived, didn't have the stature to use the newer spaceports. That worked to their advantage as most security forces focused their attention on the heavily trafficked

International Air/Spacedrome that had replaced the Dulles International airport.

Closely grouped about him, his family waited in the aging building badly in need of repair.

A few minutes passed before the door opened and another worker dressed in similar dark blue coveralls entered.

Without introducing himself, he walked to a side door, opened it and motioned Peng to enter, his actions urgent.

Hesitantly, the father gathered his family and obeyed.

Stepping into a narrow passageway, hurriedly but quietly, they followed their guide along the dimly lit hallway up a flight of stairs arriving at a dock. They stumbled through a door to a waiting van.

Frightened, the children clung to Peng and their mother.

Without windows, Peng was unable to see. He settled back in his seat deciding it made no difference other than just to be able to view the country. He envisioned slums, trashed houses, and street beggars. In reality, he'd paid no attention to the rest of the world. Working for Yang left little time for anything that distracted him from their one goal. Making his first trip to America, he wouldn't recognize features had he seen them. This was, in fact, his first time outside of his own country.

One hour later, the van stopped and along with their guide, they left the truck and entered a small room.

Surprising Peng, the man said in broken Chinese, "Wait here. This is as far as I can take you today. Another will come to help you complete your journey."

Two days and half a dozen vehicles later, Peng and his family walked into an apartment.

"You may rest here. Someone will come for you." Their guide smiled and closed the door.

Peng flinched as the lock's tumblers fell into place. Cautiously, he inspected their accommodations; kitchen with ample food, four bedrooms, and clean western clothes properly sized each. For two more days, they waited. Not being hustled from place-to-place, the children's trepidation turned to restlessness. That quickly ended with a gentle knock and the sound of a key opening the door.

Fear again gripped Peng's family.

A woman along with an elderly oriental man stepped into the room. She didn't introduce herself although the interpreter spoke words of assurance to Peng.

Another windowless van ride took them to an office building. A few steps further led them to a basement and into a well-lit conference room. Devoid of any pictures or windows, only a large table surrounded by a dozen chairs filled with unknown faces greeted him, some with smiles.

Speaking through the interpreter the woman said, "Mr. Peng, I am Holly Joiner. The names of these people," she motioned to the remainder, "will not be revealed to you. I can tell you they are all interested in your family's welfare and what you have to say. If you have no objection, your wife and children can rest and enjoy a few pleasantries while we discuss the reason for your being here." She motioned toward an open door. "If you'd like, please take a look."

Peng did so and satisfied, in hushed gentle words spoke to his wife.

Reluctant to leave their father, it took some urging to get the children to move.

Following his hostess, Peng took one of the two chairs at the head of the table, the older Chinese gentleman the seat next to him.

For three hours, Peng fielded questions about the upcoming war on New Earth and his own opposition.

Seemingly satisfied with his answers, Holly thanked him for his help.

One man stood, signaled the Chinese interpreter who again thanked Peng and told him he would guide them to their new home.

Before leaving the room, Peng asked if anyone had plans to stop the fleet and got only smiles.

As the door closed, former space Admiral Johann Liverson said, "Well, gentlemen and lady, what do we do with this information?"

"We needed confirmation of what we already knew and that's what we got," said one man. "Nothing new. But just knowing what they know, or more correctly, what they don't know is very useful."

"From what we've just heard, Yang has no idea we've altered their shipboard electronics," a third man said. "If, and I stress the *if*, our operatives aboard those spaceships can disrupt their attack, it will have all been worthwhile. We owe New Earth at least that. It will be up to those people to select the time and place. It would seem all we can do is wait."

Former space Admiral Johann Liverson agreed. "In fact," he said his face reflecting grim satisfaction, "it is time to begin our second phase. If our efforts are successful, the Chinese empire will unravel and we must be ready." That got complete agreement.

With that, the informal China Resistance ended.

"Gentlemen and lady, you know what each of you must do to put the next part into operation. This will be our most dangerous effort. Now we must involve a great number of people and keeping this quiet will be next to impossible. There will be casualties."

* * * *

Aboard the flagship, Flying Dragon, Captain Huang Liang Chen waited as Supreme Admiral Fong Chao read the message from Army Navy Commissar Yang. He chuckled and said, "Our leader grows worried. He sees enemies everywhere. Perhaps he is right." Turning to his aide, he asked, "Chen, have you been in contact with our *huángdòus*?"

"Yes, Admiral, all our spies are on alert," she said. As the only woman to reach the rank of Fleet Captain, she had earned the envy of many flag officers. Without the support of Chao, she knew a space lock waited. "Our spies tell me they have detected nothing that would harm the fleet. If we have enemies, perhaps our diligence has cowed them into submission."

"Perhaps Captain, but doubtful. Tell our *huángdòus* to double their vigilance. We want nothing to upset our great plan. Our master wants to live another three or four hundred years and we must deliver the long life secret the New Earthers have denied us." He leaned close to Chen and whispered, "If you would be at my side, I would live for that long, but if it is the hag I'm now married to, I would rather die." He laughed when Chen gave him a look that said—*behave*.

Chen walked down the passageway to her quarters after the oncoming bridge watch arrived to relieve them, changed into sweats, and headed for the gym. She spent the better part of an hour at her wushu exercises before taking a shower, dressing and then going to the officers' mess hall. She had no idea how long it would be before orders came to space for New Earth. Even then, it would take three weeks to make the journey. She had reservations about the battle plan but Admiral Chao had made it known Commissar Yang considered it worthy. He did admit not knowing what defenses they would face when they met the enemy conjured troublesome thoughts. But they would carry out their orders and attack. New Earth would feel the full force of their majestic fleet. They would succeed. After all, the People's Republic subjugated seven billion people on Earth, how difficult could forty thousand be?

Back in her quarters, Chen keyed her computer, entered her password and studied the maintenance records. Her fingers tapped the icons and the navigation electronic schematic appeared. Satisfied nothing had changed, she keyed half a dozen other sites and made the appropriate notations of her presence. From the beginning, she had opposed the invasion as unworthy of a great nation. Her devotion to country did not include the leadership. In her mind, the people of China had built the nation into a world power and created a standard of living not enjoyed before. Born to entrepreneurial parents, her intellect caught the attention of the school authorities. Appointment first to China's Experimental High School virtually assured her of attending the China Military Academy and those assignments came quickly.

Using their supremacy to conquer those who had believed her government's promises to participate as equals, amounted to lies of the worst kind and were unworthy of a great people.

8: King Grabel

Martin Grabel, dressed in a dark blue business suit, something the Kalazecis and Pagmok physique couldn't accommodate, accepted the vid pad from the Kalazecis commandant knelt before him. "So, Secretary Presk-Milar wants to kick my ass," the King said his voice carried a note of levity, something unusual for him. Surprising the assembled he added, "Can't say as I blame him." He motioned for the kneeling court to rise.

Expecting an outburst, a curious look crossed the face of Gnos Lznac, Myslac's Supreme Military Commandant. To the population, Grabel presented a sympathetic demeanor. Those close to the king often experienced his volatile personality. Grabel's reign as Myslac's king had gone surprisingly well considering how the man's tirades sent chills through those who suffered it. He tolerated no breech of etiquette or supposed slight. Any criticism remained well out of earshot.

Martin signaled the Pagmok guard standing at the back of the room to approach. Grabel's original plan dividing the Kalazecis and Pagmok on two different continents, the idea he'd presented to Maria Presk over a hundred years earlier, still held. It had proven a good solution. Pagmoks still supplied the labor to run the factories and any chores required by the Kalazecis as well as security. All Pagmok military served under a Kalazecis commander.

Kneeling before his king, the warrior waited.

"Find Rayall. I wish to see him," Martin said.

He turned at the slight rustle behind him and smiled. "Come my dear." He stretched his arm toward his wife and the court genuflected as Queen Bethany entered from a side door ushering two toddlers.

Grabel seldom used the throne room. His Kalazecis predecessors held court in just the opposite manner, requiring full dress and absolute obedience to ritual. His approach worked best for him and he believed the informality of the office resulted in people getting more done. Large by any standard, he had the room decorated much like Old Earth's Oval office—understated elegance he termed it.

"Ah, my favorites." Martin said as he picked up the two grandchildren and spun around a number of times to their squeals of glee. Running the kingdom took much of his time and the upcoming war kept him from the twins. His three sons, to his delight had proven quite capable, one a mathematician and the other two scientists, they had born him eight grandchildren all of whom enjoyed the long life gene.

After a few minutes of cuddling, a Pagmok warrior entered and knelt. "Your Highness, Rayall awaits his audience."

Grabel waved his hand and the warrior quickly arose, retraced his steps, and escorted Arnold Rayall into the office.

Amid a chorus of protests the Queen herded the children out.

Rayall, another human who switched sides, had participated in the first raid on Myslac serving on the Dragon's Claw and was subsequently captured. Having changed sides and swearing allegiance to Myslac, in the second raid he commanded the Kalazecis ship Gznosis with a Pagmok crew that boarded a Chinese battlewagon. Although outnumbered three to one, he'd led a fierce fight that resulted in its capture. Even the highest ranking Kalazecis military men paid credence to his leadership of the Pagmok. In hand-to-hand combat none were a match for them.

For his own reasons, Martin had not permitted any long life transfusions to the captured humans except for a select few. Too old to receive the long life gene, Rayall nevertheless served with distinction.

Martin had shed all the trappings of office that appeared haughty, preferring to present himself as one of the people. Those close to him knew better. On Old Earth and Orion, he had few intellectual peers. And on Myslac, none could approach, let alone challenge the man's intellect.

"New Earth has changed its strategy," he said to Rayall Maybe it's just as well." He paused. "I know President Jabari. The man is resolute and a very thorough planner. He leaves little to chance and when he can leaves himself an out. In fact, he tries to leaves his enemy a way out. The man believes a trapped adversary is more dangerous than one who can extricate himself. We should consider that when making our plans.

"What do you think about New Earth's approach, Arnold?"

"My King, given the chance to destroy an enemy, I say do so. Otherwise, he lives to fight another day. Kill him and be done with it." His voice was void of any compassion. Arnold Rayall served as sub-commander aboard on Chinese destroyer with a commander much of the same mind. For a ship of that size, it had inflicted a great deal of damage on several Kalazecis before another Myslac ship turned it into a floating hulk.

Martin nodded.

"Lznac, what say you?" he asked.

Gnos Lznac, as Supreme Military Commandant, had never led space ships into battle in fact, had barely reached his teens when the Chinese last attacked Myslac. What little he knew came from vids. Martin had at least witnessed the first fight between New Earth and the Kalazecis. He ascended the throne following the last Chinese attack and prior to that had received only cursory updates on that war. Even though President of the Pagmok nation, Martin rarely received information from the Kalazecis about the war, and treated with disdain, often ignored him. Actually, the isolation worked to Martin's benefit leaving him free to develop substantial technology for his nation. Only when the Kalazecis learned how far Martin had advanced their Pagmok neighbors did he gain their attention and the know-how that helped defeat the second Chinese attack. To say he had their respect would understate it—envy worked better.

Martin, to his credit and Kalazecis amazement, showed no animosity once on the throne. Discussions with the Kalazecis war committee caused Martin concerns, particularly Lznac's penchant for counterattacking when logic seemed to suggest the best way to defeat an enemy came from a bold assault. Using the lessons learned from Maria Presk's devastating defeat of the Myslac fleet one hundred T-years earlier when they attempted an attack on Old Earth, the Kalazecis sprung the same maneuver on the Chinese. While the results were not as astounding as New Earth's they nevertheless pounded the Chinese fleet unmercifully. The enemy would not make the same mistake twice. In the coming war, Martin understood the initiative remained with the Chinese and the Tri-Council's order of battle would focus on whatever weakness the invader presented as Admiral Presk-Milar attempted to drive them into his trap. That strategy he agreed with.

Grabel turned to the court reporter and instructed him to forward his last utterance to Kzasis, their representative on the Tri-War Council.

About the same height as his king, demeanor always respectful yet wary, Lznac said, "My King, I understand your concern of the Chinese securing the long life secret. Splitting our forces weakens the plan. It may be better if our entire fleet engaged the enemy."

"You may be right Commandant. But I believe the Tri-Council is correct that the thrust of the Chinese attack will be to clear a path to New Earth that will allow them to land troops. They understand that for the transfusions to work they must have live subjects."

Pensive for a few moments, Martin said to Lznac, "How many of our ships are capable of joining the fight?" After signing the treaty between Myslac and New Earth, shipment of badly need rare minerals began arriving almost immediately. Needed to repair their worn-out ships, a major refitting program began with the first arrival. Myslac's space worthy fleet amounted to less than one hundred ships. Getting to that number remained the first goal and problematic. Fortunately for the Kalazecis, in the first war the Chinese lack of experience in how to apply their ships led to their defeat. But that lesson would not be forgotten.

A Kalazecis appeared and knelt.

Curtly, Grabel said, "What do you want?" He showed his displeasure at the interruption.

"Majesty, we have received a message from our New Earth ambassador," he said still on his knees and eyes fixed on the floor. "It is from President Jabari."

Grabel motioned for a courtier to retrieve the vid pad. He quickly scanned the screen and chuckled. "Just like Jabari to stir things up. He wants us to put forty thousand Pagmok on the ground in case the Chinese make it to the planet surface."

Martin dismissed the court, retreated to his working office and called up the data on the drones circling Old Earth. Three years earlier, he had designed a series of satellites capable of orbiting Old Earth undetected. Having the opportunity to study the computer systems aboard the captured Chinese ships left little mystery when developing computer software to obviate detection. So far, they had escaped exposure despite their number and proximity to the planet. He considered his greatest success discovering and making contact with the China Resistance. Surreptitious communications confirmed the placement of microchips into some of the Chinese fleet's onboard electronics. Learning of Admiral Liverson's murder and the emergence of Holly Joiner left him questioning how successful any continued resistance might be.

Satisfied he'd learned well under David Rohm's tutelage aboard Orion, he smiled and punched the icon.

He gave a sigh and again touched another icon, "Yes, what is it?"

"Majesty, Lord Lzac wishes an audience," said the Kalazecis voice.

"What does he want?" Grabel changed his mind and said, "Never mind. I'll see him in my office." He paused, "in one hour."

He would let the head of his diplomatic corps cool his heels. The man tried Grabel's patience and seemed to enjoy doing so.

Fifth in line for the throne as far as the Kalazecis reckoned, his resentment toward Martin had few bounds. But then again, Martin kept the man off balance and the simpleton wasn't smart enough to deal with it.

Precisely on time, Martin sat in his office. "Show Lord Lzac in."

"My King." The Lord gave the obligatory nod expected of royalty acknowledging royalty. "I appreciate your taking the time to see me. I know how busy you are."

That, Martin knew, was the man's attempt to insult him. He thought for a minute deciding if he should let the slight go or retaliate. He would retaliate, with kindness.

Speaking in Kalazecis, which always irritated Lzac as his physique couldn't handle English, Martin said, "My Lord, you are always welcome here. I value your service to the throne. It is inestimable. What can I do for you?"

Lzac's smirk disappeared. Even he was smart enough to recognize a putdown. "My King, you received a dispatch from our ambassador on New Earth. The messenger mistakenly brought it here instead of to me. May I know the contents?"

"Of course. President Jabari wants forty thousand Pagmok warriors on New Earth in case the enemy lands troops on the planet. An excellent idea; wish I'd thought of it. And Fleet Admiral Presk-Milar wants to kick my ass. Threatened to in fact." Martin sat back in his chair, hands folded across his stomach a smile of contentment etched over his face.

"How do you think I should respond?"

"You are joking with me Highness."

"Not at all, Lord Lzac." Martin touched and icon, "Bring in the message from New Earth."

Shortly a courtier entered and started to hand Grabel the note. "Give it to our peer." he motioned toward the Lord.

Lzac grabbed the vidpad and read it. "It is true. He threatened you. I will prepare an appropriate rebuke immediately and deliver it to their ambassador. This shall not go unpunished. This demands they recall their emissaries, all of them and we will close their embassy."

"Not at all Lzac."

Mistakenly, he believed Martin would want the severest penalty against New Earth and Lzac would make the best of it.

"In fact, send him this note: "Fleet Admiral Presk-Milar, I understand your anger and were I in your place, I would kick my ass as well. Withholding significant information that could affect your war plans obviously doesn't rank high with you and rightly so. We share the same sense of responsibility. Should we meet, I will offer my royal butt for your pleasure. And oh yes, Forty thousand Pagmok warriors are a great idea. I almost wish the Chinese do make landfall and I could be there to watch. My best to you, sir. Grabel, King of Myslac."

"I will not send this," said Lzac. "To not defend the throne is unthinkable."

"Transmit it immediately." Grabel would brook no refusal as his stern look pinned the defiant lord. "If we send the New Earth ambassador packing," he scolded. "Who would we turn to when the Chinese come calling? Our fleet, deprived of the minerals only New Earth possesses, is in disrepair. Even with their help we may lose but most certainly without it. Still want to send their ambassador packing?"

* * * *

Ten T-days later, forty Kalazecis transports each carrying one thousand Pagmok warriors appeared on the far side of New Earth accompanied by four hundred Kalazecis to command them.

Admiral Presk-Milar, sitting in on a briefing by the Science and Engineering committee listened to the comm. "Yes, sir, that's what the Kalazecis Commander said. They want to land forty thousand Pagmok warriors. Says they're our insurance in case the Chinese make landfall."

Just the thought of forty thousand armed flesh eating anything roaming around New Earth brought images most didn't care to dwell on, not to mention what the Rococo and the *First* would say once they find out. "The Pagmok say they've brought enough soy meat that they won't be a burden on our resources," the voice continued.

David Rohm broke out in uncontained laughter—uncommon for the usually staid scientist. Once the outburst subsided, he told the story of his grandfather's attempt to wean the Pagmok off their fresh meat habit by teaching the Rococo and the *First* how to grow and process soybeans for their meat-eating compatriots—some wordsmith gave them the tag *tofu warriors.*

"I feel the hand of our President in this." Presk-Milar commed Jabari's secretary then excused himself. After a few minutes, he returned. "Well, for what it's worth, President Jabari asked Grabel for these warriors. Seems the man thought it such a good idea that he sent them and our president failed to mention it."

Now they had the problem of housing the warriors. Presk-Milar contacted the Interior Secretary and laid out his solution. Over the next week, engineers, carpenters, plumbers, every trade that could help along with material, headed for an uninhabited area on the other side of New Earth to build a city—a Pagmok city. There, away from humans and *First,* they would stay until the attack began.

9: New Hope

It had taken almost a month to provision the corvette and two transport ships to take one hundred New Earth people to their new home and six T-months to make the journey. Traversing around the *void* eliminated any contact with New Earth and they had no idea how their home world had fared in the battle with Old Earth. They could only hope New Earth had won.

President Jabari had made the decision to send these people, all volunteers but with certain skills, as a hedge against ending what Maria Presk and Orion had struggled so hard for so long to make for themselves—a life.

Not skirting the *void* less than ten thousand kilometers distant, to avoid detection meant many of the dangers it presented were ever-present.

"Cut our speed to one hundred meters per second," said Lionel Penrose. He sent the same command to the trailing transports. Linney as he preferred, was a brilliant geneticist. The group had selected him as their leader before spacing from New Earth. He knew firsthand the dangers the *void* presented—at least enough of them to go slowly. Asteroids in themselves were enough of a problem, but the biggest danger lay in the electrical disturbances that raised havoc with a ships electronics. Not only navigation, but also steerage proved exceedingly troublesome. "Launch a razor." Much more maneuverable, the fighter made for a better lead vessel.

Linney looked around as his number two stepped through the hatch. "What's bothering you," he said as Michael Scott stopped at the comm, a look of disgust plastered across his youthful face.

"We lost number one forward overhead external antenna. Musta got hit by debris too small for our sensors to see. Linney, someone has to go out there and fix the problem. Even with the fighter leading the way, we need those eyes."

"I'll go," Linney said. Working on the outer hull was no picnic in clean space. In the *void*, a small rock could knock you off the hull or just as bad, punch a hole in your space suit. Either meant certain death. It was a two-man job. He didn't want to assign someone the chore. Especially with the risk involved. Asking for volunteers, over twenty offered to join him.

"Who do you recommend?"

"Me, of course," Scott answered. "Next to you, I'm the best." No humor came with the retort.

"Nope, can't both of us go. Pick a name."

Michael did so, reluctantly.

Almost eight hours later, Linney returned to the bridge. "As good as new," he announced.

A nerve-wracking month later, they cleared the danger, transiting into clear space.

After another two T-months in quiet space, Lionel Penrose eased Trekker into an orbit ten thousand kilometers above New Hope and launched a survey party to the planet. "Stay in contact every minute. Everything you see, hear, or smell, relay back to the ship. Understood?"

That got the accepted acknowledgement and the small ship left the docking bay.

Lionel Presk-Milar Penrose, descendant of Maria Presk, arguable the most intelligent of the group, seemed immune to the status his name provided. The outwardly casual nature of his approach to most problems belied the intensity of the man. He had never used his heritage to gain an advantage, relying instead on his intellect and leadership skills. Matched only by David Rohm's, the two had become fast friends and collaborated on a number of scientific achievements. Stepping onto the bridge having just awakened, Linney asked, "Where's the shuttle?"

"It should dock in about ten minutes," said Brooke Fossey now at the comm, her smile in place. Brook had to argue for a place as a voyager. Her résumé lacked credibility, some said. An artist, her specialty landscapes, just didn't seem to fit the pioneer's needs. As the selectors were to learn, her debating skills were formidable. She won. It turned out that exceptional ability made her an ideal comm operator. In addition, she had mastered the craft of basket weaving and that added invaluable insight in classifying the flora. Perhaps her greatest asset remained her personality. If someone had a bad day, it didn't take long for Brooke to lift their spirits.

Linney keyed the comm, "Have Michael report to the bridge as soon as the shuttle's secured." Anxious to end the seven months cooped up aboard the corvette, Linney wanted the survey results.

A few minutes later, Michael Scott, a geologist on New Earth, strode onto the bridge all smiles. "Looks great, Linney. I say put together a building crew, get some temporary places up where we can stay and let's get off this tub."

Linney smiled, "That's the plan my friend. Didn't find any threats? Nothing that might sneak up in the night? No boogey men?"

"Nope. Nothing we saw."

Lionel suggested boundary signs to tell the people where it's safe.

The atmosphere aboard Trekker, as they'd named the corvette, reflected the people's attitude. Anxious to get started on their new life, most wanted to be included in the first building crew. Some even saw themselves as Orion's incarnation—others thought that a bit of a stretch.

"Nothing to worry about. The fauna we spotted are small and shied away. Plenty of water and it's good, air's good, everything we need is here. Plenty of wood, so I say, let's go."

"We need a name for the town," said Lionel. He keyed the comm, "Tomorrow at fourteen hundred, we will select a name for our city. Use computers to submit suggestions."

The next afternoon, in the hanger, Lionel called those present to order. Some were still on the planet and others had shipboard duty. "Okay, some of you guys were more than original and went *beyond the pale*. Some even made me blush and their entries were deleted."

That brought a chorus of laughs.

"We had to boil down the list as some of you could qualify as etymologists."

That brought another laugh.

Lionel grimaced at the over eight hundred submitted name suggestions. "Obviously, we had to prune the list. So, some we had to cut."

That brought a few derisive remarks.

"Ten possibilities are on the list. We'll use a round robin vote." Finalists received explanations when questioned. Five votes later, Alexander (Protector of Mankind) won.

Over the next two months, a frantic level of around the clock work erected enough livable quarters that only a standby crew remained on Trekker and the transports. In the back of Linney's mind, what to do with the three spaceships? They were a major part of who they were and their most valuable assets. Yet, the manpower it took just to keep them functional would detract from satisfying what they had to accomplish to become a viable community. He didn't have an answer and wasn't ready to put it to the people.

One of first buildings put up was a nursery and children's play school. Buildings were first made of timber cut from what passed for trees, but it wasn't long until they had a plasticrete processor producing slabs for walls and floors. Along with the anti-grav hoists, shortly the wooden structures gave way to the more durable buildings, all except for Linney's office. He liked his log cabin. Roofs proved to be a different problem. One of the chemists finally provided a solution. New Hope's weather had a habit of suddenly changing—in an instant from bright sun to thunderstorms or blizzards. It took a little adjusting to get used to the shorter day/night routine. The rotational period, only eighteen T-hours caused a few problems for some but they mostly adapted to the cycle. A year on New Hope clocked in at two hundred eighty five Old Earth days—ten less than what they were accustomed to on New Earth. New Hope standards were established but they would use terra as their base reference.

Gracie Fuessel walked into Linney's office. "Hey, want to join us for dinner?" Gracie, married to a physicist, came to the group with perhaps the most impressive credentials of anyone, not quite on a par with the original Orion Eight, but up there. She'd made extensive use of the library Orion had brought, virtually self-educating herself in the sciences and math.

"Sure. What time," he responded. Gracie insisted that schools have a priority—not surprising most. Her reasoning didn't apply to known skills, but those used by Old Earth's early pioneers.

Sitting at the hand hewn table, something of a novelty, enjoying a dinner of steak, potato pancakes, salad and desert, Gracie, Linney and two other couples reminisced over the trials they'd faced. Descendant of one of the ten men who assembled the Casimir engines, Gracie came by her talents quite naturally. The merriment abruptly changed when she said, "I worry why New Earth hasn't contacted us. My greatest fear is that they lost the war." She paused, "I suppose, they could have decided to leave us alone long enough to see if we were successful. They could come calling any day." Her question went unanswered. Most everyone had the same fears.

Two years of physical effort bordering on heroic, brought major improvements that dramatically changed the New Hope settler's lifestyles from frontier, which gave few amenities to some creature comforts. Linney finally had time to relax. Alexander had become a thriving city with paved streets, lighting and most important a thriving economy albeit dependent on the citizen's innovativeness and that was enormous.

An unexpected plus was Brooke's knowledge of the plant life. Her experience working with New Earth's gave her an insight into the many unique forms of flora on the planet that added to the versatility of products needed to satisfy daily needs. Most of the women, as well as a number of men, attended her training sessions.

All that time passed without a word from New Earth... until, unexpectedly, the comm sounded an alarm.

Linney, mildly startled, answered the comm. "What is it Mr. Temple?" A skeleton crew rotated on the orbiting ships spending a week on the ships, sharing their time between the transport and Trekker.

"I'm not sure, Linney, but I believe we've got visitors. There's a big ship approaching at low speed. I tried to raise it on all frequencies but so far, no answer."

Linney quickly rounded up a crew and headed for the shuttle. Experience told him to be prepared no matter what. He commed Arles Blankenship. "We've got visitors. I want you to arm everyone who knows how to shoot a weapon. This may be nothing but let's not take a chance."

Before leaving dirtside, he laid out a plan utilizing what few defensive assets they had. Building any kind of fortifications had never entered his mind. Not that it made much difference. Any armed spaceship could destroy what few buildings they'd erected. And grouped together as they were, made them an easy target. *One missile would do it he thought.*

One hour later, a shuttle settled into the corvette's landing bay and Linney ran through the empty passageways to the bridge. "Show me what you've got, Berry."

Linney studied the plot. "No answer, huh?"

Berry Temple served as bos'n on Trekker. Known for his special skills, namely street fighting, as Master-at-arms he'd effectively kept the peace. And of course, the people elected him their first sheriff. Until now, something not needed.

"Nope, we should have a visual in about an hour," he said.

"Okay, let's get the engines started and power up the weapons." Trekker carried two small energy and four laser cannons. Not formidable when compared with a ship of the line, but it was all they had.

With the engines running, he changed orbit, gaining maneuvering room.

"Linney, Looks like ours," said Berry. "Its electronic signature isn't far off the Simón Bolivar."

"Can't be," responded Linney his voice a bit hasher than he intended. "Those ships are either Kalazecis or from Old Earth. Either would have declared themselves." He paused for a moment, "I suppose they could be the Hommew." He punched a series of icons. "It's moving mighty slow. At the rate it's shedding velocity, it'll take another ten hours for it to get here. It'll be in firing range in two T-hours. Let's get some rest. This could be a long night." What went unsaid was it could be a very short one if the ship proved hostile.

Aroused from a light sleep, Linney punched the comm. "It's in range," Berry said. "Haven't powered up any weapons yet, Linney. Do I fire a warning shot?"

"No. They're not acting hostile—let's not start anything. Maybe this is a peaceful visit. If that changes, don't wait. No warning shots. Shoot to kill."

Linney entered the bridge and stopped at the plot board, as the ship took up orbit, still moving slowly, ten thousand kilometers off Trekkers starboard side.

"Look at the size of that thing," a voice said in utter amazement. Many of New Hope's people thought Trekker was large. Of course, the transports that accompanied Trekker from New Earth were bigger by a factor of ten.

"It's a destroyer," said Linney. "Probably out masses us a thousand to one. Its crew is larger than our entire population." He didn't add that the ship carried enough firepower to destroy Trekker with a single shot from one energy weapons. He counted seven on the portion he could see.

"Damn, they've launched a shuttle. They're heading toward us," he said. Trekker locked its two cannon on the approaching vessel. Now he had to make a decision—open the landing bay doors and let this unknown shuttle land or not. "Issue arms. I'll let them land. But keep your weapons handy."

Nine men waited in the loadmaster's room sealed off from the corvette's landing bay—one remained at Trekker's helm.

A few minutes after the bay doors closed sealing the area from space and pressurized, the launch's side hatch opened.

One man stepped out and faced Linney and his group. "Thank god. You've no idea how grateful we are to find someone. I am Robert Daniels." He pointed at the launch, "Twelve more people are on the ship and over four hundred on the Hope."

"Well, they speak English and look like us," said Linney. "Who are you and where are you from?"

The man started toward the loadmaster's room. "Stay where you are," Linney ordered. "Answer my questions."

"Forgive me. I'm afraid my exuberance—" He paused seemingly to gather himself.

"As I said, I'm Robert Daniels. We are all from Earth. Perhaps unbelievable but we were able to commandeer this ship following the war at Earth and set out to find you—find New Earth. It's been a long voyage."

"This isn't New Earth. How did you find us?"

A troubled look filled the man's face. "Not New Earth? Where are we? Who are you?"

"Answer my question," Linney said, his voice like a sledgehammer. "How did you find us?"

A second face peered out from the launch.

"Tell your people to stay onboard," Linney ordered.

Daniels motioned the woman back then turned toward the loadmaster's room. "You must have doubts that we could take such a vessel." He paused, rose to his full height, an obvious look of pride on his face. "When Admiral Presk-Milar attacked the Chinese fleet over Earth, he had some electronic weapon that disrupted this ship's steerage and navigation, in fact practically all enemy ships. The chaos gave us the opportunity we needed. For some unknown reason, most of this crew came from subjugated nations—all but the leadership. We overwhelmed the command, put them on a shuttle along with those who wanted no part of what we had planned and headed them back to Earth. Finally, we got control over the malfunctioning systems. It took three of us a month to come up with the right answers. By that time, the ship had drifted a long way from Earth, as did a number of others. All of us decided we'd never have another chance like this and wanted no more of the murder and degradation we had to put up with, so we decided to leave. Named the ship 'Hope'. We captured two drifting supply ships. Took everything we could stow. Good thing. We've been in space for a long time, over a year. Unfortunately, no one had the skills required for computer navigation but we tried; did our best. We thought we were headed for New Earth, got caught in an area of space that really messed up our electronics. Lost our comm. I mean we can't transmit or receive, had no radar. We had no idea where we were going. Just decided to keep at it and with a little luck we'd find New Earth. It sure made us very resourceful; captured comets to replenish our water. I was concerned about the fuel and dropped out of sub-light drive. Good thing I did. We got into that terrible part of space. Full of asteroids. Been at the lower speed for most of the year." A perplexed look crossed his face. "If this isn't New Earth, what is it? Where are we? Who are you?"

A wry grin crossed Linney's face as he closed the comm and said, "Sounds like we won," referring to the war between New and Old Earth. He opened the comm. "This is New Hope and I'm Lionel Penrose." The irony that the ship Hope found New Hope didn't go unnoticed.

Lionel understood the puzzled look on Daniels face. Before Hope's captain could respond, Penrose said, "Return to your ship. You are to send me a complete list of all the people onboard."

Surprised by the order, Daniels stood his mouth agape but the look on Linney face discouraged any argument.

An hour later Hopes shuttle returned. New Earth personnel ran the list through their extensive computer library. In his office surrounded by those wanting to see if anyone with the same name showed up, Linney studied the results. "There are some skills here we could certainly use. Adding four hundred or so people to our numbers is a good thing as well. But these four with criminal records… what do we do with them?" It wasn't a rhetorical question—he simply didn't want them on New Earth.

"What were they convicted of?" asked Gracie.

His log cabin office, originally built to handle their conference needs, provided enough room for the thirty or so people and then some. Linney flipped through the pages. "Murder, arson, murder, and assault," he said. "All swore allegiance to China, volunteered for ship duty and were released from prison." Looking around the group he asked, "Any suggestions?"

"We've got a brig on our ship and one on the Hope," said Berry. We can lock them up. 'Course that means guards and feeding them."

Linney turned and hit several icons on his desk. "Mr. Daniels, meet me on Trekker in one hour. Only you and the people on board to fly the craft." He closed the link without waiting for an answer, touched another, and ordered the shuttle readied.

Standing in the loadmasters sealed cubicle, Linney watched as Robert Daniels shuttled locked to the rails and the bay doors closed. Once sealed from space, Daniels stepped onto the deck and Linney motioned him forward.

"We have a great deal to discuss, Mr. Daniels," he said and extended his hand.

About a head taller than his counterpart, Linney guided him up the passageway. "Trekker's a bit smaller than what you're accustomed to."

They stopped in the mess hall where Linney poured both a cup of coffee. "We have our own little farm. Grow such as this," he raised his cup.

"Ha, we did the same. Made all the difference. Most likely wouldn't have gotten this far without it," responded Daniels.

Linney nodded hoping his surprise wasn't too obvious. Someone on that ship had the initiative and that he liked. New Hope needed all of that they could get.

"Your idea?" he asked.

"No, Mr. Penrose, we've got some fine, really talented people on Hope." Desperation choked the man's voice. "Sir, we can't go any farther. You have only to see the joy on the faces of these people. They believe, no they want, look forward to being a part of this new world."

Linney turned and faced the man only to see tears streak down his face.

"Please, have a seat and it's Linney. Mr. Daniels, we welcome you to New Hope and Alexander."

The man's breath exploded. "Thank God." He shook, realizing the ordeal had ended.

Linney thought Trekker's voyage from New Earth was worthy of note, but what these people had endured dwarfed anything he could imagine. He handed Hope's captain a towel. Unabashed the man wiped away his tears.

Hope's arrival did ease another concern Linney harbored. It would be many years before they could attempt to build space ships and finding the minerals to make the hulls—maybe never. Hope's arrival was a blessing in many ways.

10: Settling In

"**Put** them in number two's brig," said Linney referring to the second transport.

"How we going to keep watch on them and four ships?" asked Davidson. Each on-orbit ship required a minimal crew. Adding brig guards only added to the problem.

Linney punched the comm and asked Leonard Clark to come to the bridge. "Mr. Clark, I would like to stack these four ships. Trekker on the bottom, our two transports then Hope on top. Lock them together at the boarding hatches, tie in their life support and electrical systems. See any problems with that?"

Linney waited out the hee-haw that exploded from their maintenance engineer. "Any problems? No shit, you're serious aren't you, Linney?"

Less than a week later, with all four ships securely locked together Clark walked into Linney's log cabin. "Hey man, that went a lot easier than I thought it would. What do you want to do with the shuttles and pinnace?"

"Bring them all dirtside," he responded. We'll assign one shuttle to handle the back and forth trips."

"Still don't know what to do with four prisoners, huh?"

"Nope. I just know I'm not setting them free. Let's give it some time and maybe someone will come up with a doable idea," Linney said.

It took a month to sort out the various skills these new people added to the colony. Retraining was the order of the day. Few Old Earth skills translated to a frontier existence.

"Anything new?" asked Linney walking into his office. The place had become the informal meeting place as well as the community meeting hall.

"What's got you worried?" said Robert Daniels. "I haven't known you very long but I can tell when something's eating on a guy."

Linney had grown to like Hope's captain. It was easy to see why the people had chosen the man to lead them. He was not only smart; his leadership skills were superb. Without anyone saying so, the man had become New Hope's number two. And the best part, Michael Scott, the previous de facto number two, had accepted the leadership change without a sign of animosity. Daniels had accepted Lionel's reasoning for not disclosing New Hope's origins understanding that in due time he would be told.

"Don't know. Wish I did. Ever get a gut feel the world was about to drop on you?"

Daniels laughed. "Yeah. And there isn't a damned thing you can do about it. Yeah. Things have been pretty easy. Few complaints over job assignments so it must be something else," he added and eyed Linney.

Linney stepped behind his desk, gathered a few items and said, "Keep a watch over the place, would you? I'm leading an expedition to the interior. Seems one of our survey teams found some interesting minerals. I want a look for myself. We should be back in a couple of days."

"Sure, anything special I should devote my time to?" asked Daniels.

Linney shook his head. "Nothing exceptional going on right now. Biggest chore may be staying awake."

* * * *

Deep in New Hope's interior, immediately alert, Linney rolled over in his sleeping bag and answered the comm.

Instantly he was on his feet running to the various sleeping bodies rousing the entire crew all the time on his comm. "We'll be back as quickly as we can. How is Daniels?"

Penrose shook his head. The feeling that had nagged him for the last few days had blown into a major problem.

Leaving the campsite and most of their gear, Linney pushed the aircar to its maximum. "In detail, what happened?" he said into the comm.

Michael Scott, at the colony hospital, let out a slow breath. "Well, Linney, it seems our prison guards got careless. Somehow, the prisoners got control, out of their cells. Killed all four of the crew watching them. Brought the shuttle dirtside, disabled the remaining shuttles and pinnace, that's when Captain Daniels must have discovered them and they shot the man. The bastards went back to the ships. If the activity we're seeing is telling us what we think it is, they're disconnecting Hope from the transport and will space."

Linney ordered Leonard Clark to get one ship flyable.

Arriving at the launch site, Linney quickly learned the depth of destruction the prisoners had heaped on the pinnace and shuttles. "How long, Leonard?" Linney referred to making at least one ship flyable.

"Week. Maybe less if we get lucky. These guys knew what they were doing. Really raised hell with the engines."

"Every resource we have is yours to get one ship launchable. Spare nothing, around the clock," Linney said as he left the hanger. "I'm going to the hospital. As soon as I check on Daniels, I'll be back to help."

Every eye in the large hanger locked on Lionel Penrose. Never had they seen their leader look or heard his voice sound so threatening. There was no hint of forgiveness.

"We'll get her, Captain. You can count on it," said Leonard.

Less than thirty minutes later, standing in the hospital hallway, Linney asked, "Doctor, how is Mr. Daniels?"

Doctor White shook his head. "He'll make it. We've done all we can. It's really up to him. Good thing he stays in shape. A lesser man would be dead by now. He's one tough hombre. I'd say by morning we'll know a great deal more."

"I'll be at the launch hangar, please keep me informed." Linney thanked the doctor and made his way to the aircar.

True to his word, Mr. Clark had one shuttle capable of a launch. "No navigation." Linney knew he wouldn't need that to reach the stack of ships, now three.

Linney glanced at his watch. "Twenty hours head start. That is if they didn't spike Trekker's engines." He turned to Michael Scott and said, "You're in charge. Keep me informed at all times. As soon as we can get Trekker space worthy, I'm going after them."

"You're taking some of our best people, Linney," Michael said. It wasn't a challenge.

"To stop some of the worst," the Captain shot back a little more intensely than he intended.

"Want the brig restored or we going to lock them up somewhere else?"

Standing in the launch hatch, Linney said, "Don't waste your time. We won't need either. I'm not bringing them back."

The launch pad cleared as the small ship with ten people aboard set out for Trekker and the killers aboard Hope.

Arriving on orbit, Linney raced to the engine room. "Their mistake," he said. "Not spiking Trekker's engines will be their epitaph."

Half a day later, with the corvette loose from the stack, Linney ordered the ten-hour engine start-up procedure.

"All clear," said Clark at the end of the countdown and Trekker slowly crept away from New Hope.

"All sensors working, Captain. We'll start a general sweep to pick up their electronic emissions that is unless you might have a clue what their vector might be," said Brooke Fossey manning the helm and comm.

"Nope, you've got it right. But let's put off duty people on the plot tables. Just in case the void shoves a little static our way." Humans could spot many anomalies not programmed into the computers. Spacing Trekker with a skeleton crew remained risky, but the best people possible made up the crew.

"Aye, sir," she said and summoned three off-duty sets of eyes.

"Hope should be able to run circles around us, Captain," said Clark. "How are we going to catch them? They can make theta band and we're only beta capable. That's four times as fast as we can go."

"True. But I'm betting whoever's calling the shots aboard Hope knows we didn't refuel her and at theta, they'll have less than ten days power. If they go dead in space, it'll save us having to kill them. Instead, they'll cruise along and wait until we get close enough to shoot us. They'll try to put an end to this."

Three days later one voice said, "Got something. I think it's them."

The comm operator put his plot signal on all the boards.

For over half a day, all available hands studied the sign sorting out static and stray signals.

"Computer confirms, sir. It's the Hope."

"Miss Fossey, please go to stealth," Said Linney.

"We'll have to slow down, Captain. May lose the signal," she said.

"Please go to stealth, Ms. Fossey."

"Yes, sir." Brooke's eyebrows shot up in her chagrin that the Captain had to repeat his order.

Linney left the bridge. "I'll be in the hangar. Comm me if there's any change."

"Aye, sir," she briskly said.

An hour later, Linney stepped onto the bridge. "Distance, Ms. Fossey" he said. Everyone on the bridge picked up on the note of gravity in his voice.

"One million Klicks, sir," she answered.

"Mr. Clark, I will take the razor and attack Hope. You will have command of Trekker," said Linney.

"Captain, may I ask what you plan to do?"

"I'm taking four men with me. We'll neutralize Hope's energy cannons, board her, and take control."

"Sir, you're going to board that ship?"

"Yes. I see no other way to get her back. If we trade shots, they could well win. On the other hand, she's not much use to us as a piece of junk. However, if we can board her, all that changes. I want that ship, Mr. Clark."

"Have you ever boarded a spaceship, Captain?" said Clark. "Forgive me, I don't mean to challenge your authority or decision but please think this through. We can't afford to lose you. And I'd guess the probability of that happening is quite high." Clark's practical nature, the part that made him their best engineer, pushed his concern.

"You may be right, my friend. However, we did practice the maneuver at the academy a number of times. I have a dozen boardings under my belt, three of them hot."

No one carried the conversation further. Lionel Penrose had made his decision and it was final.

Linney guided razor down Trekker's rails into space. The hangar doors closed behind the fighter. Penrose accelerated ten thousand kilometers ahead of and above Trekker, putting distance between the two vessels. With orders to stay at least one million klicks behind Hope, Leonard Clark armed all of their weapons. If ordered to, Trekker could and would attack with every asset it had.

Thanks to David Rohm's farsighted strategic thinking almost three hundred years earlier, the razor was the most maneuverable ship in space. With internal inertial dampening, the small ship could move faster than the destroyer could target. Added to that, their high-energy cannon out ranged anything Hope had. Razor could stand off half a million kilometers and pound the bigger ship. But that wasn't Penrose's plan. He wanted in close for precision shots. Take out their weapons and board the ship. The one drawback, razor had fixed weapons and that meant he had to aim the ship. Those few seconds required to set up for a precision shot made the ship vulnerable.

"Everyone ready? We're going in." said Linney. "Body armor, spacesuits, grav-boots, pulse lasers and flechette rifles. Brady, when we board, you're at razor's controls. Ms. Fossey will have the comm and assist you at the helm."

Boomer Brady had attended Midway Naval Space academy one year behind Linney, majoring in orbital mechanics. Considered one of the best at handling a razor, crewmembers clamored to be on any ship with him at the controls.

With the inertia generators at maximum, Penrose started his attack run. Zigging and zagging, razor moved against the destroyer. Out massed by a factor of over ten thousand and one weapon against the Hope's thirty external weapons, mostly large energy cannons suitable for long-range targets, and fifteen laser pumped cannons that required precision targeting, razor had to get off the first shot. With only three crewmen aboard Hope, that meant only one external weapon could be manned. All others required ranging could only be fired from the bridge. Unmanned weapons were notoriously inaccurate under an inexperienced Captain, and more of a nuisance with an inexperienced person at the weapons station. The odds still seemed outrageously against razor.

"Boomer, you have control. Fire when you have your target."

Brady spotted Hope's top turret amid ships rotating. He had his target. Using his secondary controls, micro adjusted razor's vector, well beyond the destroyer's effective shooting range, and fired the energy cannon.

Hope's only manned weapon disappeared. "Good shooting Mr. Brady but please remember I would like a functioning ship when this is all over."

Brady laughed, "Understood, Captain. I can take out a couple of engines. With a low powered shot, there won't be much damage."

"No need, Boomer. Avoid the engines, remember, we want and need that ship. We'll overtake her in about twenty minutes. Her engines won't affect our boarding."

"Aye, sir.

"Where you gonna put us, Captain?" Boomer asked. "We don't know much about that ship."

"Hope is a duplicate of the Gandhi, Mr. Brady. We know her in detail. I think we'll go in the front door."

"Sir?"

"Put us on the forward entry hatch, starboard side," Linney said. "We'll exit to Hope's hull, make our way aft, Mabre will take the Port center hatch, I'll be at the Port forward hatch. Digger and Grason will do the same on the starboard. Hope is down to three crewmen thanks to your first shot, so one hatch has to go unguarded. We blast our way in, shoot the bastards and go home."

"You make it sound clinical, Captain," Brooke said from her perch at the plot board. "I suspect it will be anything but."

Linney chuckled and said, "Insightful as usual, Ms. Fossey. But enough chatter. We attach in ten seconds."

Banging and clanging echoed throughout the fighter as it landed and secured against Hope's hull. Four men exited razor and reached their assigned locations. Each set explosive charges on the targeted hatches, timed to explode at thirty second intervals.

Linney squatted down behind the base of an antenna array, locked his grav-boots, triggered his explosive blowing the hatch and starting the timer for the secondary blasts. He tossed in three concussion grenades and jumped through the opening.

Not waiting to identify a target, he hit the deck and rolled spraying the entire area with flechettes.

He saw his man flail as the needles shredded him. "I'm in and took out one."

"I got mine with the grenades," said Grason.

"I'm chasing mine," said Mabre. "Gimme a minute."

Linney pressed his comm.

"Mine got away," Mabre said and added, "He's headed forward"

Following a distant exchange for blaster fire, Linney touched his comm, "Digger, what's your status," and waited but got no answer and suspected the worst. That meant Mabry's man was still loose.

"Grason, which hatch did Digger have?" Linney asked. Digger's assigned location meant the enemy was starboard and opposite Linney.

Suspecting the killer had Digger's comm, Linney went to the backup frequency and ordered a sweep.

Hope's aft cross-ship passageway, almost one hundred meters long and two wide, offered the Captain no cover. Halfway into the ship ran the main fore and aft passage. A flechette fired down the steel paneled passageway would eviscerate any living thing.

Slowly, he crawled along the deck plates, his rifle set on automatic fire. All he had to do was release the stud.

He heard a laser pulse and running footsteps headed his way.

Linney stopped, took his weapon off automatic, aimed it at the crosswalk opening and waited. He pulled his comm ear bud inserted it and whispered, "Grason, Mabre, talk to me."

"Whoever we're after should be approaching your location, Captain."

"Either of you in the center passageway?" Linney asked.

Getting a negative, he aimed his flechette toward the intersection and fired.

At an angle, the knives ricocheted back and forth off the bulkheads, deck, and overhead down the passageway.

Screams told him he'd hit something, but he waited. At this range, his body armor would mean little if the enemy unleashed either a blaster or pulse rifle.

The screams didn't last long. With care, still crawling, he turned the corner into the passage and didn't need a doctor to tell him the flechettes had done their job.

"Status," Linney said. "Mabre here. All clear." A similar messaged came from Grason. "Put the dead in body bags and meet me at the airlock. Except for Digger. We'll take him home."

11: Betrayed

"**Take** every precaution my friend. We have a traitor in our midst," Liverson said. Police alerts had gone out for the arrest of the Free Council members. Their names could only have come from one of their own.

Retired Admiral Johann Liverson and Jason Bridger, the leaders of the resistance to stop the Chinese, shook hands and parted.

Liverson steered into the driveway stepped from his car, and swept up his young granddaughter into his arms.

The moment he gathered her to his body, he stumbled, dropped the child, and grabbed his chest never seeing the man who killed both instantly. Jason Bridger fared no better when a bullet pierced his car windshield.

One by one, the leadership, eleven members of the rebellion, died as they had lived over the past few years—in the shadows of the world they wanted to save. No mention of the murders made the vids or HD as banners applauded the Chinese fleet's leaving orbit for their war against New Earth. Holly Joiner alone escaped the slaughter.

In her hideout in Washington, D.C., now slangily known as *Beijing West*, worked feverishly telling the world of the slaughter. Questions flooded into the NWO in New York City, irate that retired and respected men were murdered. No matter what the NWO leadership tried, they could not quell the anger.

Peng Rui Bao, from his secret home in central Texas, fed instructions to Holly guiding the public exposé into his homeland. Knowing in detail how the Chinese apparatus worked from his twenty years as Yang's aide, he gave Holly the tools to expose the Chinese leadership with deadly effectiveness. Holly laid out the facts for the world to hear, how the Chinese military orchestrated the murder of the eleven men.

First issuing denials, the Beijing leadership misjudged the severity of the fury they now faced. Quelling riots with soldiers only added to the tenacity and determination of their antagonists. Insurrections exploded in countries thought pacified. With not enough troops or none in those areas, the rebellion gained momentum. In a desperation move, leaders of thirteen nations were gathered and publicly executed putting the revolution into full swing. Only mainland China seemed immune to the chaos that gripped the rest of the world.

Holly looked up as a helper approached. "Miss Holly, I have an unbelievable message. It's addressed to you." She accepted the scrap of paper and read it. *"'Keep up the good work. We'll be there before you know it,' Fleet Admiral Bogdan Presk-Milar, Commandant New Earth Naval Space Force."* Holly raised her arms and shouted in a joyous unusual strident voice. Knowing how things worked, she rightly suspected it would be many months before Presk-Milar and his fleet would arrive and she could meet the man. She still had a job to do.

"How you doing," asked Alex Mendenhall. "You haven't been out of this hole since you arrived. Doesn't that eat on you?"

Holly had to admit she would like a walk in a park, smell the flowers, maybe even do it in a rain. But both the army and police had a price on her head and she couldn't risk giving away their hideout. A lot of research had gone into finding this place. Local communication traffic created a confluence that allowed her electronic engineers to piggyback their messages on unsuspecting outgoing signals.

"Yes," the raven-haired Holly answered. Born to free thinking parents, they had raised her never to accept subjugation. Raised in what her friends said was the wilderness, independence came naturally. Skiing, hunting, fishing—becoming an expert with both hand guns and large caliber rifles— self-sufficiency came naturally. After the betrayal, her parents were imprisoned—something that tore at her soul. As the only survivor of the murderous onslaught of the co-founders of the freedom movement, Holly had become its leader. Betrayed by one of their own, and now hunted, she hadn't shied away from what she saw as her duty—a duty that had nothing to do with revenge but everything with freedom and honor. She could only hope another traitor hadn't found his or her way into their ranks.

"What's the world like? Let me guess. It's February, so there should be a few inches of snow on the ground. Nothing green, well the pine trees, too early for robins, so no songbirds. And it is cold. Warm and cozy in here." A touch of whimsy made it through in her voice. But that didn't alter her determination to see the end of the Chinese hegemony. If she could help to that end, nothing else mattered. She wouldn't falter.

"Would you believe a foot of snow? The city's virtually paralyzed."

* * * *

"It would seem the years Martin Grabel spent learning all the engineering he could following David Rohm around Orion are still paying off," President Jabari said referring David Rohm's time as a savant—a brilliant engineering savant. Of the engineering skills Martin Grabel learned, very little had accrued to Orion but Jabari was pleased that New Earth would reap the benefits now. As far as Jabari was concerned, Martin's commitment might mitigate the betrayal of his kind by joining the Kalazecis.

"We just got a relay from the Kalazecis. Their drones signaled the Chinese fleet is headed our way." President Jabari released the comm switch and sat heavily in his chair.

"Mr. President, I must join the fleet." Having resigned as Secretary of Defense to be in the fight, Admiral Presk-Milar had accepted the commission as Fleet Commandant. With his flair for tactics, most considered it a plus, preferring him leading the fleet instead of sitting in an office.

Pensively, Fleet Admiral Presk-Milar said, "Do you want me to recall the ships headed for New Hope?"

"No." Jabari's terse response left no room for discussion. One ship would add nothing to the upcoming fight.

A number of New Earthers had urged him to take the initiative and send a ship. Others roundly criticized him for not doing do. Jabari seemed just a little piqued with his critics. Deep down he would have like to check on them. But he knew if the settlers he'd sent were to make it, they would have to find it within themselves. That lesson he'd learned in the swamps the hard way and hadn't forgotten. And the outcome of the pending war was by no means certain. New Earth could lose.

"Jimmy-John, if we are successful, do I carry it all the way?" Both men knew that many of their young people would die, but their plan went well beyond defeating the Chinese at New Earth. They would rid the galaxy of this threat, cutting off the enemy's head. New Earth would again visit Old Earth. This time, their purpose would be different. In the first and only time the two had met since leaving Old Earth, Maria Presk had warned Old Earth that if she had to return, they would feel her full wrath. The only change in that dictum: Fleet Admiral Bogdan Presk-Milar, great-grandson of the lady would come calling.

President Jabari opened a desk drawer and pulled out a small notebook. Opening it he read, "'*In mortal combat, political or moral correctness makes little or no difference—that judgment is left to the historians—only who wins matters.*' Von Molke ." He paused, "Something I wrote down a few years ago," he continued, "*Courage is the discovery that you may not win, and trying when you know you can lose.*" He looked up at his admiral and added, "*No battle plan survives contact with the enemy.*" He paused and said, "General Colin Powell. Reading further, "*We will win because we never lose. I am a soldier. I fight where I am told, and I win where I fight*',—General George Patton."

These two military men Presk-Milar knew about in detail and admired them for their devotion, courage and commitment.

"Of course, Admiral. Take it all the way. I wish I could go with you." They shook hands.

"God speed my friend." Jabari had seen enough war to know he may never see this man or many others again. Much of the President's combat experience happened on the ground, often hand-to-hand fighting. He had stared death in the face a number of times—and won. Space was different. Even though a battleship could take one hell of a pounding, a well place hit from a distant enemy could mean instant death for all aboard. And the flagship carriers were even more vulnerable.

Brogan Presk-Milar smiled, thanked the President, saluted and left Government House.

Two days later one million kilometers above the planet, his launch settled into the flagship Lexington's huge bay.

The bosun's whistle blared through the ship's speakers and then the announcement, "Fleet arriving."

"Fleet aboard," answered Captain Swain as Admiral Presk-Milar stepped onto the carrier's deck.

"Welcome, Admiral. The fleet is fully manned and the Lexington stands to your orders."

"Thank you, Captain. Let's get them underway."

Over the next few weeks, Presk-Milar constantly drilled the fleets despite the complaints. He admonished his captains that *'no matter how good you think you are, you can get better'*. He reminded them it just might make the difference whether their ship lives or dies. He commed the utterances to the fleet that Generals Powell and Patton had made and added, "Gentlemen, I aim to win."

Admiral Presk-Milar's bulldog attitude, something tagged on him at the academy, had stuck become a hallmark for the man. He never saw himself as special and expected the same level of performance from those under his command. On occasion, his flag captain, Jeanne Swain would remind him not everyone was capable of performing at his level. That usually brought a comment that people performed as their commander expected and his expectations were his own and he had no plans to back down.

A day later, Presk-Milar ordered Captain Swain to have the fleet stand down from maneuvers. "I want all fleet captains here tomorrow on the Lexington for a meeting at zero eight hundred. Send the signal."

Sitting in his cabin, just off the bridge, he closed the comm and made his way to the CIC a Marine fore and aft accompanied him. "Admiral in CIC," quietly announced a crewman. Presk-Milar touched the comm icon and asked Captain Swain to join him. As she arrived, Presk-Milar pointed to the plot screen. "See anything you think needs changing, Captain?"

She studied the plot. "No, sir, everyone seems to be in their assigned position."

Presk-Milar nodded. "I think that's the problem. If I recall correctly from studying the history of the Chinese attacks on Myslac, they used a standard spread. All the ships were positioned much as are ours."

With that, Admiral Presk-Milar left CIC and returned to his quarters.

At zero eight hundred the next morning, almost four hundred ship captains, some who captained transports and other support ships with true ranks as low as lieutenant, gathered in the carriers assembly hall. Admiral Presk-Milar laid out the new alignment for the fleet. No one questioned his reasoning in fact all agreed—eliminating predictability was a good thing.

Five hundred million kilometers above the planet, Presk-Milar ordered the fleet to take up its new positions and Second Fleet to cloak using the same technology that hid New Earth. How effective the devices would work in space remained problematic. Astral disturbances were easily detectable and if the Chinese picked up on it as a hoax, it would expose Second Fleet and compromise the plan. Presk-Milar's strategy was to lull the Chinese into thinking that the disturbance only an anomaly and not discover its true origin. Actually, he wanted the enemy to believe their fleet had an unimpeded path to the planet by outflanking the New Earth defenses. Let them pass and then close the trap. With New Earth's energy cannons ahead of them and his fleet behind, the Chinese trapped between, he would pound them to oblivion. *And* if some of their transports reached dirtside, they would meet the forty thousand Pagmok. All he had to do now—was pull it off.

Admiral Presk-Milar ordered the fleet to the predetermined coordinates. With only one city to protect, Goldthwaite City, named after George Goldthwaite who died saving thirty children when an airlock seal broke aboard the Washington. Goldthwaite threw his body over the breach giving his life to save New Earth's most precious commodity—their children.

Home fleet took up station spreading their ships one million to two million kilometers above the planet creating an umbrella over the city and most of the hemisphere. Second Fleet stationed itself three million kilometers distant creating a clear flanking path to the planet—cloaked something they'd never tried in space and had no idea how effective it would be.

Hesitantly, the comm operator said, "Admiral, Ms. Olivanta wants to speak with you.

Anger crowded Bogdan Presk-Milar's face as he punched the comm switch.

Without waiting for him to acknowledge her presence, she blared, "Are you sure you want to pursue this? Letting the Chinese land on New Earth is an irresponsible gamble," she complained.

"Madam, I don't know how you got this frequency but in due time I will," said the Admiral. "I'm breaking this connection. Do not make another attempt to communicate with me or any other ship." He punched an icon. *How in the hell did she get our order of battle? Some bastard's going to answer for this* he thought. Speaking to no one in particular, he answered her question mostly to allay any fears she may have caused with the bridge crew, "At the least, I want them to think they have a clear shot at outflanking us for a landing dirtside. The Chinese fleet commander will have to provide cover for his troops all the way to the ground and then protect the landing. He can't do that and at the same time stop our fleet. And their troops will have no support to cover them." Without heavy firepower from space, the soldiers would have to take the flesh eating Pagmok on; something Presk-Milar did not want to see. He had his own battle to fight.

"Enemy fleet is in system," said the comm officer and added, "fifteen million klicks separation. Estimate twenty-four hours standard before engagement."

With Second Fleet cloaked, Presk-Milar could only watch and wait to see if the enemy took the bait.

Presk-Milar watched the battle unfold from his chair on Lexington's bridge. Sixty enemy landing launches loaded with over thirty thousand troops flanked Home Fleet and passed down the chute toward New Earth. He wouldn't interfere with them. Each officer knew what had to happen. The next few hours would determine the outcome. He'd re-read everything available on his great-grand mother, Maria Presk, and stood in awe at how she'd faced down the Pagmok and Kalazecis ships when she had nothing with which to fight but her guts and intellect. He would like to have known her.

"Captain, Second Fleet may have a problem," concern etched the comm operator's voice. Captain Swain didn't bother to repeat the message since

Admiral Presk-Milar heard the same thing she had. "It appears the Chinese have detected them," the voice added.

Presk-Milar switched on the overhead screen and watched a portion of the enemy fleet change its vector heading placing it in position to rain destruction on Svern's fleet. All eyes watched the vid screens as the flotilla shed delta v and change course. Beyond doubt, Admiral Svern would catch hell. Presk-Milar or anyone else could do nothing to help. Going to his aid would compromise the entire battle plan. That he couldn't do. Under his breath he muttered, *Good luck, Magnus.*

Second Fleet maneuvering to challenge the enemy wasn't an option. Lying doggo, it would take almost an hour to reposition the ships. "Bastards want to make sure they get clean shots," Presk-Milar said to no one. *This Admiral knows what he's doing. Better not underestimate him* he thought.

He ordered a squadron of Kalazecis and Pagmok ships to guard Home fleet's flanks. With their shorter ranged weapons, they were an even match for the Chinese. Reluctantly, the Kalazecis officer acknowledged the order.

Presk-Milar watched the plot as the Pagmok ships engaged a number of vessels that had tried to flank Home Fleet. Recognizing that Presk-Milar had anticipated the move and the futility of his effort, the Chinese commander quickly disengaged. Presk-Milar decided it was a feint to draw Home Fleet away from the main battle and returned his attention to the plot board.

12: Inside the Enemy

Captain Huang Liang Chen, aboard the flagship Flying Dragon, watched the plot board, Supreme Admiral Chao at her side. He returned to his chair toward the rear of the bridge.

"This is a trap," Admiral Chao said his voice full of contempt. "Send a signal to Squadron Seven. Have them vector toward this anomaly." He traced his finger across the plot screen. "Order a small nuclear missile launched there." He jabbed his finger at an area on the plot. "That will destroy their pitiful screen and expose them." He smirked at his Captain. "They think we are stupid."

She did as ordered but simultaneously watched as ten battleships with escorts headed for Second Fleet as a deadly electronic signal invaded their systems—the fleet seemed to lose steerage, breaking formation as if uncontrolled.

* * * *

Admiral Presk-Milar studied a portion of the enemy fleet vector toward Second Fleet and punched the comm button, "Get David Rohm for me." He waited a few minutes.

"Yes, Admiral. How goes the fight?" David asked.

"Too soon to tell, Mr. Rohm, but Second Fleet could use some of your magic. Have you come up with anything that might help?"

Bogdan tried to keep the anxiety from his voice and wondered if he'd been successful. Everyone had committed to winning this fight. They all had the same question; would they be around to see the end of it?

"Well, I've got something we can try, Admiral. I have no way of knowing how effective it will be. My grandfather used the same thing against the Kalazecis. We can only hope the Chinese never heard about it. One thing we do need is a clear path to the enemy ships. If any of ours gets in the way, they get the same treatment. I'll send you the headings your boys and girls need to steer clear of."

Like his scientist namesake, Rohm seldom used humor; but now a little went a long way.

Presk-Milar recalled Colin Powell's admonition, 'No *war plan stays intact once the battle begins.*' "Understood David. Give me a little time. I'll get back with you."

It took over an hour for Admiral Presk-Milar to realign Home Fleet. With the exposure of Second Fleet and repositioned Home Fleet, the

Chinese commander now had precise locations of New Earth's ships—all of them. Presk-Milar realized the new vector put the Chinese in position to rain hell on Second Fleet but it put the enemy under the weapons of Home Fleet.

Presk-Milar saw the enemy's error; its new vector would cause their port side ships to close on their starboard formation. A major tactical mistake. "Now you get yours, bastard," Presk-Milar said. "Captain, order Home Fleet to open fire, targets of opportunity."

All eyes fixed on the plot board as the Lexington shuddered from the broadside it had released.

"Mr. Rohm, you may let loose your electronic wizardry on the enemy."

Presk-Milar watched as two enemy ships lost steerage and unable to control their vessels, collided with such force gigantic tears appeared venting both to space. One by one, the enemy ships systems shut down.

As expected, the engines ceased operation one at a time, causing the effected ship to gyrate wildly from the asymmetrical thrust. With engines still engaged but steerage lost, ships sped haphazardly, uncontrolled on unintended vectors. In close formation, necessary to maintain the vector to the planet surface, collisions were unavoidable. At least two thousand people died in an instant as ships rained havoc on each other. Of more than fifty ships bearing down on Home and Second Fleet, seventeen were in trouble, speeding wildly among their own disrupted formation. None of their weapons could target a ship and have anything more than hope of inflicting meaningful damage.

With at least part of the enemy armada in chaos, Second Fleet unleashed its missiles.

In Lexington's control room, all eyes locked on the plot board, watching as the lead enemy ships flared brightly and disappeared from the screen.

"Damn, David's wizardry has destroyed the enemy's lead elements. Press the attack," ordered Admiral Presk-Milar.

"Captain," this time he pointed at the overhead screen, a few enemy ships had split from the main fleet.

Swain smiled, "We're on it, Admiral," her voice totally non-committal not wanting to talk down to her Admiral. He just couldn't stay out of the fight. "Dodger, Sizemore, and Jefferson have them covered," she told him. Those three battleships had more than enough firepower to handle the breakaways. "We just lost the Arapaho and Gettysburg," Swain added.

"Admiral, want me to continue?" David Rohm asked. "I think I can still add to their misery."

"Please do so, Mr. Rohm," said Presk-Milar.

Again, silent death raced out into space from the planet's surface. One-by-one, Chinese ships lost steerage. Actually, the enemy lost *all* their electronic systems, and that included environment. Without life support, the ships were doomed even if they avoided colliding with their own. Almost as if a giant hand slapped them around a death dance started. Mr. Rohm's devastation left the enemy helpless—some of them. Too many remained capable.

For the next ten hours, the battle raged.

"Admiral, looks like the enemy is forming up for a high speed run straight through us," Captain Swain said.

Presk-Milar studied the plot and ordered Home Fleet into a circle almost one million kilometers in diameter perpendicular to the oncoming enemy fleet. It reminded him of an old-fashioned wagon train circling, giving them sustained firing patterns against the floundering enemy fleet.

"A pinwheel," said Captain Swain. "Where'd you get the idea, Admiral? It's certainly different. Innovative. Pure genius."

"If it works," he said. "Just an idea that looked like it had possibilities, Captain—a variation from the old wet navies of crossing the T." Presk-Milar's maneuvers confirmed what his junior officers had learned over the years about his tactical abilities, for which they were thankful.

The entire order of battle all captains had memorized and put through simulations, never saw the light of day. Every maneuver employed against their enemy came on the spur of the moment as Presk-Milar saw and acted against his enemy's mistakes—fatal mistakes that only meant death—no recovery.

The new formation did open a path for the enemy troop transports to the surface and he could do nothing about it. "Looks like the Pagmok will get a crack at the enemy army."

That sent a shudder through the bridge crew.

"Sir," said the comm operator, "If I'm reading this correctly, there's," he paused, "a Pagmok ship is closing on an enemy ship." He'd tried to keep his voice calm but unsuccessfully.

Presk-Milar touched an icon and followed the arrow superimposed on the board. "Get the Kalazecis fleet commander on the comm," he ordered less than pleased with what he saw.

"Yes, we are boarding," said the voice. "We want that ship as a prize. In fact, we plan to board as many as possible. We have lost two ships and the enemy's ships will make excellent replacements."

Presk-Milar returned to his chair and tried to keep his voice calm. "Sir, we still have a battle in front of us and the outcome is not certain by any means. I suggest you keep with the plan. When we defeat the Chinese, all the ships you can handle are yours. In the meantime, I need your fleet to reengage the enemy." He gave the Kalazecis the coordinates and watched the overhead board. "Seems I need to keep a tight rein on our compatriots."

"They're accelerating toward the coordinates, Admiral," the comm operator said. "Three ships."

The admiral nodded. Given the chance, he would make sure the enemy captain knew about the Pagmok and what that meant.

New Earth's combined fleets had twelve ships out of commission with two thousand people dead—five percent of its total population. Pagmok losses were fewer in personnel. Historians had noted that any country that lost four percent of its people had effectively lost the ability to wage war. But that held no water for New Earth. They would fight to the last man or woman.

As they watched the screens, seventeen Chinese ships disappeared along with their crews, twenty floating hulks blocked the path of the oncoming ships, their crews probably doing what they could to stay alive. Those who still had control of their electronics fared little better than those who had lost steerage. Fighting New Earth's ships became secondary as the enemy fleet struggled to avoid collisions with derelicts that clogged their paths.

Home and Second fleet fired volley after volley of energy cannons along with high energy pulsed laser missiles. Another sixty Chinese ships sustained damage that effectively took them out of the battle. They still had half their fleet but many of those ships were transport and support vessels. The enemy was steadily losing the capacity to wage war.

Presk-Milar saw the enemy carriers at the same time as Captain Swain. She smiled as she said, "Permission to launch squadrons two and three. One will remain for fleet cover," her voice crisp and sharp.

"Permission granted, Captain."

One hundred fighters launched from the Lexington like a swarm of angry bees but with a much deadlier sting. Named *razors* for their ability to maneuver cutting a swath of destruction, the fighters attacked. Presk-Milar doubted the Chinese had anything to match the threat coming at them, and they had no room to maneuver and no place to hide.

David Rohm, the first David Rohm's strategic logic remained viable. Instead of mass and heavy cannons, the razors relied on agility and lethal armament. Internal inertial dampeners allowed the fighters to maneuver much as a terrestrial airborne ship. The enemy had no way to target their highly maneuverable rivals.

One by one, the enemy fighters died, their own weapons lacked the razor's range and they never got within killing distance.

Lexington's bridge crew watched as razors picked off the enemy fighters. The comm operator said the enemy fighters reminded her of fireflies, flaring brilliantly for a second and then disappearing from the plot. In less than thirty T-minutes, the razors had cleared space of the threat. New Earth's fighters turned their attention to the two massive carriers and escort battleships.

Approaching aft of the closest carrier, three razors attacked simultaneously and fired their long-range energy weapons into the huge landing bay.

Immediately ahead of the cavernous opening, massive power generators exploded in a flash the entire battle area could see. Seventeen thousand men and women died instantly, vaporized in the blast as their fuel cells exploded.

"Captain, the first Chinese transport is on the planet." This time, the comm operator's voice approached a yell, clearly worried. Still, bent on landing on New Earth, the enemy remained relentless and exploited the opening.

"I see it crewman," Swain casually responded and turned to the Admiral awaiting his orders.

"I'm sure the Kalazecis commander is releasing his warriors about now." Presk-Milar's voice whiplashed across the bridge. He punched an icon on the arm of his chair and commed the Kalazecis commander, "Admiral, can you release your fighters to aid the ground battle?"

"Half of them," the response immediately came back.

Seventy-five fighters formed up and headed for the planet. Presk-Milar's returned his attention to the enemy fleet.

President Jabari had said that a cornered enemy is the most dangerous. Not wanting to trade lives—New Earth couldn't afford attrition—he ordered Home Fleet to open a corridor, leaving the Chinese a way out.

A few hours later, he listened as the comm announced, "Admiral, they're heading out system."

"Looks like they're giving up and going home," Presk-Milar said. "The son of a bitch is abandoning their troops on the ground. Poor bastards having to face the Pagmok. I almost pity them. Almost."

Admiral Presk-Milar commed President Jabari to advise him. "You're where? Mr. President? With all due respect, sir, get your ass out of there. The

Pagmok are quite capable of handling the ground fight without you. And you're no good to us dead."

That brought a deep roaring laugh from the President. "Yes, Fleet Admiral. The Chinese soldiers tried a mass charge and that is just the kind of combat the Pagmok relish." Apparently, he thought for a minute and said, "Maybe that wasn't the best choice of words. It isn't pretty, but damn, these guys are something to watch. I guess I've seen enough so, Admiral, I'll obey your command and go back to my nice cozy office. By the way, Goldthwaite City took few hits. Tell your people they were magnificent."

Admiral Presk-Milar shook his head. "Even Presidents sometimes get carried away and forget they can get killed." With only mopping up operations and recovering escape capsules remaining, he ordered Captain Swain to assemble the fleet. "We're going to Old Earth."

He commed the Kalazecis admiral and they agreed, two Pagmok ships would be detailed to shepherd the least damaged enemy ships back to Myslac. Maybe I won't need to tell the enemy skipper about the Pagmok. He's going to find out first hand he mused.

13: Old Earth

One million kilometers above Old Earth, New Earth's fleet took up station.

"Have the fleet disperse, formation alpha," Admiral Presk-Milar ordered.

The Hommew ships had returned to their home world. During the war at New Earth, Hommew's fleet fought alongside his own ships and he doubted the Chinese had noticed. Both Presk-Milar and Hommew's commander agree they were unknown to Old Earth and it should remain that way. Admiral Presk-Milar had decided this fight would be between Old and New Earth. He would hold the Pagmok in reserve. Just knowing they were there should put fear into the hearts of his enemy if it wasn't there already.

"We've establish contact with the Chinese Fleet Admiral. It's Supreme Admiral Chao," Captain Swain said.

Seated in his flag office, Presk-Milar told her to pipe it in. "Admiral Chao, this is Fleet Admiral Bogdan Presk-Milar, New Earth. In order to avoid further losses, I am requesting you surrender your fleet. I am prepared to be lenient."

"Ha, you may have won a battle, Admiral, but the war is not lost. As long as I have the ability, I shall fight. And you will lose."

Chao knew he was outclassed and had inferior equipment, Presk-Milar figured his counterpart must have grave doubts about salvaging any kind of victory, no matter how small or insignificant. But he knew the man would try.

Ready to use the interrupter beam, Presk-Milar silenced the comm with Chao and opened another to Captain Swain. "Do we have a good lock on the Chinese fleet?" he asked.

"Admiral, we're still half a million klicks above Old Earth. Our engineers say the spread is too great to have any meaningful effect. We need to close on the enemy."

Presk-Milar ended the comm and reopened the link to the Chinese Admiral. Before he could speak, Chao's voice broke the silence. "Having second thoughts, Admiral? You should. Many of your people will die. And for a world that is of no longer of concern to you. Think carefully, Admiral Presk-Milar. Think carefully and long."

Chao broke the connection. Presk-Milar said, "Comm, try to reestablish the link."

"Admiral, no response," the comm operator answered after a few moments.

* * * *

Captain Chen waited for some word from Supreme Admiral Chao now in his cabin. She pressed the comm icon. "Your orders, Admiral? The New Earth fleet is maneuvering and will shortly have the advantage," her voice urgent.

"How many ships," he asked.

"We count almost three hundred. Two carriers, twenty battleships, mass about twice our largest, fifty heavy cruisers, a number of smaller, probably light cruiser size. The rest support, most likely supply," Chen answered. "Admiral, this fleet is far superior to ours. If we continue, it means the death of many of our people.

"Less than one hundred are New Earth," she continued. "The remainder are Pagmok."

That brought a shudder from the admiral.

An hour later, Captain Chen punched the icon, "Yes, sir."

"Captain, come to my quarters."

Outside his cabin, Chen lightly rapped on the hatch.

"Come."

She stepped through the opening, saluted and waited.

Seated with his back to her he said, "Captain, I have ordered the fleet to ramming formation. We should be able to destroy their carriers and do enough damage to the remainder of their fleet to keep them from attacking the homeland."

"Admiral, you can't be serious. Why wasn't I told?" She knew the answer. Chao knew she would object wanting to end the conflict. His promoting Chen to flag captain had earned her the enmity of the officer corps and there was little he could do to protect her. Bypassing her with the ramming order, kept her out of the chain of command and might be of some help. He had hoped the prospects of the fleet's destruction might bolster her commitment to fight and win but that hadn't happened. He now knew it was an unforgivable mistake in judgment on his part.

His chair turned slowly. She'd never seen such a look on his face— something between disappointment and hate. Chen had treated her more like a doting father than command officer. Knowing this moment might come, Chen had mentally prepared and stoically looked at her mentor.

"Sit down, Chen," his voice threatening—strident. "We will watch the carnage together." He flicked on the view screen.

Regardless of the outcome of this battle, and ramming could hardly work, with a land army of three million, no Old or New Earth force could invade the Chinese mainland. Captain Huang Liang Chen understood if this was to end, China's leadership must change. She could only wonder if she would be alive to see it happen.

* * * *

Aboard NES Lexington, Admiral Bogdan Presk-Milar studied the plot board. "Those bastards plan to ram us," he said and added, "they're forming up three abreast." He had studied in detail every space and wet navy war ever recorded, recognized the formation, and had a plan to counter it. Known for his tactical savvy, Presk-Milar had thought through how to deal with a suicide attack. His fleet had never faced a ramming—a tactic that made no sense at all in a universe of long-range weapons. Still, he'd considered it.

Without time to send detailed instructions through the normal channels, Fleet Commandant Bogdan Presk-Milar opened a comm to all captains.

"Gentlemen, it appears Admiral Chao is desperate, perhaps no longer rational. His fleet has assembled in what can only be a ramming formation. I will communicate to you verbally how we are to deal with this. I'm confident we can defeat his frantic attempt."

Over the next few minutes, Presk-Milar told his captains in detail what needed to happen and how to respond to his commands. Only on his orders would they would break current formation. He knew his fleet wouldn't get through this without some additional losses.

"If they figured out what we did to them at New Earth, they will accelerate at military power until within range of our Rohm disrupter weapons," said Presk-Milar and added, "cut their engines, shut down all electronic systems and come straight down our throat to attack the carriers at the tail end of our formation. If they do that, we'll have a problem." What ships made it through the New Earth fleet would tail-over then kick in their hyper engines to reverse course and repeat the same maneuver only from the rear of New Earth's fleet. If the enemy could take out the transports as well, it would disrupt any ammunition resupplies to the fleet. He stepped back from the plot board as if to gain larger perspective. For the next hour he seldom moved, eyes never missing the slightest change.

Presk-Milar continued speaking out loud but to no one in particular. "If they don't understand that it was our interrupts that helped defeat them, we'll destroy them.

"Launch all fighters," Presk-Milar ordered his voice breaking the silence that had reigned for an hour on Lexington's bridge.

Over three hundred New Earth and Pagmok fighters steamed from the carriers.

"Remind our pilots that the disrupters will take them out as quickly as the enemy."

Over the next few minutes, the razors assembled in a standard protect formation around the fleet. On signal from the squadron commander, the fighters would accelerate toward their enemy.

Just as Presk-Milar had predicted, the enemy would rely on their speed and thrusters to ram his ships.

"Tell the fighters they are to concentrate on the trailing ten ships and then the lead ships. Have our disrupters focus on the lead ships, they will do our work for us." The center of the enemy fleet would have no way to avoid the chaos in front of them. They would do the killing for Presk-Milar.

Presk-Milar stood over the plot board as the enemy fleet raced toward them. No effort was made to disguise their purpose. Any slewing vectors would further expose the enemy to broadsides. Still, he intended to make them pay.

Arms folded across his chest, fingers tapping a cadence that seemed to mark the enemy ships approach. On they came and yet the admiral waited.

"Admiral, shall I order the fleet to disperse?" said Captain Swain somewhat nervous.

"Yes, Captain."

As the Chinese battlewagons entered cannon range, the razors executed a starburst, then reversed course, attacked the trailing vessels and then streaked for the ships at the lead ships. Coupled with the missiles and cannons that rained down on them, the badly wounded ships could do little against the carnage that ravaged them. The combined weapons utterly destroyed them, as dying ships clogged the approach route to New Earth's fleet.

"Disperse," ordered Presk-Milar. At the same time, he told his lead battleships to standby to activate the electronic disrupters.

Three hundred spaceships parted, opening a one million kilometer separation between them and the attacking ships. "Activate Rohm's electronic disrupter. Sweep their entire fleet," he ordered.

The trailing ships, which had been the last to get up to military speed were easy targets for the fighters. Ravaged by the fighters they streaked into the maelstrom of broken vessels left by the disrupters and their own malfunctioning steerage systems. Collisions not visible on the plot left little evidence but the clutter left no doubt as the trailing ships drove into their lead sister ships.

New Earth fighters raced among the maelstrom killing any ship that showed signs of life. Presk-Milar grimaced as the fighters reported. Not one ramming ship escaped undamaged.

Captain Swain touched an icon and studied the plot. "Admiral, we've lost one hundred fighters, ten destroyers, one cruiser and one battleship. Minimal damage to the carriers."

"A terrible waste," said Admiral Presk-Milar. "Criminal."

* * * *

Chao turned his chair away from her. Chen pulled a pocket neutralizer from her tunic, stepped to his side and handed it to the Admiral.

Despair laced his voice as he said, "Have the fleet stand down. You are now in command."

Supreme Admiral Fong Chao placed the weapon next to this head, pushed the stud, and tumbled to the deck. Even though she knew what he intended, Chen gasped. She collected herself, touched the comm and summoned the doctor. Her finger again pressed an icon, "This Captain Chen, Admiral Chao is no longer able to direct the fleet. He has authorized me to assume command. Stand down from your attack. Comm, signal our surrender."

* * * *

"Ms. Joiner, this is Fleet Admiral Bogdan Presk-Milar again," he said and released the comm, a giant grin across his face.

"Admiral, you've no idea how happy we are that you're here." She waited until the cheers ran their course.

"Holly, what is the situation?" Presk-Milar asked.

Over the next hour she laid out the turmoil racking Earth. Learning of the defeat at New Earth when the Chinese fleet returned, full-scale wars broke out in many countries. Some were under martial law and the outcome still in doubt. Only the Chinese mainland remained immune to the upheaval. At last word, the PRC had ordered three million troops to maintain order.

"What do you want us to do? We're anxious to meet with you. As you must suspect, or know, the national government still has not yielded. The Army is everywhere ruthlessly putting down uprisings. If you can contact Washington, it might help." She sent the necessary frequency.

"Your showing up has really changed things, Admiral," Holly said. "Without spaceships to move their troops, with you having control of space, they can't effectively shift their forces to put down the rebellions."

"Holly, I do not intend to put troops on the ground. Each nation must consolidate its hold and get some semblance of order. Our first chore is to finish what we came to do—deal with the PRC. A squadron of our forces will remain in low orbit just in case you can use our support.

"We've already made contact with the military command, Holly. Do you have any formal structure that can take power? Someone on the ground must step forward. They don't have to be in the city, in fact it's better if they're not. They will need vidcom capability."

"Yes, we can arrange that Admiral."

Over the next few hours, in contact with the Chinese Army, Admiral Presk-Milar laid out what was to happen. "I remind you, sir, your responsibility is to protect the citizens. You are to restore order with as few losses to the public as possible. I will personally hold you responsible for anything less than that. Do you understand?"

General of the Army Wha Zan responded curtly, in English, for the American pig to go to hell and he looked forward to personally killing him.

"Your call, General. You've unnecessarily condemned many people to their deaths.

"Captain Swain, target the General's headquarters and fire. We'll see who dies first."

* * * *

"General Mackenzie, the nationwide vidcom is ready. You may broadcast," Holly Joiner said.

Mackenzie reminded the Army officers of their first responsibility to keep order regardless of their political leanings. "Any who swear allegiance to the United States will lead that effort. Those who chose otherwise must accept the consequences," he told them.

The majority of the Army yielded to Mackenzie's orders. Skirmishes between the loyalist forces and those commanders who chose to stay with the Chinese broke out across the nation. Within one day, the rebellion had shifted from guerilla action to full-fledged war raging across most nations. Nobody expected the fighting to end quickly or soon. Admiral Presk-Milar dispatched ships to aid loyal commanders on the ground. Scorching firepower destroyed those enemy troops caught out in the open or in their camps. But those areas were few compared to the fighting in the cities. Dislodging bunkered soldiers meant door to door fighting in thousands of cities.

"When will the Chinese Commander be on board?" Admiral Presk-Milar asked.

"Her shuttle left the Flying Dragon an hour ago. Should be here shortly, Admiral," Captain Swain said and added, "She doesn't have the blessing of her government."

"Too bad. It would go easier if she had. She'll never be able to return to her homeland. What do we know about her?"

"She was a protégé of Admiral Chao. Resented by most officers for the favoritism she received—" Captain Swain hesitated and Presk-Milar with his back to her, turned in his chair. "Captain—?"

"Holly Joiner says she knew of the sabotage on their ships but never warned the Admiral." Swain referred to the microchips on the Chinese fleet that destroyed their navigation and steerage.

"Has this been confirmed?"

"We have no way to verify the information, Admiral."

Presk-Milar let out a low whistle. "I don't know how to respond to this. If it's true, others may know; no they will know. They'll brand her a traitor. I almost wish it were not true."

Captain Swain didn't respond, apparently not knowing what to say if anything.

"She'll be lucky to live out the day. Certainly not much longer. One of her own will kill her."

Jeanne Swain stepped to the Admiral's desk and touched an icon, "Yes."

"Captain Chen is onboard," a voice said. "She has two officers with her."

"Escort the Captain to the Admiral's cabin," she ordered.

"Does she speak English," Presk-Milar asked.

"I don't know, sir."

"We don't know much do we?" he said his manner circumspect.

"It would seem so, sir."

"Loosen up Jeanne. This may be the only time you get to accept the surrender of your counterpart."

Presk-Milar motioned Captain Swain to the center of the room and took the chair behind his desk, clearing the top as the hatch buzzer sounded. He punched the comm switch. "Come."

Tall and attractive Presk-Milar thought as the black haired Asian stepped through the hatch, came to attention, saluted. Her eyes glistened.

Captain Swain returned the salute and motioned her to a chair.

"I am Captain Huang Liang Chen, People's Republic of China, acting Commander of the People's Fleet," she said in perfect English. "I surrender."

14: The War comes to Old Earth

"**Captain** Chen, I accept your surrender," said Captain Swain.

Fleet Admiral Presk-Milar remained silent seated behind his desk. "We have some documents for you to sign. Please be seated." She motioned toward a table and chair.

Chen, dressed in her full parade dress uniform, visor cap tucked under her left arm, sat, read the papers laid out before her and signed. She turned to face Presk-Milar. "You understand I do not have the approval of my government to sign on their behalf. I doubt this ends the conflict."

"Understood," he said. "What is the condition of your fleet? Do you require any humanitarian help?"

"No, we have many casualties, but I think our medical personnel are adequate. It will be some time before some ships are capable of maneuvering under their own power. Your tactics proved most effective."

She had no smile with what he thought an admonition.

Presk-Milar had no regrets. "Captain Chen, make sure your captains know we will destroy any ship that resumes hostilities." It was his people or hers and that was no decision. He'd do it again if any if of her officers started shooting.

She nodded her understanding.

Presk-Milar walked from behind his desk and offered his hand. She stood and hesitantly accepted.

"I understand you were against this war. Is this correct?" He tried to present a relaxed demeanor and yet maintain a military bearing.

She nodded. "I am not proud of opposing my government. Had matters played out differently, we might not be having this conversation." She left no doubt loyalties remained with her country but voiced her contempt for the leadership. The only solution lay in a complete change at the top.

A sizeable chore suggested Presk-Milar. "Have you any suggestions as to who should head your government."

"The key is the Army Navy. General Yang Kuo Nu intimidates the politburo. None dare oppose him. Any attack on the homeland will only secure his grip. The man controls the Army and is ruthless. He will not hesitate to kill the President or Prime Minister if they so much as speak out against him.

"Perhaps you should ask Ms. Joiner," said Chen.

Presk-Milar's eyebrows shot up. "Holly Joiner? How do you know her?" Before the Captain could answer, he added, "You seem to know a great deal about the American operation. I'm not sure I should let you return to your ship."

"Admiral, information has a way of getting to the right source at the right time."

"A Chinese saying?"

She didn't answer.

"Captain Chen, I am prepared to offer you asylum," he said.

She started to speak and Presk-Milar held up his hand. "I suspect your life is in peril. In fact, I'm surprised you lived this long. Undoubtedly, not all of your crew and officers feel as you do. I could give you sanctuary here on the Lexington. I'm making you that offer. You are more valuable to us, alive, even locked up."

"Thank you Admiral. But I must refuse. If my actions mean anything, I must try to convince the fleet of their correctness. I will return to my command."

"So be it, Captain. I wish we'd met under different circumstances." Presk-Milar motioned toward the hatch signaling the meeting was over.

Chen stood, saluted both officers, made a crisp military about face and headed for the hatch. She stopped, turned and said, "I would have been proud to serve in your command, Admiral. You exemplify what I've always believed an officer should be." She stepped through the hatch.

Presk-Milar cocked his head and smiled. "Hear that Captain? I ain't so bad ta serve under." He laughed as he said it.

Jeanne answered with a prodigious yawn, her eyes closed.

As quickly as the light moment appeared, it ended.

"Captain, we'll leave Second Fleet here to keep an eye on the enemy. Have the remainder join up with the Lexington. We've got to finish what we came to do."

It took the better part of the day before Admiral Presk-Milar okayed the fleet alignment. "Admiral Svern, no breach of my orders. Kill any ship that disobeys. Understood?" The acknowledgment came quickly. Captain Swain conveyed the warning to Captain Chen and got the expected reply. Slowly Home Fleet positioned over the western Pacific.

"Get me a secure channel to Holly Joiner, with vid if possible." Presk-Milar left for his day cabin just off the bridge.

Slipping off his tunic, he poured a cup of coffee and sat at his desk. Joiner had definitely gained his respect. What she had accomplished bordered on miraculous. He punched the icon and her face appeared, "Ms. Joiner, finally I get to see who I'm talking with. You're much younger than I expected." And he meant that. For the load she had taken on, he anticipated an older person. She'd be a seasoned veteran before this was over if not already that.

"Thank you Admiral." He was paid with a smile and shrug.

"Not going to tell me your age are you?" he laughed as he spoke.

"Nope and a gentleman wouldn't ask."

"My apologies, Ma'am. I must admit your youthfulness caused me pause."

"Captain Chen suggested I contact you. She indicated you may know someone who could help me." He didn't ask how an enemy flag captain knew about her and the operation she headed.

"To do what, Admiral?" Holly's demeanor changed and he saw what made her such a determined person. This was no one to mess with.

"I plan to attack China. I understand the Army Navy Commissar is the guy to take out. That he's the real power."

"That agrees with my information, Admiral. Getting rid of him will be a formidable challenge."

"Any suggestions?"

"I know a man who was his aide for twenty years. Knows him as well as anyone."

"Well, Ms. Joiner, do I get to meet him or do I relay my questions through you?" Presk-Milar tried to moderate his tone but the lady seemed reluctant to give him much information.

"Admiral, this man is in a secret place with his family. We have avoided giving anyone access to him. He sacrificed everything to bring us invaluable information—"

Admiral Presk-Milar interrupted her, "Forgive my bluntness, Ms. Joiner. I have lost over two thousand damned good people in this war and it isn't over. And that's out of a population of forty two thousand. As you can see, our loss is significant. That sacrifice went beyond family. I intend to do what I came to do. You have information that could help save lives and I need it."

His pronouncement didn't seem to faze the woman.

She's one hard case though, Presk-Milar. But then, to accomplish what she had took just that kind of person.

"I understand, Admiral. Give me some time to make contact with him and I'll get back to you," she said, her voice terse. She cut the connection not waiting for a response.

"I could have handled that better," he told himself. The loss of people was his first concern, but then probably for Joiner as well. She had her own problems and he must consider that next time.

Bogdan smiled as Holly's face reappeared on the vid screen. "Ms. Joiner, please again accept my apology for my earlier behavior. I have no excuse to offer other than that of man who has become accustomed to giving orders and never having them questioned. That makes me an overbearing ass."

"So it would seem, Admiral. Apology accepted." She paused for a moment. "Our man will help. But he insisted that you take him and his family aboard your ship. He believes it will take a running dialog to accomplish anything meaningful." She gave him a look that seemed a bit incredulous. "There is a caveat. He wants the long life gene for him and his family." She cocked her head and shrugged.

"Does he realize he can never return to Old Earth?"

She smiled, "Old Earth. You make it sounds rather anachronistic. And yes, he does. In fact, he believes boarding your ship is the only way he can save his family. He's probably right."

"Okay, it's done. How do we pull this off?"

Ideas passed back and forth with no resolution. Holly didn't want to give away the man's location fearing it would compromise too many assets ruling out Lexington's shuttle retrieving the family. Finally, Presk-Milar said, "Is Scaled Components still around?"

"Not only around, they are a major builder of sub-orbital ships. I think you've hit on it, Admiral."

Presk-Milar got the company's secured frequency, commed the fabled builder and made arrangements for them to shuttle Yang's aide to an orbit of two thousand kilometers where they'd meet with Lexington's launch.

Seven days later, Peng Rui Bao and his family boarded NES Lexington.

For over a week, Admiral Presk-Milar, Captain Swain, the ships intelligence officer along with an interpreter, grilled Peng. According to Peng, Yang a renegade, gained the upper hand through intimidation and threats. He had used sappers from the Army to take care of many who opposed him.

"Got a lot of insider information," said Presk-Milar. "It looks like someone needs to shoot the bastard in order for us to make much headway."

Through the interpreter, Peng said, "That may be possible," startling Lexington's officers.

The smallish man laid out an idea he thought might work but reminded them getting an assassin that close was problematic at best.

Over the next few days, working with Holly Joiner, Peng's idea moved forward.

"We can't rely on this even if it does work," said Presk-Milar. It's going to take more and that has to come from us." With that, he dismissed his staff and retreated to his cabin—to think.

Mulling over possibilities, rejecting every thought, two days later, Admiral Bogdan Presk-Milar finally hit on an idea. Recalling his staff and Peng, he laid out his plan.

Addressing Peng he said, "We need to get in contact with Yang's enemies, antagonists, anyone who is willing to speak out or hopefully, take action even if Yang isn't killed. Knowing that someone at least made the effort should embolden the population. And if they need prodding into action, maybe we can do that. With assurances, we will back them all the way, it shouldn't take too much convincing. That is if they're the right people. I need names, Mr. Peng."

Even without assurances these men and women would act, Bogdan Presk-Milar put his plan in motion.

A month later, Presk-Milar took a vid from Holly. "You were right, Admiral," she said. "Missed killing Yang, but he's on the run. Looks like enough of the higher-ups, and a few others took the challenge. They're after the guy and even called for new leadership. Seems they've stirred up the populace. With Yang showing weakness, even the Army has hesitated to put down the public uprisings."

Presk-Milar had watched the vids throughout the day. Twice he'd sent warnings to the Army field commanders he would use all his resources to stop any effort made against civilians. He keyed the comm and sent a third. "If you want to fight, at least fight with your own kind. And I'm here just for that reason. Any action you take will be met with an appropriate response."

Presk-Milar continued to watch action unfold. "Looks like we need to convince a few diehards, Captain."

"What? Something like a few shots across their bow," said the intelligence officer.

Wanting to minimize collateral damage Presk-Milar said, "No, let's send First Squadron."

Over one thousand enemy fighter rose to meet Lexington's one hundred razors. Against ships they'd never seen the likes of, the air-breathing fighters stood no chance. The fight, if you were naive enough to call it that, the outcome was predictable. Those who could get away, lived. Those who couldn't, died. After the initial encounter, not one enemy rose to resume the challenge.

Presk-Milar continued to monitor events on the ground. Not surprising, most of Earth's population waited to see the outcome. Only the most determined came forward to take a stand for their freedom. At best, the battle seemed chaotic and sorting it out would take some time. People, governments, and companies with parochial interests continued to resist. Presk-Milar didn't interfere, knowing the tide favored the rebellion. With the Chinese Army Navy contained on their own turf, they presented no threat to establishing something approaching order.

"Open all channels to the Chinese leadership," said Presk-Milar four weeks after the Chinese fleet's disastrous attempt at ramming. Dressed in full parade regalia, an interpreter at his side, he stood before the camera and for the first time addressed his enemy. "Gentlemen, I am Bogdan Presk-Milar, Fleet Admiral of New Earth's Space Navy. By now you must realize that your only hope for securing peace lies in a change of government. Your domination and warlike policies will no longer stand. I have exercised great tolerance waiting for you to accept the inevitable. But my patience has reached its limit. You cannot win in conflict against us. You attacked our world without provocation. We defeated your fleet twice and are prepared to begin selectively destroying your country. For your own selfish reasons, you have brought this upon yourselves.

"Send the coordinates," he ordered. Presk-Milar had decided to send the locations of the installations he meant to destroy to his fleet. Not for humanitarian reasons, his enemy had shown no reluctance at killing New Earthers and its own—he wanted them to talk. Destroying over a million of their service personnel wouldn't enhance that possibility.

Presk-Milar broke the signal. "Captain Swain, the fleet has its targets. You have the timetable and may commence your attack as designated." He would wait for a response.

Twenty-four hours later, Home Fleet, now some fifteen thousand kilometers above Old Earth, unleashed a rain of energy cannons. Over five hundred military bases worldwide, land, air force, and naval, disappeared in an instant.

"Open a vid channel to the Chinese high command," he ordered.

Standing before the camera in battle fatigues this time, he said, "Gentlemen, you have seen the destruction I can visit on you at will. If you make any attempt to interfere with the schedule being transmitted, my fleet will start systematically destroying your country. And it will begin with your official offices, then your residences. Your army is to stand down. Maintain domestic order but do only what is necessary to minimize civilian casualties. Please do not test my resolve. I will tolerate no violation of my orders. Presk-Milar out."

Sitting in his wardroom Presk-Milar received the comm noting the governments of the world were ready to talk. Omitted was any mention of the Chinese.

He commed Holly Joiner. "Madam, what's going on? I assume you have monitored events."

"We have indeed, Admiral. Representatives of the major nations are ready to talk—all nations. It would seem this is your shot to call. How do you want to handle this? A gathering of world leaders?"

"I understand the Nelson Mandela is still in service. Is my information correct?"

"Give me a few minutes and I'll verify."

"Thank you. If so, put it on orbit at fifty thousand kilometers. A contingent of Marines and flight crew from my fleet will arrive to take control. Whoever brings it up will surrender the ship and return to Earth. And Ms. Joiner, if someone should be stupid enough to hide, trying to stay on board, my Marines will summarily shoot them on the spot. We are capable of detecting any explosive material should someone think it's possible to disrupt this meeting in such a manner. I will tolerate no breach of my orders." Admiral Presk-Milar's reputation for doing exactly as he said by now was well known.

* * * *

"Come," said Bogdan.

The hatch opened and an orderly entered carrying a half meter stack of papers placing them on the Admiral's work desk.

"What in the hell is all this?"

"Captains, and squadron commanders' reports, sir."

"Whose idea was this? I didn't order this."

The orderly cleared his throat. "Sir, your orders clearly state after any hostile engagement, the respective captains are required to submit a fitness report on their ships, crew along with their evaluation of their part in the fight."

"I said all that?"

"Yes, sir. You were quite precise."

Presk-Milar frowned but decided not to respond to the orderly's effort to suppress a grin.

15: The Assembly

"**Ms.** Joiner, is the NWO capable of leading a delegation?" asked Admiral Presk-Milar.

"To what end? They've shown a little backbone at times but Beijing appointed all of the current leadership. There are influential individuals of various nations that are showing real promise but lack the backing to pull off much. I mean by that they are not elected. Mostly just people who took the initiative and stepped forward when the situation demanded action. Probably natural leaders. They may be the best we have to offer at the moment."

"You missed one, Madam. Ms. Joiner, I am appointing you to head Old Earth's delegation," Presk-Milar said. "You are to select the most capable leaders, the number is unimportant, for a meeting with me aboard the Nelson Mandela. Take whatever time you need in making your choices. I will give the necessary details for transit when you are ready. Shortly, a broadcast will leave here to every nation and the NWO advising them of my decision. Do you have any questions?"

"What? Admiral—me? Why?" she stammered.

"Who better? Ms. Joiner, you've taken all the chances and shown the leadership when no one else did. You have led the charge and everyone knows it. How could I pick anyone more involved or as capable? Presk-Milar out." He broke the connection with a broad smile.

"That may be the right decision, Admiral but a little high-handed," said Captain Swain.

"So it was. I acknowledge that. But it doesn't change a thing. She's the best to lead Old Earth through what I have in mind. It's going to take someone not only strong but tested. And she meets all of the above as far as I'm concerned."

The Nelson Mandela arrived on station minus any stowaways and booby traps. A New Earth crew took the better part of a week to prepare the ships hangar for the meeting. Presk-Milar modified his earlier transmission, allowing five reporters, all selected by Ms. Joiner, to join the delegation.

Days later, Holly Joiner commed that eighteen people would make up Old Earth's delegation to the Mandela. A few more than Presk-Milar had hoped for. Leaders of NWO objected to being excluded but a few words from Presk-Milar put a stop to their truculent posturing.

Lexington made shuttles available to those attending members who needed transportation to the rendezvous point outside Washington. One razor left the Lexington to bring Holly Joiner ahead of the other attendees—for as she said, 'the ride of her life'.

An hour later, a launch deposited the remaining members in Mandela's hangar.

Marines in full combat regalia with pulse rifles lined the perimeter of Mandela's hanger decked out in flags of every Old Earth nation and centered on New Earth's ensign. Imposing by any standard, eyes straight ahead, anyone doubting their purpose had only to see the determination reflected in their precision as the Marine Major announced, "Attention on deck. Fleet Admiral Presk-Milar, all rise."

In full parade dress blues, gold shoulder braid with matching epaulettes Presk-Milar strode in accompanied by six Marines and took his seat at the head of the conference table.

"Be seated," the Major said and ordered his men to parade rest.

"Ladies and gentlemen. I am Fleet Admiral Bogdan Presk-Milar, New Earth Supreme Military Commander. As of this moment, I am declaring Old Earth under military command of New Earth and instituting worldwide martial law. Any act taken against any New Earth ship or personnel will meet with deadly force. If you know of any pending actions against my authority, you will do your people a service to issue immediately orders to stop any illicit acts. Any disobedience of my orders or those serving under my command will receive harsh treatment."

Hearing Old Earth used, while not intended to be a metaphor to define who they were, it did cause heads to turn.

"Who are you to issue such ultimatums?" The Chinese representative stood, shoving his chair back.

Presk-Milar made a slight motion and four Marines along with their officer stepped forward positioning themselves behind the ambassador. "Sir, we have defeated you in battle twice. Over fifty thousand of your people have died in an effort one can only say for a reason that was vain in the utmost. If you do not sit down and maintain silence, my Marines will remove and return you to the planet."

Presk-Milar waited as the ambassador seemingly contemplated his choices and sat.

"There is a folder in front of each of you," the Admiral said. "It is in your native language and English. Please open it and take a few moments to familiarize yourselves with the content." Still sitting, he leaned back in the chair, his eyes sweeping each delegate.

"Sir," said Presk-Milar acknowledging a raised hand.

"I am former United States Ambassador Reginald Covington. There are over one half million foreign and mercenary forces still on American soil. How are we to rid ourselves of these troops?"

"As have we." A chorus of members spoke up.

Presk-Milar tapped the conference table with one finger for a moment. Speaking to the American, he said, "As we speak, naval transports are assembling on both of your coasts. As ships become available, they will provide the same evacuation to your respective countries. Ambassador Woo Ling, there is a vid phone in front of you. Issue orders, *now*, to your field commanders. They are to go to the nearest military post and leave their weapons. Upon completion, you will receive instructions for debarking to one of the fleets and return to China. Your soldiers will be under the protection of the allied militias." That was the best he could offer.

Woo Ling didn't move.

"Do it *now*, sir."

Woo Ling still didn't move.

"Major," Presk-Milar said his voice harsh, "Place the Chinese ambassador under close arrest and remove him from these proceedings. If he should resist, shoot him." Presk-Milar's order could not have riveted the group beyond the stark realism of its severity.

It took only seconds for the Marines to comply with the order. Once they had handcuffed the ambassador, his guards bodily carried him from the hall.

"Ms. Joiner, is there anyone who can act for the PRC?" said Presk-Milar.

"Only me, Admiral and I must first clear this with Beijing."

"Please do so." Again, he leaned back in his chair and waited. Holly, using Woo Ling's vid phone made contact and as the entire delegation on the Mandela watched, informed the PRC government of what had occurred and received their tacit approval to convey any information affecting them. Not a compelling endorsement but it would have to do. Following Presk-Milar's instruction, Holly commed the Chinese military command giving explicit instructions for the withdrawal of troops from every occupied country for reassignment to their homeland. He purposely avoided language suggesting they were to surrender. Less than an hour later, she had acknowledgment from Chinese Army field commanders in one hundred countries stating acknowledgement and compliance.

Over the next two days, Admiral Presk-Milar laid out a plan to restore order on Old Earth, which included open and free elections, establishment of police and national guards, a judicial structure and a functioning economic system. Every government was to submit their plan and he would review them in detail.

The delegates returned to Earth, satisfied with the conference and, with some trepidation, eager to move ahead.

* * * *

Alone in his office, Admiral Presk-Milar summoned Captain Swain. "How are matters working out for Captain Chen?"

"From what I hear, quite well. It would seem, after three attempts on her life, her enemies have gotten the message. They want nothing to do with the Pagmok you assigned to protect her. By the way, she's now a full Admiral. Happened just after the big conference. According to Peng Rui Bao, enough of Yang's enemies have decided to speak up for her. It seems they point to her backbone and the fact she placed her life in jeopardy for the benefit of her country when the leadership failed to do so."

"She's damned lucky to be alive," said Presk-Milar.

"Captain, Ms. Joiner, what's your opinion of her?" he asked.

"Remarkable woman. Frankly, we could use a few more like her," Jeanne said and added, "About a dozen would do it.

"You've something more in mind for her."

"What do you think of putting her name before the world leaders to head the NWO?"

Captain Swain sat pondering the idea for a few moments. "That bunch. They've never lived up to expectations and their bias is legendary."

"Don't care much for them or the idea, huh?"

Swain shook her head. "Assuming she would accept the role, which I would not do, what makes you think she could muster the kind of muscle it would take to make it work?"

"How about a dozen of our ships on orbit and a couple of thousand Pagmok warriors for her on hand muscle?"

"Damn, Admiral. Pagmok warriors on Old Earth." she again shook her head. "I can't even begin to imagine how that would go over. I thought having them aboard the Flying Dragon to protect Captain, Admiral Chen was a reach. And according to what I'm hearing, several delegates have expressed similar sentiments. Might create more of a stir than Ms. Joiner wants to deal with."

"Holly Joiner has many of the same qualities as Admiral Chen. Maybe more. She's acted when no one else could or would."

"Admiral Presk-Milar, you like that woman don't you?" Captain Swain was half out of her chair and turning toward the hatch.

"Sit down, Captain."

"You should know better than to invade the personal prerogatives of your commanding officer." Presk-Milar paused, stood walked from behind his desk and stopped facing his flag captain. "Have I been so obvious?"

"My apologies, Admiral. My intention was not to involve myself. Although, on a personal basis, I'm happy you could have those feelings for someone like Ms. Joiner."

"Yeah, two different worlds, and a long life means something entirely different to each of us."

Jeanne's features softened. "Does she know how you feel?"

Presk-Milar's cleared his throat in that special, resonant way. "How would she unless some nosey flag captain talked too much."

"We women have our ways. It's a sixth sense only we possess. You men could never understand it."

"That's an arrogant attitude. What makes you think you're so superior?"

"Only in certain matters, Admiral. Like affairs of the heart."

"Captain, surely there's something useful you should be doing." He tried to make his appearance brooding—sinister but failed miserably.

Captain Swain headed for the door. "Golly, can't you hear the newsies now talking up how a love affair plays out at long distance." She saluted and hurriedly stepped through the hatch into the passageway.

PART TWO: The War

16: Parting of the Group

"**Doctor,** how is Mr. Daniels coming along?" Linney walked into Robert's hospital room.

"Why don't you ask him? See if his diagnosis is any different than mine."

"There's just no substitute for a doctor having such faith in his patient's judgment but doctor, maybe it would be more meaningful coming from you," joked Daniels standing next to the window.

"He's doing just fine," the doctor said. "Should be able to send him packing in a day or two. About a week of rehab, which he can do at home, and you can put him back to work. Now, I have patients who need me, so if you gentlemen will excuse me, I must be about my appointed rounds."

Both men laughed as the doctor left.

As the door close, Linney dropped the goodguy attitude. "Robert, we need to have a very serious talk."

"Wow, Linney, what has you so geared up? First I must apologize for my lack of diligence in allowing the prisoners to escape and more certainly to kill five of our finest."

"Accepted, Robert. But it could have happened to any of us. What is important is your blood," he responded solemnly.

"The doctor said I needed to talk with you about my transfusion. He wouldn't elaborate. Is there a problem?"

Linney led the way into the sitting room, Daniels assigned a suite of three. Taking one of the chairs said, "Sit down Mr. Daniels. I have a story to tell you."

Robert's questioning face stared at his leader. "What could my blood have to do with anything?"

Over the next few minutes, Lionel Penrose told him the blood transfusion he'd received carried the long life gene.

"You mean that's true? Those people actually left Earth for that reason?" Back on Old Earth, the telling and retelling of the reason for leaving Earth had become as much lore as truth. Not everyone accepted the idea as many of Earth's people rejected it as just a fascinating story.

"Yes, my friend. It's true. All New Hope's original settlers carry this gene. And with your transfusion, you have joined us. What we have to decide is how to handle this with the rest of Hope's people."

As Linney and Robert expected, there was a mixed reaction. For those people who were too old for the gene to have any effect, there was a sense of despair. Inevitability quickly handled that problem. By far, the majority of Hope's people welcomed the news.

Over the next year, assimilation of Hope's entire crew into the long life home style went apace. Many had special skills that greatly enhanced New Hope's capabilities. Almost daily, life became easier and certainly more routine as people adjusted and grew in their new existence.

* * * *

"Robert, I think it's time for a trip to New Earth and your introduction," said Linney sitting with feet firmly planted on his hand-hewn desk. In fact, Penrose had received a comm requesting him to come to New Earth. It was his idea to include Daniels.

"Well, I've certainly heard enough about the place that seeing it would be a treat. How and when?"

"How? I thought we'd take Hope and when, almost anytime. Do you have anything going here that requires your presence?"

Robert shook his head. "Nothing that others can't do. I could be ready in about an hour."

Linney laughed. "I imagine it will take about a month to prepare and provision Hope. The trip itself, probably six months. We don't want to rob New Hope of its best talent, but we'll need good people to navigate the *void*."

"That I understand," said Robert. Having brought Hope through in its search for New Earth, he knew about the hazards only too well. "I've seen little of space and nothing like that. No way around it is there?"

"Yes, if you want to add a year or two to the trip. Otherwise, its straight through at dead slow. And that's still six months."

* * * *

Almost one month later to the day after inviting Robert, Linney address the leadership of New Hope. "David, you're in charge. Keep the drone transceivers active day and night. We'll set drones as we go through the void and attempt to stay in constant communication. We intend to take our time."

* * * *

"Entering the *void* in twenty minutes," said Brooke. She'd become a superb helmsman and comm operator. Preparing the ship for the rigors offered by the region had occupied most of the crews time for the last T-week. Double shielding around ultrasensitive instrumentation along with reinforcing the ships external antenna and sensors was completed with little time to spare.

"Setting first drone." The less troublesome areas would consume a drone every one hundred thousand kilometers. As conditions worsened, the procedure would repeat itself down to ten thousand kilometers. The entire trip through the void would consume an enormous quantity of the devices. Crews remained busy around the clock assembling, testing and launching the transceivers.

* * * *

"Clear space in one T-day," said Brooke.

"We'll stop here and announce our presence to New Earth," said Linney as Hope exited the *void*.

Most of Brooke's idle hours at the helm, and there were many as at times Hope could only proceed a few meters per second, were spent collating data taken on Trekker's trip through the *void* along with Hope's return and would provide a comprehensive log for future voyagers.

Less than two T-days later, the words they wanted to hear broke the silence. "Mr. Penrose, by all means, proceed. You and your crew are most welcome. Your vector heading is included at the tail end of this transmission. New Earth awaits your arrival."

Two weeks later, Hope slid into its assigned slot awaiting the orbit master's inspectors. That completed, Brooke guided the ship into the parking orbit ten thousand kilometers above New Earth.

"Everyone dressed in their finest?" asked Penrose. "We want to look our best." This wasn't a meaningless gesture on his part. Linney wanted New Hope's presence to be something more than friends returning. Success had many faces.

"Look at the crowd, would you," said Daniels. "Your return is something special Mr. Penrose. I'm guessing there must be at least ten thousand people waiting." Gazing through a porthole as the launch neared the landing area, he asked, "Who are those," he paused, "I don't know who or what to call them, waiting in the background?"

Linney put the scene on the overhead screen and laughed. "Mr. Daniels, you are about to meet your first non-human aliens. Those are Hommew, Kalazecis, Pagmok, and the Rococo and the *First*."

Lionel Penrose stepped from the launch to the strings of New Hope's state song followed by New Earth's national anthem.

"Welcome home ladies and gentlemen of New Hope," said President Jabari talking over the boisterous cheering crowd.

Linney stuck out his hand in greeting but instead received a very smothering unpresidential hug from the huge man. The crowd roared its approval.

After a brief welcoming speech from the President, Lionel took the dais and in fewer words, thanked them all. With the ceremony concluded, and the launch crew milling with their hosts, Linney and Robert joined the President in his aircar for the ride to Government House.

Minutes later, sitting in the President's office, Robert Daniels related Hopes adventure and acceptance into the New Hope society.

"That's quite a story, Mr. Daniels, said Jabari. "You are to be commended for your foresight and daring leadership."

Daniels thanked the President for his kind words but mostly directed his appreciation to Lionel Penrose for allowing them to become a part of New Hope.

President Jabari's manner change as he leaned back in his chair and said, "Linney, you come at a most prodigious moment for New Earth." For the next hour, he told of the changes occurring. Of how Old Earth had adapted to the rules Admiral Presk-Milar imposed on them and most importantly, that shortly a diaspora from Old Earth would occur and how that would affect New Earth.

"We have made our decision," he said. "It may seem unneighborly but the inhabitants of New Earth have decided to move on. We have discovered an M-class planet that meets our requirements and needs. In the near future, we will move and make it our home. This may seem extreme to you, but we have decided not to share our long life gene. Since keeping our current location secret is impossible, relocation best serves our objectives." Off-handedly, he interjected, "Before Presk-Milar left Old Earth, he erased all references to our location from their database." You have become a viable civilization in your own right. You will not know of our new location. You must decide on your own whether to join what will become a galactic community or not. Our recommendation is that you not. We believe that our forebearers are not ready for the long life information."

Linney stared at Jabari. "I don't know what to say Mr. President other than your decision seems extreme in the utmost."

"You may be right. But New Hope's location is well off what most likely will become the beaten path these new explorers will take." The President made no mention of the part New Earth played in Hope's adventure.

"We believe, with proper attention, it may be years before someone discovers your planet's location. The *void* provides a natural barrier that should keep your secret. Mr. Penrose, we want you to honor our decision and make no effort to find our new home. We will make contact with your world when there is reason to do so."

The strained conversation continued for over an hour with Penrose reminding the president it was his idea to establish New Hope. That brought no meaningful response.

Leaving Government House, Linney said to Robert, "I'm dismayed. They gave no reason for this move. I recognize they've practiced isolation since landing on New Earth but," he paused, "I think we were due, at the least, some reason. Looks like we won't make this trip again, ever."

"It's very generous of them to give us every scientific discovery and engineering advancement they've made," Robert said hoping to lighten the moment. "From what little you've told me, these guys are way ahead of the rest of us."

"No doubt about that. Many of these people are descendants of some of Old Earth's best and brightest."

"What happens to New Earth?" said Robert. "They just going to walk away or destroy everything they've built?"

"Going to turn it back to the Kalazecis, Pagmok, and Rococo and the *First*. It will be called Usgac again."

One month later, Hope, along with a transport loaded with many marvels of science, departed New Earth having given their word never to return. Forty-five New Earthers chose to come along to make New Hope their home.

17: Alone

A somber group of six hundred people faced Lionel Penrose and listened to what he'd learned.

"For their own reasons, the people of New Earth decided to go it alone much as they have for almost three hundred years." These people, their ancestors, were the first humans to venture into deep space. They made a home for themselves. When their existence was threatened, they took on the most powerful nation on Old Earth and soundly defeated them and then imposed rules to make Terra function as a reliable citizen of the galactic community. This was no small feat and mostly attributable to superior intellect with the will to win.

"My personal feelings are mixed as some of you have made known yours. I was looking forward to being neighbors with these people. People who I could gladly call friend. Many of them are blood relatives. But, now we must go it alone. Our fate is entirely in our hands. New Hope's location does give us some comfort. By that I mean, we are in an isolated part of space created by the *void* and most likely, it will be years before anyone learns of our presence. We have the means to cloak our planet making it invisible to current science. Terra has declared it will send ships into space to populate newfound worlds. A diaspora is in the making. Part of that is to ensure the continued existence of the human race. In part it is to fulfill what some believe it is their destiny." Linney stopped, looked out over the crowd. "I know you must have many questions. I'll do my best to answer them. Just understand, there is no going back. As much as you can, be positive in your questioning as we must look to the future. And that we must create for ourselves."

Linney fielded questions for over five hours. The many concerns showed the people were worried while clearly trying to be positive. As long as New Earth was there, hope and wishes for something approaching a normal existence remained high. Now, that was gone and they were alone.

Part Two Prologue: Second Beginning

Raybold Presk Penrose accepted the mantel as second leader of New Hope. Lionel Presk-Milar Penrose had ably led their world for all of its three hundred year existence.

The diaspora, begun by Old Earth, now commonly known as Terra, populated over thirty new worlds. Unfortunately, the human predilection to wage war with its neighbors remained intact with certain worlds choosing to live outside the bounds of legitimacy. Pirating had become commonplace, with some nation states providing safe harbor for all, including some of worst of humanity. New Hope was, of course due to its isolation, not one of them. But they were not free from the influence created by these rogues who killed and stole almost at their pleasure. Hubris demonstrated by these villains seemingly placed them above common law.

With increased frequency, ships traversing between the known worlds edged toward New Hope. It was only a matter of time before their one of these spacers discovered their location. Still, only the second planet to carry the long life gene, they must decide whether to declare themselves and join the galactic community or continue in their self-imposed isolation. True to their scientific heritage, New Hope had improved on the technology left them by New Earth, allowing their people safe harbor even when venturing out to observe the going's on in their part of the increasingly crowded galaxy. Protection provided by the *void* certainly added to their isolation, but the citizens watched human science advance. It was only a matter of time before outside science learned to deal with the *void* disturbances reducing the prospects of maintaining their secret existence.

18: Discovery

Raybold Penrose walked up the steps of Government House; a trip he'd made many times but his first as President.

"How sails the ship of state, Mr. President?" Dedus Rhineholt asked. Rhineholt had served as leader of parliament for the last twenty T-years, something of a record.

"We are blessed with a sure and steady wind, Mr. Speaker. What brings you to my doorstep?"

"To invite you to our humble chamber. Some of the members think it a face-to-face meeting is in order. I believe they want to hear your views on a number of subjects. Your being new in the presidency alone raised certain questions."

"Flexing their muscle, is that it?"

"We are minions compared to your lofty office."

"Mr. Speaker, without question, it is easy to see why you have served so long. You have no peer when it comes to addressing an issue. I will be pleased to accept your invitation."

"On both counts, Mr. President, I thank you."

Dedus Rhineholt had served in the shadow of Lionel Penrose, their recently deceased leader, and placed him in the hierarchy of New Hope's governing elite. Something he seemed to cherish. Whether that made him a political foe for Penrose remained to be seen.

One week later standing in the *well*, Penrose submitted to questions regarding his position on a myriad of subjects from his view of New Hope's place in the galaxy, indeed if it should join the community of worlds that had formed. Knowing he would follow the ailing president, his uncle, Raybold had intentionally kept distance from all offices of government. That, in itself, raised question. Lionel Penrose was a man of the people. In fact, for all but a very few who came on the initial voyage of Trekker, he was the only leader they had known. Reluctantly, Raybold knew he would have to take on some of that mantel even with his dislike for publicity. Raybold Penrose was by his own admission, a loner.

Apparently satisfying his inquisitors, the President graciously accepted their applause after a number of hours of grueling questions.

Returning to Government House, he took his seat behind the hand-hewn desk. The only desk the office had ever housed. He reached for the comm button and said, "Yes, Dee."

"The communications office wants to know if you can come to their place to accept a restricted message?"

Dee Shaparov had worked for Raybold in every job he'd held on New Hope. Most people relied on her to see that any commitment the man made to them, didn't get lost in the shuffle and she would do the same as the President's secretary. Married to a botanist and childless, on weekends she'd participated in classifying the planets flora. That endeared her to Raybold's wife who had a liking for gardening.

"A what?"

"Restricted message, sir. They say they cannot forward it. Some kind of electronic lock on it. Don't ask me what or why. You know I don't understand that stuff."

He punched the icon.

"Missy Mosier here Mr. President. How can I help you?" The tease was obvious in her voice. Yet, in her own way, she was a delight. Few dared take her on in a debate; most often, words like 'ruthless,' and 'coldblooded' described her. Granddaughter of Brooke Fossey, she came by her oratory skills quite honestly.

He forwent the usual greeting. Dee had stepped into his office and could hear anything that passed between the two. Something he'd prefer not happen but with the comm still open he had to say something. "I understand there's a message for me. Any idea who it's from?"

"No, Mr. President, or should I say Captain or maybe Raybold?"

"Thank you, Missy." He released the button.

"No wiggle room, huh," he said to Dee.

"Your popularity knows no bounds, Mr. President and your calendar is clear for the next two hours. Seems you have no excuse to hide behind. Sounds like you have an admirer." There was no doubt Missy's question of addressing him would occasionally get mentioned.

"Me hide? How dare you suggest such a thing? Have you no respect for this office?"

"Only history, Mr. President. Only history. I know how things work. Well, some things."

"Where is the communications office?"

A few minutes later, following Dee's directions, Raybold entered the comm office.

Located two floors down, a siege mentality seemed to exist in the windowless chambers. Virtually everything these people did or touched was in some way secret. And of course, that added to the mystique surrounding their jobs.

"Mr. President, we have a message that is not decodable," a clerk said.

"Then how in the hell am I supposed to read it?"

"Oh, it's in English, sir or so the interrogatory says. It's just that some cipher is required to open it.

"Somewhere there should exist a list of keys that you alone are privy to."

"If so, I've not seen it." He commed Dee.

"Sir, your uncle kept an information data chip. I assumed you had it," she politely answered.

"Well, I don't." Unchecked irritation invaded his voice. Raybold had to discover where Lionel kept the damned thing. He returned to his office and over the next few hours, occasionally interrupted by official business and visitors, investigated every nook and cranny, scouring every centimeter of the office walls that might hide the secreted chip.

Knowing his uncle's habits, Raybold decided the chip must be in plain sight. Given to the understanding people usually made the worst of most situations, Lionel would have put it where most would never think to look. He changed his tactics and began investigating everything in the room. Gazing around, he said, "Well, shit. After all this time, there it is. And keeping with his understanding of people, in plain sight."

Raybold stood from behind his desk, walked to a gallery of pictures hanging on the wall, and from one depicting an artist's rendition of a typical scientists mind, plucked a small virtually unnoticeable chip. With it in hand, he returned to the code room.

With the message, he stepped into an electronically isolated room. After a few instructions, the operator excused himself and left, locking the door leaving Raybold alone.

Precisely following directions, he activated the message.

"President Penrose, I am Bogdan Presk-Milar, the third, President of New Earth. Congratulations on your elevation to President of New Hope. I had the pleasure of knowing your uncle. Remarkable man. He kept his word and made no effort to contact us after he departed our original home. I'm sure you know the story. It is time for our two worlds to meet. We have much to discuss."

Raybold paused the message and sat silent—stunned better described his feelings.

Restarting the message he memorized the meeting coordinates and date but could only wonder what prompted New Earth's contact. Surprised that they had selected a location in the void, the message said New Earth would rendezvous with them a day or two after Trekker arrived at the designated spot.

Raybold leaned back in the chair and let his pent up breath slowly escape. Using the computer, carefully, he transferred the message to the data chip. That night, he would listen to every entry. Most likely, it was everything his uncle thought significant—information he needed to govern.

He destroyed the paper message, erased any track left in the computer, stood and rapped on the door.

A few minutes later in his office, he pondered what the future held. How to handle this? Who would he leave in charge? Many questions clouded his mind. He would think this through as thoroughly as possible.

"Dee, would you please advise security I'm taking a drive."

Never had a threat been made on the president's life, but parliament had decided caution had its merits and established a watchdog group strictly to ensure the president's safety.

"And would you please ask Robert Daniels to join me. I'll pick him up shortly at his residence."

Daniels was the one man his uncle trusted implicitly. Personally, Raybold had never let anyone get that close to him but things had changed. He needed someone who could and would listen and give his best advice.

Raybold guided the aircar to a stop, security close behind in their own car.

Robert Daniels, cane in hand slowly settled into the vehicle. "It's so good to see you Raybold. What's it been, over two years?"

"Something like that Mr. Daniels. Too long I assure you."

"What's up?" Something must be bothering you. You're much like your uncle in that regard. He could not hide it when something got his dander up."

"I think that's the first time anyone has said my uncle and I had anything in common."

"Ha, you're more alike than you're willing to admit. I should know. I've known both of you for many years. So, out with it. What can I do for you? Don't ask anything physical; words are my only unencumbered asset these day. And I have few of them." Daniels health was failing. The aging gene had run its course and time was not on his side.

"Mr. Daniels, I received a comm from New Earth. They want a meeting with me."

"Really? That is a surprise. It was they who wanted no contact between our worlds. Wonder what's changed."

"Since I have to guess, I say it's about how we plan to conduct our business. They will not like our concept of off-planet marketing."

To generate income, Raybold planned to build an orbital factory and make New Hope's main effort to push scientific development in areas of interest to other worlds. Using agents from Odysseus, he'd decided to name it, they could establish strong relations with other planets using surrogates—all in truth, New Hope. Their customers would have no reason to believe they weren't dealing directly with the source. He didn't mention that Presk-Milar knew of his becoming President. How they learned that was troublesome to say the least. Who—nagged at Raybold.

"I'm betting New Earth learned of it and has something they want to say," said Raybold. "Probably won't be anything that we want to hear."

"What can I do? They have no reason to listen to me. I'm the outsider."

"True, but I'd like for you make the trip with me. It'll take almost a year."

"I'm flattered, Mr. President. But I doubt I'll live that long."

"Mr. Daniels, our scientists have come up with a booster that extends the long life gene. We don't know for how long, as the discovery is very new. If you're willing, we're offering it to you. It is our intention to make it available to our entire population as they reach the proper age. Our scientists do want it tested."

"I'm the guinea pig. If it works on me everyone gets it."

Raybold cocked his head and shrugged.

"Give me a few days to think about it. I've had a most productive life but one should know when it's time to go.

"Raybold, I'm wondering if somehow New Earth may have learned of this latest advancement. Maybe that's why the want a face to face meeting."

"Let's hope not, my friend. If you're right, that gives us a problem I would rather not have."

Robert's face lit up as recognition of where his comment led. "Ah, yes."

Penrose smiled. "We've freely, willingly, exchanged information, science with New Earth. Why would anyone gain by taking such a risk—even to our New Earth brothers. Although, whoever, assuming you're right, it would have had to take place off planet. That greatly reduces the number of possible suspects. But we're getting way ahead of ourselves. Our speculation is a waste of time."

He saw the quizzical look on Robert's face and added, "If anyone transmitted from New Hope, the clocking shield would light up sensors on the planet like a Terra Christmas tree. We'd know it immediately."

The two parted with Raybold asking Robert to sleep on his suggestion to take the added long life injection. "If you decide to make the trip to meet New Earth with me, you'll need it. As I said, we'll be gone about a year."

19: Old Friends Meet Again

Cloaked, Trekker entered the *void* and made its way to the coordinates specified by New Earth.

"Cut our emissions to zero," said Raybold. He'd not made known the reason for stopping and going silent, but his experienced spacers had it figured.

"If someone's looking for us, Captain, we're not making it easy for them. They'll have to be damned good to find us in this mess," said Missy Mosier. Her proficiency as astrogator had made her the obvious choice to handle the helm despite her proclivity for him. Trekker's voyage had taken two months to reach the area and another making their way to the rendezvous coordinates. "How long do we wait, Captain," she asked.

"Until they find us," Penrose gave her a knowing smile. "Set the watch. Four on four off. Starboard has the first turn. Man each plot board. Look for any anomaly."

Boredom plagued the entire crew as they rotated duty chores for the next thirty T-hours. Robert Daniels, standing at the hatch entry, looked around the bridge and caught Raybold's eye. Strolling over he asked, "Any idea how or where or what caused the *void?*"

Penrose knew his friend well enough to understand it wasn't really a question nor was it meant as rhetorical.

"I have a feeling you're about to tell me."

"So I am." He cleared his throat. The long life injection Robert received had improved his condition. No longer slowed by aging, now robust in his movement and mental alertness, he took the mate's chair next to the Captain. "You know I've made a study of this phenomenon off and on over the last one hundred years. Learned a lot." Those who knew the man also knew a lengthy lecture was coming and they were right. Robert Daniels had earned a reputation for extended oration and yet still enjoyed the respect of the people. His having stepped down from active leadership did not lessen those interested in the government from seeking his opinion.

Raybold leaned back in his chair, scrunched around until he found the most comfortable position. "Go ahead. I'm ready. After all I have nothing else to do."

"You make fun of my diligent study. I put in many hours poring over every scrap of information to reach a well thought out conclusion."

"No offense Mr. Daniels. Please go ahead. I too have studied the *void*, if not as diligently as you. I will be very interested in your conclusions."

Appropriately unapologetic, for the next two hours, Robert laid out his findings. Finally determining the *void* was the remnant of a unsuccessful planetary system formation, the planetoid evidence of that effort, a much larger maverick object, most likely another planetoid or maybe a planet, intervened disrupting the formation and resulting in the *void* assuming its current shape. The disrupting object obviously had gone on its way into space and was no longer a factor. Robert judged the *void*'s age at approximately three to four hundred million years old.

"It would seem we are very much in agreement," said Raybold. "Very astute study, sir. Why don't you enter your findings into our computer database. Others may wish to review your study."

Daniels agreed his effort should stand up to peer review although neither man would have admitted anyone other than Raybold or Daniels had the expertise to perform a meaningful critique.

"Sir, there's a disturbance fifteen thousand klicks off our starboard bow," said Missy. Despite not knowing if this was New Earth, her voice remained moderated. "Coming in slow. If I'm reading this correctly, looks like it's unpowered."

Penrose punched an icon on his chair arm displaying the disturbance, more than an anomaly, on the overhead screen. He didn't like the idea that a ship could get that close before detection. Especially with Trekker laying fully cloaked in stealth mode and making no electronic noise itself.

"If they're interested in us, they'd better start showing some signs," mused Raybold.

"Only making one kilometer per hour, Captain," said comm and added, "They'll pass a few thousand meters off our bow."

Raybold pressed the comm icon, "Boat bay, how long will it take to launch the razor?"

"Less than ten minutes, Captain," came the immediate response.

"Launch when ready. I suspect that ship's dead. See if you can board and stop her."

Penrose ordered the three men who survived the boarding of Hope to lead the attempt.

Less than an hour later, using a hand laser, razor signaled they had boarded the ship and saw no signs of life.

Then by whisper tight beam, the boarders gave their grim message. "Looks like pirates hit them, Captain. Hell of a mess. All dead, seventeen people. Bastards, bastards," said a voice full of revulsion.

Using their thrusters, razor stopped the ship, a corvette of unknown registry.

Following a burial service and cleanup, Penrose boarded the ship, and discovered it was HMS Backlash out of Braeden.

With the corvette locked to Trekker, they continued the vigil, waiting for the New Earth ship.

Feasting on the information retrieved from Backlash's computers gave them a new image of their part of the galaxy. Terra's diaspora had populated over one hundred planets with half a million people. New Hope had distant neighbors—their own kind. Questions bombarded Raybold Penrose wanting to know if contact was possible. Quite often, yearnings to become part of the galactic family had made it to him. Having the long life gene again lurked in the background. But he had other concerns. Raybold felt an obligation to rid the galaxy of this scourge that raided ships and occasionally planets and took the lives of innocent people.

"Captain, picking up a tight beam whisper comm. Must be the New Earth ship," said the operator. "Best I can estimate, dead ahead one thousand kilometers."

"Put it on speaker. Ship wide," he ordered. "Those folks have certainly improved on their stealth capability."

A quiet voice announced, "Squawk on assigned frequency."

Penrose gave the comm operator the necessary information who punched the transponder icon and a single signal left Trekker.

Within seconds, the speakers belched out their tight whisper transmission, "Greetings Trekker. This is NES George Washington II. Please standby to receive our delegation."

Emotions ran high on Trekker as they readied the hanger bay for the launch. With the recent funerals fresh in his mind, and never one to be careless, Raybold armed ten people with flechette rifles and stationed them at the three hatches that gave access to the landing bay.

The hanger bay doors closed and the area pressurized as one somber uniformed man stepped from the launch. Itiki Masamoto, Lieutenant Commander, NES Navy announced himself and received permission to board. He looked around the empty hanger bay and nodded seeing the armed reception committee at the three hatches.

"Diligence, very good," he said. "Nothing wrong with being alert and ready. Space can be a very dangerous place." He motioned and three people exited the launch and joined him. "On behalf of Marsha Mason, Captain of NES Washington II thank you for agreeing to this meeting."

Still no Trekker crewmember moved from their assigned locations.

"Captain Penrose, as you know NES Washington is a battle cruiser. We out mass you by a factor of fifty and our weapons by even more. Had we meant any harm, you would be space dust by now."

Markam took the comment as humor even though the officer seemed somewhat stoic. Trekker massed about forty thousand metric tons.

Raybold, standing in the loadmaster's quarters, nevertheless smiled and spoke into his comm, "Stand down." He opened his hatch and stepped into the hanger bay. "Commander, I am Raybold Penrose. Welcome aboard Trekker." In long assured strides, he walked to the launch and extended his hand. "We've looked forward to this meeting for over a year."

New Earth's delegation numbered forty people, mostly naval but included some civilians. After a few minutes of exchanged greetings, they all moved to the conference room.

Small talk dominated the conversations. Commander Masamoto and Raybold joined in obviously enjoying their crew's elation. The conversation hadn't changed Raybold's sense that this was more than a friendly call. He let it run its course, stood and tapped on the table bringing immediate silence. They had yet to discuss anything of substance.

"Captain Penrose, Captain Mason extends an invitation for your crew to visit the Washington. Interested?" asked Masamoto.

"Most certainly." Raybold issued the instructions that permitted all crewmembers the opportunity. Something approaching a riot followed as each made their case to make the first visit list.

He joined Commander Masamoto on the first launch back to the Washington and totally unexpectedly faced full sideboard honors.

"Permission to board," Raybold said. He saluted the flag and OD.

"Permission granted, sir." Raybold listened as the Bosun's voice blared from the speakers, "New Hope Fleet arriving, New Hope President arriving." The piercing whistle echoed off the bulkheads.

Along with twenty crewmembers, they stood to attention as the strains of both worlds anthems in turn died away. Raybold's mannerism reflected how he felt; after all, this was the first time he'd ever been through such a ceremony. But then this was the second time he'd ever set foot on a foreign vessel as a distinguished guest, Hope being the first.

A tall slender woman with startling penetrating black eyes, in underway khakis, stepped forward. "Captain Penrose, I am Captain Serona Mason. Welcome aboard the Washington. You've no idea how much your world has been in our thoughts and discussions."

In the fifteen minutes it took for the group to the reach the conference room, both captains learned most of each other's pertinent history or so Penrose thought. He accepted a chair at the head of the long conference table between Mason and Masamoto. Robert Daniels was seated a few chairs down from him on the left side. Trekker's crewmembers set about looking for relatives and in general getting acquainted.

Captain Mason opened the meeting with a greeting from President Bogdan Presk-Milar II.

"Please convey my best to your President. What a magnificent ship, Captain. If you have an extra, I think it would make an excellent addition to our fleet," Raybold said.

"So it would, sir. But we've not added a new ship to our fleet in over fifty T-years and adding one ship to your fleet is not why we are here."

Puzzled by her response, rather coy he thought, Penrose decided there had to be more.

"Commander," she said to Masamoto, "since you to have a number of matters already under discussion, please continue."

Penrose turned his head toward Commander Masamoto and said, "As pleased as we are to finally meet with you and as much catching up we want to do, I need to know what prompted this meeting? We were told never to make contact with you and yet you've done just that."

Masamoto took his time spelling out the concerns of New Earth, which mostly dealt with how space was changing as Terra continued to send people to newly discovered planets. New Earth was as far off the travel routes as New Hope, but they knew it was a matter of time before the explorers would show up and their isolated locations discovered. "By the way, I see you captured Backlash. You probably plan on keeping her," Masamoto said referring to the ship attached to Trekker. "May not be a good idea. If the Braeden Navy finds out, you can expect a visit. They're a very possessive bunch."

"I'm claiming salvage rights and taking it back to New Hope."

Quizzically, Raybold looked at the Commander and said, "How do you know about the ship?"

"We neutralized the pirate ship's electronics that hit them. That's a fancy word for saying we screw the hell out her—everything that needs electricity or electronics to work. Boarded the ship, disarmed the crew, spiked the ships external weapons, set their controls for Braeden space, and sent her on the way. She's broadcasting giving all the details. We tried to make it easy for Braeden to find and take the pirates. Of course, we told them that Backlash made the *void* and we lost her."

"Won't the pirates tell them about you?" asked Raybold.

"They never saw the Washington. What do you think of our stealth capability?" Raybold nodded and Masamoto continued, "No one has ever seen our uniforms before and we made sure there was nothing to identify us. That will raise questions, but so be it. We're confident Braeden will have no idea who their benefactor might be."

Penrose spoke about their concerns over the increased pirating. Masamoto assured him they would give New Hope their latest stealth advances and in fact, a number of new technological improvements.

Slightly pushing his chair back from the table, Penrose said, "Sir, with all that you've said I still do not believe you've told me the nature of this visit."

Masamoto smiled. "You're quite correct, Captain." He paused long enough that Penrose glowered at him.

"It is my hope, New Earth's hope that what I have to say will not destroy the trust we want to build between our two worlds." Somberly, he looked at Robert Daniels, bringing Raybold upright in his chair.

Raybold Penrose's head jerked around toward Captain Mason his voice cold, demanded, "Captain, I must insist this meeting be adjourned."

Shocked expressions stood out from most attendees, unsure and unknowing what had provoked such a response from Penrose.

"Captain? May I ask why?" Totally caught off guard with Raybold's demand, she remained seated as he moved his chair back from the table. Only Masamoto seemed to have anticipated the reaction not flinching or otherwise displaying any sense of alarm. Questioning looks were cast at Penrose as the room cleared not waiting for Captain Mason's agreement.

20: The Test of Wills

Raybold stood back from the table putting distance between the three. "You son of a bitch," he snarled at Masamoto. "Who is it? Who's been feeding you information?"

"Captain, your manner and language are out of order," sternly said Captain Mason.

"If you'll give me a chance to explain I'm sure this can be cleared up to everyone's satisfaction," Masamoto quietly responded seemingly embarrassed matters had gotten out of hand.

"Don't count on it, Commander. We can raise a little hell of our own." Penrose touched his comm, "General quarters," he said.

Captain Mason held up her hand, "What's going on here? Captain Penrose, please." This wasn't a plaintive plea but from someone who knew she had the wherewithal to get her way and how to use it.

"And what does that gain you? You risk losing your ship and crew as well as New Hope their leader—is it worth that?"

Masamoto had hardly moved, his arms still on the table his voice remained subdued. "Please, Captain, there's much more to tell that concerns your interests."

Raybold understood how military and political muscle worked. You could dislike a person but more was at stake—relations between two worlds that had every reason to get along.

"Captain Penrose, whatever caused this dustup I'm certain it will be evident we are not adversaries. If you'll give me a moment I think I can dispel what has earned your ire."

Raybold studied him for a long moment and then reclaimed his chair.

"Commander," said Captain Mason, "if you know what is at the root of this problem tell us now."

"Yes, Commander, start talking and this time leave nothing out," Penrose added.

Captain Mason, now standing, reminded Penrose she was still in command of the Washington and would give the orders.

Captain Mason fully understood what was going on and Masamoto nodded acknowledging his Captain's order addressed Penrose.

"Sir, you have no traitor in your midst. Hope and Captain Daniels did not arrive at New Hope by chance. Once we were aware of their intention to make New Earth, our engineers and scientists electronically invaded Hope's computers and navigation equipment. We directed them away from New Earth and made sure they found New Hope. Once they arrived at your world, we took advantage of the opportunity, with access to New Hope's computers, and made the most of it. That includes accessing Trekker's data base as well." New Earth set up an elaborate scheme to keep track of your efforts and extract information. Before exiting the planet's cloaking shield we transferred data to Hope or Trekker's computers and when well away from the planet, transmitted to our drones including those in the *void*.

"And I'm supposed to believe we have no way of discovering this? You don't think much of our abilities."

"You failed to see our approach today." He cocked his head knowingly. "We anticipated you'd make discoveries. I can tell you we did not develop the stealth capability. That came from one of Orion's original scientists, Martin Grabel—a genius mathematician who defected from New Earth to the Kalazecis. Later became their king. But I'm sure you've studied your history. So, you see, it wasn't long after you developed the add-on long life serum that we knew about it."

Raybold wasn't sure about his own feelings—embarrassment that this man upstaged every argument he presented—anger that New Hope couldn't do anything on its own. "Captain, if you know so damned much about what we're doing, why didn't you just take the long life data. I'm assuming you do know the details of our research."

"Unfortunately, that scientific information wasn't included in Hope or Trekker's computers," she said. "We trust you will share the information."

Raybold studied the woman at length. "That's certainly a distinct possibility if you're leveling with me. That is a subject much discussed but the way you cut us off and made no effort to maintain any kind of contact suggested that was unlikely. Of course, we had no idea that Hope's arrival changed all that."

"Right or wrong, New Earth's leaders believed you had to make it on your own. Wet-nursing you would only increase your reliance although we did equip you with everything we had at the time. Adding the four hundred from Hope to your population greatly increased the possibilities you could and would survive. I personally believe our leaders were right and you more than met our expectations. We greatly admire what you've accomplished."

Raybold studied the Captain and Commander looking for anything that suggested duplicity and finally decided he believed the commander.

"There is another matter of concern," she continued. "There is a world named Cullen that we fear may know, or at the least suspect, our new location. They declared themselves an open port and give sanctuary to some of the most despicable human trash known to mankind. Cullen may have discovered some of our drones stationed above our world. Unfortunately, perhaps during a transmission, they exposed our presence. That allowed them to triangulate the area of space toward which the signals were sent. More and more, we have detected their ships in our vicinity. One day, they would discover us. New Earth did not see them as a military threat. We could destroy their world with little effort. It would mean more of our people die and for what? It doesn't bring back our dead or our world."

"And you think they will pay you a visit," said Penrose.

"These cut-throats are wanted by nearly every legitimate government. They are the worst kind of people. Regularly, they pay mercenaries to gather intel, which they consolidate and then sell to the interplanetary scum. Few ships or planets are safe from them and you should assume that includes New Hope. As I said, New Earth could have handled Cullen along with their allies. You however, are not strong enough to oppose them. In time, the Kingdom of Braeden should be able to stand up to these outlaws but that will be some distance off.

"We've considered taking out the pirates and that would put a dent in Cullen's capabilities. We got the one who jumped the Braeden ship. They won't bother anyone again."

Raybold smiled as Mason seemed to enjoy their dispatching the killers. "Do we get the location of New Earth? It seems only fair. That would go a long way with our people to show that we're equals." New Hope had lived in isolation for so long, that the prospects of having someone, particularly if they were a kindred spirit, satisfied many of the longings of their people.

"I'm afraid what I have to say will result in just the opposite, Mr. Penrose," said Captain Mason. "We are in the process of relocating again. I know, it seems like we're running and perhaps we are, but understand, our sole purpose is to survive. When President Jabari named your world, it had purpose. What he wanted established must not die. "How many worlds know of New Hope's existence?" Mason asked.

Penrose shrugged. "Just one, yours," he responded.

"Even though we left, at least a dozen worlds suspected New Earth's location as a result of the war with Terra. Yes, that has heightened the interest of some. And that should tell you why we must seek a more remote location."

"Again you mean. This is your second move. Friends are hard to come by," Raybold said. "Particularly when you share a secret that keeps you from making more."

Captain Mason turned to face Penrose and looked at him for some time. "There is more, sir. Mr. Penrose, what you do not know," Captain Mason stopped and seemed to sort out her words.

"Before we made our first move, "Danstan Grabel, Martin's son and his family, were assassinated by the Kalazecis. In fact, all the humans on Myslac suffered the same fate including our ambassador. It doesn't speak well of Danstan's rule, first that the Kalazecis were dissatisfied enough to rebel and the totality of their revenge. Of course, we had no clue it was coming, so we share some of the blame. Without Danstan, the Pagmok were leaderless and easily managed as the Kalazecis had control of their food source. The Kalazecis attacked New Earth while I had my fleet on maneuvers near the *void*, and First Fleet was on diplomatic jaunt to the Hommew world. New Earth had only Home Fleet for protection and they were no match for the enemy. The Kalazecis destroyed virtually everything except the Rococo. So, you see, we didn't leave as such. We could have returned to New Earth but little worthwhile remained. With the combined fleets, we could have retaliated and put an end to the Kalazecis once and for all. But instead, we joined up with First Fleet and made the decision to move on." He paused and looked at his captain.

Captain Mason said, "With Cullen suspecting our new location and that they will sell it to others, we want to join you on New Hope if you'll have us. Our choices are limited and you, along with New Hope's location, seem a logical solution. We will submit to your authority; what we have will belong to New Hope. You have proven most resilient in building a home for your people."

Raybold Penrose sat staring at the Captain. "I hardly know what to say. But rest assured, you are most welcome. Why didn't you say so at the beginning of the meeting?"

"We number about twelve thousand, Mr. Penrose," said Mason. Can you absorb that many people? It means a great deal of dislocation for your citizenry. And frankly, some of our people voiced concerns that you might see us as forcing ourselves upon you."

Penrose understood the enormity of these people coming to New Hope and her delimma. He also knew they could and would be a tremendous asset, technically. Their presence would greatly enhance the idea he was forming for New Hope's future.

"This matter has neglected something personal," Masamoto said. "Mr. Penrose, you and Captain Mason are cousins, a number of times removed of course." Apparently intending to ease the tension, Masamoto managed a smile.

Raybold blanched slightly and cast a glance at his grinning counterpart. Occasionally, he'd thought about relatives on New Earth. With a new commonality established, Masamoto added detail to his earlier words and answered all of Penrose's questions.

Once he had time to think it through, Raybold was ecstatic with New Earth's people and fleet coming to New Hope. The meeting adjourned. Raybold and Captain Mason made their way to her cabin. She spent the better part of an hour giving him the history of the family—the good and the bad. For the next few days, crewmembers generally enjoyed what remaining time they had with discovered relatives and newly made friends but mainly letting the scientists and engineers work together as the two worlds exchanged discoveries and explained their intricacies.

Having upgraded Trekker's cloaking devices to match NES Washington, Trekker's crew, now more than friends, said their goodbyes. Knowing their progenitors would soon join them, buoyed everyone's spirits as they headed out of the *void* and home.

The news of New Earths destruction brought mixed comments from New Hope's people but having the survivors join them was great news. Most thought they should concentrate on building the planet's defenses in anticipation of an attack that Raybold knew would come in time.

* * * *

Six months later with some elements of New Earth having arrived on New Hope, sitting in Government House, he turned to his guest, "I know how to grow our business and I think keep our secret."

Baskom Wazalewski had served as vice-president for the last three years. Tough minded, he'd come to Raybold's attention after the man had put together the draft on New Hope's economic plan. It was of the first order and once implemented, the nation's economic status had change dramatically for the better.

"And how is that?" questioned Baskom.

New Hope had made the most of the information gained from the Braeden ship. Of particular interest were those worlds that could benefit from the electronic talents New Hope had to offer. The remaining ships from New Earth should arrive in another month. The addition of scientists and engineers would make his task easier.

"Soffett has a new ruler. And the word is, he wants to make the place into *the* entertainment spot of the galaxy. That means all new construction, gaming equipment, everything that makes a place like that work. And it all takes electronics. And no one is capable of producing the sophisticated equipment that we can. I need to sell them on the idea. While I'm gone, Baskom, come up with an orbital factory. We'll put it around that small star we plotted a couple of years ago. Call it Odysseus. We'll claim it's our home world"

"While I'm in that area, a call on Saragosa Prime and Braeden should pay off. Prime has announced its intention to purchase one hundred freighters to haul fish protein. And that means electronics as well. We should be able to corral that work as well. Keep our people busy for ten years with the initial work and the follow up maintenance should be as good."

With that decided, Penrose prepared the nation for his absence, a year in space, turned the government over to Baskom Wazalewski and headed into space.

21: One for the Money

If nothing else, Jasper Weingarten knew how to make a fortune. He had done so a number of times... and lost almost as many. A businessman of the highest order, enemies often accused him of being a con man. He thought of himself as a first rate opportunist.

Leaving Terra penniless after losing his last fortune, he earned his way to Soffett as a lowly deckhand on a space freighter. From there, having recently gained control of Soffett, quite honorably at the gaming tables—an honest game of Texas Holdem'. He set out to change Soffett from an open port to any and all spacers to a recreation world second to none.

Short and stocky, the man seemed almost as broad as tall without a gram of fat. His thin slits for eyes, without a hair on his head, and that included eyebrows, gave him the look of someone with unnatural strength and power.

Notorious for its illicit gaming and recreation offerings, Soffett catered to the worst brigands in the universe—a cesspool of self-indulgent interests. Disgraceful mess that it was, there were differences between Soffett and Cullen. Soffett allowed no weapons dirtside. Anyone caught trying to smuggle arms onto Soffett was sent packing with the admonition that spacing would be their sentence if caught again. The planet's reputation for running clean games and keeping their word discouraged most would be gunrunners. Unlike Cullen, Soffett made sure no pirate benefited from information that could place a ship or planet in jeopardy.

Sitting in his office Weingarten hit the comm button on his elaborate desk, "Yes, Jessica, what does the best right hand in the galaxy want?"

"Mr. Weingarten,"—that told him this was official business—"Mr. Roscoe Gladden is here to see you."

"Send him in, by all means." He stood and walked from behind his desk, gigantic smile in place, to the center of his ornate office and waited.

"Mr. Gladden, welcome to Soffett. You've no idea how I've wanted to meet you. Please join me." He motioned to a form-fitting chair.

Gladden towered over his host, his expression suggesting dominance. Meaningless small talk died quickly. Weingarten apparently intended to get a specific message across. Previous attempts by the former rulers to establish some kind of working relationship with the planet Cullen all ended in disaster, usually to the detriment of Soffett. But that was then and Weingarten intended to change that.

Jasper Weingarten started to speak as Gladden held up a hand. "Mr. Weingarten, I am a simple man. My political instincts are non-existent. I tell you this in order that we may bypass the usual nonsense and get down to the reason you have asked me here. As Cullen's point man, it is my job to determine if there is substantive reason for any further discussions between our two worlds. Your messenger was not very specific but shared enough so that our leader wanted to know what was on your mind. It may have merit, then again, it may not, that there is reason for the meeting to continue." Roscoe Gladden's manner, abrupt, verged on dismissal.

Weingarten's demeanor hardened. He'd faced, in fact faced down, some the most notorious bastards known. Despite Cullen's reputation for taking what it wanted the man did not intimidate him.

"Very well. Here's what I have in mind." Jasper laid out his idea for turning Soffett into a first class recreation spot; one like nothing known in the galaxy. Years earlier, he'd spent time in Terra's Las Vegas. That was what he wanted to build on Soffett. The planet had excellent, perhaps even the galaxy's best weather and beaches that matched old Hawaii. He believed it was ideal to become the galaxy's recreation spot for legitimate sporting people. "Of course, to do so, meant all forms of notoriety must be eliminated. The planet had to be squeaky clean and be seen to be so.

"I want to attract the cream of society; make it the place to come. Gaming will be the centerpiece with the relaxing beaches and indulgent services second to none, with magnificent hotels and recreation for even children. No whores, we shoot thieves, pirates, shysters or anyone else who might come to take advantage of the type of guests we see necessary to make the idea palatable. Visitors will not be allowed to bring weapons of any kind to the planet." He stopped and with something less than a glare looked at his guest.

"And what does Cullen gain from this?"

"Same as everyone else. One hell of a good place to bring your family and friends to enjoy the pleasures."

"We could do that on our own. Why do we need you?"

"Mr. Gladden, with Cullen's reputation, there aren't enough credits in the galaxy to sell that idea. Besides, we, or I happen to know that the Kingdom of Braeden is seriously considering kicking your ass. And don't overlook Saragosa Prime. They're a major supplier of fish protein and word is they're about to cut a deal with Braeden to establish a transport fleet to greatly expand their business. Big money is involved and what I'm hearing—if Cullen screws with any part of the operation—well, I wouldn't recommend

Cullen take on any long-term commitments. Add Prime's navy to Braeden's and your days may be numbered. If you threaten that, boom and your planet is history."

That didn't seem to faze Weingarten's guest. "If what you say is true, why do you want, indeed, grovel for our approval."

"Your words are insulting. But that is in keeping with your reputation. Cullen does exert great influence among the types of people who could make my idea much easier to implement or harder. The right words in the right places and many potential problems never plague us."

Espousing the potential threats to Cullen did have its effect. Yet recognizing Cullen's influence seemed to please Gladden as his hardnosed attitude noticeably changed and he relaxed.

"We'll take a piece of the action and you can add that as protection. Not a majority interest, but enough that our voice can be heard without undue distress." Gladden stretched out, his demeanor more than casual, insolent.

"No," said Weingarten, his voice flat and unyielding. "Maybe you didn't understand what I just said so I'll put it in plain English even though threats are not called for."

"It seems to me that is precisely what you've done."

"Good. We understand each other."

"We do not like threats. Surely you must know we have people, very influential people, in virtually every corporation of any substance with the means to control deliveries, prices, just about everything that can determine your success or failure."

"As I said, Mr. Gladden, the Kingdom of Braeden has bought into the idea and offered us protection. Most likely because it will eliminate a blight that has plagued this part of the galaxy. They've offered to station portions of their fleets off Soffett to ensure our efforts go ahead without unwarranted interruption. You need to comm Cullen and tell them of this conversation. See what their reaction is. You can forward their response. This meeting is over, Mr. Gladden, and you should be thankful it has lasted this long. Now leave."

Weingarten wasn't pleased that the get-together had turned surly but that wasn't his responsibility. Without FTL comm, something he hoped to add, it would take two weeks for a message to reach Cullen and that long for a response. But with Braeden's boot on Cullen's throat, he felt certain he knew the answer.

Weingarten punched the icon his voice carried a bit of an edge thanks to his aggravation with Gladden, "Yes, Jessica."

"Sir, orbital control is reporting a problem."

"Patch it through."

"What's going on?" said Jasper.

"Not sure, sir," said the voice. "An unregistered ship asked for an orbital slot and we assigned one," there was a long pause. "It came in cloaked. We never picked it up on any of our sensors. For whatever reason, a Cullen ship wanted to know its port of registry. Told them they couldn't orbit without clearance from Cullen."

"Those bastards," exploded Weingarten. "And?" Gladden was trying to let Weingarten know his displeasure with the meeting by showing a little of Cullen's gall and muscle. Weingarten had to admit the man had reacted quickly—almost as if he'd planned the reaction before the meeting.

"It was ignored."

"Good, and?" Jasper knew a talk with the orbit master was in order. Getting information out of the guy was like talking to a Galen mastiff.

"The Cullen ship ordered the unnamed ship to remain in high orbit for boarding and inspection. I told the Cullen ship it didn't have the authority and that its threats amounted to piracy. They told me not to interfere; all the time heading for the incoming ship. I asked the ship its name and the vessel responded 'Trekker' and that it was spacing under open port registry. Just before the Cullen ship attached to Trekker, our sensors detected a disturbance and the Cullen ship apparently lost its navigation and steerage. We had to use one of our tugs to control her. Damned near had a ramming."

Jasper laughed. "Order that incoming ship to go ahead and take its orbital slot and tell the Captain I would be pleased if he would be my guest at dinner this evening."

* * * *

Raybold Penrose knew he was taking a risk and this trip would result in many questions. Disrupting the Cullen ship would certaintanly be a topic of discussion and his hosts would want to know his home planet. His intention wasn't to bring New Hope into the galaxy family, at least not now and not this way, but it did need freedom to conduct business without fear of interference or worse, unwanted governments and corporations showing up unannounced. Pulling this off would be tricky. The only way he saw to do that was for their ships to gain acceptance with open port registry. Much depended on the outcome here at Soffett. If it worked, Saragosa Prime would be his next stop, followed by the Kingdom of Braeden. The Federation of Aligned Worlds recently voted into existence would follow—a tall order he agreed.

"Standby to receive port inspection," said the watch.

Raybold Penrose stood in the hanger deck with the OD and three crewmembers.

"Welcome aboard, sir. We stand to your inspection. If you require assistance, these men are at your disposal," Raybold pointed to the three men. "If you require anything, you have only to ask."

The inspection thanked him and directed the six inspectors with him to their areas of responsibility. Speaking to Raybold he said, "Sir, I have some questions for you—private questions."

Penrose nodded and motioned for the man to follow him. Once in the conference room, Raybold said, "I have no secrets, you could have asked your questions in public."

"Perhaps. But we have no knowledge of any ship with galactic clearance as your open port registry claims and your ship didn't register on our sensors. Care to tell how this happened? While you're at it tell me how you obtained open port registry. We know of no government with this kind of authority."

Penrose didn't hesitate and said as casually as possible, "Our ambassador made the request of worlds with which we currently do business. They granted us this as a privilege. We saw fit to extend it to Soffett." About this Raybold wasn't lying unless omissions amounted to that.

"Doesn't make sense to me. Have you a list of these planets and what do you sell to them? Neither your planet nor ship are on the interplanetary ship registry." Eying Penrose, he studied him apparently watching his reaction.

Penrose told him who they sold to and a general idea of their commodities. He did leave out electronic devices were high on their list. "About your sensors not seeing us, perhaps they're due for a rigorous maintenance inspection." He handed the inspector a vidplate and then surprised the man with of all things a sheet of real paper carrying the Kingdom Of Braeden seal. Of course, Raybold had only to copy the heading and seal off documents found earlier on the Braeden ship Backlash. But it did the job he wanted and indeed needed.

Apparently not satisfied, the inspector shook his head but seemingly realized that was all he was going to get and had no authority to force Captain Penrose to tell him more. Preparing to leave he said, "Mr. Jasper Weingarten extends his welcome and would like for you to join him for dinner this evening. May I give him your answer?"

"Of course. It's yes. May I ask Mr. Weingarten's official title?"

"Mister," said the inspector with a shrug. "He's very informal. His launch will call for you. Dinner is at eight bells on the dog watch."

Precisely at twenty hundred, dressed in a dark blue business suit, Raybold Penrose stepped from the launch onto the lawn at Government House.

"Mr. Penrose, I am Jasper Weingarten. Welcome to Soffett."

Shorter by a head and a half than Penrose, Weingarten grasp his guests outstretched hand. At first, Penrose thought a vice had trapped him.

"Ha. Your handling the Cullen ship was magnificent. Care to tell me what you used." Weingarten, arms on hips, wide grin looked every bit the bruiser of his reputation.

"I'd prefer not," Raybold said with as much humor in his voice he could muster.

"You'd make a good poker player."

Penrose reminded the leader he'd never won a planet at poker. Weingarten gave a belly laugh and slapped Raybold on the back causing the victim to grab the man's arm to stay upright.

"Cullen thinks it can have its way at whatever it wants. They do not give up easily. I had a dust-off with their emissary a few hours earlier. I'm sure their attempt to control you was really meant as a message to me. You've no idea what your response to that scurrilous effort may mean in the long run for both our worlds. Cullen will not forget nor forgive this slight."

Weingarten seemed withdrawn into his own concerns for a few moments, so Penrose kept silent.

Finally, he broke his self-imposed quiet, "Enough of that. Let's eat. My chef has prepared a feast and would fricassee me if I let it get cold."

"I wouldn't dare denigrate Trekker's chef. Somehow those remarks always seem to get back to the wrong ears. But, after a month of the same fare, I will welcome your cook's efforts."

The two men were silent as they entered Government House. Built before Weingarten took control, the imposing structure sat on a slight rise overlooking the only inhabited area, Soffett City. Past governments had strictly controlled the number of citizens believing it easier to control what generally was riotous gatherings. Something Weingarten championed as well. Even though a gaming planet, Soffett had earned a reputation for not allowing the mayhem to overrun their business. It was on this reputation Weingarten planned to build his gaming and recreation mecca.

"Mr. Weingarten—"

"Jasper, please," he interrupted.

Penrose nodded and said, "Raybold here.

"We heard of your plan regarding Soffett's future. We would like to be a part of that. Our engineers have superb experience in electronics and I can assure you they can deliver you gaming devices that crooks would find difficult or impossible to rig or cheat. We will manufacture guaranteed fraud proof equipment." He sat back and waited for a response.

"Enough talk," said a giant of a man entering leading an array of cooks carrying trays of food his huge red Chef de cuisine hat plopped on a matching head. And stop talking they did.

Tasting the exotic cucumber soup, Raybold nodded his approval only to find the mushroom salad took no back seat. But then, the chef presented his piéce de résistance: grilled salmon, sautéed in a honey mixture, covered with a delicate lemon accentuated sauce and served with an ancient Pinot Noir.

Finishing the delicious meal Raybold said, "I believe you got more than a planet at the poker table. I have never had a more delectable meal. How may I repay you and your chef?"

Weingarten acknowledged the compliment and had the chef join them for a toast to his efforts. He then bombarded Penrose with questions for the next two hours. "What do you call home?" Jasper asked.

"Odysseus," said Raybold. "From the beginning we made it an orbital factory and built to accommodate families as well. I guess you can say it's an artificial planet."

"Never heard of it." Weingarten pensively responded. "We need to know that you can meet our technical and delivery needs."

Penrose bent to the chore needing to convince his host they could and would meet all the requirements. To induce him further, Raybold offered to put credits in escrow in a Soffett bank as a guarantee. That seemed to make the difference.

"I think, sir, we can do business," said Jasper as he reached for Raybold's hand. "Our aides can work out the details."

As they walked toward Raybold's aircar, he asked, "What kind of government does Soffett have? Are you it; absolute; without challenge?" Knowing would tell him who else they might have to deal with.

"We're leaning toward a governance," said Weingarten.

"Never heard of such a thing. I thought governors governed states or provinces," responded Raybold.

"I admit it is different," Weingarten paused for a few moments then said, "What I envision here, in part to attract the kind of money and people who have the credits to pull this off, the amount of your investment determines your amount of say-so in how the planet if governed. We'll call that bunch the Upper House. And so the general population isn't left out, there will be a Lower House elected from those who don't own businesses. So, I thought it proper to call the leader, governor and the form of government, governance."

"Unusual to say the least," said Raybold. He shook Weingarten's outstretched hand and entered the launch for return to Trekker with what he came for. Now all he had to do was convince, Saragosa Prime and the Kingdom of Braeden that Odysseus could meet their requirements without telling them too much. From what he'd heard from Weingarten, Saragosa Prime wouldn't be the problem; Braeden, though, had a reputation of throwing their weight around.

22: The sojourn continues

Aboard Trekker, Raybold Penrose stepped through the hatch onto the bridge ordering the astrogator to break orbit for the month long trip to Saragosa Prime. "We should have a similar reception as Soffett," he said to no one in particular. With Prime about to order over one hundred huge freighters to carry their fish protein throughout the galaxy, the need for electronics should rank high on their want list. And Odysseus could deliver everything they would require.

One T-month and one week later, Trekker spaced from Prime on a vector for Braeden. Even with contracts from Soffett and Saragosa Prime in hand, making a deal with the Kingdom of Braeden would be the real test.

A month later, as Trekker approached Braeden's picket ships, Raybold ordered the astrogator to kick the ship over and begin shedding delta v for its approach to the Kingdom. Raybold wished he'd been more diligent learning about the kingdom. Everything he knew was hearsay and that gave him little comfort. Originally populated by some of the worst mankind had to offer, Braeden, then called Omicron Alpha—the first settlers saw themselves as beginning something that they intended to keep their end of the galaxy for themselves. That is until Barrymore conquered the planet and renamed it Braeden in honor of Philip Braeden who had saved his life years earlier. Barrymore saw himself as a righteous man and his mission to rid the galaxy of sin and sinners. Over the years, that fervor lessened in those who sat on the throne. Today, only a few of the population still championed the original purpose. The comm operator contacted orbital control requesting a parking slot. "Sir, orbital control is challenging our registry," he said.

Raybold touched the icon on his chair. "Orbit master, this is Raybold Penrose, Captain of Trekker. Our papers carry verification from Soffett and Saragosa Prime. In fact, we have contracts from both worlds that should be of benefit to your kingdom. Assign us an orbital slot and you can verify everything I've said." He shut the connection.

"Negative, Trekker. Authorization to approach Braeden is denied. Maintain your current position and do change or our pickets will intercept and stop you. Kill your engines. An inspection crew will arrive within the hour. Braeden Orbit Control out."

"It seems they're cautious with the welcome mat," Raybold said pondering the order. "Wonder what's going on?"

Raybold and three crewmembers waited in the loadmasters perch, sealed off from the hanger, as the Braeden launch settled onto the clamping rails with some difficulty. Obviously, the launch pilot failed to shut down their on board grav system, creating interference with Trekkers gravity field. Since Trekker out-massed the smaller ship by about ten thousand times, the launch got a sever bouncing around. A few seconds more and the hanger doors closed allowing the area to pressurize. Dressed in an inspector's uniform, one man stepped onto the deck followed by six armed Marines.

Just before Raybold opened the booth, his comm buzzed. "Captain, there's a destroyer approaching and she's powered her weapons."

Raybold, not liking what he was seeing, opened his comm ship wide as he stepped into the hanger and waited, his attitude conciliatory, eyes locked on the seven men. Normal procedure had the inspector saying something that included submitting to an inspection by the Royal Orbital Inspector.

Instead, "By order of the King, this ship is impounded." As he spoke, a Navy officer followed by fifteen armed Marines, men and women, exited the launch.

Penrose stepped toward the inspector, again his manner retiring, anything but confrontational and said, "Sir, may I ask the meaning of this? What reason can account for your actions? We have violated none of your laws."

"You may not. This ship is under the command of his majesty's Navy. The Royal Navy will take control of the vessel. You will obey all this officer's orders without question." The officer motioned his entourage forward joined by three Marines. Facing Raybold he said, "Sir, you will lead me to your bridge—immediately."

Penrose shrugged, without a word, turned, and exited the hangar bay. Minutes later, entering the bridge he said, "We've been taken hostage. This officer now has command of Trekker. His authority, the three armed Marines." This was the first time he'd uttered anything remotely defying the ships capture and it brought a glare from the commander.

"You'll keep a civil tongue, sir. Obey my orders without question and you may live a long life."

"Commander, you've sited no laws we've broken, you have no warrant other than the armed Marines. It seems to me your high handed manner in taking a vessel with open port registry is no more than hijacking."

"Put this man in the brig," ordered the Commander. With that, one Marine drew a blaster pistol and said, "Sir, you know where the brig is, take off."

Raybold Penrose turned to the bridge crew and with his comm still open said, "All hands, this is the Captain. Do nothing that places yourselves or the ship in jeopardy. You are to follow implicitly orders given you. Do nothing you are not ordered to do." Little could the commander know Raybold's words would mean his spacers would have to give detailed instructions to Trekker's crew for anything to happen; not a screw turned, a bolt tightened or the ship moved without detailed orders to do so and how to do it. Penrose knew it wouldn't take long for the Commander to understand and the man would not be happy. Passive resistance was the order of the day.

Normally, confining someone with a Captain's rank meant in his quarters under close arrest: an armed sentry at the door. Something else was going on but Penrose didn't have a clue as to what it was. And certainly no idea what to expect.

As he and the Marine made their way down the passageway, Penrose asked, "What happens next?" and turned his head toward the Marine as he spoke.

Without missing a beat, his guard said, "Have no idea. This is a first for most of us. We don't normally treat visitors this way. You must have really pissed someone off."

"Apparently. It didn't take long or much either. We've been on high orbit only a few hours."

Later, a Marine appeared at the brig and unlocked the bared cell door. "Sir, if will follow me." He stood aside and motioned Penrose out.

"Which way," asked Penrose.

"To the hangar bay."

"Is someone coming or am I leaving?" he said.

"Leaving."

A man of few words.

Raybold boarded Trekker's shuttle now occupying the hangar bay, the Braeden launch having left earlier. He'd not seen the Commander and no one saw fit to tell him anything more than the Marine's orders.

Not waiting for instructions, he took a seat and strapped himself in. If the pilot knew what he was doing, the grav system would shut down while the shuttle parted from Trekker and he didn't want to be floating around.

His guard was not overly attentive and his blaster remained holstered. Something had changed.

He leaned back against the metal bucket seat and relaxed for the trip dirtside to Braeden.

Raybold watched from the porthole as the shuttle circled for landing. Someone's attitude had changed. Only a staff hovercar, driver and uniformed officer waited.

Exiting the launch, the officer saluted and said, "Sir, please join me in the car."

Raybold nodded and stepped through the door held by the driver followed by the officer and sat. "Your name Marine?" That he got along with the man's unit.

"Tell me, what are the King's Grenadier Corps? You charged with King's personal safety?"

"Yes, sir. Among other things. We get special assignments on occasion. Usually the small nasty stuff," he said with a smile and manner that Raybold took as bragging.

Penrose pondered that a moment. "Why you and not the regular Marines?"

The officer laughed and said, "Sir, the brigade is on maneuvers so we got the call."

"Oh, well, you can't win them all."

"Not bad duty, sir. It beats hell out of sitting around polishing your brass and boots and standing inspection," he said with sincerity.

"Are we going to see the King?" Penrose asked. He didn't know what that meant other than the stakes had gone up.

"I have orders to deliver you to Soffett's Embassy. We get calls to do some odd jobs frequently. Our ambassador seldom sees anyone. He's the King's brother. Leaves the heavy lifting to others and that includes the Navy and Marines. We have a standing Army, but about all they do is drill and serve long tours off-world. Poor bastards."

The car slide to a stop and a steward waiting in front of an imposing building hurried to open the car door.

Following the man, Penrose started up the long stairway. He paused and thanked the Grenadier and driver then resumed the lengthy climb.

Reaching the top, the steward's hand motioned him toward a waiting woman. She signaled him toward a door. Inside, obviously a reception room, she pointed toward a chair. So far, not one word passed his way. He had no idea who he would see, let alone why.

A few minutes later, the only other door in or out of the room opened and the same young woman entered. "If you'll come this way, the Ambassador will see you now," she said in a practiced official voice.

"Come in, Captain. I'm Romo Finnman, Soffett's Ambassador to Braeden. Since your world isn't officially recognized by Braeden, Soffett has agreed to represent your interests. I did receive a comm a month ago from Mr. Weingarten and later from Saragosa Prime so I knew about your visit." Apologetically, he said, "Sorry about your being locked in the brig." He paused with a quizzical look and asked, "What is the name and where is your world? You are an unknown quantity in this part of the galaxy. Enlighten me, please."

As the Ambassador talked, Penrose pondered how he would answer that very question. "Odysseus, sir. We're located in an isolated area about four parsecs from here. I can't give you the coordinates since this is our first time to Braeden and we have yet to calculate our route home." With breath held, he waited to see if the Ambassador would buy the explanation.

"I've never heard of it. In due time, I suppose I'll know. I don't understand all those arc seconds, kilometers and parsecs. It's just gibberish to me."

He punched an icon on a slightly raised area of his desk and the young women entered. "What would you like to drink? Bring me a glass of iced coffee, please," he said and looked at Raybold who ordered plain water.

"I assume you're here to consummate an agreement with Braeden to supply the electronics needed on Saragosa Prime's freighter order. Am I correct?"

"Sir, what about my ship and crew?" Raybold tried to keep his voice calm but doubted he'd done so.

"The ship, Trekker I believe you call it, is in our custody. I see no reason for it not to be returned to you. In fact, that is being finalized as we speak. Your executive officer is in command of the vessel."

Penrose visibly relaxed.

"Now, about Braeden's concerns. They lost a ship some time ago. Rumor has it you took the vessel. If so, they would like it back." He didn't seem antagonistic, but simply matter of fact. "Do you have the ship? Backlash I believe it's called."

Since Braeden had already decided not to grant an orbital slot, the question of Trekker's home port was never resolved. At least they couldn't accuse him of deception or worse, lying.

With the contract to supply Saragosa Prime's freighters electronics in the balance, prudence dictated that Backlash be returned to its original owners. Raybold decided not to mention the cost New Hope had incurred to make it spaceworthy and agreed to return the ship.

"I'm here to discuss a possible contract. Braeden will build transports for Saragosa Prime and we are to supply the electronics. That means we must have access to the ships. Spacing them to Odysseus without proper nav equipment isn't an option. Yet, Braeden's navy remained unforgiving and argued against using Braeden's shipyards to install the electronics.

A day later, Trekker prepared to leave Braeden orbit for New Hope with Raybold realizing the fruitlessness of arguing anymore. He'd finally agreed to build an orbital installation some five hundred million kilometers away from Braeden.

Taking care of all the customs requirements, Raybold Penrose turned as the orbit master approached, "Mr. Penrose, there's a Cullen ship ten million kilometers outside Braeden space. We've attempted to contact them but they've declined to respond. They're a nasty bunch and you can never tell what they're up to. Just thought I'd let you know. Oh, yes, our navy says you're on your own. You're not very popular with them."

23: The Enemy

"**Sir**, there she is," a sullen Missy Mosier at the astrogator plot said. Not one given to histrionics, she was ready to take on the Cullen ship.

"They're one million klicks off our port," she added. "On an intercept vector. Matching acceleration. They've ordered us to stop, cut our engines, for boarding."

"Is the hailing frequency open?" Raybold took his chair at the back of the bridge.

"Yes, sir," answered the comm operator.

Raybold punched an icon the chair's arm. "Cullen ship, this is Captain Penrose of the Trekker. I have no intentions of stopping and if you think you can board us, come on. You do so with this warning: I intend to comm this conversation and the results of any boarding attempt to Braeden and Cullen."

"They've powered up weapons."

"General Quarters, battle stations," ordered Penrose. "Power all weapons. This Cullen ship is about to find out he's completely outmatched. He'll never know what hit him."

Raybold Penrose ordered Missy to a vector that allowed Trekker to bring its forward energy cannons to bear. "Range?" question Penrose. Lacking the range of Trekker's weapons, the Cullen ship stood no chance. Raybold issued the order. "Half energy, fire forward one, and two cannons."

Trekker gave a slight shudder as the weapons discharged their deadly message.

"Put it on screen," he ordered. The bridge crew watched as the enemy ship glowed and slewed sideways. He then ordered engineering to release their *package*. It was the same electronic emission that David Rohm had used centuries earlier against the Kalazecis and Bogart Presk-Milar against the Chinese in both the attack on New Earth when Admiral Chao attempted a ramming maneuver when out of options at Old Earth. Already damaged by Trekker's energy cannons, the Cullen ship lost all steerage and navigation.

"Let's go home," Raybold said. "It will take them a month or so to make that ship space worthy. No sense in us waiting around." Missy punched the console bringing Trekker to their original vector that would take them to New Hope. He added, "We'll make our visit to the Federation of Aligned Worlds later."

After four months in space, Trekker sent the signal that dropped the cloak hiding New Hope. They were home. Once the relief team boarded, all the crew headed dirtside. Raybold secured the watch and said, "Mr. Fitzmore, you have command."

"Aye, sir, I have command of Trekker. Any orders? Anything that need attention?"

"Few things. The log has it all. If you have any questions or problems, you know where to find me."

With the ship in good hands, Raybold Penrose headed for the hanger bay and home. He waved at the crowd surrounding the launch pad as he stepped from the ship and spent the better part of an hour accepting homecoming greetings. Finally, that ran its course. Entering an aircar, he told the driver to take him home.

Raybold arose early but not before Dee who already had coffee and pastries at his side table. She was overjoyed with his return and the news that New Earth's people would join them.

"You're up early Mr. President," said Baskom Wazalewski entering the office extended his hand. "I'd think you would hide for a few days before coming in. After a year in space, you deserve some time to rest up."

"No, I'm ready to get back to work. How did it go? Anything of interest happen while I was gone?"

"Not really. I prepared a synopsis for you." Baskom handed Raybold a vidpad. "Any questions you have, I'm prepared to answer in detail."

Raybold laid it aside and launched into a brief recap, giving the salient results of his efforts at Saragosa Prime, Soffett, Braeden and the run in with the Cullen ship. He asked Baskom to lay out a plan for implementing the contracts with Soffett, Saragosa Prime and the Kingdom of Braeden. "How's Odysseus coming?"

"Sixty percent completed," Baskom said. "Should be ready in about eight months. When's first delivery?"

"Soffett is first, the dates are in the contract, and most of that should not present any major hitches. Training their people may be a different matter. What do you think, should they come to Odysseus or do we send people to oversee the installation?"

Baskom thought for a few moments. "I think we should bring them to Odysseus. We run less risk of blood contamination if we have total control. Besides, if they do the installation, our liability is only for the design and fabrication. We spend most of our time teaching them how to troubleshoot and repair the gaming equipment. The fancy electronics we plan for their casinos and the rest of what they have planned is all straightforward and any competent electronics tech should be able to handle it. We can make holos to assist both the gaming and construction."

"I agree." Raybold leaned back in his chair. "We had a run in with a Cullen ship. The details are in my report. I think we should pay more attention to that bunch. Mister Weingarten says they have contacts in virtually every corporation or world. Helps them keep on top of matters of interest. Maybe we should consider doing the same thing."

Baskom agreed and said he'd submit his ideas for Raybold to add to his thinking.

"Yes," said Raybold pressing an icon.

"Sir, our deep space monitors are reporting a ship at five hundred million kilometers. It has zero acceleration, speed one thousand klicks per second. Current vector will keep that relative distance," said the voice.

"Any indication they know we're here?" Raybold said. He held the icon.

"We've not detected any long range sweeps, sir. We are passive." That meant they had only the mystery ships emissions for any kind of analysis and that could be a problem.

"Have you run its signature through the computer?"

"Yes, sir. No match, but it comes close to Cullen ships."

"Check it against Trekker's computer," he ordered and waited. Routine procedure meant Trekker would collect every bit of information possible on any ship it encountered.

"Got a match, Mr. President. No name but is does match Trekker's data."

"Keep me posted." Raybold thanked the comm operator and closed the connection. "Looks like I didn't give that Cullen captain we had the run in with enough credit. The bastard followed our radiation spoor," said Raybold.

"And it ends here," said Baskom. "He's got to know that ship is somewhere around. What do you suggest?" Concern edged the vice-president's voice.

"We can be sure the captain has maintained contact with Cullen. So we can't take it out at least while it's still in our sector. My fault for selling this guy short." Raybold pursed his lips and stared at the ceiling.

Almost as an afterthought, he touched the icon again. "How long will the ship be in system?"

"At current speed, three T-weeks," came the response. "We're now picking up electronic sweeps. They may take longer to clear our space."

He punched an icon on his hand-hewn desk and said, "This is Raybold Penrose. Is Backlash space ready?"

"Take four or five days to have her prepped and provisioned, Mr. President," came the answer.

"Get it ready, please," he ordered, stood and added, "Braeden wants that ship back. I think if Cullen has it, that might work in our favor." He returned to his desk and hit the comm switch, "Get me the electronics lab, please."

Moments later, a distracted voice answered, "I'm very busy. What do you want and who is this?"

"This is the President. I'm sure you are quite busy but I need your superior intellect right now."

"My apologies, Mr. President," said a contrite voice. "Of course. How can we help?"

Penrose wanted to know how long it would take to modify Backlash's radiation signature to replicate Trekker's pattern and as quickly return to the original.

Assured that they could do it without much effort, he ordered the work to go ahead immediately.

"What you got in mind? You don't think you're going to fly that ship do you?" asked Baskom.

"Why not? Who better?"

"I'll call out the population if you try."

"That's mutiny, insurrection. That's not you."

"It is in this case. I'm serious, Raybold. I will take it to the people. There are others just as capable who can carry out any instructions you may find necessary to issue."

"Relax, Baskom. I have something else in mind. Who do you think is capable of being a covert spy for us—on Cullen? We need four people as a minimum crew to space the ship but one will do as a spy. The others have no need to know one of them is on a covert mission."

"I have no idea. I wouldn't know how to approach selecting a man."

"Doesn't have to be a man. We have some women who could do the job quite well."

Baskom shook his head and said, "You never cease to amaze me. Would you send a woman?"

"Of course. I'm no chauvinist. Besides, Cullen is a male dominated world and most likely would never suspect a woman as an informant. All I want this person to do is find some way to keep us informed about what Cullen's up to where it concerns New Hope. He or she won't be expected to steal state secrets, just have clandestine meetings with informants."

Baskom threw up his hands. "Do it your way. I'll put the word out and see if any volunteers step forward." With that, he turned to leave the office, stopped and asked, "How do we get these people back? We can't ask them to be there forever."

"They must plan on that possibility. They can start negotiating for their release immediately. How that turns out depends on how resourceful and convincing they are."

"When it comes to New Hope, you know no bounds, Raybold. I don't know if I could make this kind of decision." He left the office seemingly questioning his own resolve if he could lead faced with such decisions—for him a dilemma.

Raybold turned to the matters of state piled before him. His selection of Baskom Wazalewski to run the country as interim President during his absence had received parliamentary approval with few dissenting votes. Wise or not, the framers of the government had not found it necessary to have a functioning vice-president. That decision remained the province of the president. Baskom had proven a master administrator. Each item waiting his attention was concisely summarized, easing the task before Raybold. Whether Baskom could lead in a crisis remained a question.

24: The Chase

Raybold Penrose looked up as his secretary knocked and walked into his office. "Yes, Dee, what is it?" he asked more tartly than he intended. He apologized.

"Sorry, Mr. President. There's a delegation here from parliament. They want to see you." New Hope's unicameral legislature had the reputation of debating issues *ad nauseum*. Seldom did they make any effort to involve the president until an issue was fully vetted. If that was the case now, he could only wonder the issue. He'd heard nothing suggesting a major difference of opinion existed between the executive and legislature.

"Without the usual bureaucratic requests, responses, and negotiation? That must be a first," he said somewhat dourly.

"Mr. President, if I'm reading this bunch, they are not in any mood for give and take. They are polite but not acting very happy."

"Well, in that case, I should put on my space armor? Any idea what they want?"

Dee shook her head in dismay. "You're not taking me seriously and they haven't said why they're here."

Raybold gathered himself and took on a serious air. "Forgive me, Dee. Send them in and have a steward bring coffee or something for all of them."

"Too many for this office, sir. I can put them in the conference room."

He nodded approval, stood, slipped on his coat and made his way to the waiting delegation.

"Gentlemen," Raybold said shaking hands with each member. "Please be seated."

The Speaker took the chair at the opposite end of the table facing the President as the rest sorted out their own pecking order. Mackinzie Dunston had succeeded the late Dedus Rhineholt, taking office just after Raybold spaced for Soffett, Saragosa Prime and Braeden. Raybold didn't know the man well. In fact, had only spoken to him once or twice and had no idea how to deal with him.

"Well, Mr. Speaker, to what do I owe this visit?" He didn't say what was on his mind that must have them so stirred up.

"Mr. President, we are concerned that the contracts," he paused, "the contracts you entered into on your just completed trip will expose New Hope. We fear the prospects of our location remaining secret, no our very existence, seem diminished to say the least. We believe your effort will inevitably lead to our discovery. We think this is a mistake and should not go forward."

Raybold somberly looked at each member. He had anticipated this reaction from a few Members of Parliament, but the Speaker seemed to have a majority. Otherwise, he would have not been quite so straightforward. He wasn't here to negotiate. Yet, Raybold had to wonder why he didn't come alone. Why such a large delegation? Was it to show he had his fellow parliamentarians behind him? Or maybe it was for the benefit of the House—a way of showing his flag.

"Mr. Speaker, Members of Parliament, I think you are correct in your assessment." The reaction wasn't what he expected. Uninhibited prattle, bordering on ranting broke out among the parliamentarians. Heads nodded as they exchanged acclimations of agreement.

"Gentlemen," said the Speaker waving them to silence. "Forgive my intervention, Mr. President."

Raybold nodded and stood to address the delegation. "More and more, it has become a major effort for New Hope to keep our presence a secret. Our scientists have been most successful in developing devices and advancing the science of cloaking, just to mention two areas. I personally think we've been as lucky as good. I too think it is inevitable, only a matter of time until we're discovered. Space is becoming a very busy place. We happen to occupy a seldom-traveled area but that is bound to change. One day our secret existence will end. It has been and is my intension to prepare our world for when that happens. It seems to me a robust commercial business is a very good way to enter the known universe. It is my plan to use the remote orbital factory to introduce our world to the rest of the galaxy."

"You have ably led our world but I, we, the Parliament, think you are wrong with this move. Granted, New Hope would benefit economically for years to come. But what you propose is too high a price to pay."

"What do you propose, Mr. Speaker?" Raybold stifled his temper.

"Nothing. Leave it alone. We have managed to keep our being, our presence unknown. I see nothing that threatens us."

"Are you aware, sir, that a Cullen ship is systematically scanning this sector of space as we debate? It suspects something or wouldn't be here." What Raybold left out was that the ship had followed him from Braeden and when Trekker's radiation disappeared, it started a systematic search scanning the entire Acraconda Sector.

"No, I wasn't aware. But we've managed to outwit others. The scientists can do it again."

"And if we can't, the scientists, I mean? I'll ask again, Mr. Speaker, how would you handle New Hope or the rest of the galaxy once our existence became known?"

Getting no answer, Raybold said, "Perhaps you would like some time to think about an answer. I plan to proceed until someone presents an acceptable alternative. Gentlemen, as I said our discovery, and exposure is inevitable." He watched as the delegation filed out amid looks of disgust, which he interpreted as antagonism.

Back in his office he commed Baskom Wazalewski. "What can you tell me about Mackinzie Dunston?" New Hope's population now numbered over one hundred forty thousand souls and between his trips off planet and affairs of state, there were many people, even in Parliament, he had little or no opportunity to know much about.

"If you have the time, I would prefer to come to your office and have this discussion, Mr. President."

A few minutes later, Dee gently rapped and opened the door, "The Vice-President is here."

The gentle giant strode boldly in, thanking Dee.

"Okay, Baskom, this must be serious. Out with it. Tell me about the Speaker."

The Vice-President seemed to mull over the question.

"The Speaker is a bit of a puzzle. As interim President, I had to ratify the vote that elevated the majority leader. Only two people voted against him. Rather unusual. I was told that little discussion preceded the vote and no one saw fit to run against him. Yet, I'd heard little about the man. He's introduced no legislation," Baskom paused and looked at Raybold, both knew Parliament can only recommend for consideration." He paused again, then added, "Franklin Douglas, I think you know him fairly well, told me that the day before the election, Dunston told him he expected no opposition. A bit irregular wouldn't you say?"

"Baskom, you are the most obvious person I've ever known. You believe he's up to something don't you?" Raybold's observation brought a smile from his number two.

"Did he ever contact you as Speaker?" Raybold continued.

"Yes, in fact, he seemed more interested in what crossed my desk than what went on in Parliament."

Raybold cocked his head. "Now, that I would say is irregular." Penrose had no fears the man sought the presidency. He was free to do so under their constitution. If that were the case, his methods were just as irregular.

Wheedling and worming would never get it done. The people of New Hope had become accustomed to results. But then, they had never had to deal with a con man. Was that what Dunston was—a confidence man. If so, his first effort seemed to have failed miserably.

"There's more. Markam Zenester is the real power behind Dunston. According to my information, he organized Dunston's bid for Speaker. Seems he has a group, very active bunch that does his bidding. He's no con man but tough as hell. Isn't above intimidation. I'd say he has cowered enough of Parliament that he might be a threat. That's the only reason allowing Parliament to enact legislation should be delayed until we sort this out."

"Markam? He headed up our intelligence a number of years ago. I have no recollection of any wayward behavior in that job." Raybold sat silent pondering. Markam Zenester had earned a reputation for running a tight, thorough operation. Prior to that, he started a company that specialized in detection equipment: something that had served New Hope quite well with advanced warning against ships scanning their area of space. "It would seem his many skills have been put to use. To what end, I can't imagine. Should I have him arrested? I could have Legal issue a warrant for his arrest."

"Your humor is lacking, Mr. President. There is something wrong in our legislative body. Men who sought out my opinion no longer do so. People whom I called friend for years now turn down invitations to my home. It has been customary for Parliament to keep the President informed of its deliberations. Have you received any such comms or vidcasts?"

"There were none on my desk when I returned. So you think the Speaker was here this morning to show some muscle, is that it? If it was, he failed miserably. Had he come alone I might think differently. But with a delegation to back him up, no way." Raybold's demeanor had changed completely. He no longer took exception to Baskom's concerns. If there were any move to circumvent the constitution, he would deal with it and not be gentle in doing so.

"What do you suggest?"

"You must have ways of getting information that will not place undue hardship on members of Parliament you've known and dealt with for years. I suggest you make use of them and find out if there are, in fact, matters of concern to you and the Republic."

Baskom had never demonstrated the finesse required of a politician. He was and always would be an administrator: the best Raybold had ever worked with. That wasn't a bad thing, but this matter required a different skill. One

Raybold had in abundance—political maneuvering, using comprises, negotiation, and downright guile to make sure the Republic stayed free of anyone who would do it harm. "Or maybe, we just need give Markam something else to think about. Something that would use some of his latent talents."

Baskom gave a quiet laugh. "And how do you propose to do that?"

"Offer him something he can't refuse. Something that isn't obvious to any who support him. Something that he may cherish. The opportunity to represent New Hope in a life or death confrontation as a negotiator."

"You're thinking about him being aboard Backlash when it spaces to meet the Cullen ship? Preposterous. He'd never do it."

"I like my idea," said Raybold. "You've had more contact with the man, why don't you approach him and make the offer. He'd stand out among his peers like never before. See what he says. One added benefit, we'll see if the Speaker can manage on his own."

Raybold studied his friend for a few moments. "Baskom, on another matter. I've been thinking it's about time to make a change in the constitution. Give Parliament the power to offer legislation that can become law. The president would hold veto power but a two-thirds majority could over-ride. What do you think?" Penrose had a commission working on that very matter. He'd not talked with them since returning from this last junket. Maybe it was time to do so.

"I have no problem with that. In my opinion, it is long overdue. But how does that fit in with my concerns?"

"With Markam away in space, we'll certainly be able to determine the depth of our Speaker. Find out what he's capable of accomplishing."

"Raybold, you are the most, the most impossible man I've ever met. You'd stick your head in a Bovian gryphon's mouth just for the hell of it."

PART THREE: Living With the Enemy

25: The Deception

"**It** would be a chance of a lifetime for someone who has over the years developed their shadowing skills," said Baskom.

Markam Zenester eyed the Vice-President. "This wasn't your idea was it? I feel the hand of our intrepid President."

"You're right. But that doesn't diminish the need. We have a real problem with Cullen. At least we believe it will develop into that. Mr. Penrose and Cullen's emissary to Soffett crossed verbal swords and Trekker disrupted their navigation and steerage on orbit over Soffett. And then did the same thing to one of their ships over Braeden. Those people are not accustomed to that kind of treatment. Raybold underestimated them not realizing they were following Trekker's radiation trail. So, we need to put a stop to their scanning. There's always the risk they'll discover our planet. That must not happen."

"So I take Backlash, with its electronic signature masked to mimic Trekker and suddenly show up."

"That's the idea."

"And what do I tell them?"

"Depends on what they ask. Just make sure you get to Cullen. We must know what they have in mind for New Hope. There's always the chance you may not make it back. I think you know that. And of course, perhaps most importantly, the long life issue. Everyone on Backlash must do whatever is necessary to not let that knowledge out—whatever."

Having served on three other worlds Markam knew what that meant. Asking others to make the ultimate sacrifice, taking their own life to keep the secret.

"Yeah, I realize that. But I must admit, the spy business does get my juices flowing. I must be nuts to even consider something so risky." He sat silent looking at nothing. "Okay, I'll do it."

Baskom stood, walked to the man and offered his hand. "You know, Markam, I must be as nuts as you. I almost envy you. Our life on New Hope sometimes is dull and routine. What you and the others are about to do makes this truly mundane. Here's the name of a woman that can be a big help to you."

Markam read the name, Darcy Lipscomb. "How do I find her and who is she?"

"Darcy runs a small dispatch business in the capital. You shouldn't have a problem finding it."

Two days later, Backlash, on near orbit waited until the Cullen ship disappeared behind New Hope and launched for deep space. Once away from New Hope, Markam handed the comm operator a chip. "Send this now. Use a sweeping tight beam toward the Braeden sector. No coding. It's our insurance," he added. Any Braeden ship intercepting the signal would know Cullen had taken Backlash.

Braeden's ship design reflected the latest in spaceship technology. When it came to spacing the most formidable ships in the galaxy, their engineers had spared nothing. All they lacked to take on Cullen were numbers. Plentiful and spacious recreation areas along with a mess hall, second to none, with every delicacy to temp the taste buds. Of course, that made the gym a must for those paying attention to their waistline. Rumor had it, Braeden sailors who avoided working out earned the wrath of their captain. Would be video directors made use of the studio providing offbeat productions to entertain the crew. Markam admired the bridge. Not laid out in a traditional plan the console placement formed a semi-circle that fronted the area with the captain's chair the focal point giving him immediate access to every station with few steps. A large view screen centered on the bridge hung from the overhead.

"Rotate," he said preparing to shed delta v. Two hours later, having stopped dead in space awaiting the Cullen ship's appearance from behind New Hope, Markam set an intercept course. "When we get within one million klicks, open a channel." He had no doubt the Cullen ship would spot them. When Backlash transmitted to the Cullen ship, it would come as no surprise.

Backlash usually required a crew of twenty, but that now numbered four in addition to Markam. All volunteers, he had hoped to use the transit time to Cullen for schooling his neophyte spies on some of the intricacies to avoid discovery. That seemed in doubt and he could only hope these volunteers could hold their own against any questioning. Actually, if things went as planned, he'd be the only one to remain on Cullen. The rest would repatriate to Braeden or Saragosa Prime. The possibility existed they all might be jailed. He had to prepare them for either eventuality. Missy Mosier had the helm, Danny Davis, on engines, Millard Case, had responsibility for medical along with the galley, and Reece Emery electronics. All were skilled in their areas of responsibility and he couldn't object to their being part of the crew. Except for Missy. Just the thought of what might happen if Cullen discovered their real mission… he knew what happened to women captives.

Markam served in New Hope's investigative service for over forty years. In that time, he'd volunteered for covert duty on Saragosa Prime and Federation of Aligned Worlds when it first formed on Galactica. Before leaving New Hope, he admitted to President Penrose his behind the scenes maneuvering to get Mackinzie Dunston elected as speaker of Parliament amounted to no more than overcoming boredom.

"Backlash, stop and prepare for boarding." The order didn't surprise Markam.

"Missy, bring her about; full thrust for twenty minutes, then take the engines to idle until were dead in space."

And hour later, he keyed the comm, "Missy, stay at the controls. The rest of you join me in the boat bay. No weapons and have your nicey-nicey faces on."

Instead of landing in the hanger, the Cullen ship attached to the outer overhead hatch. Markam along with the other three men, moved to the area and secured it against the improbability the Cullen boarders might be careless enough not to get a good seal between the two ships. He undogged the hatch and stepped back in line with this crew.

Seven men armed and in full armor dropped through the opening. "Who's captain?" asked one man. He raised his blaster pistol.

"I am Captain Markam Zenester. I am returning this ship to the Kingdom of Braeden. Pirates took it and we found it abandoned. Tried to claim salvage rights but Braeden raised so much hell, we decided to give it back."

"I don't give a damn about what you were doing." Sarcasm laced the man's voice. "Why were you going away from Braeden?"

"We were heading for Galactica and the Federation. Going to hand it over to them. It's about two months closer than Braeden. Makes sense doesn't it?" A lie but Markam tried not to stare at the man as he studied his reaction. He'd had enough experience to have a good feel if his antagonist believed him or not. And as usual, this man had his orders. Most likely, he lacked the rank to make any decisions on his own. Just the mention of the Federation of Aligned Worlds would put enough doubt in his mind that nothing harmful would happen. In fact, Markam and his crew's lives depended on that reaction. The next few minutes would tell how successful he had been.

"This squad will remain on board and you'll follow us," the soldier said.

"To where? We're expected at Galactica in just over a t-month," said Markam. That was less than the truth. But he knew Cullen had a habit of taking ships and they were not about to contact the Federation or Braeden to ask questions.

"Cullen," the soldier said curtly and added, "You," motioning to Markam, "Get your gear. You're making the trip aboard Lancaster." Aiming his blaster pistol at the remaining crew, he said, "You'll follow this Sergeant's orders. Don't and he'll shoot to kill."

Markam soon appeared with his duffle bag. "Reece, you're now captain," he said then followed the officer through the hatch, secured it leaving his crew and the six soldiers behind.

* * * *

Reece introduced the crew and pointed toward the area where the soldiers would find bunking accommodations. "I guess you'll want us to run the ship. You can't do that and guard us too."

"Just do your job and follow Lancaster. Get out of line and you heard the Captain, we'll shoot anyone who disobeys even one order."

Reece nodded and motioned for the two remaining crewmembers to follow him. Entering the bridge, one soldier close behind, he said, "Brooke, the Captain is on the Cullen ship. I'm now Captain. There are six soldiers aboard with orders to shoot to kill if we don't follow orders. Make sure you understand all orders. Don't do anything unless told. Any questions?"

"Well, well, what have we here?" said a soldier stepping through the hatch onto the bridge. "This trip ain't going to be as boring as I thought. Looks like we've got a plaything." He leered at Missy.

Reece stepped to the comm and punched an icon, "Lancaster, we have a woman aboard, she's our astrogator. One of your soldiers seems to think she's his plaything. I expect you to make it known to this soldier, and the others, he's here on the bridge now, that they will suffer the consequences if she's molested." He held the comm open waiting for an answer.

"Soldier, you are to restrict your contact with the crew of Backlash in line with your orders. Do you understand?"

The soldier responded with a crisp, yes sir. His look at Reece said anything but that.

Reece made a motion indicating he closed the comm as the soldier said, "You son of a bitch. You'll regret that."

"Soldier, your name," the comm blared.

Reece thought for a moment the man would shoot but finally obeyed. As instructed by the speaker, Reece opened the ship wide comm and asked the sergeant to come to the bridge. The voice over the comm gave specific instructions regarding Missy except they didn't use her name. The speaker made it known anyone not obeying would face a court-martial.

The soldier walked to the comm and checked its position. Turning to Reece he said, "He didn't say anything about you. I just might shoot you for that stunt. Might get me a medal."

The sergeant called the soldier by name and said, "I'm not getting my ass in a sling because you can't keep your pants on. As far as the Captain is concerned, you stay away from him. I'd hate to have to shoot one of my own men. Do you understand?"

Cursing, the soldier stormed from the bridge. "Captain, stay away from him," the sergeant said and left through the hatch.

Reece settled into the captain's chair. "Missy, when you move through the ship, keep your comm open at all times. I think we can trust the sergeant but beyond that, take no chances."

She nodded, her eyes on the comm tracking the Cullen ship as it moved away from Backlash. Shortly, coordinates and speed received, she turned toward Reece. If what had just happened alarmed her, it didn't show on her face or actions. Her voice steady, she said, "Captain, I think we should wait at least one hour before going into hyperspace. It's the safest thing to do. There's too much chance of overrunning the other ship. If they have any problems, we won't know in time to avoid a collision."

Reece commed the sergeant.

Entering the bridge, he informed him about the delay. "I'd like for you to be here when we tell Lancaster. You can hear their response along with us."

"Makes sense to me," he said obviously pleased how Backlash had handled their concern.

Reece gave the order and shortly they had their response. "Keep one transmitter on line and it only to receive on the frequencies we will supply shortly."

Reece knew that meant nothing as far as meaningful communication went, but it would eliminate the possibility that Backlash could send an unauthorized message. Actually, he thought the Lancaster captain knew his business—had done what he would have. What only the crew of Backlash knew: the tight beam transmission that went out to Braeden preceding contact with the Cullen ship had already alerted Braeden and that Lancaster had headed for their homeport. Three months gave Braeden enough time to intercept the two ships. He suspected matters would get dicey before the space dust settled.

26: The Spy Plan goes Forward

"**Signal** from Lancaster," Reece said manning the comm station. He called the sergeant to the bridge and played the message.

"Backlash, you are to kill your acceleration immediately and cut your transmissions to zero. You are not to make your presence known; do not acknowledge this message."

"Do it," said the sergeant. "Wonder what's going on?" he added.

Reece shrugged and reclaimed the captain's chair as Missy entered the commands.

Shortly after entering hyperspace, the problem soldier attempted to stop Missy in the mess hall.

Assigning another soldier to accompany her when off the bridge had taken care of the problem. She'd done her part making sure the escort remained nearby. However, when not accompanied, the sergeant approved Brooke's carrying a blaster pistol.

For over a five T-hours, Backlash heard nothing then a jolt as a ship attached to the hull. Reece and the sergeant quickly made their way to the overhead entry.

Securing the area and shutting off the grav force, Reece looked at the soldier as someone banged on the hatch. A nod and Reece released the catch. Six Braeden Marines along with a captain dropped onto Backlash's deck.

"This ship is the property of the Kingdom of Braeden. We are now in command. Sergeant, assemble your men. You will leave immediately," said the Marine.

Following a salute, the soldier commed his men and within a few minutes climbed through the hatch leaving Backlash. Reece noted how eerie it seemed. Not one word had passed between the two commanding men other than the Marine's order. But then, Reece hadn't spoken either and had no idea how this would play out.

Addressing Reece, the Marine said, "You people can go with the Cullen ship or remain aboard."

"We'll stay on Backlash, Captain. But what about our captain? He's aboard the Cullen ship."

Triggering his comm, the Marine raised the question. They waited. "Zenester isn't wanted by our government, and Lancaster insists he stays so that settles it." Touching his earpiece, he paused. "A crew is coming aboard to pilot Backlash. All of you are relieved of your responsibilities. Behave yourselves and it should be an uneventful flight to Braeden."

"Any idea what happens when we get to your planet?" asked Reece.

"Probably repatriation. Where's home?"

"Odysseus. But we'll take Soffett or Saragosa Prime and make our own way back," Reece said.

"Odysseus? Never heard of it."

"You will," said Reece. A smile crossed his face. "We have contracts to supply the electronics on the transports you're soon to build for Saragosa Prime."

* * * *

"Captain Zenester, you have some questions to answer but they can wait until we reach Cullen," said Dominic Morfrain. "It seems a bit odd to me that a Braeden ship would find us as easily as they did. Any comment, sir?"

"Braeden has the best in technology, Captain," responded Markam Zenester. "They've been looking for that ship about a year, so, no, I'm not surprised at all.

"You said Cullen had a warrant for my arrest. What are the charges?"

"You will find that out when we reach our world. Although, I suspect it's for pirating Backlash."

"Not so, sir. We found that ship abandoned. We think pirates boarded her, killed the crew, and for their own reasons cut the ship adrift. That's how we found her."

"And the name of the ship you were on and her captain?"

"She was the Hope and Mr. Daniels captained her."

"That ship is unknown to me. Where were you bound for and where is it now?"

"Captain, I think I've answered enough questions until I know the charges against me."

"So be it." Captain Morfrain motioned toward the guard. "Return him to his quarters," he said with a menacing look. "And captain, if you do not want to spend the next three months in the brig, don't do anything stupid."

"You have my word, sir; I have no intentions of giving you any reason to restrain me further." Pausing at the hatch, he added, "With your permission, may my guard and I occasionally take a stroll? Three months in the same room isn't much different than a cage."

Morfrain spun toward Markam, his appearance even more threatening, and then seemed to have second thoughts. Looking at the guard he said, "An occasional stroll is in order."

* * * *

A month into the trip to Cullen, sitting in his quarters, a general area he called the living room, with a recessed nook that housed his bunk, a kitchenette and bath with toilet made up his prison, Markam keyed the comm, "Yes."

"Captain, come to the bridge."

Markam could only wonder why Morfrain wanted him but glad to be anywhere else, he quickly opened the hatch and informed the guard.

As Markam stepped onto the bridge, Captain Morfrain gestured toward the navigation console and Markam followed him.

Pointing toward the screen he said, "See that? It's a ship. Been following us for two days. Any idea who and why?"

Markam shook his head. "No, sir. Maybe it's a pirate. But on second thought, at the speed you've been holding, I doubt it. No idea, Captain." He backed away from the console scratching his chin. Why would anyone follow a Cullen ship? Notorious for not tolerating any interference, only a warship would do that but why. Braeden now had Backlash and they had no interest in him. So who and why remained a question, maybe a problem.

"What do you suggest?" asked Morfrain.

Markam looked quizzically at this counterpart. "Seems, sir, you have two options, hold your course and keep an eye on them or cut your speed and see if they care to approach."

"And which do you prefer?"

Markam suspected this had something to do with breaking the monotony. "I'm the curious type. I'd slow and hail them. I'd want to know, as you do, who they are and why they're interested in us."

"So be it. Helm, cut our speed to one thousand klicks per second. Let's see if this mysterious ship takes the bait."

Ten T-hours later Morfrain stepped on the bridge. "Whoever they are, they didn't take our cue," he said as the ghost ship changed its vector and accelerated away. The Captain keyed his comm, "Run their signature through the data base," he ordered.

Shortly the response came, "Nothing, Captain. It's unknown to us."

"Return to your cabin, captain."

Dismissed, Markam followed the guard.

His ventures through the ship were to the gym and mess hall, with an occasional stop in the vid room but mostly the gym. A crewmember frequented the place and seemed skilled in martial arts. He and Markam soon became sparing partners. Between allowing time for bruises to mend and frequent bouts, Markam's skills became appreciatively better. In fact, his opponent judged him to be one if not the best he'd encountered. Certainly on Lancaster with over six hundred crewmembers. Otherwise, no interruption marred the trip and two months later, the ship took up orbit over Cullen.

Transfered to a launch, Markam watched from the porthole as they prepared to land. The airdrome could easily accommodate at least ten spaceships.

Exiting the launch a man from the provost's office took custody of him and they settled into an aircar. For the first time, the man addressed him. "You're going to the Space Marshall's office."

"Any idea why?"

"For questioning."

Markam thanked him for the heads up but said no more.

Once inside the austere building, the guide led him to a barren room that matched the outside with only a table and two chairs.

As instructed, Markam sat and waited for over an hour. He turned as the door opened and a small, mousy looking man entered.

Taking short choppy steps, the man took the chair behind the table.

"Name and rank?"

"Markam Zenester. Captain of Backlash."

"Where are you from?"

"Odysseus."

That brought a hard look from the pinched eyes.

Markam changed his first opinion, instead of a mouse, the man's appearance reminded him of pictures of an Old Earth Weasel.

"We've never heard of Odysseus. Tell me about it. Where it is, who founded it, how long it's been inhabited—everything." With that, a smirk appeared and he leaned back in the chair, arms folded across his chest and curtly added, "I'm waiting."

"Odysseus is a man-made planet orbiting a planetoid about two parsecs beyond the defined boundary of the Galactic sector. We had suffered severe damage making our way through an asteroid cluster. Had to make repairs and made it to a small uninhabitable planetoid orbited a star. We discovered enough minerals that enabled us to build a repair facility and decided to stay there rather than on the planetoid. The concept worked so we expanded it making it our home as well. About a thousand people live and work on Odysseus. We've been there about forty T-years."

He stopped prompting a vindictive stream from the weasel.

"Sir, you asked me a question and you have my answer."

"Listen you smart assed son of a bitch, don't think for one moment I buy your bullshit story. Now I want the truth." Weasel said, running his mouth again.

Markam sat silent eyeing his antagonistic inquisitor. "What I've told you is the truth. Take it or leave it. I don't care which." And then, just to piss off the man further, he smiled.

Weasel slammed his fist on the desk. "We have ways of dealing with people like you." He stormed from the room.

Markam knew what he'd done could lead to some real interrogation. *Probably should have held his temper.* But he'd been through some tough grillings and this guy couldn't begin to match them.

The door opened and a large soldier entered. Markam braced for the beating. Instead, the man said, "Come with me," and motioned toward the door.

Following a corridor, they walked for a few moments. Passing through a door, they entered into a different world. The halls painted, floors tiled and pictures decorated the walls. Steps further, they entered another room, this one well decorated and with soft form-fitting chairs.

He sat as instructed and the guide left.

Shortly, a side door opened and a well-dressed man entered. A woman followed.

"Mr. Markam, I am Felix Deverour, Charge-de-Affairs for Saragosa Prime Embassy. As you may or may not know, Odysseus isn't known to these people, let alone recognized by Cullen. Since Odysseus has diplomatic credentials with Soffett, they have extended that courtesy to Saragosa Prime. I came as quickly as I could. I trust you've been well treated."

Markam stood. "I've had harsher and better treatment. I'll admit I'm surprised that they allowed you to see me. So far, all I've gotten is a good butt chewing." He nodded to the woman.

"Please be seated. I am aware of Odysseus's contracts with our world. I also know how your ship, Trekker, treated the Cullen ship at Soffett and above Braeden. In fact, I'm here trying to smooth over Mr. Weingarten's blow-up with the Cullen representative. Our conversation is being recorded as we speak at the demand of Cullen. This woman is my assistant handling the devise. I insisted our time with you be alone. Cullen insisted on the monitor."

Markam acknowledged the lady and said, "Yes, I heard about the dressing down by Weingarten of the Cullen guy. And of course how someone handled the Cullen ships. How's it going?" Both incidents were common knowledge on New Hope. He'd considered it a bit of a coupe that the Soffett Governor refused to be intimidated by the insolent Cullen representative.

"Not well I'm afraid. These people are not accustomed to that kind of treatment, particularly denial of what they want. What brings you to Cullen?"

"I and a crew of four were headed for Galactica to return Braeden's ship, the Backlash. The Cullen ship Lancaster intercepted us, took me aboard their ship and we spaced for Cullen. A Braeden Navy ship caught up with us and they took control of Backlash. I was told Cullen had a warrant for my arrest and wasn't permitted to return to Backlash, so here I am. Any chance of getting me out of here? And do you know why I'm being held?"

"Don't know about your first question and as to the second, it's because of Trekker's assaults against the Cullen ship at Soffett and Braeden."

"I had nothing to do with either. I wasn't aboard Trekker." He knew his plaint would cut him no slack, not with Cullen. An insult is an insult is an insult. He would pay the price for Penrose's action.

The Charge-de-Affairs was quiet for a few moments. "I'll see what I can do but I'm not hopeful. Don't antagonize them although I know that admonition isn't necessary. You don't seem like an impertinent man."

Markam thought about Weasel but kept it to himself. No sense in discouraging the only hope he had for release.

27: The Spy

Markam made the best of the next few days. Questioned relentlessly, his answers never changed. Surprisingly, his interrogators never asked for Odysseus's spatial coordinates. He surmised they already knew.

A week later, released into the custody of the Saragosa Prime Charge-dé-Affairs, he professed his appreciation.

Meeting him at the Saragosa Embassy, a Marine and a staff aide led him down the marble-floored corridors. Frescos of the home world adorned the walls and ceiling, depicting life on their world. The aide gave a running scenario of the renderings many he recognized from his years as a spy on that planet.

Shortly a man joined them, dismissing the guides.

"Mr. Zenester, I'm Grover Happan, Chief of Embassy Security."

Markam grasped the extended hand.

Stern, unsmiling Happan said, "Welcome to Saragosa Prime Embassy. You can make this your home as long as you are on Cullen. I must caution you, do nothing to antagonize these people. Your release is conditional. We are responsible for you and frankly, we have enough problems without adding to them." His smile, anything but cordial, left no room for doubt. Markam had to be on his best behavior. If Cullen caught him spying, he wouldn't be the only casualty; Odysseus's contracts with Saragosa Prime or even Braeden might suffer or worse, canceled.

The officer left and Markam retreated to his suite and made a cursory inspection. Three generous sized rooms. *Better than a hotel*, he mused.

Markam made a good faith effort to fit in. Purchasing a wardrobe ranked high on his needs list. With that done, he frequented the bistros and casually made acquaintances, but did nothing of significance. Purposely, he avoided seeking out Darcy Lipscomb in case Cullen officials were watching.

* * * *

It was still early and he wasn't ready to call it a night. He walked a few blocks from the embassy and commed for an airtaxi. Dressed in slacks and a pullover he said to the driver, "I need some action. Got any suggestions?"

"Yeah, but it'll cost ya."

Markam handed the man a twenty credit.

"Thanks, but I was talking about the action. Is it gambling or women you're wanting?"

"I'm not much of a gambler," responded Markam.

That brought a laugh from the driver. "Just as well. You can't trust the tables or dealers. There are some houses that have both gambling and women and a couple of them have a reputation for being up and up. They cost a little more but your being alone, I'd recommend one of them." He paused for a moment, "You ain't carrying a pulser or blaster are you?"

"Not me," Markam exclaimed.

The driver raised his hand and displayed a monster pulser pistol. I have to carry one. All cabbies got a permit. We get some real losers once in a while. Knocking off a cabby is a full time sport around here."

"Why stay in the business?" asked Markam.

"Wait 'till and see how many credits it costs for hauling you around."

"Well, you being unarmed means one of the better clubs. Don't *ever* go into one of them with a piece. On the other hand, don't go into one of the scum places without a weapon and it's best if you have someone with you. There are some really bad people on Cullen and a lot of them. You must be new."

"Yeah. Just a few days."

"Why here?" asked the driver. "I sure as hell would leave if I could. I used to be a spacer, originally from Mercer, it's a little planet on past Soffett. Served on big transports and even did a stint with the Saragosa Prime Navy. I'm one hell of a good engine man but I'm stuck here now. If you ain't tied in with one of the families, it's damned near impossible to get a permit to leave. Ya gotta have connection on this planet. Mostly, as I said, with one of the families."

"Families?"

"Yeah, but they ain't real families. They use that brotherhood bit. Ain't nothin' but scum and I don't want any part of them."

"Same with me. I'm here and can't do anything about it, so I have to be on my best behavior."

Steering the aircar to the curb and letting it settle to the ground, the driver turned to face Markam. "Mister, I don't know a thing about you, but I'll tell you this: Cullen ain't no place for an honest man and that's how you come across to me. These bastards can find fault with anything you do. So be careful. They ain't nothing to mess with."

"I know," responded Markam. "They questioned me for over two weeks."

"What did you do to get that much attention? Usually, anyone sparking that kind of interest would still be locked up." He took a long look at Markam.

"Don't know," he answered. "A Cullen Navy ship boarded my spaceship, took control, made me go with them and brought me here. Won't let me leave." Markam studied the man's reaction.

"They got spies everywhere and informants by the hundreds. Got to be careful who you talk to and what you say."

"Aren't you taking a chance with me? I could be an informer."

"Neither of us has said anything that could get us in trouble," said the driver. "Besides, no government agent would want to go to the gaming houses, at least the worst places. They have a way of disappearing if someone gets the chance to nail them."

"Is the Interior Ministry really that lax about internal security?" Markam asked. "As notorious as Cullen is, its reputation in the galaxy, I've heard the worst of the worst come here. You'd think the government would really ride herd on them."

"They've tried a number of crackdowns. Last time, lost over a hundred cops the first week. Backed off. They've got every kind of electronic gadget you can imagine all over the city, I'm told around the planet as well, watching. The government does its best to keep an eye on you."

"What keeps the place from exploding? With that kind of trash running around, and from what you said, armed and ready to kill," he paused, "How does the government keep control?"

"Simple. Get caught doing something wrong and they shoot you. Happens all the time. An hour doesn't go by without a shooting. They don't tail a person like they used too. You go into one of the sleaze joints and you'll see armed guards all over the place. Work for the owners. They keep order. Believe it or not, there's kinda an agreement between the citizens and the government. Behave. If someone tries to harm you, do what's necessary to keep alive and they leave you alone. Stealing isn't enough to get you killed. That happens regularly," he said that with finality and put the car into the air.

"What's serious enough to get you shot without a trial?" asked Markam.

"Man you are new. Get caught spying and they shoot you. A trial? No way. Happens every so often. Believe it or not, that's the law. Been that way as long as I've been around here. No sir, it's legal. Funny part, the people expect the government to abide by the laws and raise hell when it violates its own rules. I guess that's why there aren't very many... laws that is."

"Spies on Cullen," mused Markam. "Who, I mean, I don't know what I mean. What has this bunch got that would cause someone to send spies?"

"Not so much what they've got but who their going to attack next. It's no secret that Cullen makes its money takin' from others. Ever thought about why we pay no taxes. First, they can't collect them. Too damned dangerous. So they raid and take from other worlds."

The drivers words added to Markam's resolve to get the information New Hope and Odysseus needed.

Neither said much for the remainder of the ride. The driver finally stopped in front of a building lighted from top to bottom, mostly with designs of gambling devices.

"Here you are. You should be safe here. Just don't start anything." He handed Markam a card. "When you're ready to go somewhere else, comm me. I'll come get ya."

Markam paid him and understood the earlier remark about the cab fare but still gave the driver a tip and offered his thanks with assurances he would contact him when he'd had his fill of the evening.

Gaudy fell short of describing the décor. Flashing lights enticed at devices Markam had never seen.

Testing various games, he decided on a blackjack table. An hour later, and fifty credits ahead, he moved to roulette. His luck held and he increased his winnings another two hundred credits. Ambling up to window to cash out, a man he'd seen walking around the parlor said, "Not going to give us a chance to win back our money?"

Markam stopped, thought a moment, "Sure double or nothing, you and me. Want to gamble."

That brought a look of surprise and then a chuckle. "Why not? What's your game?"

"Flip a credit. Heads you win, tails I win." Markam took one of his chips from his pocket, ready to flip it. "You can do the honors if you'd like."

By then, a small crowd had gathered watching the two. A few cheers of take 'em mac to beat the bum sparked the action.

"Your credit, your game, you flip it."

It came up tails. "Not a bad night," Markam said. They stepped to the window, got the count and with the house credits, Markam asked all five hundred credits be sent to the Saragosa embassy in his name. He wasn't about to carry that kind of money.

"You'll have to come back. Give me a chance to redeem myself," said the man.

"Count on it," responded Markam with a wide grin. Reaching the door, he pulled out the airtaxi driver's card and commed him.

Ten minutes later, he slid into the bright yellow cab's rear seat.

"Leaving early," he said as they sped toward the address Markam gave him. "Lose all your money?"

"Nope, made a few. Leaving with their money." He related the evening highlights.

"You actually got one of their catchers to gamble with you? Mister, you are one lucky man. I thought you said you weren't much of a gambler. Doesn't sound like it to me," the driver said with a hearty laugh. "Didn't find a woman to your liking I take it? I can show you a place that will please ya." He turned slightly facing Markam.

"Not tonight. I don't want to push my luck. But I would like to have dinner. Know a good place?"

Once they'd agreed the cuisine, the airtaxi rose and sped away. It stopped at a large building surrounded by columns.

"Impressive," said Markam. "I'm not dressed for a place like this."

"Won't make any difference. As long as you don't smell like a recycler, you'll be okay."

"Good thing I'm on an embassy expense account." He left the cabby with another tip and repeated assurances he would comm him when ready to leave.

Once seated by a hostess, Markam, a waiter brought three plates filled with tidbits of multicolored fruits, vegetables and bread. Markam ordered a glass of wine.

Shortly, the maître dé approached him. "Sir, I know this is most unusual, but we are quite busy, and, well, you have three empty chairs and I have a couple waiting. Would it be too much of an inconvenience for them to join you?"

"I would appreciate the company. Send them over."

Approaching the table, Markam noted they were young and made a handsome couple. Both carried themselves like people accustomed to being watched, which many patrons were.

He stood and graciously accepted their apologies for the intrusion as the man introduced his wife and himself as Mr. and Mrs. Edward Branford.

"So you're with the Interior Ministry," Markam said after the introductions were complete. "That must keep you quite busy." It certainly put Markam on guard.

Following the waiter's suggestion, they ordered a dinner of baked fish, Markam had no idea what kind, but sautéed in butter and sprinkled with what he judged as Cullen's answer for old bay and garlic, it made a king's feast.

Dinner went quickly with small talk dominating the time. "This has been a most pleasurable dinner and discussion, Mr. Zenester. I apologize for your subjection to such intense questioning. Some of our people are very zealous and over protective. You must let us make up for our intrusion on your evening. Perhaps you would join us for dinner some night soon." He handed Markam his card.

Markam glanced at it. Startled, he said, "Sir, you failed to tell me you are Minister of Interior."

"Sometimes titles get in the way," said Branford. "I prefer a low key approach. Makes for better discussions, don't you think?"

This man would require cautious handling. Young for such responsibility, he must be quite capable. Cullen had a reputation that suggested only the best made it to the top and Interior Minister, in their constitution, placed third in the line of succession to Supreme Leader.

Markam suggested the invitation be sent to Saragosa's Embassy. As they left the table, the minister's wife asked, "Mr. Zenester, are you married?"

His surprise brought a smile from both.

She added, "It helps knowing about the other guests."

"I'm single and I agree. Very thoughtful of you," he smiled and nodded.

They parted and Markam signaled the waiter for his bill only to learn the minister had taken care of it. Undoubtedly, the waiter received a generous gratuity but he left one as well. Despite the official attention, tomorrow he would set in motion his scheme to learn Cullen's plans as they concerned New Hope and Odysseus.

28: Getting Acquainted

The airtaxi stopped at the address Markam gave, and with assurances he'd use the driver again, sped off into the night. Markam returned to Saragosa Prime's embassy.

After breakfast, he walked into the kitchen, chatted with the cooks and accepted treats. At every opportunity, he made it a point to engage the staff. Crumbs of seemingly meaningless information might prove useful as he developed his plan to learn Cullen's intent where Odysseus was concerned. Most important, it helped keep his real purpose secret.

He delayed visiting the communications installation not wanting to attract unwanted questions. Over a period of a few weeks, his visits to various parts of the embassy became routine. Concerned for his fellow Backlash crewmembers, the embassy permitted a transmission to Saragosa Prime—they had spaced for Odysseus. With the first trip out of the way, his inquires became commonplace as did permitting him to use the equipment.

Approaching his suite, he watched as a clerk drop an envelope into his mail slot.

Retrieving it, he saw the Cullen emblem. Inside, the promised invitation from Cullen's Interior Minister to dinner two weeks in the future.

Markam approached the embassy side exit. "Going out, sir?" said the Marine.

"Got some shopping to do," said Markam as the guard opened the door.

Retrieving an assigned aircar, he began a tour of Celestial City.

Laid out in a tradition pattern with Dartmore House, named after the first Supreme Leader, government offices spread out in all directions with embassy row not far from the center.

Casually, he drove past and toward the local shops. He decided a private dinner required a gift for his hostess and had no idea the minister's wife's preferences.

An hour later, having selected antique wine amber gold leafed carboy demijohn, he returned to the embassy.

Having checked the city register, he signed out another aircar and began a systematic tour of the city and outlying areas, identifying sites that required a closer look, Markam would make a detailed surveillance of those on foot. Of particular interest, a dispatch business. Learning that Cullen did not monitor civilian dispatches, and had a habit of trying to intercept embassy transmissions, gave him the reason he needed. It was time to go to the Off-World Dispatch and check out Darcy Lipscomb.

He pushed open the door and stepped inside.

Drab by any standard, one picture of the Supreme Leader, a global map of Cullen, and a wooden counter with a vidpad for writing out messages made up the decor.

An attractive woman sat behind the counter, although from her plain dress and hair piled atop her head it seemed she had done her best to hide her looks. He judged in her early thirties.

Markam introduced himself as she entered from the back. "I'll be opening a business soon and will need to send confidential dispatches," he said.

She informed him civilian dispatches were usually unmonitored by the authorities. She added that many customers required the same thing and assured him off-world dispatches would be private.

Never taking her eyes off him and seemingly indifferent, she gave him a rate sheet and invited him to use their office any time he wanted.

Returning the embassy an hour later, he learned the Ambassador had received a dinner invitation from the Cullen Interior Minister as well. The invite wasn't just a social payback and the Interior Minister joining him for dinner earlier wasn't coincidence—certainly worth consideration.

Opening the door to his suite, he stopped. Someone had been there and it wasn't the maid—she'd cleaned his room while he had breakfast in the dining hall. Whoever, they were sloppy with the search. More than a habit, he always arranged the dresser top the same way and such that unless they'd paid detailed attention, returning it to his pattern was virtually impossible.

Markam decided the time had come to move out of the embassy.

Two days later, unfamiliar with the better living areas, he rented an aircar, eliminating the need to report his destination to the embassy, and returned to the dispatch office.

"Back so soon?" said the lady.

"I'm looking for an apartment, kinda nice one, not too expensive and I don't have a clue where to go. I could end up in a tough neighborhood. I don't know many people yet." He could have asked at the embassy and hoped she wouldn't question him. "Can you give me any advice?" he asked.

Moving from behind the counter, she offered her hand and said, "I'm Darcy Lipscomb." All the while, her eyes never left him. She returned to the back room and shortly reappeared. "My clerk will watch the place. I'll be glad to show you around."

Cullen's weather remained balmy and she took only a shoulder wrap.

"Do you often take time off to show customers around?" he said once in the aircar. From the corner of his eye, he studied her reaction.

"No. You need help and business is slow: actually I'm bored stiff." She gave him a smile. "We don't get many new customers. Most are regulars. You seem like a nice guy, so why not? Show you around that is."

He cast a glance at her and got only a nod that said behave.

As they drove around the city, he learned she had opened the office five years earlier after her father died. Her mother had died years before.

They toured the more desirable apartments, stopping to inspect some, bypassing others, as they just didn't look right. Markam knew what he wanted but purposely hadn't told Darcy: an entrance that afforded some privacy with his coming and going; ease of observation of anyone approaching and yet denying those who might pry on him the same opportunity. To his question as to why the government didn't monitor civilian dispatches, she told him about official efforts to tail and keep track of a number of desirables and undesirables angered far too many people. "As you know by now," she added, "Cullen has more than its share of bad people, thugs really, who come and go as they please. The government relies on them for a great deal of information. On occasion, the civilian spacers are conscripted to assist the navy in its forays. These dregs know what's going on, the private and secret."

"Forays? You mean when they raid another planet."

"Yes." She didn't elaborate and he didn't push her. Anyhow, the cabby had given him enough information that he had a clear picture of Cullen's warlike attitude.

"How about dinner? All this tromping around made me hungry."

"Like this? I can't go to a restaurant in this dress," she protested.

"Where's home? I have some errands to run while you change."

Markam left her at a small nondescript house. He backtracked to one apartment he particularly liked as it met most of his wants. In less than an hour, he completed the lease under an assumed name and still had time to freshen up at the embassy.

He returned to Darcy's house. Knocking on the door, he heard her shout, "It's unlocked. Come in."

"Isn't that a little dangerous? Leaving your door unlocked doesn't seem like a good idea."

Out of sight, she said, "I saw your aircar coming and slid the bolt. Have a seat. I'll be out in a few minutes."

Markam took a chair that gave him a view of the street. The room was about what he'd expected of an independent small businessperson: nothing spectacular yet not common. Evidence of Darcy's handiwork, mostly art dotted the walls.

Before he could ask if it was her work, he noticed an aircar slide into view at the corner, just enough showing to permit the driver to watch the street—the same maneuver he'd seen while renting his new apartment.

Cullen's Interior Department or Saragosa's embassy? He could only wonder but someone had an interest in him. Knowing Cullen's reputation for disciplining citizens, he hoped it hadn't put Darcy in jeopardy.

As she walked into the room, the sound of footsteps turned his attention away from the window and whoever tailed him.

"Wow," Markam said as she spun around, the dress billowing giving him a very good look.

"Like it?" Dressed in a black, high-necked knee length lace trimmed outfit, the plain looking woman had transformed into a raving beauty.

"Would you please tell Darcy I'm still waiting?"

She cocked her head and said, "It's the real me."

He stood and extended his crooked arm, "Madam, dinner is waiting."

She placed a matching shawl over her shoulders and they walked down the few porch steps.

From the corner of his eye, Markam watched the aircar sitting at the corner. As they drove away, the tail entered the street and sped past. He knew another car lurked somewhere to take up the watch. He would not let them, whoever they were, ruin what promised to be a very fine evening.

29: Being Watched

Markam parked the aircar in the Saragosa Embassy garage and casually walked to the grav-lift where the security officer, Grover Happan, waited.

Taking Markam by the arm, they walked to the center of the large area.

"Mr. Markam," Happan said, his voice subdued, "are you expecting to move from the embassy?"

"Well, that answers a question. *You* had me followed. I imagine there's been a tail on me every time I went out."

"We have and yes, that was our man."

"Not very stealthy. I easily spotted him."

Ignoring Markam's retort Happan drove ahead. "I should not have to remind you Saragosa Prime is responsible for your actions. I ask again, are you contemplating a move from the embassy?"

This guy will keep after me until he got his answer. "When I returned to my suite yesterday afternoon, it was obvious someone had searched it. Privacy is important to me. Besides, even with your admonishment to behave, I had no idea it meant intimidation. What would you suggest?" Markam could only guess where this conversation would lead. Keeping him under surveillance meant restricting everything he did. That wasn't acceptable. He could never get the information he needed nor could he transmit to New Hope under this kind of scrutiny.

Extending his hand, the man repeated his earlier admonishment that Saragosa had to answer for his behavior. He added, "Cullen has people working in our embassy. Take care who you talk to and what you say. I suggest you keep this residence, buy some clothes for your new apartment. Maintain a regular appearance at our embassy."

Markam accepted the overture as a warning but was thankful since it meant approval.

Entering the grav-lift, exiting on the second floor, he retreated to his rooms. Something wasn't right. Convoluted might better describe his concerns.

Someone had him under watch—a Cullen spy in the Saragosa Prime Embassy.

Markam mulled this twist for a few moments. How would he deal with it? Damn, evidently, Cullen hadn't believed his story. That didn't surprise him but Saragosa's reaction did. Could Raybold Penrose have alerted Saragosa? Was it Trekker that followed the Lancaster for a short time as the

Cullen ship was on a vector to its home world? More seemed to be going on than he had anticipated and most important, that he didn't know about. One positive thing, for whatever reason, Cullen apparently didn't know about the apartment. Maybe the Cullen Interior Minister didn't think Markam was enough of a threat to put a full time tail on him. Naive? Markam doubted that. The man seemed too sophisticated to be that easily fooled.

Early the next morning, Markam entered the embassy dining room. He went through the line getting eggs, pancakes, bacon, coffee and a couple of slices of bread. Picking a table near the kitchen door, he sat.

"May I join you?" He looked up at the voice: the clerk who delivered the invitation from the Cullen Minister stood with tray waiting.

"Please," he said standing. "I'd enjoy the company."

"I hate eating alone," she apologized, adding, "I'm Coleen Marin. We seem to be among the few early risers. I never can sleep late. You the same?"

"Markam Zenester," he said. "No, I usually sleep in. A lazy sleeper. I like to take about thirty minutes to wake up. You know, kinda wallow around, stretch, doze, don't want to get in a hurry to face the day."

That brought a chuckle. "I know your kind. My ex-boyfriend had the same problem only worse; he never got out of bed."

"Not around any longer, I take it?" Markam said pausing to take a swig of coffee. It seemed like a come-on but he let it pass. Getting involved with an embassy employee didn't rank high on his needs list. Then there was the evening with Darcy Lipscomb.

"Yeah, I booted him. He had no drive, lazy. I'm a go-getter. You don't seem like a lazy person, well maybe other than getting out of bed. That doesn't sound all that bad. In fact, lazing around might be fun."

"Room for another?" Markam looked up to see Grover Happan with a tray of food.

Motioned to a chair, the security officer took a seat.

Markam had finished his meal and decided he'd better get the hell away from Coleen and let Gordon handle her. "Hate to eat and run, but I've an appointment and can't be late."

"Call me sometime," she said her voice sensuous, seductive.

"I'm spoken for," Markam said. It was a lie but he suspected anything less and he'd be the topic of conversation all over the embassy. He had to wonder if she was the kind to keep a liaison quiet, and quiet he needed. He couldn't have her running around asking when he would be back.

Gordon seemed to enjoy the moment.

Markam leaned toward her, said goodbye, nodded toward the security officer, took his tray to the rack and left.

In his aircar, he headed for the shopping district. With heavy traffic along with crowded stores, it took longer than he'd planned to buy a wardrobe but so be it. By late afternoon, the apartment held the clothes and food he thought needed.

He checked his chrono and decided to call Darcy. He accepted the polite admonishment for not doing it earlier.

"I was beginning to think you were disappointed."

"No way. I meant to call earlier but I've been really busy. But I apologize. It was wrong of me not to find time." And it surprised him realizing he sincerely meant it. The evening had been everything he could want. Well, almost.

"How about dinner tonight? I know it's late to be asking."

"Only if you let me cook for you."

"It's a date. Want me to pick you up or just come to the house? And what time?"

She told him to come to the house around seven..

"I'll be there and bring the wine."

* * * *

Darcy opened the door and he repeated his "Wow. Gorgeous absolutely stunning."

Dressed with a tan skirt and light green pullover that set her deep green eyes ablaze, she invited him in.

His timing was perfect. Dinner was ready and he helped set the table as she brought in a concoction of seafood and what he judged as pasta bathed in a delectable sauce.

Light talk about their lives passed between them, neither asking delving questions.

Later, finished with dinner, Markam pushed back from the table and raised his glass, "My compliments. An excellent feast. As for the company, it couldn't be better."

Darcy smiled, sipped her drink and set it on the table. Without preamble she quietly said, "A man from the Interior Ministry stopped by the office today."

He sensed nervousness in her voice.

Feigning a surprised look he asked, "What in the world for? The way you said it, he must have questioned what I or we were doing?"

Somberly, she responded, "Yes. Quite insistent that I tell him in detail where we've been, what we did. Everything. I suspected he already knew and wanted to see if I would tell him or lie. I told him everything."

"So he knows we went apartment hunting. I see nothing out of place about that. Anyone who's been around an embassy has to know there's no such thing as privacy. That's the only reason I considered it." He hadn't told Darcy about renting the apartment and that appeared for the best. The less she knew, the less danger he placed her in. Even at that, deceiving her didn't please him. Markam looked questioningly at her. "I take it there's more?"

"He wants me to report each time we see each other and what we do."

"Everything?" a faint smile touched his lips.

"I suppose there are some things better not told: most certainly to a stranger."

Surprisingly, her demeanor hadn't changed all that much. She seemed to handle the adversity in stride.

"They have no plans to let you leave and want to know everything you do." Her voice showed little alarm.

Markam agreed and told her about Backlash, the harried trip from Odysseus to Cullen, them detaining him, the intensive questioning, and the Interior Minister dining at his table. He left virtually nothing out including the dinner invitation.

"You must be right. Only something approaching their attack would raise their interest to the level of the Interior Minister."

Markam had to know if Raybold Penrose notified Saragosa Prime and they in turn contacted their embassy on Cullen. If Saragosa knew why he was there, maybe others did. Maybe the Cullen spy had access to their most private information.

"I considered asking you to accompany me to the Minister's dinner but I fear they could decide your interests might not be toward Cullen. You don't need to be tainted with my problems particularly since they see me as a threat." Markam meant what he said as far as concerned Darcy. Being a small business operator, the government could destroy her and never blink an eye. She was nothing to them. He rethought that, in fact she was a primary source of information. Maybe that in itself was enough to ensure her safety. The more time Darcy and he spent together, the less time Interior needed to watch him. Maybe this could work to his benefit without harming his lady.

Through her, he could feed them the information he wanted. Treacherous for her. If Cullen learned of her role, they would see it as treason. If they knew the information she gave to them amounted to nothing but lies—"

"Darcy, I have to contact Odysseus. I need to know just how much information was given to Saragosa. Is it possible for me to contact them through your dispatch office? If you think it will get you into trouble, I won't do it."

"I don't see a problem. So far, my dispatches are not monitored." She paused for a moment and then added, "But that could change, could have changed now that Interior has asked me to keep them informed. And the man did suggest, very strongly, that I keep his visit from you."

Markam considered that for a moment. "Perhaps I can persuade Saragosa to let me contact my home world."

Together, they walked into the living room. He took her in his arms and kissed her. Darcy smiled as he led her to the bedroom.

Four hours later, Markam kissed her again and left for Saragosa's embassy.

He glanced at the dash chrono as he parked the aircar in an empty stall near the guard office—two a.m.

"Out late, Mr. Zenester. Hope you had a good time," the guard said casually and without any implication.

The only reservation Markam had was that he'd not explained his real reason for contacting Darcy. But when he felt the time was right, she'd be told. The man from the Interior Ministry showing up didn't bode well and he needed to be sure how Darcy would handle the contact.

"As a matter of fact, I had a most rewarding time," Markam responded as the Marine waved him past.

At his regular time, he left the cafeteria, not having seen the woman who'd plagued him the day before.

He made his way to the security office.

Finding Grover Happan, he quietly asked about contacting Odysseus expressing his concern that the Cullen spy might have access to his messages.

"That won't happen I can assure you, sir. Come with me, please."

Markam followed Happan into an office. "This room is secure. Once a document is put in here, it stays. Nothing can get in or out without my approval." He motioned toward some chairs, inserted a chip into the computer and waved his hand signaling for Markam to join him. "You can use this but security protocol requires me to be present." Calling up a file he said, "Here's the dispatch we received from home just after your arrival."

Markam read the entire document. "I take it Cullen's spy hasn't seen this." He told Grover his concern that Cullen had stepped up the surveillance of him; specifically what Darcy had told him.

"Damned right she hasn't. Only a handful of people can get into this room. And as I said you can be assured the Cullen spy is not one of them."

Eyeing the man, Markam said, "You know the spy's identity don't you?"

"We do. It may surprise you but we make no effort to curtain her activities. She has access to every room in the embassy except this room and communications. We are well aware of her actions. She is monitored day and night."

"After she leaves here?" Markam asked.

"As I said, day and night," the security officer emphasized.

"Are you going to give me the name of the spy," asked Markam.

"You had breakfast with her yesterday." A broad grin stayed plastered on Grovor's's face.

"Well, I'll be damned. At least I now know." Markam leaned back in his chair. "Okay. Raybold Penrose did contact Saragosa and that information made its way here. That explains a number of actions on your part but not the Cullen Interior Ministry's involvement." He doubted either government would lose interest in him.

"We have people in the Cullen Foreign Ministry. They believe it more than coincidence that Braeden intercepted them and retook Backlash. That coupled with what Trekker did to their ship at Soffett, is in their judgment, enough to keep you detained." Grover paused and added, "Now that you have an off-campus apartment, you'll need some income." He smirked and added, "We won't cover the cost. Got something in mind?"

"Money exchange," Markam responded with a grin. "I plan to get the necessary licenses today and open an office."

Soon Braeden would begin building massive transports for Saragosa Prime to haul fish protein throughout the galaxy and Soffett to transform itself into a recreation mecca, Odysseus would become the focal point for a lot of money movement. That's where Markam planned to make his living. He could discount where the Cullen government had to stick with the official exchange rate.

"Markam, I can be of help to you. Of course, it would have to be kept quiet. If it got out that the embassy was anyway involved in suspicious or nefarious activities that involved Cullen, I suspect we'd all space the next day for home. That is if the Supreme Leader didn't have us arrested and shot."

"What makes you think I need any help? I'm here because Cullen refuses to grant permission to leave."

"Just remember, I'm here if you need me."

Markam suspected Grover Happan, at the least, knew more than he was telling about his presence on Cullen. "I need to send a secure message to Odysseus." The embassy had recently installed FTL communications equipment substantially reducing the time for an answer.

Giving the necessary instructions, the security officer moved away allowing Markam a measure of privacy.

Done transcribing the chip, he inserted it and the message transmitted automatically. Even with FTL communications, it would be days before he would know how much he could tell the Saragosa Prime security head.

He bid the officer goodbye and left the secured area.

Getting his aircar, he headed for the Interior Ministry to complete the necessary paperwork licensing required for his business. Not having found an office and therefore lacking an address, he called Darcy.

"I know just the place," she said.

Ten minutes later, he stopped the aircar at Darcy's dispatch office to pick her up.

She gave him directions and they pulled up at an office building. Another hour and he'd rented a three-room suite.

"That was easy. You sure know your way around the city and how to handle these people," Markam said and added, "Good location, not too far from the Treasury Ministry, good price, nice view, everything a guy could want." His comment wasn't an indictment, just an observation.

"My father owned the building. Well, before he died, that is. His estate handles all of the holdings."

He returned Darcy to her business, and drove to the ministry to complete the licensing.

Early the next morning, leaving the embassy, he steered his aircar into the traffic and drove to his office. He spent the day putting the place in order then called Darcy asking her to dinner. He'd pick her up at seven.

Promptly at the appointed time, Markam punched the pad on her door. "Wow," he said as she appeared in the opening. "That seems to be the only word that fit you. Great looking outfit and what you do for it. Gorgeous, my lady," he said beaming.

Dressed in a bright red sheaf, matching shoes with a pearl necklace, she was a thing of beauty and his words brought her thanks. She handed him a matching wrap that he draped around her shoulders. "Where are you taking me this evening?"

"To the Place de Meze," he said. "It came highly recommended. Know the place?"

"I've been there. It's a good choice. Dinner's excellent, desserts aren't all that great. Kinda pricey as well. You sure you want to spend that kind of money on me?"

"I think you're worth it. As to the dessert, we could make it dinner and have our treat later," he paused casting a glance toward her, "somewhere else."

"Any particular place in mind?" She put her hand on his arm.

"After dinner, you pick it."

Her hand still on his arm squeezed. "I'll be delighted."

Seated at the Meze, (in Greek it literally means little pieces or little bites) the Chef wheeled a portable cooking plate next to their table and diced the prime beef then sautéed it in butter with garlic, adding smothered onions along with green peppers. He then covered it with sauce from the pan. With the addition of Cullen's best wine, the feast began.

With dinner over both waved off cart loaded with tempting treats and walked to the entrance.

"Okay, we still have dessert to deal with. Where to?"

"How about my place?"

"I couldn't have picked better."

An hour later, in Darcy's bedroom, Markam slid the straps from her shoulders and let the dress fall to the floor. He touched her firm round breasts, and then smothered her in kisses. Her tongue slipped onto his as he laid her onto the bed.

"Leaving so soon," she quietly said in a silky voice.

Out of the clear she asked, "Who are you, Markam Zenester. You say I'm an enigma: you are as much of a mystery. Who are you?" the softness of her voice seemed to belie her question.

He stopped buttoning his shirt and sat down on the bed next to her. *How in the hell do I handle this,* he wondered. He considered telling her his real purpose for being on Cullen. He knew the imperative spying required after years of having done so on Soffett and Saragosa Prime.

"Would you believe I'm a guy who's on Cullen against his will? A guy who would leave if he could. A guy who's starting a business knowing it may be years before he gets to leave. A guy who's falling for a beautiful lady and can't help himself." He lay on the bed, pulled her close.

His decision made, he told her why he was on Cullen and about both Odysseus and New Hope. He left out only that the inhabitants carried the long life gene.

Markam's description of what Cullen had planned for Odysseus momentarily took her breath.

"I had no idea," she gasped.

"Where and how did you meet Baskom Wazalewski?"

"Haven't met him." She didn't elaborate.

Gently, he pushed her away. "Are you going to tell me about Baskom? How you two got together?"

Apparently, she was stunned by his disclosure about Cullen's intent. "My planet has threatened to make a cinder of Odysseus?" It wouldn't be the first time the rogue government had destroyed or taken over another world. No other planet had a navy big enough to stop Cullen although Braeden was building a fleet that one day could challenge them. Saragosa Prime had a fledgling fleet but was light years away from being a factor. With the formation of the Federation of Aligned Worlds, most people believed one-day Cullen's rule of terror would be brought to an end. But that was some time off.

Darcy recovered her composure and said, "I don't know how Baskom Wazalewski learned of my opposition to Cullen's behavior. My father was of a similar mind as me. Only a few people knew our true feelings. That's only added to the mystery of how Wazalewski became aware. One day, I received a dispatch from Baskom and over a period of a year we exchanged communications. Finally, we gained enough confidence in each other and made our positions known. I agreed to help Odysseus."

"In what way? I mean, did he ask you for information?"

She looked pensive for a few moments. "Baskom was convinced that once Odysseus's capabilities with electronics became known, Cullen would see it as a threat. He wanted me to ingratiate myself into the War Ministry and learn what I could about their intentions. But then he sent a dispatch that said to disregard his earlier request. It wasn't long after that he told me someone from Odysseus would be come to Cullen, someone skilled in that sort of thing." She smiled knowingly at Markam.

"Do you know Raybold Penrose?" He intently watched her.

"Penrose, no. I've never heard the name. I began to think they'd called it off. Sending someone, I mean." She seemed to relax. "And then you showed up."

"Are you sure you want to get involved on Odysseus's behalf? It isn't your problem."

"I've been an advocate for change most of my adult life. We are the pariah of the galaxy. Every world looks down on us. I'd like to see that change.

"What exactly is it that you're here to do? And what do you want of me?"

"If they plan to attack Odysseus, I must know when. I've got to find some way to learn Cullen's timetable." He knew there was no way he could infiltrate the government, particularly the part that would have the kind of information he needed. He'd have to find someone who could do the job.

"And that's what you want me to do—find out for you." Doubt seemed to crowd her voice.

"I don't know if I should involve you. I don't have enough information and no plan on how I'm going to pull this off." About that, he was honest. Asking her to become a spy would put her in extreme danger. He had no way of knowing if she was willing to take that step, let alone if she had the skills. Spying took a special make-up. Not everyone had the nerve it took to do it, particularly when it came to their own world.

An hour later, Markam entered the embassy. Up early the next morning in the cafeteria, Coleen approached his table. "See you're up early again. Mind if I join you?"

"Please," he motioned toward a chair.

30: The Questioning

Coleen leaned forward and slid a scrap of paper toward Markam. In a whispered voice she said, "I'm free this evening."

He glanced at the note: her address and comm number. Remembering that Grover Happan had her under surveillance, day and night, he had to find some way to say no without alienating her. His earlier assertion that he was spoken for seemingly carried little weight with her.

"Hey, Coleen, I'm flattered with your interest in me." Markam tried to keep a reasonable level of sincerity in his voice. "But, it would be wrong. I told you I have someone who is very special to me." Seemingly as lame as his plea sounded, it was a lie but all he could come up with.

"Okay, but keep that," she pointed to the scrap, "If you change your mind." Her smile suggested she didn't believe him or at the least had her doubts.

Small talk passed back and forth. He learned she'd worked at the embassy for two years, before that as an off-world travel agent on Saragosa Prime. It was that knowledge of Prime that got her this job. Making matters worse, she worked on Prime during the time he was there. Could she have met or seen him? Damn, that was a complication he didn't need.

Finishing his meal, he excused himself, deposited his tray, and searched out Grover Happan. "You wanted to see me?" he said.

"Yes, there's a coded dispatch for you. Let's go to the *room.*"

Clearing the security devices, they entered the secured area and Happan set him at a computer, punched in his own codes and then took a chair across the room giving Markam privacy.

The message, in personal code, he read. 'Grover Happan is cleared to know about New Hope and your purpose on Cullen if you find it advisable, Raybold Penrose.'

Markam sat at the console, one arm folded across his chest, his left hand tugged at his chin.

"Anything you want to talk about?" Gordon questioned.

"Can't say. I'm not sure." So far, only Darcy knew about his purpose. Anyone who knew was a risk, and an anathema for a spy. But the security officer is in a unique position. He heard things and had access to information Markam might otherwise never see or hear.

He made his decision.

"We need to talk." Markam turned to his host. Over the next few minutes, Zenester gave Happan everything, except leaving out Darcy Lipscomb's involvement. He did omit they'd been to bed twice.

"Well, I suspected something, just didn't know what," said Happan, his manner grave. "Asking questions will undoubtedly attract attention and intense scrutiny by the Interior Ministry. They miss few cues. These people have more informants than any three worlds. They are experts at collecting and piecing together bits of information. If it weren't for the bureaucracy involved, I could envy them."

"Cullen is a big place. With a population of over a billion people, how effectively can they track everyone? I think most of their rhetoric is meant to intimidate the people. Keep them in line with threats."

"I hope you don't believe that. They are as ruthless as you've heard."

"Any idea how you're going about getting what you need?"

"Nope. None. But as I expand my business, I'll come up with something. What I need is a well-place contact within the Interior Ministry."

"Dangerous and hard to come by." Happan paused then added, "But there are people."

Markam's head slowly turned. "You know someone who could do the job don't you?"

"Maybe." Moving his form-fitted chair close to Markam Happan stared hard at him. "It'll take your approval and if it were me, something I wouldn't sanction."

"That bad?"

"I suppose it depends on your attitude."

"Come on Happan. Cut the mystery. What's on your mind?"

The security officer looked at his hands, the floor and then Markam. "Your Darcy Lipscomb."

Markam's head jerked up, his body tense. "Shit. No way. She's a clerk. That small dispatch business in no way qualifies her. Come up with someone else." He had no intention of telling Happan Darcy was known on New Hope and his contact. His feelings remained mixed about involving her further and if he let this man know that, the Ambassador would be told. Information had a way of finding its way to the wrong people.

"Maybe *she* should make that decision."

"Why do I have the feeling you're about to tell me I don't know this woman?"

"At least you're perceptive. What has she told you about her past?"

Markam glared at Happan and then decided he'd better let the man talk. "Obviously, not what you're about to tell me. Go ahead."

"Darcy had operated as an undercover agent, and I don't mean undercover like the two of you have, twice—"

"You bastard," interrupted Markam. "My personal life is my own—"

Gordon held up his hand. "If you have feelings for her, that's your first mistake. As a spy, you ought to know better. Take what you need but keep your personal feelings out of it."

"I don't need a lecture from you." Markam realized New Hope, specifically, Baskom Wazalewski would have made that information available to their people on Cullen. He scolded himself for not realizing it.

"Perhaps, but we both know you can't let anything distract you and get in the way of what you have to do. Otherwise, you'll most likely fail and the consequences for Saragosa would be as disastrous."

Markam knew the man was right and it didn't take years of honed practice to tell him so. Years working with aliases, lying, taking what he needed and discarding people was ingrained. This time, things hadn't played out as he had expected. Even though he'd momentarily considered using Darcy to feed the Interior Ministry what he wanted them to know, never had he given a thought to her infiltrating the agency. What the two had shared in bed was more than casual sex but he'd pushed it from his mind until Happan brought up her name.

"I'll have to think about it. I simply hadn't anticipated this or would never have gotten personal with Darcy." This conversation firmed up his resolve, He would not ask Darcy to undertake such a dangerous chore.

"Okay, let me know what you decide."

They left the secure communications room. Markam, angry with himself, started down the hallway without another word. Out of the corner of his eye, he spotted Coleen behind a column watching the two.

Markam retraced his steps and smiled at Happan now standing in the hallway. Turning his back on Coleen, he told the security officer she was watching them and then about her serving on Saragosa Prime while he was stationed there neglecting to add he was spying on Saragosa. He had no idea if she'd recognized him.

Happan returned the smile, slapped him on the back as if they'd exchanged a lighter moment and the two parted.

* * * *

Checking out an aircar, Markam drove to the treasury office and parked. As he stepped onto the pavement he observed that Cullen used very little plasticrete as old-fashioned concrete was much cheaper. In fact, that was very much the story of Cullen. Technically, only their means to wage war, check on their people and those areas associated with both could match modern science. Beyond that, Cullen was a backward world. Few technological conveniences made their way to the people.

He dug into building his business but did take time to honor the Interior Ministers earlier dinner invitation. Darcy did not accompany him, prompting the minister's wife to introduce him to a variety of single ladies.

Over the next year, he established himself as a formidable estimator of the probable exchange rates between Cullen, Saragosa Prime, Braeden, Soffett, and Odysseus. Darcy had moved into his apartment and their lives took on a routine that helped mask his probing into any Cullen action against Odysseus and New Hope.

Entering the Treasury Ministry, he stopped to view the exchange rates displayed on the overhead vid.

"Ah, Mr. Zenester, it's been some time. I trust your business is prospering."

Markam looked away from the board toward the voice he recognized. "Minister, good to see you. And yes, business has been good to me. I may want to stay here."

"Not go home? Well, that is a change. From what I hear, you've been able to tap into sources that apparently give you good insight and have made it pay handsomely."

"Reasonably well, Minister." Markam doubted their bumping into each other was coincidence. He'd learned nothing this man did was left to chance and decided to push it. "How can I help you, sir?"

Edward Branford eyed Markam with a false smile. "You have spent a great deal of time at the Space Registry. Why is that?"

Markam made it a point to know when a ship spaced, where it was headed and if possible its cargo. Few ships ventured into space without publishing their destination, ETD and ETA. If they had trouble, and mechanical breakdown were all to frequent, the prospects of finding them were much better is their course was known. But everyone knew that. What Markam watched for was the massing of Cullen's navy and the armed merchant fleet. If that happened, it was a sure bet a raid on one planet or another was in the offing.

"I make it my business to know when minerals are moving, Minister. It's a good indicator. If a shipment is late, it affects prices. Prices affect exchange rates. Simply taking care of business." Markam returned the smile, a bit unwillingly and that seemed to aggravate the minister.

"Take care, Mr. Zenester. Even you make mistakes." Again, the minister's smile seemed more that a warning—it was a threat.

Trailing the minister by a few meters, they both left the treasury building. Markam got his aircar and drove to the Saragosa Embassy. It had become common knowledge he had another apartment and his appearances at the embassy were not all that frequent.

The Marine guard's salute and grin was welcome enough. "Back so soon. This is new for you, Sir."

"So it is, Corporal. Everything in order?" a rhetorical question. He didn't anticipate anything but a yes sir.

"Not quite. I guess you heard Cullen isn't very pleased with us. Says we're interfering in matters that don't concern us. I think they're worried about our navy interfering with their raiding forays. They sure are a sorry bunch." He ushered Markam into the embassy elevator.

Markam thanked the Marine and got off at the second floor, walked down the stairs to the first toward Grover Happan's office.

"You're nothing but trouble, Markam," said Happan as the two shook hands. "Just got a nasty note from Cullen's Interior Ministry. Seems you spend too much time checking out their fleet movements and they don't like it."

Markam related his brief conversation with Cullen's Interior Minister. "His meeting me in their Treasury Registry building wasn't coincidence. Bastard had the audacity to threaten me."

That brought a laugh from Grover as the steered them into his office. "Audacity? Hell, he could have had you arrested and there wouldn't be a damned thing we could do about it."

"How's our mole doing?" asked Markam referring to the man they'd recruited in the War Ministry.

"He's dead. Now you know why the minister gave you the upcommance," said Gordon. "At least we believe he's dead. It was time for him to report and he didn't show. Wasn't at his home or anywhere he should have been. No one's seen him for three days. I think it's reasonable to assume the worst. Most likely was tortured. May have given us up. From the way Cullen's acting, we should assume they at least suspect our involvement. Things could get nasty."

"I need to contact Darcy on your secure line."

The two left for the communications room.

Markam sat at the console encoding the transmit chip and inserted it into the device. He turned to face Happan. In a few words, he told Happan some of the history of how New Hope came about. He left out they were from New Earth, and that the inhabitants carried the long life gene claiming instead the ship Hope's landing founded the civilization.

Happan shook his head in amazement. "You must have some very sophisticated science at work to have avoided detection all these years."

Markam only acknowledged that with a nod. "Cullen's assembling their fleet. They're pulling ships in from the Galon Sector and arming the merchant fleet. That can only mean Odysseus and New Hope are the targets. It will take them the better part of a year to get it together." The only other possible objectives were Saragosa Prime, The Kingdom of Braeden, Soffett and Galactica and both knew those would not be targets. Take the little guys. Never take on someone who could interfere with their little forays as they called them. A few more years and Braeden would be strong enough to challenge Cullen.

"I need to warn New Hope and then get my butt off Cullen. Darcy goes with me." With the void between Cullen and home, any FTL had to go to Soffett and from there to Odysseus. It would take one T-month for the comm to reach New Hope.

"How you going to pull that off, getting off Cullen?" asked Gordon. "Nothing moves without approval and that includes suborbital pleasure flights. It's risky no matter what you come up with and—I'm not optimistic. Got anything planned or do you not want to tell me?"

Markam assured him when it was time Happan would be fully informed. Of that, he was not certain. What he had in mind might not give him the time and he did regret that. Saragosa's security chief had given him help that put them at risk.

He checked out of the embassy, got his aircar, and drove to his apartment.

Darcy stood in the door waiting for him. "Do they know?" she asked.

He admired her grit. Little seemed to upset this lady, a trait he admired and shared—among others.

Before he could answer she added, "Our cabby stopped by. Apparently, he has a soft spot for us and warned me the Interior Ministry suspected you of spying. He reminded me there's no trial for spies. They just shoot them."

"They suspect us but don't have anything concrete. We'd be locked up or dead if they were sure of their facts. Pack your jewelry, valuables, what you can carry in your purse. Everything else you'll have to leave. As soon as I can put it together, we're leaving Cullen."

"Care to tell me how we are going to do this?" There was more than a brazen tone to her voice.

"You don't believe me," he said, his chin raised, appearance haughty. The truth of the matter, he didn't know himself but wasn't about to tell her that.

He laid out how their behavior should appear to the authorities. "Do nothing suspicious, nothing that would cause them to move against him or her. Not only be casual but repetitious. Do what you normally do. Go to work on time, no detours other than what you normally would take. Be your usual beautiful self," he said tenderly kissing her. "But be ready to go on a moment's notice. We won't have much of a window."

Markam explained that he could get fake passports. It was a lie. He knew they could never get off Cullen acting as tourists.

"Terribly risky," she said. "I'll be ready."

31: The Minister's Fist

"**Mr**. Zenester, a moment please."

Markam turned toward the voice still walking toward the building entry. Dressed in a business suit a man about his height strode toward him. He didn't offer his hand or name.

Markam stopped and faced him fully.

"I am from the Interior Ministry. The Minister wants to talk with you. My car is nearby. Please come with me," the man said. His voice wasn't menacing nor him manner threatening. But it was equally obvious he meant for his instructions to be followed. This was no rank amateur.

"Oh, why"?" asked Markam. "Have I violated one of your rules? I'd think after two weeks of interrogation that you people knew everything about me. What else could possibly interest you?"

"My car, please."

Markam nodded and followed the man. The man said nothing during the trip and Markam asked no questions.

They entered the ministry from the garage, cleared security, and took the elevator. It stopped at the top floor. They stepped into a plush reception area and approached the receptionist.

Markam's eyes swept her desk, an ingrained habit.

The woman smiled and motioned them toward double doors a few meters distant.

Markam's unnamed escort opened one door and together they entered into a circular reception area except there were no desks or chairs. Framed hand drawn renderings, charcoal, and graphite—clay he thought, at least twenty—hung around the perimeter.

Tall glass doors opened when they approached; the escort stopped.

Another woman stepped forward from behind an equally fine highly polished desk and asked him to follow.

The origin of the carpet he couldn't place, but the light blue texture offset perfectly the light golden colored walls.

She stopped at the only door, gently rapped and opened it.

Markam stepped through into the Interior Minister's office.

The entryway was common compared to what he now saw. Items of antiquity sat in niches around the room. Obviously, the Minister had a fancy for history. His desk, what Markam thought of Old Earth, or now the more commonly used Terra, design.

Markam walked into what could only be described as the most luxurious office layout he'd ever seen. Artifacts, most likely take from conquered worlds, adorned the walls between the recessed antiques. He recognized the deep plush rug, with the Interior Ministry emblem woven into it and therefore purchased, as being from Mackenzie's noted rug industry.

"Mr. Zenester, thank you for coming," said Edward Branford.

"I didn't have much choice," Markam said, fighting to keep his anger in check at his treatment.

"I could apologize for the summons, but you should know by now, that's the way we do things here on Cullen. Please have a seat."

"Minister, good to see you again. I take it this isn't a meeting to get better acquainted."

That brought a subdued chuckle. "No, something perhaps less tasteful. Let me get right to the point." He slid a picture across his desk.

Markam partially stood, leaned toward the desk and picked it up. It was of him on Saragosa Prime.

Now Markam understood Coleen Marin's intense interest in him. "That's me. Whoever took the picture should have given it more exposure. Must have been an amateur."

The minister didn't smile.

"So you know I was on Saragosa Prime. I've been there a number of times. Nothing unusual about that, Minister." Markam's senses peaked. Every bit of training and experience would come into play. If discovered, he'd be dead or in prison and no one other than the minister or his minions would know.

"We count at least three trips. What was you purpose there?"

"Business. As you know, Odysseus has contracted with Saragosa and Soffett to supply electronics for projects currently started. That's no secret. In fact, my business here on Cullen is to get a part of the action."

"This," the minister pointed to the picture, "precedes those contracts." His words were menacing, accusatory.

"Contracts don't just happen. Just getting acquainted and then convincing them we could handle the job took a number of trips. After all, Odysseus wasn't known to them. It was one hell of a selling job. I wasn't the only one to make that kind of trip." Markam hoped he sounded convincing. Much of what he'd said was true only he hadn't been on those two planets for that purpose. "It took many calls working with the engineers at Saragosa and Soffett to finalize what they wanted. As I said, it was no small chore."

"And that demanded your presence? My people tell me you are no engineer or scientist."

The minister gave no sign he was convinced. "About your business, Cullen must abide by the official money exchange rate since we set it, and you discount. Undercut Cullen."

"You make that sound ominous, Minister. It is a legitimate business. Happens on all worlds." Despite Markam's concern for where this questioning might head, he remained relaxed and casual not wanting to alert further the Minister. The result of this conversation or interrogation might put an end to his efforts and him.

"Have I broken some law?" That wasn't the issue and he knew it. The Interior Minister did not summon people to his office for petty infractions.

"Probably, but that's not why you're here. I want to know why you are on Cullen. Saragosa's ambassador warned you that your presence was conditional. They are responsible for your actions. Yet, you roam freely about Cullen. You've opened a business, taken a mistress, rented an apartment, all the trappings of someone who plans on a long stay. You've not made any personal inquiries about leaving our world—the embassy has to handle those. Again, Mr. Zenester, what are you up to?"

"Since I'm here against my will, and little hope of leaving, I have to make a living." At least he now knew Cullen was aware he'd rented an apartment and he and Darcy were living together. He shrugged, "You know everything I have done over the last year, sir. There's nothing I can add. The Saragosa Charge dé Affairs told me it would be some time before I would get to leave and that I needed to find a means of support. So I have. As far as why I'm here, the only thing I know is it's because of an indiscretion that had something to do with two of your ships at Soffett and Braeden. And for that, which I had nothing to do with, I'm being detained. From what the embassy has told me, indefinitely. You could remedy that; just let me leave Cullen."

"That isn't possible, Mr. Zenester. I'm cancelling your business license. As we speak, your office is being close. You can no longer trade in the money market." The minister walked from behind the massive desk and stopped a few meters from Markam. "Consider yourself an unwelcome guest on Cullen. As such, you will be given more latitude than a criminal but less than a citizen. Therefore, know that my office will scrutinize everything you do. I do not trust you. There is something about you," he paused and stepped closer, "you are a devil. That is what I see in your eyes. You may be more of a threat to Cullen than any man I know. I shall be watching you very closely." He waved his hand dismissing Markam.

Markam left the Interior Ministry knowing exactly where he stood in the eyes of the government. Hell, nothing escaped even Grover Happan so why Cullen's snoops.

Keeping his efforts, supposedly secret, had taken on a new meaning. If he were to succeed, he'd have to change his ways.

Then it occurred to him; instead of hiding, be obvious. Markam knew what he had to do.

He dug out the card and commed the hack.

"Hey man, I thought you'd forgotten about me. What's it been, two weeks?" said the cabby.

"Nope. And we need to talk." He related what had happened at the ministry.

"Man, you're in their crosshairs. One wrong move and someone shoots you. Without that embassy protection, they'd have shot you anyway, just on general principle."

"Yeah, but all I have to do is make sure they see everything I do. Well, almost everything." Both laughed.

"How you gonna do that?"

"It starts with you." He leaned forward toward the driver.

"Why me?" No surprise registered on the man's face.

"You're a slick bastard," said Markam. "You were at the ministry today. I saw your card on the receptionist's desk. You're one of Interior's best informants now that you've made contact with me. You need to tell those people to be more careful with what they leave laying around."

"So, what do we do now?" Markam noticed he'd move his hand from the joystick to the seat, sure that was where the blaster resided.

"You won't need your pistol. I'm no threat to you. In fact, I'm going to tell you everything, where I go, who I'm with and most of what I do. When I'm with Darcy is off limits."

"I don't get it." He seemed to mull over what Markam had said, the added, "Maybe I do. The Minister thinks you're up to no good. And you plan to use me as your cover."

"Bright fellow. My congratulations."

"I got to tell you, I ain't doing this because I want to. They've got me in a vice. Suppose I don't go along with it?"

"What's not to go along with? All you have to do is haul me around and report to the ministry. What could be easier? You'll be telling them the truth, and you'll be getting two paychecks I need to know your name, though. I can't keep calling you cabby."

"Disdan Weisman."

"Okay, Disdan, what you were telling me about being a spacer, a good engine man, was that true?"

"Damned right it was. I served in Saragosa's Navy. You can check that at the embassy."

"I will. Now, let's set some rules. When I'm with Darcy, you stay away. Clear out of earshot. Do you read lips?"

That brought a laugh. "No, but I may learn just to keep my butt out a jamb."

"Zenester, the minister doesn't trust you." Disdan shrugged, "but I don't trust him either. He says you're a devil—can see it in your eyes. Personally, I think he's seeing what he wants to. These guys think there's a spy behind every post. He says that you were a spy on Saragosa. Were you?"

"Would it make any difference? I always reported to my world anything that I thought would be of interest, particularly if it could or would affect them. I would expect any citizen to do the same."

The man nodded. "Where do you want to go?" All of the humor seemed a thing of the past.

"I'm returning the aircar to the embassy. Follow me."

With that done, he returned to the cab. "To Darcy's dispatch office."

Neither spoke during the ride.

Arriving at the place, Markam told him he'd be right back.

Shortly later, with Darcy in tow, they entered the cab.

He formally introduced the two and told Darcy about his trip to the ministry and the discovery that his intrepid cabby was an informer. Maybe even their star informant where he was concerned.

Darcy let out a slow breath, eyed Markam, then sat back in the seat and looked straight ahead her arms folded across her chest. Clearly, she wanted no more dealings with this man.

"It's lunch time. Drop us at the Village Bistro. Care to join us, Disdan?"

"I'll pass. They have knives in there and I think your lady would prefer to stick one in me instead of her lunch."

Darcy's stare hadn't changed. She'd not moved and his appraisal didn't faze her nor did her demeanor seem to deny it.

Once inside, Darcy quietly said, "Markam, you are in grave danger. I suspect that I am as well. What do we do or more importantly, not do?"

He told her the ground rules he'd laid out with their cab driver.

She didn't seem impressed. "And you expect him to go along with this?"

"No. I fact, it's most likely he'll get fed up and dump us."

Over the few weeks, Markam and Darcy called Disdan Weisman at every hour of the day and night. Often they made up reasons to summon the cabby.

"I give up," said Disdan. "You two are a pain in the ass. No, actually, I think you're good people. Just on the wrong side of the Interior Minister. My telling on you was supposed to be my ticket off this hellhole but unless I come up with something good enough to put you in prison, they've threatened to renege. I've told that bunch they can find someone else to keep track of you two."

"Disdan, something tells me you would do most anything to get off this god-forsaken rock. Am I right?"

"Almost anything," he laughed. The cabby turned to face the two. "You've got something in mind, don't you?"

"Maybe, maybe not. Depends on you." About that, Markam was sure. He needed someone who could move freely and had the confidence of the Interior Ministry. Disdan Weisman was that person.

"You don't know me. I may run to the ministry and tell them."

About that, Markam was also sure. But he suspected the ministry would soon find some reason to arrest him regardless of what Disdan reported.

"Hell, they didn't need a reason," said Disdan.

"Even if it means a good chance to get off Cullen—alive? Maybe your only chance."

"Mr. Zenester, these bastards have every route off this cesspool covered. I don't see any way to escape."

"There is one," said Markam. He studied the man for a reaction.

Disdan looked off into the distance for a few minutes. "Mr. Zenester, I've pretty much given up on the idea. But I can tell you, I'd kill if it meant getting off this hellhole.

"I'm with you. What you got in mind?"

"All the way?' asked Markam.

Disdan looked at Darcy. "Until death do us part." A big grin came with the vow.

"Since the ministry closed my business, I need a job. I'll hire on at the Space Repair Facility. Instead of quitting as a snoop drop your cabbie job and you get hired there also."

"And what does that do for us?" said Disdan thoughtfully. "With your record, there's no way you can get a job there."

"Get me to a computer that's tied in to the grid and my record and Darcy's will get corrected—cleansed," Markam said. "Can you do that?"

Disdan thought for a minute. "Yeah. Risky but I can.

"You still haven't told me what happens at the repair place," said Disdain.

"We leave this place," said Markam his voice like a hammer..

"How? This all seems too impossible," Darcy said, her voice crowded with doubt. "As ruthless as these people are, and as much the Interior Ministry seems to fear you, what makes you think this will work?"

Disdan again turned in his seat. "Ms. Lipscomb, with as many people the ministry keeps tabs on, and with all the snoops doing the looking, people fall through the cracks regularly. They try to make everyone think they watch everyone all the time. But I know better. It's hit and miss. They're not nearly as good at keeping tabs on people as they want everyone to believe. They rely on intimidation as much as real information."

Markam knew the odds were against escape but he had to try.

32: Leaving Cullen

Markam and Darcy walked down the steps to the aircar. He kissed her and gave her a pat on the rump.

Rising a few meter above the ground, he steered away from the apartment complex. He pushed the joystick hard and jabbed at the thrusters as the blast threatened to overturn the aircar.

Gaining control, he swung around spotting Darcy lying on the ground. Fearing the worst he sped toward her. Pushing back the panic that gripped him, he leapt from the vehicle to her prone body. He checked for any wounds and breathed a sigh as she said, "My god, they tried to kill us. The people, the others."

He cradled and lifted her into the aircar. Looking back at what had been home, he knew there was no reason to see if there were survivors. What had been twelve apartments was now nothing but a pile of smoldering rubble.

"Anyone inside could never have lived," he said. "We're getting out of here."

Strapped in, he said, "Looks like we've got their answer. Evidence or not, these murdering bastards willingly kill their own to get rid of us. I'm sorry our living there cost some people their lives but it wasn't our doing. It's this bastard government. It isn't on our heads." He raced the aircar away from what had been home.

"Where will we go?" Badly shaken, she spoke pulling out her comm and told the clerk to immediately close the dispatch office and go home, fearful it too might be bombed.

He steered the aircar into a parking garage. "Come on. Hurry."

They crossed to the other side and entered a skimmer. Markam pulled a small box from his pocket, turned it on and slowly walked around the car. Satisfied there were no bugs to give them away, he drove onto the street.

An hour later, he entered another garage located under a government building.

Darcy stared at Markam. "What is this place?"

"An overhaul and repair station. Fixes parts and sends them up to the fleet. People and equipment move back and forth from orbit at all hours of the day and night. We are going to become some of these techies."

"I have the feeling you'd tempt the government just for the hell of it," Darcy said.

"Hide where they'd least expect us. If you were looking for us, would you look here?" Markam got out of the skimmer, opened a panel and brought out some grey coveralls, shoes and caps.

"Here, change into these." He handed her a small bag. We're going to get off this cesspool and go home—to your new home."

"Odysseus or New Hope?" she asked.

Markam didn't answer her but instead handed her an ID card. "There's a chip embedded. Gets us through the doors."

Darcy looked at it. "Already got my picture on it. How did you arrange that? And how long have you been planning this?"

"The picture? Swiped it off your end table when, about a month ago, I hit on this idea of using the repair facility."

They walked toward the entry some fifty meters distant.

"And once we get off Cullen, how do we get a ship?"

"Haven't figured that part yet," he said as an apprehensive grin crossed his face.

"You, Disdan and me," she paused, "Markam," she paused again, "I don't see how the three of us can make it happen." Fear laced her troubled words.

He smiled.

"What makes you think we can trust Disdan? Notifying the Interior Ministry would be a real coup. Might even get his a sizable reward, maybe even his ticket home. Cullen uses money to buy loyalty."

"No, not loyalty, just service. Loyalty is earned and for his own reasons, I'm convinced Disdan is totally with us. I think he knows they will never give him permission to leave. That just isn't their way."

He'd better be, thought Markam or they would never make it. Worse, prison and he'd heard plenty about the treatment state prisoners were subjected to.

Cozying next to Markam Darcy asked, "What're our jobs? And what do I tell people about being new."

"I'm assigned to the astrogation refit group. My primary job is to test the equipment before and after installation on a ship. You'll be in the gopher group. You get to drive an airscooter. Most of your time will be spent delivering parts and other supplies. Sometimes, that includes going on orbit.

"Learn the layout. When it's time to make our move, getting to where you need to be will be crucial.

Approaching the garage entry, he inserted his card and motioned for her to do the same.

They stepped into a brightly lit hallway blocked by a metal cage. He pointed to a retina scanner. Each turned to faced it and waited.

A green light appeared along with a click signaling the cage door had unlocked. Once through they continued down the hallway.

"Nervous," he asked.

She nodded. "Just a little. I hope I don't make a mistake that will give us away."

"Disdan will guide us through the indoctrination. He'll make sure you get what's needed. Trust him. He's the difference maker. If he gives you instructions, even if you question them, do as he says. Deviation makes you suspect."

At the elevator, he punched the call button.

Both stepped off on the main floor and stopped at the information desk.

Following directions, they continued down the pristine hallway. One thing the government had done was provide first class conditions for the workers. That didn't apply to the general population. Most people lived in little more than hovels: all but the government workers and those few who had the government's ear. Markam didn't recognize the flooring, but it was clean and had a soft texture muffling their steps. Mixed pictures of space, Cullen and other worlds adorned the walls.

"Here we are." Markam guided Darcy into a large room lined with tables. They sought out Disdan and took the chairs opposite him.

The ex-cabby acknowledged both, gave each a vidpad telling them to complete the forms, then patiently waiting until they'd done so.

Darcy looked questioningly first at Markam and mouthed, "Our real names?"

Disdan tapped the table and nodded.

Immediately, professionally, Disdan explained their responsibilities, work areas and most importantly, what was off limits. Under no circumstances were they to attempt to enter a restricted area. That would bring security and that meant intensive interrogation. In a stern voice, he repeated his earlier warning. "Memorize the areas that are off-limits. They're noted on the back of your ID chit. Again, do not insert your card into a receptacle for which you are not cleared." He punched an icon on the table and told them to go to a waiting area.

One of the perks working at the service center meant government supplied living quarters. Since that same government had blown up his apartment, it seemed only right to Markam that they provide another place, even if they were doing so unknowingly.

"Our real names?" questioned Darcy as they made their way to the waiting area. "How? They'll spot us. We have to be on every wanted list."

"We were but no more. Disdan got me access to a government computer and I fixed that problem. These guys are not very technical. Every system they have must have been stolen from someone else. Their computer security is nothing. All references to the government's interest in us, I removed."

Shortly after, a woman appeared. "Follow me. I will take you to your work places."

Markam and Darcy trailed her into the hallway. Quite pleasantly, she welcomed them to the Space Repair Center.

Entering another elevator, she said "fourth floor," where they got off.

"Ms. Lipscomb, this is your assigned area. Mr. Downy is your supervisor. He'll complete your instructions. He's a good guy. I think you'll enjoy working for him."

She and Markam continued down the hallway again entering an elevator. "Basement," she said.

"Your supervisor is Dr. Wilson Davidson. He's not an easy man to work for. Very critical of most people's performance. He thinks everyone should perform at his level. Of course, most can't and that angers him. If you, no when you become the target of a tirade, just take it. Everyone has tasted his temper. When it's over, just do your job."

"And if I meet his expectations? What happens?"

"You'll be the only one," she laughed. "It hasn't happened that I know of. But, I suppose you'd be a favorite if such exists. Think you can make the grade?"

"Why not? If it's never happened before, I can be the first."

"Good luck." She turned into an office, introduced Markam and left.

"Sit," ordered Davidson." He punched an icon and studied it for a few seconds. "Astrogation. What do you know about spatial navigation?" He watched Markam, a smirk crossing his face.

"Ask me a question?" responded Markam.

Davidson laid out a tactical spatial problem and told Markam to provide a solution.

With extreme precision, Markam stepped him through the answer.

Dr. Davidson leaned back in his chair. "Well, well. What have we here? You certainly handled that. Why haven't I heard of you before?"

"I had my own company. Tried to make it in the business world. Didn't happen. Couldn't compete with the government." Markam hoped the man wouldn't decide to dig into his background. The cover he put in the government computers wasn't very deep. It couldn't stand much scrutiny.

Davidson leaned his elbows on the desk. "Maybe you can do the job. Time will tell." He summoned and aide, "Take this man to the navigation section. Put him to work."

Markam accepted the dismissal and left.

After the workday ended, he commed Darcy and had her meet him at the skimmer. A few minutes later, he steered into the parking slot of their new quarters less than a kilometer from the repair center.

Darcy, her hand held to the side of her face exclaimed, "We've got nothing. No change of clothes, no toiletries, what will we wear tomorrow. How can you shave? What about eating? There's no food," she asked.

"There's a government store on the main floor. Let's go shopping."

Entering, Markam quickly turned, took Darcy by the arm and steered her behind an aisle end cap. "There's a man I saw at the Interior Ministry. I can't let him see me."

They maneuvered around the store, picking what they needed and all the time keeping an eye on the man. Heading for the checkout exposed them. Too late to backtrack, the man turned away from them. Finished, they left the store. Had he spotted Markam?

Over the next month, Markam delved into the detail intricacies of the Cullen's navigation systems. Some elements were rudimentary, some archaic. He offered some minor changes that improved a few systems, immediately gaining him another session with Davidson.

"You didn't say you were an engineer. What else have you not told me?" asked the director.

Navigation was one thing and Markam had satisfied Davidson on that count but engineering was something altogether different. "I spaced for ten years on freighters. With limited crewmembers, I had to learn not only how to navigate, but fix the equipment and that meant learning something about the designs."

"What company or corporation employed you?"

"Neither. It was a loosely formed conglomerate. They called themselves the Twelve. Corporations came and went based on whether they had ships ready to space on short notice. There was a core group. We were responsible for assembling the fleet and if they had problems, it was up to us to solve them. Had to learn a lot of different navigation systems."

Davidson seemed to accept the explanation. Markam's expertise had gained the respect of the navigation people, including Cullen's engineers.

Often he was included in discussions concerning problems. Many had come to rely on his recommendations.

* * * *

Some time later, Davidson called Markam to his office, punched an icon, then turned the vidscreen so both could see a schematic. "We have a problem on the transport, Supreme Reflection. It had to be sabotage. That part cannot fail," he pointed to a specific area, "in the manner it did. That only happens when someone tampers with it. See if you can find a way to prevent this happening again. Report back to me when you finish."

For the first time, Markam was permitted to check out a shuttle and go on orbit. Sabotage meant government inspectors and he had to stay away from them.

It took him most of the day to come up with a recommendation to prevent another failure and make the repair. He commed Davidson and told him the results.

With that, just hours before the state inspectors arrived, he returned to the planet and reported to his supervisor, avoiding the Cullen officers. That had been too close. His luck had held this time, but he couldn't let his guard down for an instant nor could Darcy. Questioning by government agents wasn't on his agenda.

On the return to Cullen, he had reported into the orbital master as he did on the way up. They told him the report wasn't necessary, he had proper clearance.

Markam jokingly told the master he preferred to be on the safe side and not become part of the space debris. What he wanted was familiarity with him making the trip. He wanted enough contact that when he made his escape, those on duty wouldn't question him and the get-away would go undiscovered until they were out of system.

33: The Plan

Markam's expertise gained him assignments on increasingly critical systems. Days went by quickly. He took every orbit job he could get, giving himself some cover. He couldn't do anything to help Darcy but encourage her to be casual and alert.

Moving back and forth from the planet to orbit, if the Interior Ministry agents showed, at least he'd have some chance of avoiding them. Darcy didn't have even that. Not much help for either, he admitted, but what else could they do?

At his workstation, he keyed his comm. Davidson wanted him in his office.

Markam cleaned up and left with no idea why the antagonistic manager summoned him.

Arriving, without looking up, the receptionist motioned him in.

"Sit," Davidson ordered. "You captained Backlash so you should know it well. We now have a Saragosa ship and it carries Braeden's engines and astrogation. They are superior to anything we have. Our scientists have finished reverse engineering the equipment. How it came into our possession is of no concern to you. The War Ministry decided to install the engines and astrogation equipment on a new ship just released from the yards, CNS Perilous. It should exceed Backlash's performance when completed. We have encountered unanticipated problems with both the engines and astrogation. There seems to be some unknown interference. As you know, I'm sure you do, the engines can generate unwanted electrical disturbances and those are affecting astrogation. You are to resolve any issues."

Markam accepted a folder, realizing this was the break he needed. "About the engines, Mr. Davidson. As you said, sir, Braeden's engines should have a great deal to offer. I understand you have a man with experience with those engines or at least some like them. I don't know his name."

Davisson punched a series of icons and studied the screen. "It seems you are right. Disdan Weisman and he's rated as an engineer. How is it you know of him and I didn't?" There was no doubt the question was an accusation.

"Heard some guys down in the tank talking about it." The tank was an area that provided near zero gravity and matched the space vacuum required to test engines before disassembly and transfer to an on orbit ship.

That seemed to satisfy his antagonist. With a few more jabs at the screen, Disdan was assigned along with Markam.

Dismissed with a wave of a hand, Markam left.

Darcy met him at the skimmer. "What has you stepping so lively?" she asked.

He didn't answer until he'd seated and completed the check for bugs. "I've got our way off Cullen," quietly he said. "And Disdan is going with us."

"How, I'm sure you'll tell me, but I still can't bring myself to trust Disdan. It just seems too convenient, his change of attitude."

"Maybe you're right. I'll find some way that might tell if he's with or against us."

"And if it doesn't?"

"Then we put the plan to work even if we have to go without him," he said as they left the parking area.

"Really! Just like that. Push the button and off we go?"

Markam ignored the touch of sarcasm and said, "Have you prepared your family?"

"Yes. I've told them what I could. They don't know that I'll be leaving Cullen, only that it may be some time before anyone hears from me. They think we are being assigned to a top secret project that will keep us away for an extended time." Darcy's voice trembled. "I really hate deceiving them."

"In a way you're not. It is top secret as far as what we intend. But I know what you mean." He reassuringly patted her hand now resting on his leg. Cullen had a history of retaliating against families of traitors, which is how they would brand her. Darcy's father's stature would mitigate some of that reaction. Considered a loyal citizen, that accrued to the family. Darcy's defection would put that to the test.

Over the next month, Markam and Disdan dug into the problems that plagued the installation aboard the newly commissioned CNS Perilous. The War Ministry was pushing for completion. Cullen's fleet numbered over one thousand ships but many of them were armed merchants and transports. They didn't bring much to a fight, particularly against ships of the line. Their primary purpose was to carry off materials looted from conquered planets. The armament was meant to discourage anyone who might be brave or stupid enough to attack them.

"Darcy's bringing a shuttle up later today," said Markam. "It's the parts you requested. Should be the last run."

"Yeah. I think I should go down and check it out before bringing it up," said Disdan.

With these parts installed, Perilous would be ready for a shakedown run.

"In the meantime, I'll contact orbit control for clearance," Markam said. The weekend was approaching and sub-orbital pleasure flights would start considerably adding to the traffic.

Markam went to a stowage compartment and pulled out a small package. "Leave this with the dock master."

A year earlier, thinking he'd been invited to a private dinner by the Interior Minister, he'd bought a gift for the man's wife. As it turned out, the invitation was anything but a private affair. With the harassment the man had shown toward him, a little payback jab in the butt seemed justified.

With the delivery chip embedded, Disdan could only wonder who it was intended for. "Sure, any instructions?"

"Delivery first of next week," said Markam.

By the time the packaged arrived at its destination, if all went right, Perilous already have accelerated out of system headed for the *void*. Once inside that that maelstrom, discovery would be next to impossible.

If Disdan planned to sell them out, a better opportunity couldn't be found. "Consider it done," said the engineer.

* * * *

Disdan commed for a shuttle to take him dirtside.

One hour later after clearing with the orbit master, he emerged on the tarmac fronting the repair center's docks.

Inserting his ID chip, he entered the building and headed for the dock supervisor's office.

Spotting Darcy checking the manifest, he changed directions toward her.

She turned at the approaching steps. "Disdan, just in time to help me check this cargo. Of all the times for things to get mixed up, it had to be now. How are things on orbit?"

"So far, good. What's the problem?" He accepted the vidpad and studied the screen. "Have to check with the dock crew." With that, he strode off toward the office. Minutes later, a security guard appeared.

Darcy's heart sank fearing. Had she been right and Disdan betrayed them?

"Ms. Lipscomb, who delivered this load to you?" brusquely asked the guard.

"I don't know. It was here when I arrived. Why?"

"Whoever it was brought the wrong pallets. Anything already loaded on the shuttle must be removed. I'll have a crew take care of it. You need to go into that office." He pointed toward a door.

Darcy did as he said.

As she entered the small room, Disdan motioned for her to join him and turned his attention back to a woman studying a vidscreen. It didn't take long to get the matter resolved.

"Seems we take a launch instead of the shuttle. Let's go see if we can find our ship."

Two hours later, the giant hanger doors opened and Disdan guided the launch onto the tarmac with Darcy in the copilot seat. He let the ship coast to the designated take-off coordinates and waited for clearance.

Minutes later, he acknowledged approval and cracked the throttle gaining lift. At one-thousand meters, he went to one-quarter power and headed for orbit. A check with the orbit master confirmed their routing to Perilous. Not one word had passed between the two since he first approached her at the shuttle. "You don't trust me do you?" he said.

"I'm slowly changing my mind," Darcy responded.

"Can't blame you. I'd have been suspicious as well."

Quiet settle over the cockpit. They had an hour's flight to orbit. "Ever been to Odysseus?" he asked.

"No. I fact, I have no idea where it is or how long it will take us to get there. Do you?"

"Nope. But I do know Markam has squirreled enough food and water on this ship to last a long time."

Darcy wasn't about to mention they may be going to New Hope. But then, she only knew of the place from the one time Markam mentioned it. She had no idea what to expect. This would be her first trip into deep space.

Disdan guided the launch into Perilous's hanger next to the shuttle and cut the power as a worker locked the holding rails.

The three unloaded the cargo. With that chore done, Darcy headed for her quarters, Disdan and the worker set about distributing the parts to the various work groups. A few hours later with all assignments completed, Markam commed the workers and assembled everyone in the hanger.

"It's done. You can return to Cullen," he told them. He designated the one man qualified to pilot the launch as captain and the fifteen workers boarded.

A few minutes later, with the hanger secured he made his way to the bridge.

Darcy and Disdan settled onto seats. "This will be dangerous," Markam said. "It's now or never. I'm ready to go home. With only three of us to man this ship, the risk increases." He had spaced Backlash with a crew of five and that had tested them to the limit and they were all experienced spacers. "If either of you want to change your mind, now's the time."

He waited.

Darcy cocked her head and said, "Why are you asking? Do you want me to leave, return to Cullen?"

"No, my dear. Most certainly, I do not."

"I'm in for the ride, all of it," said Disdan.

"Then, let's do it. Disdan, you're on the engines. Darcy, at the plot console and I'll take astrogation and steerage."

As Disdan headed for the engine room, Markam took Darcy's hand and they walked to the bridge.

Settling into their stations, Darcy cleared departure control under the guise of Perilous taking a short shakedown cruise. Ten thousand kilometers out from Cullen with the engines at ten percent power, Markam commed Disdan. "All the boards show nominal. Do you see any problems?"

"Nope. We can begin to increase the power settings," the engineer said. "I'd recommend ten percent steps for one hour each. That will give me time to make any necessary adjustments.

Markam entered the vector that would take them to the *void* and started the run. He keyed his comm. "Yes, Disdan, go ahead."

"Markam, looks like we've got a couple of passengers," he said.

Darcy's head turned toward Markam, "Stowaways? How?"

"I don't know," he said and left the bridge. "Where are they," he asked into his shoulder comm.

"Right here in front of me," responded Disdan. "I've got a pulser on them."

Markam raced to the engine room.

Opening the hatch, he saw a smallish man and woman sitting on the deck.

"Who are you and how in the hell did you two get on this ship?" he demanded, making no effort to hid his anger.

Standing, the man introduced himself as Wayland Gooding and his wife as Merriam. "We hid on the launch. We wanted to get off Cullen and planned to steal the shuttle—make it to the colony on Cestess Two."

Markam interrogated both for over an hour. Leaving Disdan to his engines, he herded the two to a cabin, locked them in and walked up the passageway to the bridge.

"What are you going to do with them?" Darcy asked.

"Haven't decided. She's a nurse and he says an excellent cook. He's a simulator operator."

As he settled into this chair, the comm came alive. "Perilous, this is Cullen Departure Control. You are on an unauthorized vector. You are ordered to return to Cullen."

"I've picked up two blips on the console," Darcy said. "If I'm reading this correctly, they're ships and headed for us."

Markam commed Disdan and told him they'd been ordered back to the planet. "I need full power. Think the engines will take it?"

"Don't know. Considering the alternative, what do we have to lose? I think I'd rather take my chances with the engines over being shot."

Disdan laughed. The man often used humor to ease tension.

"Okay, I'm going to full power. If things go wrong, use your controls as you see necessary," Markam ordered. It would take one hundred seconds to attain full speed and if it worked, the Cullen ships would have little chance of catching them. Disdan had assured him, no Cullen ship could match Perilous's speed.

34: Going Home

Perilous easily outdistanced the pursuing Cullen spaceships.

Markam left the bridge and opened the cabin door. "Mr. and Mrs. Gooding, please come with me."

They followed to the bridge and sat where he pointed.

"Don't touch anything," he cautioned.

"What am I going to do with you two? I can't let you leave: it's against my morals to shove you out an airlock." Markam had already decided their fate. They would remain onboard all the way to Odysseus. "Your presence does present another problem. Food and water. Perilous carries enough for the three of us to reach safely our destination. With two more mouths to feed, we will have to begin rationing. Did you bring anything with you? A change of clothes perhaps?"

"Yes, our baggage is still in the shuttle. We moved it from the launch. I apologize, sir. What little food we brought was only enough to see us to Cestess. About seven T-days worth. Not very much," he said apologetically.

"My wife, as you know is a nurse, and an excellent cook," he placed his hand on his wife's. "I can do some chores. Neither of us has been in space before so we're not of much help in that regard."

Markam shook his head. "How did you expect to pilot a launch if you've never spaced?"

"I have a manual in my bags. It sounds ridiculous, I know, but I have considerable time instructing pilots in simulators. That was my job on Cullen."

Markam stared at the man. "You sir, are an idiot. Not even an experienced space pilot would attempt to fly a ship in which he had no experience. You and your wife should be thankful Mr. Weisman discovered you before you could pull such a stupid stunt."

Markam reflected on that a moment since that was exactly what he was doing. Not only was Perilous untested as a viable space worthy ship but he'd never flown it.

"Markam," said Darcy, her tone admonishing. "Be kind. They will be with us for a few months."

"Okay." Clearly, he'd vented his frustration with the two.

Opening his comm, he said, "Disdan, Mr. Gooding can assist you in the engine room." Markam motioned for the two to follow him. He gave them a quick tour of the ship pointing out the areas of danger and what to avoid.

Stopping in the crew area, he said, "These will be your quarters." He opened the hatch and gave them a quick look into the cabin. Next, they entered the engine room and leaving Wayland there, led the woman to the galley.

Punching on the vidscreen, the list of provisions appeared. Quickly, he wrote an algebraic equation, "Use this to measure out each person's ration," he said making short work of the unwanted but necessary chore.

Something between apologetic for having upset their plans and pleased they wouldn't be returned to Cullen, Mrs. Gooding said, "Odysseus? I've never heard of it."

Markam let out a breath of exasperation. "Few people have, ma'am."

Over the next month, everyone settled onto their routine chores. Much to everyone's elation, the engines performed with only minor glitches. Twelve T-hours on and twelve off shifts were wearing, but everyone came up with ways of relaxing, easing the taxing hours. By now, on a first name basis, Wayland had proven an able assistant to Disdan. Merriam's cooking was everything her husband claimed and everyone looked forward to meals instead of mind-numbing flight rations.

* * * *

"Rotate in ten minutes," said Markam. No evidence of Cullen ships had plagued them although he doubted they'd given up the chase. Perilous exceeded every operational parameter most especially speed.

Slowed to one kilometer per second, Perilous entered the *void*.

Markam settled into the pilot's seat operating the controls. Darcy had proven a fast learner and quite capable of handling the ship in open space. Markam alone took care of the navigation. An error here could well be their last.

Aided by thrusters, using short-range scanning radar, he guided the ship.

"About a month," said Markam in response to Darcy's question on the time it would take for them to make it through and that was assuming they didn't hit something.

Darcy and Disdan spelled him at the controls after he coached both relentlessly. Avoiding asteroids, some no more than small rocks, but potential disaster if one hit the ship, was not taken lightly. The intensity required to piloted twelve on and twelve off wore on the nerves.

Alone on the bridge, Markam studied the plot. "Someone, another ship has been through here—and recently," he said to no one. He punched a series of icons and called Darcy to join him.

Within minutes, brushing hair from her face, she stepped through the hatch onto the bridge. "I was asleep. Why waken me?"

"I'm picking up a weak distress signal. Someone's in trouble. I need you on the plot console." He pointed toward an array of asteroids.

"All I see are a bunch of dots," she said.

"And they're in a line. A ship's been through here and not long ago. It used an energy cannon to clear a path. Obviously, it can't change its course." Again he touched the plot cutting off all radar and lidar.

He keyed his comm, "Disdan, there's another ship in the *void*. Cut emissions even if you have to shut down the engines." He watched as the engine instruments showed engine cut-off.

"Got something," said Darcy. "At least I think I have."

Markam smiled. "Put it on my plot."

"Lady, you are right," he said scanning the board. "Even with all this interference you picked them up. Good job. They're about a thousand klicks ahead of us. Not very far and just barely moving."

"How do we know they haven't spotted us?" Darcy asked.

"We're directly behind them; out of their radiation pattern. They're blind as hell to us."

"What do we do?"

"Nothing. Well, almost nothing." He again commed Disdan. "Give me everything you can on the thrusters."

Markam turned on the hull forward vidcameras. A ship's hull appeared on the screen as Perilous closed on it.

Steering Perilous to within a few hundred meters of the ship, Markam bolted upright. "That's Trekker. That's our ship. Disdan, get up here," he shouted into the comm.

The engineer came through the hatch. Out of breath, he scanned the overhead screen. "That ship's dead in space. No engines running."

Markam agreed. "Something serious has happened. We're going to board her."

Markam steered Perilous toward the hanger and keyed the comm on Trekker's frequency.

"Trekker, we are a few klicks behind. Open the hanger doors?"

"No answer. I'm putting us on top. Disdan, you handle the grappling hooks. Try not to puncture the hull any more than you have too. Trekker has clamps on her exterior that will permit a secure mating. We have to be outside to activate them. Spacesuits with grav-boots."

Markam showed Darcy how to keep Perilous in place until the two ships were safely secured together. "You two," motioning to Wayland and Merriam, "if Darcy needs help, do exactly as she says."

He and Disdan quickly donned spacesuits and exited through the airlock.

With the ships firmly locked together, Markam opened the hatch and dropped into the airlock followed by the engineer.

Once inside, he activated the pressurization and gravity controls.

Nothing happened.

Disdan opened and stepped through the hatch into Trekker's passageway and Markam followed. The interior was a wreck.

They double-timed to the bridge climbing over massive damage and no sign of the crew.

Markam undogged the hatch entered the bridge spotting six bodies: one still sitting in the captain's chair.

"Raybold. My god what happened?"

He got no answer and eased his friend onto the deck. "He's still alive," he said comming Darcy to suit up Merriam and get her to Trekker.

Disdan met her at the docking bay and led her to the bridge.

"We may be able to save some of them." Markam strained to keep his voice calm. It seemed to take forever but the nurse arrived along with Darcy and Wayland.

"Looks like apoxia and decompression got them," Merriam said. "Their air supplies ran out. Get replacement oxygen bottles on them immediately."

Pulling the emergency medical pack from the bulkhead, she immediately set to work. "I've stabilized this one's vitals. He should regain consciousness shortly."

Raybold's eyes slowly opened. A faint smile touched his lips. "About time you came home. Ouch, I've got one hell of a headache. I don't remember getting hit."

Markam told him the diagnosis.

"What the hell happened? Where's the rest of your crew?" Markam asked. He feared the worst.

"Hopefully alive. We had cleared a path when our anti-matter containment failed," said Raybold in a whisper. Markam got enough of the particulars and motioned for Disdan and Wayland to follow. Over the next hour, they found twenty-eight people alive and helped where they could. Four hours later, all survivors were in secure quarters. Seventy people had died or beyond help, dying.

"Another ten minutes and we would have been too late," said Merriam.

"You did a fine job, lady. A lot of people owe their lives to you," Markam patted the woman's shoulder, now sitting on the deck, exhausted.

Searching the ship, they sealed off all areas exposed to space. It took several days for the headaches to stop but once up and functioning, Trekker's bridge crew took much of the load off Markam and Darcy, spelling them as the two ships, securely locked together, continued through the maelstrom. Disdan tried to make sense of the disaster.

"Seems a fatigue fracture in the containment vessel and when the shield failed, well, you know what happens when matter and anti-matter get together. Good thing the fail safe kicked in when it did. Had it taken a second longer it would have left noting for us to find. One hell of an explosion. That's all I can find," he said entering Markam's cabin. "Nothing more will happen. There isn't enough of the engine compartment that's worth saving. Tore hell out the place. I've cut all power to the area and sealed it off. They're damned lucky to be alive. Nothing but good fortune kept the explosion from tearing the ship in half."

Raybold thanked him and Markam offered the engineer a cup of coffee and turned to Markam, "I need a little favor,"

"Anything," Zenester said.

"Don't tell Missy that I almost died."

"Okay, but that goes on the *you owe me list*." That brought a nod and grimace. Markam had a knack for calling favors at the most inopportune times.

"Disdan, you've not been formally introduced to our President. President Raybold Penrose, Disdan Weisman, engineer."

"My pleasure Mr. President." Disdan added. "What in the galaxy is the President of Odysseus doing in the *void*." Disdan had traveled that troublesome space before and knew the dangers.

"We had planned to mine an asteroid that had some rare minerals we need." With a smile, he looked at Disdan. "Thank you and I'm President of New Hope and I guess Odysseus," responded Raybold.

That brought a quizzical look from the former cabby.

"I think it's time for these four people to know what's ahead for them," said Markam. "Since there's no going back, they will become citizens of our world."

Raybold nodded.

Markam pressed the comm icon on his desk, "Darcy, Merriam and Wayland, please come to my cabin."

One by one, they entered and took chairs, each supplied with coffee.

Markam took a deep breath and said, "All of you have heard the story about the people who left Old Earth, Terra, years ago to find a new home."

"That old tale," said Disdan. "I never believed it. You can hear twenty different versions from that same number of people. Some even say they had found a way to live a long time."

"It's true," said Markam. "The Trekker crew and me are part of what's left of those people. And we do have the long life gene. I am one hundred forty four years old. Raybold is approaching three hundred."

That brought a gasp from Darcy, the others stared at Markam. He gave them the highlights of how they came to be on New Hope, taking the better part of two hours. Raybold had pulled a pipe from his pocket and casually smoked while sipping his coffee, occasionally interjecting a salient point.

"You can refuse the blood transfusion," said Markam. "That's your right. In the same respect, if you want to live another three hundred years or so..." He left the unfinished statement to their imaginations.

The dead weight mass Trekker added attached to Perilous slowed the remainder of the journey though the *void*. A month later, Markam sent the signal that shut down a portion of the cloaking screen over New Hope and they settled into orbit. "We are home," he exclaimed slapping his leg. He hugged Darcy. "We did it." Thanks and shouts of *well-done* went back and forth amid talk of what life would be like for the newcomers.

Eyes switched to Markam and quiet settled over the bridge crew as he took Darcy's hand and to everyone's absolute delight, knelt before her and said, "Darcy, will you marry me?"

Tears ran down her face. "I was beginning to think you might never ask. Yes, Markam, yes."

It took a few minutes for the near pandemonium to end as crewmembers took turns embracing the betrothed. With a semblance of order restored, Markam asked, "Want the ceremony here or dirtside?" still embracing Darcy. "I suppose once on the planet you could have a proper wedding."

"Let's not wait. We have Captain Penrose and these folks are all the family I need," she delightfully responded.

Raybold Penrose nodded his assent, letting everyone know he'd always wanted to perform a wedding ceremony in space and being on orbit was close enough.

Darcy spent the better part of the day preparing herself. It didn't take Markam long to get ready. About the same size as Raybold, he borrowed a suit.

Disdan disappeared for a couple of hours and reappeared waving a ring he'd forged from some exotic metal taken from Trekker and a good sized diamond removed from the master navigation sensor.

Assembled in the hanger bay, radiant in a makeshift full-length wedding dress, made up of borrowed lace, pieces of curtains donated by one female crewmember from her cabin, and a corsage the product of an ingenious person, Darcy made her way down an aisle on Disdan's arm as Markam waited and watched. The strains of "here comes the bride," somehow, someone had managed to get a rendition, played. Raybold completed the ritual and the two kissed. Cheers echoed off the bulkheads.

"Ladies and gentlemen of Perilous and Trekker, I present to you Mr. and Mrs. Markam Zenester."

A few hours later, the on-orbit crew arrived, allowing Markam and Darcy to de-orbit to New Hope.

"I have to brief a delegation from Parliament and the security council." Markam apologized, then kissed Darcy. In the back of his mind, he wondered if he'd condemned these people. People who meant a great deal more to him now than when their voyage started. Cullen could assemble a fleet twice that of New Hopes just by calling on the corporations responsible for most of the pirates. The addition of New Earth's fleets certainly helped, but the technology used against the Chinese on both on New Earth and at Old Earth was destroyed when the Kalazecis destroyed New Earth., No one knew when Cullen's attack on New Hope and Odysseus would come, just that it would.

35: New Hope

Markam Zenester stood at the end of the conference table, his manner intense. "Gentlemen, Cullen is massing its fleet for an attack on New Hope and Odysseus. There is no other world that offers them what we have, namely our electronics industry. They want to be the supplier to Braeden, Saragosa Prime and Soffett. With the fleet to enforce their will, they doubt that those worlds have any choice but to go along." He explained that Cullen had experienced people who recognized what items they should seize completely stripping Odysseus and New Hope, how to identify skilled key people who are critical to electronic research and engineering. "They plan to transport them to Cullen. That has been their way for over one hundred years. They have the Navy to make it happen and a merchant fleet equipped to carry off everything of value they want."

Raybold Penrose listened as Markam Zenester informed New Hope's Parliamentary delegation and recently formed Security Council of the impending threat.

"Mr. Zenester," said the Parliamentary Speaker, Mackenzie Dunston, his manner pompous, "You have been New Hope's nefarious tool a number of times. However, that doesn't preclude your misreading Cullen's intentions. You may well be over-reacting—too many years playing the role. We could waste valuable assets preparing for a war that may never happen. I think confirmation is required. Or we could go to Cullen, send someone," he paused, "less biased to talk directly with them."

Markam lowered his head most likely to keep his anger from showing. He wanted to tell Dunston he lacked the mental tools to question him. He knew only too well his antics had put the man in a position of power for which he was totally unqualified. He'd realized it at the time but manipulating parliament was a challenge he couldn't resist. The satisfaction from having done so, now came back to haunt him.

Markam successfully quelled his rising temper, which, for those who knew him, was no small feat. "Mr. Speaker, I have given you the facts. These are not figments of my imagination. Cullen is a renegade world that has raped and ravaged a number of planets at will. You can assume anything you want, I know of what I speak. Cullen is preparing to attack and destroy us."

"I agree with you Mr. Zenester," said Raybold. "I have sufficient independent verification. We will prepare to defend ourselves. Mr. Speaker, I expect you to use your fine office to move our efforts forward."

The President apologized for the interruption as he keyed the comm. "Yes, Dee. I hope this is important," he casually managed despite the anger roiling in his gut.

"Mr. President, the hospital called and said if you want to be there when your son is born, you had better hurry."

Not bothering to excuse himself, Raybold bolted from the conference room on a dead run.

People scattered even as he tried to avoid collisions racing down the hallway. Taking steps three at a time, not waiting for the elevator, he made it to the capital roof. The ever-capable Dee Shaparov had the helo-car crew standing by and they wasted no time getting into the air.

Minutes later, it settled atop the hospital. The pilot had called ahead alerting the personnel to the president's arrival. Doors stood open with attendants pointing the way.

At the nursery room, a white clad helper held up a swaddled baby for him to see. Raybold stopped, mesmerized, and stared at the red faced, red headed squalling boy, his son. He was a father.

Two days later, he summoned the chaplain to christen Joshua Fossey Penrose. Mother, father, and baby left the hospital to an uncertain future.

* * * *

Pacing the opulent office, the Supreme Leader turned on his Interior Minister, Edward Branford "Someone will pay for this," he yelled. "You told me the man couldn't be trusted. Why was he not arrested? How, did he steal our newest ship? I want to know." Standing, he leaned heavily on his desk, hands balled into fists. "Well, Minister!"

Third in line to succeed the Supreme Leader, Branford did not shrink as he faced Cullen's ruler. He was the one man on Cullen who had the means to keep the man in check. Namely, his police provided the Supreme Leader's security. "I do not have all the details yet, sir, but it appears he was able to disguise himself sufficiently and get a position in our Space Repair facility. His accomplices', Darcy Lipscomb and Disdan Weisman, were instrumental in making good the theft and escape."

Supreme Leader knew of Darcy, more particularly her father had on occasion handled special missions for Cullen. He was considered trustworthy, a loyalist. "Weisman, isn't that the man who you had watching Zenester?"

"Yes, sir. For some time, he was our informant. His information proved useless. His service was conditional, tied to permission to leave Cullen. When he proved unsatisfactory, the permit to leave was rescinded. He quit as informant. Somehow, Zenester managed to get into our computers and erase any mention of the three as enemies of the state and put false information in its place. That made their hiring at the Repair facility routine."

"I want all the details. Now get out," ordered the Supreme Leader. He punched an icon, "What is it?" he snapped.

"Saragosa Prime's Ambassador and Charge-dé-Affairs are here to see you."

This was just the man, at least the ambassador, he wanted. "They aren't on my calendar," he said quietly. "Tell them to go through our Foreign Ministry for an appointment." He detested the man, and his face showed contempt, contorted, teeth clinched, lips apart. Toying with the ambassador gave him a great deal of satisfaction.

"Our Foreign Minister is with him, sir," the quavering voice said.

"Show them in," he said and took his chair.

The Supreme Leader did not offer Saragosa Prime's Ambassador and the Charge-dé-Affairs chairs, or his own minister for that matter. Not bothering with the most rudimentary courtesies, he drummed his fingers on the ornate desk casting a sneer at the man.

"Supreme Leader," said the Ambassador, "information has come to us you are assembling your fleet for an attack on Odysseus. If this information is true, my government protests in the most strenuous terms." Saragosa's Ambassador was not a big man but years in the diplomatic corps had earned him the reputation of a man who meant what he said. Polished, his manner and choice of words were those of a diplomat, and those who knew him understood a will of iron backed them up.

"I must warn you, any attack on Odysseus and Saragosa Prime will have an appropriate response."

"Warn me? What Cullen is doing is none of your business," said the leader. "You sure as hell aren't going to intervene. If we decide to move against Odysseus, you're not in any position to challenge let alone stop us."

He stood, folded his arms, "This Zenester was your responsibility. You are accountable for the theft of our ship. You will compensate Cullen accordingly." He faced his Foreign Minister. "This man," pointing to the ambassador as hate dripped from his words, "willfully allowed this Zenester to spy, to run loose on Cullen. Rescind his credentials. Get him off Cullen."

The ambassador didn't back down. "By treaty with Cullen, we are authorized to handle all matters of interest to Odysseus and an attack certainly meets that criterion."

"You will leave Cullen," said the leader. "Your government is no longer welcome on Cullen. You have one week to close your embassy."

Both men knew Saragosa Prime would suffer as a result of this confrontation. The ambassador and charge-dé-affairs left without comment.

The Supreme leader walked to the back of his office where two men waited in an alcove. "Make sure it looks like and accident," he said.

The word spread quickly that Saragosa Prime was *persona non grata* and the ambassador told the diplomatic community, leaving out little including the Supreme Leader's intent where Odysseus was concerned.

Before the week was out, the Supreme Leader ordered security to stop the stream of diplomats who hounded his offices anxious to know if they were anyway involved. Most, if not all, had faced the Supreme Leader's wrath and worried the issue might affect them.

"I have a chip from Braeden's ambassador, Supreme Leader," said the aide. He too had faced the man's temper and not wanting to be the next casualty, stood in the partially open door.

"And?" his smirk reappeared.

"It says, 'Want to try us?'"

Cursing, he pressed his finger against an icon. "Close the Braeden embassy. I want them off the Cullen immediately!" It was a decision the man would regret.

The day before Saragosa's ambassador was scheduled to leave Cullen, in his palace watching the vid news, Supreme Leader inwardly applauded.

'Quite mysteriously, Saragosa Prime's Ambassador and Charge-dé-affairs died in separate aircar crashes. The Interior Ministry has launched an investigation.' Another decision the Supreme Leader could add to his list of regrets.

"Tell the War Minister I want to see him immediately." He released the icon and sat heavily. He had overreached and put Cullen at risk. Deep down, he feared the worst. Saragosa alone wasn't a concern but having Braeden as an enemy and Saragosa, could be problem for Cullen.

Shortly, Hiram Phazen arrived. Large and swarthy, the man presented an imposing image that backed up his reputation for aggressive battle plans.

"Sit," said the Supreme Leader. "You know what's happened over the last few days. I may have given you a problem; one we didn't need."

"Braeden is a problem. However, we have confirmed information that requires a complete change in our thinking. It seems there is more to that part of space than Odysseus." Phazen outlined that their ship had tailed Penrose's ship, Trekker after he had disrupted their electronics at Soffett.

There was a major anomaly in the region. Comparing information from other sources, they now knew the disturbance was caused by a cloaked planet. Their battle plan would have to include New Hope.

"Another planet?" exclaimed the Leader and sat as if thrown into his chair.

"Not just another planet, sir, it is *the* planet. It's about a parsec from Odysseus on the other side of the *void*. As I said, it's cloaked and apparently, with technology well beyond anything we possess. Originally populated with people from New Earth. A bunch of smart bastards. I've not had time to fully understand the impact, but it doesn't appear in our favor."

He stopped to give the Supreme Leader time to consider what he'd said.

He flicked on a small notevid and studied if for a few moments. "Braeden has over four hundred battle ships. They can commit one hundred. It would take six T-months to recall the rest as they are assigned to outposts. And not all are ships of the line. Along with the few Saragosa's can offer, they could challenge us at Odysseus and New Hope." He explained that protecting the merchant transports was a major problem. "Once we committed the fleet against the planet, the transports would be unprotected and vulnerable," he added in a steady voice.

"Yes, I'd say alienating Braeden gives my fleet a problem that will haunt us."

Phazen, as next in line for Supreme Leader had shown little interest in leading Cullen. He was a spacer and made no bones about wanting to stay in his job. That in itself made him a favorite of the Supreme Leader.

"Are there any markers we can call in? What about Cestess? Don't they owe us? If not, just lean on them. They have a few ships."

"I have contacted several of my counterparts, including Cestess. Their offers have been miniscule to say the least. Supreme Leader, other than the merchants and transports we have conscripted, Cullen is in this one on our own." Phazen's reputation left little room for the Leader to argue. The man would push every world that he thought could help to the maximum. Few would have denied him, fearing retribution."

"Supreme Leader, your kicking Braeden off Cullen was of no consequence. They would have supported Saragosa and Odysseus regardless. As you know, Braeden is and has been aggressively building its fleet. This day was bound to come. Cullen should not be surprised that some worlds are prepared to stand against us. We cannot deny our actions have earned us the wrath of many worlds."

"You disagree with our way, taking what we want."

"It isn't a matter of disagreeing, Leader. I am a pragmatist if nothing else. Kick enough people and one day you will meet someone who kicks back. And we have kicked many."

The leader eyed his minister with a look that bordered on disgust. "You think we will lose this war." Anger filled his words. If the man finally realized the severity of what they faced, he wasn't allowing it to show. Getting to be Supreme Leader did not come easily. The loss of a few more was of little consequence.

"As I said, these two worlds will have two hundred ships of the line to bring against us. Our fleet out-masses and outguns them, but New Hope has that damned stealth technology. That gives our enemy a distinct advantage in their initial attack. Once they engage, they lose that ability. Our test will be to survive that short period, then we have the advantage in numbers and superior firepower—unless New Hope has more forces than we're aware of. I would prefer they not abandon Odysseus. That would require them to divide their forces defending New Hope and Odysseus, but a good strategist will not do that. Our sources on Braeden tell me Barrymore will recommend Admiral Rawlings to head up the defense. I know the woman. She will sacrifice Odysseus and concentrate her forces. We will take maximum damage. Conservatively, we will lose all of the transports and possibly half out fleet."

Supreme Leader scuffed his shoe across the deep piled rug. "You think I should cancel the attack."

"Sir, win or lose, Cullen will be a second rate navy if we go ahead with this attack."

"You make that sound inevitable, Minister."

"I shall personally lead the fleet and do what's possible."

"If anyone can prevail, it is you. Once you've set your order of battle, let me know," said the Leader.

After Hiram Phazen left, the leader again punched an icon. "I need to see you."

He wasn't ready to concede a loss.

An hour later, a solemn faced man sat in front of the Supreme Leader. After a shortened briefing of the impending raid on Odysseus and New Hope, he stood. "Make sure the fleet doesn't quit the fight." The man nodded and left.

36: Preparing for War

"**Come** walk with me, Markam," said Raybold. They made their out of Government House and entered a grove of well-manicured flora.

"This is new. I like it," Zenester said. "Who's handiwork?"

"The wife's. She's always wanted an arboretum and got tired of waiting on me to put it together. Shows you what can be done, particularly if you lean on the ship captains calling on Odysseus to bring specimens from different planets." The President's voice carried a tone of satisfaction.

Markam picked up on the man's wistful words. "Mr. President, you didn't bring me out here to see the trees and shrubs."

Raybold stopped and faced his friend. "I want to appoint you to parliament. There's an opening and we need a voice that understands what New Hope faces. I fear the Speaker doesn't take your warning seriously."

"And?"

"You know me too well. Maybe this isn't a good idea."

"And?"

"Run for speaker. Mackenzie Dunston is not the man we need in that job."

"I knew it. You want me to undo what I did a couple of years ago. You never do something without a reason lurking out there somewhere." These two had known and worked together for over fifty T-years. Little happened that in some way didn't carry their mark—certainly their tacit approval.

Two days later, Markam settled the aircar to the ground and left it to the parking attendant. It took a few minutes to clear security and Dee showed him into the President's office.

"What happened?" asked Raybold motioning toward a chair. "I understand there were hard words."

Markam sat, relaxed with a grin. "I must say, Dunston tried. Want to hear it all?"

"Word for word." The Speaker had been an irritant for over two years and this could be the salve Raybold needed or couldn't resist.

"The Speaker raised up on his toes, I'm taller than he is, and barked at me, '"Mr. Zenester, we've had our differences. I know you have the President's ear but I trust that will not be an impediment to our working together. I have an agenda that needs the attention of parliament and I intend to bring it to fruition.' Markam had seen and studied the Speaker's upcoming proposals. Really, it wasn't all that bad, new schools, parks, recreation areas and a new university: all good ideas but not when annihilation faced New Hope.

"I asked him, what about the President?"

"The guy became flustered." 'What about him? If you're referring to your assertion Cullen will attack us presentation, well, let's say I still believe with Braeden offering their navy to protect us, Cullen will reconsider. After all, they are not fools."

"I agreed but told him I believed he was. Then I said I would oppose him."

"A new member against the power of the speaker—it will be no contest."

"I told him he didn't understand. I said I would run against him for Speaker." Under New Hope's constitution, any member of parliament could challenge for the speaker's chair.

"I never saw anyone so startled. But not for long. He lashed out," 'Preposterous. Do you think for a minute that these trusted members of parliament would support you? You sir, are delusional. I look forward to thrashing you."

"I told him I put him in that office, and I would take him out," Markam said.

"He told me to leave. I of course agreed. He didn't offer to shake hands.

"I walked into the *well* where a number of well-wishers congratulated me—many of them in fact. I spotted the Speaker watching from his partially opened door, nodded and proffered my biggest smile."

Raybold thanked Markam and the man left. A short time later, as the President strode from his office, there was a notable bounce in his step. Purposely, he would avoid all Members of Parliament while Markam worked to become Speaker.

Those members of Parliament who had been a part of Markam's *little joke*, as he called it, electing Mackenzie Dunston Speaker, were ready and willing to make the change. Two months after his swearing in as a Member of Parliament, Markam Zenester faced the High Court Justice and took the oath as New Hope's Parliamentary Speaker. Following the resounding defeat, Mackenzie Dunston, to most members' satisfaction, resigned his seat.

"Congratulations on your election," said Raybold. "Had time to get yourself organized?"

"Yes, Mr. President. Dunston may not have been an effective leader, but he was a capable administrator. I had little organizing to do. Changed aides, but that was about it."

Preparations for war moved quickly. Raybold ordered New Hope's ship stealth technology be sent to both Braeden and Saragosa Prime. All agreed: if you can't find a ship, you couldn't shoot it. Every available scientist and engineer assembled energy cannons. Raybold cheered their efforts but secretly suspected they were in vain. If Cullen decided to make this a winner take all fight, they simply had too much firepower, weapons that from low orbit could wipe out every living thing on the surface.

"Markam, Braeden's Ambassador along with the Saragosa Prime Naval representative will arrive shortly. That's why I asked you to come. I want you to set in on the meeting. We have less than a T-year to prepare out defenses. Not much time I'm afraid. I've appointed Bev Rawlings our Minister of Defense. I know she's new to us, but comes highly recommended."

Confirmation that Cullen planned an attack came late, not that it would have made much difference. The addition of Saragosa Prime's ships meant Cullen would still have the advantage of mass and firepower but it wouldn't be a walkover. If New Hope achieved a stalemate, they could consider it a victory. It took years to build the kind and size of fleet that could oppose Cullen, not to mention a great deal of credits. Even New Hope's political and governmental infrastructure was unprepared and lacked the expertise for a full-fledged war. Rounding up enough people to man the ships would be an even bigger chore.

"I've not met her. I thought I knew everyone who had any say so around here."

"She's from Braeden. I guess you can say I borrowed her, well, at least her services from Braeden. She's a full admiral, got shot up in a scrap. In a gravchair: injuries were beyond regeneration. But it hasn't affected her mind. I understand she's a first rate strategist. And no, she doesn't know about the long life gene. Even if she did, her age would keep it from doing her any good."

"And the Kingdom felt they could spare her?"

"Yes. Barrymore believes Cullen must be stopped and he's determined to make it happen. He has a high regard for her abilities and believes that her involvement can make a difference. I'm confident she can help us."

"Works for me. When do I get to meet her?"

Raybold punched an icon and asked Dee to show the officer in.

Admiral Bev Rawlings entered the office in her gravchair. Markam stood to greet her. After they exchanged pleasantries, Dee commed that the Ambassador and Naval attaché had arrived.

Shortly, they entered. Raybold thought he could have picked out both men in a crowd.

Ambassador Derrick, tall and regal, looked every bit the part, as did the naval officer. He nodded to Admiral Rawlings as did Saragosa's Attaché, also a full admiral. "Beverly, it's very good to see you again. I trust matters are going well for you."

"A well as can be expected, Ambassador. This contraption does allow me to be of some use. How is your brother?"

"The King is well and sends his regards."

That did answer a number of questions for Raybold. The ambassador was somewhere in the line of succession to the throne.

"He asked that I remind you of the fifty credits you still owe him from the last poker game."

She smiled. "I always honor my debts. Please inform the King of such."

The ambassador nodded.

"Gentlemen, please." Raybold motioned to the chairs and took his seat.

Before taking a chair, Ambassador Derrick stepped toward Raybold and handed him his credentials bound in a blue felt textured folder with the gold Braeden royal crest emblazoned on the cover. "King Barrymore extends his hand in friendship. Braeden is pleased to be allied with your world. We are acutely aware that Cullen represents a formidable enemy not only to New Hope and Odysseus, but to Braeden and Saragosa Prime as well. It makes sense for us to combine our efforts."

"Ambassador, Admiral, New Hope is indebted to you. This isn't your fight—"

"Pardon the interruption, Mr. President but it is most certainly in our interests to stop this unwarranted aggression. We," he motioned to toward Saragosa's attaché, "have committed to doing what is necessary to put a stop to this bunch of butchers. Not to mention, New Hope's ability, no the advances you offer in technology must not fall into these scurrilous hands."

"Thank you, Ambassador," Raybold said. "We fully understand the threat these people represent and our acceptance of the blood offering from both worlds puts us in your debt."

"To the matter of who runs the war" Raybold said ready to move on. "Admiral Rawlings certainly is qualified and I have complete confidence in her taking the reins."

"Good, we are of the same mind. But you should know, having her around is not without risk."

Raybold's quizzical look prompted the ambassador to continue.

"Admiral Rawlings is a formidable poker player. Are you familiar with the ancient game called Texas Holdem'? If not, either learn or reject any attempts she may offer to have a game with you."

"Ambassador, how could you be so cruel?" said the Admiral. "We've known each other for thirty T-years. Have I ever cast you in a bad light? Perhaps I should let the President learn that in certain circles it's known that you have a bad habit of extraneous pegging in Cribbage matches."

"That is nothing but unwarranted gossip," said the Ambassador his chin raised as he stared at the ceiling.

Raybold laughed and slapped his desk. "You two are better acquainted than I was led to believe. But you have given me fair warning and I intend to make good use of it."

"Perhaps we should get to more serious matters," said the ambassador. He added, "Before anymore slanderous accusations are offered."

With the levity put aside, matters turned to the upcoming war with Raybold leading the discussions.

Markam gave what information he'd gleaned while at Cullen's space repair facility. "Cullen's technology is second class, mostly what they've looted. And they've done little to improve upon it with the exception of shielding their electronics. Those systems they have tried to shield. They don't want a repeat of what our President did to their cruisers at Soffett and Braeden. Their scientists are fearful of changing anything. And the engineers seemed of the same mind. Their Supreme Leader is very unforgiving if something doesn't work. But don't sell them short. The war minister is ruthless and demands the same from his admirals."

"Mr. Zenester, what effect will their beefing up the electronics have on our using this device?" asked Admiral Rawlings.

"We call it a disrupter," Markam informed them. "No way to tell unless we make a mock-up and run some tests. What concerns me more is if they figure out that all they have to do is shut down their electronics. Come in-system hot and before they get in range of our disrupters, shut down everything and coast to the launch point. Their missiles are not affected so they can still get them off."

Markam's remarks brought a pause. Raybold said the engineers would run the necessary tests to determine the effect of New Hope's electronic disrupter.

Looking at a vidpad, and then Raybold, Admiral Rawlings asked, "About the screens. What kind of punishment can they withstand?"

"Thirty-two separate generators feed the screens and each overlapped handling three sectors," he responded. "To shut down a section required all three generators be off line simultaneously," he added. "However, if they hit a sector with enough energy, it will shut down long enough for missiles to penetrate and get to the surface. It won't take them long to figure that out."

Markam remarked that Cullen's missiles were limited to fifty thousand kilometers effective range. Beyond that, targeting remained happenstance although, if they targeted the planet, it would be impossible to miss.

Both Admirals agreed they had to engage the enemy fleet well before they could employ their cannons. They would take it to them at one million kilometers.

"Around Odysseus, we have five hundred energy cannons in near orbit, ten thousand kilometers, here surrounding New Hope, one thousand at the same distance," Raybold said pointing to an area on the plot.

"Odysseus is virtually indefensible," said Rawlings.

Raybold winced at her words.

"I suggest we set our defenses for New Hope. Move all those weapons," she said eyeing the President's reaction. "Sorry, Mr. President, but that's the way I see it."

Raybold nodded but beyond that gave no indication of his concerns.

"Once Cullen masses for an attack on either location," Rawlings continued, "which I think they will do, that will leave us free to attack with our entire force. With our ships in stealth, Cullen won't know our defensive strategy until we counterattack. That gives us an edge during the opening minutes of hostilities and we must make the most of it."

"Once the enemy commits to the attack, I suggest we take out their transports with fighters. They may leave some ships, probably destroyers, maybe a cruiser to provide protection but we can deal with that."

Saragosa's naval attaché recommended a few minor changes, which Rawlings quickly incorporated. It was apparent they had a great respect for what each brought to the table.

"How do you see their attack commencing," asked Raybold.

"If it were me, I'd hit Odysseus first," Rawlings responded. "I would enter the system on a vector that would do two things. Allow a maximum missile launch without slowing, hit them with everything I could bring to bear and keep going. Then, on that same vector, jump to hyperspace for New Hope. Wouldn't wait long enough to see the effect of my barrage. Such a broadside should overwhelm Odysseus's shields and once breeched, the following missiles would have the opening they require. That should completely destroy the orbital factory." Almost anticlimactic she said,

"One broadside." Saragosa's attaché nodded in agreement.

"New Hope's a different story. After attacking Odysseus, they have to reload their missile tubes. While one firing won't deplete their onboard stores, a second one will. They have to replenish. That means their transports come into play. It takes almost five hours to transfer that many missiles. That's when we should hit them. We'll be in stealth mode, so they shouldn't see us coming. Our fighters will attack the transports, leaving the battleships, and cruisers to attack their main fleet. Our destroyers will provide cover for the carriers and take any strays." She paused and added, "Bear in mind, Cullen has never faced an opposing fleet when raiding other worlds. So we have no real experience about their tactics. But that works both ways. They have no experience in a slugfest. But then, nor do we. It could be a free for all."

The two admirals summed up their thinking on how the attack might come, and New Hope's response. The discussion centered on strategy and tactics, sometimes heated with an occasional argument. Matters well beyond Raybold and the ambassador's tactical understanding left them sitting silently.

Finally, they came to a meeting of the minds and Raybold suggest they break for dinner.

All readily agreed.

As they left the conference room, Ambassador Derrick guided Admiral Rawlings gravchair. She looked up at him and smiled. The two joked back and forth but clearly, their mutual respect was evident and they made no effort to hide it.

In Raybold's private quarters, his wife and Darcy joined them for dinner. The atmosphere remained solemn despite Darcy's attempts to change the talk away from the impending war. This was a somber gathering.

37: The War

Hiram Phazen stood on the bridge of CNS Dreadnought and keyed the comm, "Supreme Leader, we await your command to space for New Hope." He removed his finger from the plot and waited.

"Proceed, Minister. I know you will be victorious. Cullen has never lost and we both agree this little joust will be no different."

Phazen released the comm icon and pensively gazed at the blank view screen. Not one given to speeches, he knew this foray, as the Supreme Leader described it, was different. He said, "I shall address the fleet."

That brought head around. Men who had served with him for years stood silent. In earlier raids, all they have ever heard the War Minister say was 'attack'.

"Men and women of the Cullen Navy. Today we space for a world called New Hope. Emigrants from New Earth originally populated it. These people will not be easy to defeat, but I'm confident you will do your usual best."

None knew the minister's true thinking—most of them and their ships would not survive this raid to return home.

"Saragosa Prime and the Kingdom of Braeden have joined with New Hope. Braeden's navy is formidable. They are first class fighters in first-rate ships. But the defending fleet must wait until they can see our opening tactics. That is to our advantage. Our first salvo will cause confusion, as they must then position their ships. We will make use of that and strike while they align their fleet for a counterattack. "We shall be victorious.

"Admiral, get the fleet underway." He closed the comm and without another word, left the bridge.

Admiral Ephram Lowry, sitting in his command chair, stood, stepped to the comm console foregoing the control on his chair, motioned the operator to key the mike, waited as the bo's'n piped, 'pass the word' and spoke, his voice commanding, "Captains, set your course for New Hope and engage at thirteen hundred." He returned to his chair.

Dreadnaughts' bridge design, a straight line of consoles', had not changed in all the years he'd spaced. Entry hatches behind and to the sides provided access from the ship's main passageways. A center hatch led to his 'underway cabin'. It would take ten T-hours for the entire fleet to align for the jump to hyperspace. Allowing for the slower transports and going around the *void*, passage to New Hope would take five T-months.

Admiral Lowry touched the icon. "Yes, Minister."

"Join me in my cabin when you have a moment."

"On my way, sir. Captain, you have the bridge."

Exiting through a side hatch, he briskly walked the few meters to the minister's cabin, pressed the stud and receiving the okay, entered.

"You wished to see me, Minister?"

"Yes, Admiral. Please be seated."

Less than plush but better equipped than any other cabin on the ship, the furnishings were quite nice. Form-fit chairs, a bar, all within easy reach of a large wooden desk sitting on one of Mackenzie's finer short pile rugs gave the appearance of a dirtside office.

"Coffee?" He motioned toward the bar.

Lowry nodded, fixed a cup and returned to his chair. He waited as the Minister looked at him with eyes that seemed ugly, frustrated.

"Ephram, I am about to lead our Navy into a battle that may be very costly. We could even lose."

It was the first time the Admiral could recall that the Minister had called him by his first name and certainly, the first time the man had ever admitted possible defeat.

With that the minister stood, leaned on the desk. "I should have told our Supreme Leader, no. But I didn't. Maybe I'll be lucky enough to get killed."

"Minister," chided the Admiral, "if you don't make it, that means I most likely won't. And sir, I'm not ready to go. There are things I still wish to do. Many things in fact." To say he questioned the Minister's words didn't quite measure up. In fact, his experience with the man was just the opposite. Tough, unyielding, 'giving no quarter' were words most people, including him, used to describe the aging Minister. This was the first time he'd ever spaced with the man. Previous, encounters, and there had been many over the years, were always in formal settings. Admiral Lowry suspected he knew the reason.

"Yes, of course. Forgive my outburst. Braeden's Navy is quite capable of doing great damage. With Beverly Rawlings in command, we must expect the unexpected. She is a brilliant strategist. I do not sell her short nor should you."

"I've studied her campaigns, Minister. She does seem to have preferences, maybe even habits that we can exploit."

"Yes, yes, I know. But my thoughts are on Odysseus and New Hope. Once we are in system, all she has to do is watch, see how we form up and once we commit, pounce on us. The advantage goes to her. I had a chance to shoot the woman a few years ago and chickened out. Should have done it."

"All isn't lost, Minister. Our order of battle is thorough, covers multiple contingencies. We've beefed up the electronics on all ships including the transports to avoid another occurrence like happened at Soffett and Braeden. Our captains and crews have trained for over a T-year and since learning of New Hope's existence, adjusted our plan to make maximum use of our assets. We will deliver as good as we get. I am not overly confident, but satisfied of the outcome."

"I've given more thought to how we are using our missile sleds."

"Sir, we've minimized their application as the time it takes to reload only puts out supply ships and those ships replacing their missiles at greater risk. Granted, it gives us considerable fire power, but once expended, they become a liability."

"Admiral, I want the order of battle changed."

"At this late date, sir? Our fleet will need time to prepare."

"Don't think so. At least not for what I have in mind. We'll enter the system at sub-light speed on a vector that passes Odysseus and one that will also take us directly to New Hope. That will add some transit time but should be well worth it. At Odysseus, We'll deploy half the sleds. Once in missile range, we fire them all simultaneously, reel them in and jump to hyperspace for our next target, New Hope. That will give us ample time to reload the sleds minimizing the exposure to our resupply ships."

"Then you must believe our missiles can take down the screens surrounding Odysseus."

"I'm counting on it. I find it hard to believe that electronic shields can withstand such a devastating attack."

Admiral Lowry wanted to say the idea was untested and too risky but kept quiet.

"We can use something similar at New Hope. Except, instead of a broadside, our vector past Odysseus will be just that, we deploy the sleds for the initial attack. Let them take out the shields. And then our battleships and cruisers can carry the fight to the planet. We can tuck the transports in and around, close enough that resupplying will be faster as will the time to get our troops dirtside to get the equipment and personnel we came for. With ten thousand Marines, it shouldn't take too long."

"Six thousand Marines, the rest are mercenaries. A rough lot I might add. I think this is the worst bunch we've ever commanded." Lowry didn't try to hide his dislike for using hired guns. At least Cullen's Marines responded to discipline. The private army they'd hired made the same claim but it was only that. "These people were some of the worst."

The minister ignored his remark. "Change the order of battle accordingly, Admiral."

"Aye, sir." Lowry stood, "by your leave."

"You don't agree with my thinking."

"It's untested, sir. That makes me nervous."

"As you should be but it will work." What went unsaid: it had to work.

As Admiral Lowry left, he at least agreed with the Ministers first statement. Many of Cullen's ships and crewmembers would not survive the fight.

A few steps up the passageway, he stepped into his cabin. Keying the comm and asked his flag captain to join him. Once there, he outlined the War Minister's change to the order of battle and instructed the captain to implement the new plan.

The Captain saluted and excused himself.

Lowry took a small comm unit from his inside coat pocket and keyed it. "Yes, sir."

Just getting a response meant the man could speak freely. "Are you aware a civilian came aboard on the last launch?"

"Yes, sir. In fact, I know of the man. He's an assassin. Works for one of the families."

"And he knows you?"

"No, that I am sure of."

"He's here to keep me from withdrawing the fleet. If I order the fleet to cease hostilities, he's to kill me and my flag Captain is to take command."

"I'll take care of it, Admiral."

Admiral of the Fleet, Ephram Lowry smiled as the comm went dead.

38: New Hope's Legacy

President Raybold Penrose sat in his office mulling over New Hope's future. He touched an icon, "Yes, Dee."

"The Speaker is here, Mr. President."

Markam came in followed by Dee with a fresh pot of coffee. She put the pot down and left.

"Just the man I wanted to see," said Raybold pouring both a cup.

"Why the sudden call?" asked Markam. "I was just about to take Darcy and our baby for a stroll through your arboretum. That sure has proven popular."

"Sorry about the inconvenience. Give my apology to Darcy and I'll pass your comments along to the wife. And it's her arboretum," he chided Markam.

Raybold ambled around the room and sipped from his cup. "I was thinking about President Jabari's decision that started New Hope when New Earth faced a situation similar to ours. I'm considering doing the same thing. The problem I have is there isn't a planet to send them to. Any ideas?"

Markam seemed jolted. He sat his cup on the end table, stared at Raybold and clamped his teeth tight stifling an outburst.

Everyone knew the history of New Hope. President Jabari provisioned a corvette along with two transports and sent them to what is now New Hope prior to the war with Old Earth or Terra.

Markam let a slow breath escape. He sat for a few moments ignoring his brew. "No, Mr. President, I don't. I'd never given the idea a moment's thought." He paused, sucked in some much needed air and continued, "but we may have someone who could help. Disdan Weisman. He's traveled a goodly part of our end of the galaxy."

"Good. It's past time that he and I renewed our relationship. See if you can find him."

Markam left and returned with his friend the next day. Dee ushered them in.

Raybold stepped from behind his desk and extended his hand, "Mr. Weisman, I apologize for not having invited you here sooner. Since our arrival, Markam has told me a great deal about you. He attributes the successful escape from Cullen to your efforts."

"Thank you and he overstates my contribution, Mr. President. It was his idea. All I did was tune the engines," Disdan responded courteously.

Seated, Raybold asked if he knew how New Hope came to be.

"Yes, sir. Four months in space with Markam provided ample time for me to learn your, our history," with a smile he corrected himself.

"Mr. Weisman, I'm considering the same tactic that got us our start. Except I don't have a clue if there is a habitable planet that a ship could make it to that doesn't already have inhabitants. Our long life gene remains a concern.

"Any suggestions?"

"Maybe. Unfortunately, my information isn't complete and there isn't time to refine it. There are several possibilities and I stress, possibilities. I can't give you precise locations. A ship could head out on a vector and find nothing."

"Would you give what you have, what you suspect, what you've heard, to out scientists. We have a very active astrophysics program. Perhaps, with your input, they can come up with some locations that are probables."

Disdan agreed and with that, he and Markam left Government House.

* * * *

A month later, Markam, Disdan and three scientists from the astrophysics group waited as Dee announced them.

With the formalities out of the way, Raybold asked if they had a recommendation.

Markam deferred to the lead scientist to tell what they had found.

"Mr. President, we've identified, thanks to Mr. Weisman's input, two star systems with a high probability of having at least one habitable planet in their systems."

They gave the particulars. One, at hyper speed, required two T-years transit and the second an additional T-year. Either choice would take them on a heading well out from Saragosa Prime, ten light years past the Vega region on the edge of the Galon Sector a seldom traveled area. Raybold asked a number of questions and the briefing ended.

"Markam, would you remain, please?" He stood, shook hands with the four men and reclaimed his seat.

After the door closed, Markam, with an apprehensive look said, "You're going to send ships, aren't you? And," he added, "with me to lead the group."

"Like I said, you know me too well. Will you do it?"

His friend became pensive, stood, walked to a window and remained there for a few minutes. "Okay, but how do I get over the feeling that I'm running out when New Hope may face destruction?"

244 Kenneth E. Ingle

"You won't. I read Lionel Penrose's diary. He never got over the feeling he was running away on New Earth." Lionel Penrose had led the group sent by President Jabari almost four hundred years earlier. "New Earth wanted to preserve what Maria Presk had begun and I want to make sure that effort survives."

"What do you want to call us?" asked Markam.

"Keep the name New Hope. If by some miracle we survive, having two called the same may sow enough confusion that it will help us both."

A reluctant Markam Zenester left Government House. The feeling of betrayal already firmly implanted.

Raybold issued the necessary orders that would send Hope and two transports on a journey that hopefully would ensure the seeds of Orion not end under his reign.

A goodly portion of New Hope's population had gathered at the launch site. Four hundred people, all volunteers, had said their goodbyes and were aboard Hope or one of the two transports. The three ships carried the DNA of virtually every plant or animal from multiple worlds stored in cryogenic tanks, supplies, equipment, replacement parts, for a four T-year voyage. Safely tucked in Hope's bay a complete duplicate of New Hope's computer database. Everything that New Hope knew went with the travelers.

Markam stood apart from Raybold, seemingly, lost in private thoughts. He turned toward his friend and leader. "Ten blood descendants of Maria Presk are onboard Hope. I guess it's time."

Raybold handed him a microchip. "Activate this and if anyone from New Hope survives and is listening, well, you'll know what to do."

Markam again made known his feelings about leaving. A great many of New Hope's inhabitants would have traded places with him and he with them except his President had asked him to do this and he would not let his friend down or more importantly, abandon the legacy of Orion. All New Hope had agreed. What had started mankind into the universe must not be lost. If New Hope did not survive, at least a few of its seeds would—or at least have the chance.

"God speed, my friend," Raybold said. They shook hands and Markam boarded the launch.

* * * *

One hour later, he stepped onto Hope's hanger deck. "Captain on Deck," said the Marine. "As you were."

At the elevator, the bos'n's met him and apologized for his absence. "Not a problem," Markam said. "Is the ship ready to space?"

"Yes, sir."

"Post to your station. We'll get underway within the hour." He made his way along the passageways to the bridge stepped through the hatch and took his chair.

"Astrogation, is the course laid in?"

"Aye, sir."

Markam keyed the comm. "Ladies and gentlemen of Hope. We are embarking on a journey that twice our forefathers have taken. We carry the seeds of Orion and the responsibility of perpetuating our heritage. We will face perils. Our responsibility is to prepare as best we can to meet these challenges. I know you will all give your best. Bos'n's order the ship."

The bos'n's piped his tattoo and Markam signaled the astrogator to get underway.

A day later, Hope left the region on a vector that would take them to what they hoped was their new home.

Despite two months preparation, matters were chaotic as each crewmember took to their posts. Key positions had been assigned and the people trained, but once underway, reality set in. Knowing what to do and doing it proved hazardous. Mistakes were made that delayed the jump to hyperspace. It took another month before Markam was confident enough in the crew's ability to do their job and not put the ship at risk.

"Engage hyperspace engines," ordered Markam but not casually. He kept his eyes on the overhead plot constantly checking the ships performance. After an hour, he decided matters were in good hands.

"Missy, you have the bridge."

"Aye, Captain." She left her astrogation station and took the captain's chair. Missy Mosier wasn't Raybold's first choice but she had experience at the helm. Now if she could only forgo her over familiar attitude toward her male counterparts, he'd be quite satisfied. No one expected a miracle.

Markam had read Lionel Penrose's account of their journey and decided to use the constitution Trekker had drawn along with the Uniform Code of Military Justice as the governing laws. Occasional captain's masts were required and implemented with the UCMJ. Fortunately, no capital crimes occurred requiring him to convene a court martial.

Asteroid and comet catching became a regular matter replenishing water and minerals. Problems plagued the agrarian project using tenfold the water anticipated. Botanists finally found a solution, putting Botany Bay, named after Orion's first farm, in order. Fresh vegetables soon appeared on the menu, putting an end to catty remarks that the beleaguered workers had endured.

* * * *

"Captain, I recommend we slow and go to stealth. There's a ship ten million klicks aft and overtaking us."

Already running partially under stealth, Markam ordered the three ships out of hyperspace and to go passive shutting down all electronics. Coasting at three tenths c, the approaching ship quickly came abeam of Hope, one million kilometers distant.

"Registry," questioned Markam.

"Sorry, Captain. Unknown. Its pattern isn't in our computer," responded Missy. "By its mass and speed, it's definitely a war bird. Weapons are not powered and show no signs they have detected us."

"Looks like they've kicked over. They're either stopping or about to change vector," said Markam standing at the plot console.

For a few hours, all bridge hands took turns watching the red blip. The possibility existed the ship had detected an anomaly and grown suspicious. "Changing vector," Missy said and a few minutes later added, "they've gone to hyperspace."

A collective sigh crossed the bridge as Markam ordered, "Resume course, Missy."

"Aye, sir." Hope resumed its voyage.

Markam, Disdan and Missy made up the bridge crew. "If Admiral Rawlings's estimate was correct, New Hope is at war." Markam hoped his voice didn't betray his worst fears. "We can only wait. One day we'll know the outcome." With the *void* separating the two worlds, FTL transmissions were impossible.

"Captain," said Missy, "I overheard Admiral Rawlings aides, I wasn't snooping," she hurriedly added,—"

"And," Markam waited.

"It wasn't what I wanted to hear. I think they knew they would lose."

Markam glanced at the two but didn't comment. Disdan, Missy and he had become more than shipmates, they were friends. Missy's proclivity for flirting with her male counterparts was gone. He suspected a relationship was developing between she and Disdan. It might work although both were very independent souls and he'd not seen either develop close relationships.

Over the next year, Hope made its way across the outer boundary of the Galon sector without encountering another ship. Work became routine as crews gained experience. They had all become highly competent at their assigned duties. Any captain would be proud of the preciseness. They had molded into able spacers.

* * * *

"Bring us out of hyperspace," Markam ordered. Studying the plot, he pointed to a dot. "That's the system we're looking for. Start running sweeps. Let's see what we've got."

Hours later, astrogation reported, "Looks like the fourth rock might just be it." Disdan turned to face Markam beaming his massive grin. After all, it was his input that had made this possible.

Half a million kilometers above the planet, Markam launch the recon team. "Get a complete orbital survey and then return to the ship," he instructed the crew.

Markam left the bridge for his cabin. Darcy had just finished giving their son his bath.

"Looks like this place may be habitable," he said. "We may have found us a home."

An uncertain look crossed her face. "Everything will be fine," he said embracing her. "It will soon all be over and we can start building normal lives."

"I know it sounds crazy but I'm not sure I want to leave the ship."

He held her hands. "I've read the logs from Orion's journey. When they reached New Earth, most of their people had never been on a planet. All they knew was the spaceship. Had never walked on dirt. At first, a number of them refused to leave. They had no idea what a life off the ship could be. It isn't crazy. This has been home for two years. You've nurtured our son, seen him grow, the crew is more than that, neighbors, and friends. I understand what you're saying. I have some of the same feelings."

Holding their son, he pulled her closer against him.

Markam punched the comm. "Yes."

"The survey crew will be aboard in a few minutes, Captain."

He thanked the caller and signaled the launch. "Briefing in the conference room at fourteen hundred."

"Okay, let's hear the news. Good I hope," Markam said taking a seat at the head of the conference table. He touched a series of icons and opened the comm ship wide for the entire crew to hear.

"Yes, sir, with pleasure," said the survey leader. "No signs sentient beings have ever been there. Breathable atmosphere, plenty of water, we brought back samples for the lab, orbit time three hundred T-days, rotation twenty-six standard hours. Three large landmasses cover approximately twenty-five

percent of the surface. Two mountain ranges and a couple of desert areas."
Except for learning no sentients had preceded them that was information all
of Hope knew before the survey team left the ship but Markam didn't
interrupt.

"Flora not too unlike New Hope; fauna, sighted a healthy mixture of
small creatures and a few large ones, some of both sizes appear carnivorous.
We collected some bacteria but didn't bring it aboard. The lab wants to study
it first."

Questions abounded, some answerable, some not and would have to
await further analysis. Overall, Markam was satisfied they had found their
home. He assigned survey teams to make detailed studies of the planet.

After the site selection group presented their recommendations, Markam
okayed their first choice as the base location. Following a lottery to select
those first to land on their new home, Markam assigned section chiefs and
work groups to begin building houses. One week later, the second group of
residents set foot on the planet.

Work proceeded rapidly and a month later, with the exception of the on-
orbit crew, all of Hope's inhabitants were assigned housing.

Markam walked into the crowded conference room, one of the first
buildings erected.

"We've platted out a city," said the surveyor.

"Maybe you can settle an argument, Captain," someone said.

"Okay, what's the problem?"

"Some want a church built first, others a laboratory and there's a group
calling for a place to store crops."

"We need to move the food goods still on the transports dirtside," said
Markam. "I'd suggest a larder, refrigerated. That would cut down on running
back and forth to orbit for food supplies."

He acknowledged the moans and groans. "We'll be able to build what
you want, but the communities survival needs must come first. After a place
to store foods, I would suggest the laboratory. We need to know what we're
dealing with, living with if you will. Some of what we come in contact with
may be harmful. We need to know that and timing can be important. We
can't afford an epidemic. Concurrent with the lab, the shields that will keep
us hidden from prying eyes must be built."

"That seemed to put an end to the arguments. As Markam moved toward
the door, a hand grabbed his arm.

"Captain," it was the newly elected rector of the church. "We must have a place to meet. I feel you think little of our parishioners' need for a church, a place of worship."

Markam cocked his head and looked dolefully at the man. "How many in your congregation, Reverend?"

"We have a membership of over one hundred."

"And how many regularly attend the services?"

He paused, swallowed and mumbled, "Usually about thirty."

"I want no argument with you," said Markam. "When Lionel Penrose faced this problem on their arrival at New Hope, he offered the president's office. We have not elected a president but feel free to use my offices. Will that be satisfactory?"

A grimace accompanied a nod.

* * * *

Markam arrived at his office.

"I've been trying to reach you," said Missy. "Do you have your comm shut off?"

Markam checked his unit. "So I have. What's up?"

"Hope has picked up a ship. On its present vector, it will come within ten million klicks."

On orbit, the three ships had been electronically passive since arriving. The planet radiated nothing. The clocking generators were not operative so they were no problem. Markam couldn't risk communicating with Hope and using a shuttle was out of the question as the poorest equipped ship would detect it. He would wait, anxiously.

Runners sped off on foot to warn everyone not use communicators or fire a laser. Even at that distance, the visitor could detect the discharge.

Finally, the visitor spaced and New Hope was alone in its end of the galaxy.

39: The battle for New Hope

Anticipating Cullen's track into the system, Admiral Rawlings positioned Braeden's fleet five million kilometers above New Hope. Cloaked and emissions at zero she would wait until the enemy committed its fleet and approached within effective range for her weapons. Then she would attack. Her first shots would be the most important. If nothing else, it would disrupt the enemy's plan. Particularly since Cullen would not see her coming. Experience also told her once hostilities began, the order of battle would be nothing more than an exercise.

"They're in system," said the comm operator. He put the plot on the overhead screen.

"Count?" said Admiral Rawlings.

"At this distance, I can't give an exact number, Admiral, but a good guess is at least four to five hundred ships, maybe more."

"Heading?" asked Admiral Rawlings.

"Well, this doesn't make much sense but on their present vector and speed, they'll exit the system in about fifty T-hours."

She nodded and added, "Run these." She recited a series of numbers, then waited for the astrogator's results. She had anticipated this move and would have Braeden's fleet positioned where it could be most effective.

"Sir, looks like another ten hours standard and they'll reenter the system on a heading that will take them past Odysseus at approximately fifty thousand kilometers and on a vector to New Hope. Clearing Odysseus, if they enter hyperspace, they'll be here in one T-day. Should enter our system one million klicks above the planet."

"Just as you predicted," Raybold said to the Admiral.

Standing in CIC next to Admiral Rawlings, Raybold watched and listened as she issued orders. "It doesn't look good," she said. "Over six hundred ships of the line. We may be in for an old fashioned ass kicking."

Beverly Rawlings, as Fleet Admiral, had led Braeden's Navy some years before her injury. Prior that assignment, she served as director of their war college and later as the King's naval aide. Leaving that job, she commanded a flotilla in a battle against a loosely conglomerated squadron of pirates. Her ship suffered major damage. Hospitalized, gave her less than a ten percent chance of living and even less to be more than a vegetable. To everyone's amazement, she defied all odds and not only lived but returned to duty. Something King Barrymore said was due solely to her resolve.

"That bad?" said Raybold. He didn't ask her if what she was seeing changed her order of battle. He understood what the numbers meant. With Odysseus abandoned, the people and all useful equipment removed to New Hope, she didn't have to concern herself with trying to defend it. Non-combatants had moved to New Hope's underground shelters and that included Raybold's wife. His fifteen-year-old son Joshua, like most citizens, manned some form of weapon. Many had volunteered to serve on Braeden ships but with ample thanks, she declined the offer. Braeden had what it needed—first class warships and highly trained crews.

"I'll be in my cabin Captain. Let me know when we have an in-system vector. President Penrose, would you join me, please." Admiral Rawlings guided the gravchair to the exit.

Two marines lifted it through and Raybold followed. Located a few meters behind the bridge, the hatch to her quarters had been modified to accommodate the gravchair.

Raybold opened it and the two entered.

The ships engineers and maintenance crews had remodeled the cabin making everything as reachable as possible. To eliminate troublesome corners, they had arranged the three rooms in circles. Even the shower, which was visible, she could easily access.

"Mr. President, I fear this will be a blood bath."

"Admiral, the Cullen fleet will be between your fleet and the dirtside cannons. It seems to me we have a distinct advantage. I assume you'll open with our disrupters. One shot with them and the numbers will definitely be to our advantage as some of their ships will lose steerage. That should create considerable chaos. Give your fighters an excellent opportunity to pick targets of opportunity."

"And if not? What if they anticipate that move and shut down their systems? I never underestimate my enemy." She maneuvered toward a chair. "I have to get out of the damned contraption ever once in a while. Can you assist me, please?"

"Gladly, Admiral." Following her instructions, Raybold eased the admiral off the chair onto the recliner.

"Aah," she muttered as he positioned her. "I sometimes think I'd have been better off if paralyzed from the neck down. Having feeling and still not able to move is wearisome."

Instead of discussing her concerns about the upcoming battle, Admiral Rawlings talked of her childhood. How she'd been raised as a privileged child with no brothers or sisters, and pampered beyond belief. Upon entering the

Naval Academy, she was ill prepared and became the butt of many jokes. Tricks were commonly played on her. "That was until I kicked the crap out of my most enthusiastic antagonist. That damned near got me booted out. I did get six months detention. That was no picnic. But you know, in a way it wasn't much different than the life I now live with all this." She motioned at the gravchair and modified quarters.

"Tell me," she continued, "about life on New Hope."

Raybold poured each a cup of coffee, doctoring hers with ample cream and sugar. He pulled a chair close to the lounge and spent two hours relating life on his world particularly how he'd grown up.

He stood and quietly eased from the now dozing Admiral's quarters.

* * * *

Beverly jolted awake and hit the comm button. "Yes?"

"The enemy is in-system, Admiral. Another ten T-hour will put them within fifteen million klicks."

She thanked the caller and spent an hour freshening up before going to the bridge. In her gravchair, the Marines eased her through the hatch. She steered to the plot console and nodded at Raybold.

"No trailing transports," said the operator. Unexpectedly, Cullen had positioned the transports and merchant ships within the fleet, giving them maximum protection.

"Are the fighters ready to launch?" she asked. New Hope had equipped three hundred Braeden's fighters with inertial grav-units and their most advanced energy cannons. They would lead the attack or counterattack depending on what the enemy did.

"Yes, Ma'am," the weapons officer said. Overall direction would come from him once the battle started and Admiral Beverly Rawlings would be at his side.

"If you're going dirtside, Mr. President, you should leave," Rawlings said.

"I agree." They shook hands. "Good hunting, Admiral."

She thanked him and moved her grav-chair next to the plot board.

"They've powered weapons," said the electronics officer."

Quiet settled over the bridge.

Cullen's fleet, was at three tenth's c, and would be five hundred thousand kilometers above the planet.

"They're deploying missile sleds," said the Weapons Officer. Rawlings moved to his side, her eyes sweeping the entire plot.

"Not good news," she quietly said. Only the weapons officer could hear her. He turned his head toward her, a questioning look on his face. With her voice lowered she said, "Our disrupters have no effect on those damned sleds."

All eyes were focused on the overhead screens. Admiral Rawlings saw nothing that would change the plan. She had no defense or offense against the missile sleds, now numbered at fifty and each carrying eighteen missiles. Cullen could and would easily penetrate the shields hiding the planet, permitting destruction of the energy shields and exposing the entire surface to bombardment.

"Admiral, they're shutting down. They've cut their electronic systems."

Admiral Rawlings worst fears unveiled before her as one by one, the enemy ship blinked off the plot screen. They had come up with the answer for neutralizing any disruption of their onboard electronic systems.

"Drop the cloak and attack," she ordered.

The weapons officer repeated the order. She nodded and he opened the comm fleet wide and started the attack.

First squadron, consisting of thirty battleships, fifty heavy cruisers and as many destroyers, all supported by fighters, raced toward the enemy fleet. They would engage in twenty minutes.

The engineering officer pointed toward enemy ships on the extreme edge of their fleet. "I recommend we put the fighters on these. In their current configuration, those ships can do us considerable harm."

Rawlings authorized the attack. "Enemy missile launch," said the weapons office. "Screen impact in ten seconds."

Once the screen was penetrated, New Hope's energy cannons would enter the fray. But then, Cullen's ships would have unimpeded access to the surface. New Hope was in for a pounding.

"Launch all missiles," ordered Rawlings. Cullen ships began disappearing from the plot. "Enemy fleet changing vector," said the weapons office.

"Incoming missiles," he said. Everyone knew, Braeden ships and people were about to die.

Over the next hour, Admiral Rawlings monitored the casualty reports. As she expected, it was a blood bath. Ten Braeden ships were destroyed in the first enemy salvo. Six Cullen ships had disappeared.

"Direct all fighters to attack the transports," she ordered. Cullen was attempting to replace the fired missiles. If she could disrupt that transfer, New Hope might survive, at least some of it.

Twenty hours later, the comm station reported contact with the planet had been lost. Not a sound could be heard on the bridge.

"Sir," said the engineering station, "The Cullen fleet, or what's left of it is withdrawing."

* * * *

Ephram Lowry sat in his command chair on the bridge. "Communications, order the fleet to disengage. Form up on my ship. We're heading for Cullen."

With less than two hundred ships remaining from a fleet of six hundred capital ships, many of those having taken sever damage, Fleet Admiral Lowry would take no more loses in a losing cause. Braeden's fleet still numbered over three hundred ships. He would not see his entire fleet destroyed.

"War Minister on the bridge," said the Marine.

"What's the meaning of this? I've ordered no withdrawal."

Admiral Lowry stood and faced his irate leader. "We are losing, Minister. I will not forfeit any more ships and crew to a war we cannot possibly win." He knew the consequences when the fleet returned to Cullen. It would be on his head alone. Undoubtedly he would face Supreme Leader's wrath: most likely a firing squad. But the sacrifice was already too great and anything more would be simply suicidal. To continue was beyond the sense of right and wrong.

He stared at the pulser the War Minister pointed at him. "You will rescind that order immediately."

"No sir. I will not. And before you shoot me, the man behind you will kill you."

The Minister turned toward the hatch. The duty Marine stood with his weapon pointed at the Minister.

"Minister, the man you brought aboard to kill me has been disposed of. He was sent him out an airlock over an hour ago."

With that, War Minister seemed to collapse, and dropped his pulser, his will gone.

"Take the Minister back to his quarters and lock him in. If he resists, put him in the brig. Set a course for Cullen," said Admiral Lowry. At least some of his people would not die in a war they had clearly lost.

* * * *

Cheers erupted from the bridge with the announcement. Despite the losses, Admiral Rawlings had defeated a larger fleet. She turned her attention to New Hope. "Try to reestablish contact," she ordered.

"We've been trying, sir. I have an incoming comm from a fighter that's on the surface."

"Pipe it in to me." She took an earpiece and listened, her face betraying her. She let out a short breath. "Dispatch all available medical personnel to the surface. Save those that you can," she said.

For a seven T-days, rescue and burial crews scoured the planet looking for survivors and interring the dead. Many bodies were no more than cinders and burial made no sense.

"We've not found any alive, Admiral."

"Put signal buoys on every ship," she said. "Some can be salvaged. We'll be back. Some may be hulks, but a few are worth saving. Let's go home," she said. With that, the remnants of her fleet vectored away from what had been New Hope.

Two days later, a freighter bound for Galactic, orbited New Hope. "Someone had one hell of a fight," said the captain. "Take a shuttle and check the surface for survivors."

40: The Descendant

Joshua Penrose, descendant of Maria Presk, and Raybold Presk Penrose, regained conscious. The entire overhead structure, of what had been the spaceport headquarters, had collapsed into the bunker leaving nothing but debris blocking access to the surface. Disoriented, he heard rumbling above. Not knowing if they were New Hope people or Cullen looking for survivors, he banged on the girders blocking his path. And then the noise from above stopped.

It took him the better part of the day to make his way out. Having suffered through the devastating Cullen onslaught, he expected the worst— but his imagination hadn't been capable of holding the magnitude of the destruction.

Bodies, burned beyond recognition lay among the smoldering ruins. Silence added to the eerie scene. All around him nothing but remnants, bits and pieces of what had been New Hope and home.

He stumbled over rubble. Off in the distance, he saw a shuttle and the crew boarding. Fearing they were about to leave, he scrambled toward the tarmac waving his arms and yelling. A few meters from the ship he tripped over a protruding girde. His head hit the ground knocking him unconscious. When he awoke, Joshua was aboard the transport and in space. Only later was he to learn he was the sole survivor of New Hope, one hundred fifty thousand people slaughtered. Cullen would burn in his mind forever.

"Well, young man, you are certainly very lucky. Another minute and we would have been off the surface," a white clad man said. "I'm Sam. Both cook and medic. You don't seem to have any serious injuries. How you feeling?"

Joshua tried to sit up but overcome with dizziness laid down. "Whew, I guess I'll lie here for a while. What ship is this?"

"The freighter Samson. Out of Mackenzie."

Joshua Penrose quickly melded with the crew. Showing exceptional talent, he gained assignments in astrogation and engineering. Five years later, the first mate died in an accident and Captain Combs promoted him as his number one.

* * * *

"Captain," the plot operator voice reached a high pitch. "There's a ship approaching. It hasn't responded to my signal." Everyone on the bridge stopped and waited, suspecting the worst.

"Freighter, cut your engines. We're coming aboard," the speaker blared.

"Pirates," said the Captain." He ran his hand through his thinning hair.

"Looks like we've drawn a dead hand. Bad choice of words," he added. Pirates had never boarded one of his ships, or any ship he'd been aboard for that matter. Nevertheless, he'd played it over and over in his mind and knew how he would deal with it. He keyed the comm and issued the order to idle the engines. Ship wide he alerted the crew. "Don't do anything to anger them. Obey their orders. Maybe we can survive this."

Resolved to do his best to save his crew and ship, the Captain assembled the non-essential personnel in the cargo hold. Along with the few men, he stood waiting in the docking bay.

Metal to metal clanking echoed as the boarding ship, not to skillfully, locked onto the freighter. The sounds suggested the two ships were not properly secured together. Through the open hatch, four body armored and heavily armed men in dropped onto the deck. One sour looking man scanned the waiting Samson group. "Where's the rest of your crew and how many?" one boarder said.

"Twenty and all nonessential members are assembled in the cargo hold. Three are still on duty," responded the Captain.

"What's in the hold," the pirate questioned. Captain Combs took him to be their leader.

"Soy seed. We're bound for Braeden."

"Braeden?" questioned the rough faced man. "I don't mind taking something belonging to them. You Captain?" he said.

"Yes."

"Take me to your valuables."

With three pirates following, Captain Combs led them to his cabin, opened the hatch, stepped in and pointed to the ship's safe."

"Open it."

Seconds later, the Captain stood aside as one pirated scooped the contents onto the floor. "Not bad. Must be a few thousand credits and some gold. Very good. Where's the rest?"

Most Captains had at least two places for their valuables.

"On the bridge. It's mostly vids and chips required for various port entries," said the captain.

Once on the bridge, with the safe's contents now thrown over the deck, the pirate charged his blaster. "You're lying. This ain't everything." He turned on the Captain, "This can't be all. Maybe you don't want to live. The rest."

"Sir, that's all there is. It is my intention to obey all your orders. I want my crew and ship to survive this boarding."

The pirate's derisive laugh didn't bode well. "Get everybody, and I mean everybody in the cargo hold," he ordered.

Captain Combs did as told. Standing in front of the entire crew, twenty men, he faced the same number of pirates.

He could only watch as the pirates removed Samson's food stores and pumped their water into the pirate ship's tanks. "Blow the engines and comm gear," the pirate ordered.

"Where's your weapons?"

"Follow me," said the Captain.

The pirate left four men to guard Samson's crew and followed Captain Combs along the passageway toward the bridge.

He stopped and pointed to a hatch. "In there."

"Well, don't just stand there, dammit, open it."

Combs swung the hatch open, reached inside and switched on an overhead light and stood aside. In less than an hour, the locker was empty and the weapons aboard the pirate. With the Samson stripped, the pirate ordered his men to return to their ship.

One by one, the pirates entered the docking bay and climbed into their ship, the pirate captain being last. As the man started through the opening, Joshua stood by to close the hatch. A violent explosion broke the pressure seal separating the ships. The pirates had set too large a charge on the engines and the poorly attached ships parted. Instinctively, Joshua grabbed the pirate, pulling him back into the docking bay.

Aided by the pressurized bay and vacuum of space, he quickly closed the hatch saving the pirate captain's life and his.

Shaken, the pirate captain turned on Joshua. "I owe you."

Joshua nodded. "Would have done it for anyone," he said without emotion.

Quiet settled as they waited for the ships to reattach.

"Get aboard the Pasqual," he ordered.

"No, I'll stay with my shipmates," Joshua curtly responded.

"Get your ass aboard my ship." He pulled his blaster and made a motion toward the open hatch. "At least with me, ya gotta chance of living. Something this crew don't have much of."

Joshua didn't move. The pirated armed his blaster. "Move or I'll start killin' your buddies."

Joshua looked through the open hatch into the cargo hold at Samson's crew fearful he'd never see them again.

On board the pirate ship, the captain ordered him put in their brig. Shortly after that, the captain appeared. "My name is Gristler. Yours?"

"Joshua Penrose."

"Like I said, I owe you. Behave yourself and I'll let you out of there."

Joshua could detect no malice in his voice. "What choice do I have? Can't leave."

That brought a chuckle from the pirate as he unlocked the cell door.

A pirate standing behind the captain took him to his quarters. Not far from the brig, Joshua glanced down a passageway, and noticed a small shuttle. Most ships this size couldn't house a ship of any size. Apparently, someone had modified the Pasqual to handle the smaller vessel. Arriving at his quarters, the man angrily said, "Better than the rest of us got. Just you and the Captain have descent quarters. The rest of the crew has to sleep in hammocks strung around the ship."

Joshua kept quiet not wanting to antagonize the man further. He entered the room and his escort left. *Not bad* he thought. *One room with a bed, its own head and what passed for a kitchenette.* Better that what he had on the freighter. An empty feeling ate at him thinking about the crew, all friends aboard Samson.

Six uneventful weeks passed and Joshua was accepted by most of the crew. Assigned to the engine crew, his skills were quickly recognized. The comm came alive, "Engine room, I'm going to maximum power."

Joshua aided by another crewmember, homed in on the instruments ready to make any adjustments necessary to keep the engines from tearing themselves apart. He had no idea how long the old engines could take the strain. In concert, the two turned knobs, adjusted flow rates, punched blinking icons, and moderated temperatures but it was a losing battle. "Captain," said the engineer, "We can't hold her. You're have to cut 'em back."

Both men breathed a sigh of relief as the captain reduced power. "We can hold that output," the man commed the bridge.

Seconds later, the comm again came alive. "Everybody to their stations. Looks like we're gonna be in a fight. There's a Braeden corvette mixin' it up with couple of other ships. Probably raiders like us. I'm gonna help them out. I've always wanted to kick the shit out of a Braeden ship." Pirates had the gall to call themselves raiders.

The corvette outgunned the three pirates, but they were not doing well. Apparently shot up, although Joshua could not see any damage, six escape capsules streaked out from the corvette ending the battle.

Not wanting Braeden's Navy always after him, the pirate abandoned the field.

"We've got to hole up somewhere, the Captain said. The Pasqual had taken two hits, venting a number of compartments to space, and needed repair.

"There's a swarm of asteroids about a day from here," said the astrogator.

Hidden in the asteroid cluster, Gristler assigned work crews, Joshua included, to make the necessary repairs. Patching the hull proved difficult and tiring. Wearing gravboots and bulky spacesuits only added to the misery. Crews rotated every two hours.

Joshua knew he'd never have a better chance to escape. With a shuttle he could steal and a corvette nearby, he was ready. During his six weeks aboard, he used every excuse to be around the shuttle. Getting off the ship would be tricky but if he could get the hull doors open, the rest would be fairly straightforward.

Alone in the passageway, he opened a bulkhead panel and disabled the circuits that signaled the doors open. Mentally, he ran the sequence: shuttle door open, hit the hull door button, and quickly into the shuttle. There wouldn't be time to start the main engine, he'd use thrusters. Hopefully, he'd be either out of range or behind a big rock away from anyone manning the top laser turret.

Joshua relaxed, hit the hull door button and dashed into the shuttle.

He activated the thrusters, backed out of the Pasqual and headed out of the asteroids. Now all he had to do was find the corvette.

He switched on the radar. Within minutes, the naval ship appeared on the screen.

Eighteen hours later, secured to the corvette, he checked the vitals. No air. It was open to space. Anticipating that, Joshua had stowed a spacesuit aboard the shuttle.

Outfitted, he opened the hatch and entered, made his way to the stern an opened the hanger door. Shortly he'd retrieved the shuttle and had it safely locked to the rails.

It took him a few minutes to find a replacement oxygen bottle for his nearly depleted supply. Another day and he'd closed or sealed the significant vented openings. It was still a mystery why the crew had abandoned the ship.

It had taken some direct hits but nothing that seemed that severe. Inspecting the engines, he stopped dead still. One shot they'd taken had twisted the hull enough to put a crack in the anti-matter containment housing. "No starting the engines." Damn, he was glad he'd spotted the fracture. Apparently, the fail-safe had worked and shut down stopping an explosion. It was still a major hazard. Anything that rocked the ship the wrong way could open the crack and that would be the end of the corvette and everything within a few thousand kilometers.

Joshua found an ample supply of food and water. The ship's safe had more than enough credits to pay for the repair. It was common for ships to carry credits as cash money was the only currency in deep space. All Joshua had to do was find someplace to hole up and fix the ship. It would be a major effort to repair the containment housing. He estimated at least six T-months.

A week later, following a space beacon, he entered orbit above Belo's Crossing. Eschewing the protocols required to go dirtside, as a ship in distress he was granted privilege and put the corvette into an on orbital repair station.

Joshua claimed salvage rights and completed the papers giving him legal title. HMS Interdictor was now Marauder. Quite to his surprise, the space overhaul crew removed and replaced the core containment housing. Marauder could space. That was, as soon as he found a crew. He'd not been idle in this regard and immediately hired Bolster Kochee as First Mate and Jerboas Finney as Master cook and medical tech. Over the next few day, he hired twenty more for various jobs. Ready to leave orbit, he took a comm from dirtside. An applicant for astrogator wanted to interview. He'd considered doing the job himself but reconsidered. At first glance, he was glad he had granted the interview and hired Michelle Barstow.

Marauder spaced, Joshua intending to offer his services to haul high-risk passengers. A very lucrative but dangerous business. He requested an orbital slot above Cestess IV, which was denied. That was when he learned Braeden had issued a warrant for his capture and arrest. The Kingdom of Braeden wanted its ship back and rightly believed Joshua must have had some connection to the pirates who'd attacked it in order to make his timely "salvage".

Simply returning the ship wouldn't be enough. They'd lost sailors and Marines in the battle and the people called for revenge.

With over a million credits invested in repairs and crew payroll, Joshua said no. This same scene repeated itself at Saragosa Prime except at Saragosa, he did manage to get permission to orbit and contact Soffett's embassy. He stopped at a bar for a drink. A group of inebriated spacers got into a fight. A bystander mistakenly named Joshua as the man that had made a pass at his wife. Joshua denied the accusation to no avail. He did admit to looking the woman over, carefully.

He left before the police arrived and headed for the Orbit Master's office. He'd gotten permission to de-orbit when the accusing man appeared. Joshua wasn't looking for a fight but had little choice. Distinguished looking couples scampered unsuccessfully to escape the melee. Knocked to the floor, one man dropped a package. Joshua picked it up intending to return it to the man when he heard the orbit master call for Marines.

Penrose made a dash for his shuttle still clutching the package.

Once onboard Marauder and on a vector away from the planet, he inspected the package. A silver plaque given by Winner White to the citizens of Saragosa Prime denoting their vote making their world a republic. Saragosa Prime filed warrants claiming that Joshua had stolen this most priceless historical artifact.

Denied access to most ports, and needing supplies, Joshua Penrose did what he'd always done, adapted. He'd take what he needed and became a pirate.

Made in the USA
Charleston, SC
07 February 2012